O9-AHW-010

**"Andrew? I've got something.
Or rather, I don't have something."**

Leaving my trowel to mark the location, I picked up what would have been the last bone in the hand proper and looked at it carefully. The edge was imperfect, though not because of some trick of preservation.

"Butchery marks," I said, holding it up to him. "It looks like the middle finger was cut off. See, you can see where this bone was nicked. It happened shortly before his death, I guess, there's no sign of healing."

Andrew stared at the bone, a startled expression on his face. "My God, you're right. But I think our friend here had worse things to worry about. Look there."

I followed where he was pointing, to the top of the long part of the breastbone. At first I couldn't see anything, but as my eyes adjusted I realized there was a hairline crack in the bone that widened almost imperceptibly as my gaze followed it. Where it stopped, close to the center of the sternum, I could see the faintest discoloration.

Rust. "There's a piece of iron in there," I announced.

"He didn't die of old age, that's for certain," Andrew said. "Someone tried to bone our friend here like a frying chicken. And pretty well succeeded."

Also by
Dana Cameron

SITE UNSEEN

ATTENTION: ORGANIZATIONS AND CORPORATIONS
Most Avon Books paperbacks are available at special quantity discounts for bulk purchases for sales promotions, premiums, or fund-raising. For information, please call or write:

Special Markets Department, HarperCollins Publishers, Inc., 10 East 53rd Street, New York, N.Y. 10022–5299.
Telephone: (212) 207–7528. Fax: (212) 207–7222.

DANA CAMERON

GRAVE CONSEQUENCES

AN EMMA FIELDING MYSTERY

AVON BOOKS
An Imprint of HarperCollinsPublishers

The quotation from "Church Going" by Philip Larkin is reprinted from *The Less Deceived* by permission of The Marvell Press, England and Australia.

This is a work of fiction. Names, characters, places, and incidents are products of the author's imagination or are used fictitiously and are not to be construed as real. Any resemblance to actual events, locales, organizations, or persons, living or dead, is entirely coincidental.

AVON BOOKS
An Imprint of HarperCollins*Publishers*
10 East 53rd Street
New York, New York 10022-5299

Copyright © 2002 by Dana Cameron
ISBN: 0-380-81955-4
www.avonmystery.com

All rights reserved. No part of this book may be used or reproduced in any manner whatsoever without written permission, except in the case of brief quotations embodied in critical articles and reviews. For information address Avon Books, an Imprint of HarperCollins Publishers.

First Avon Books paperback printing: November 2002

Avon Trademark Reg. U.S. Pat. Off. and in Other Countries, Marca Registrada, Hecho en U.S.A.
HarperCollins ® is a trademark of HarperCollins Publishers Inc.

Printed in the U.S.A.

10 9 8 7 6 5 4 3 2 1

If you purchased this book without a cover, you should be aware that this book is stolen property. It was reported as "unsold and destroyed" to the publisher, and neither the author nor the publisher has received any payment for this "stripped book."

Acknowledgments

I AM DEEPLY INDEBTED TO MILDRED JEFFREY, CATHY Bennett, Beth Krueger, Pam Crane, Peter Morrison, my agent Kit Ward, and my editor Sarah Durand, for their thoughtful comments on my work and their continuing support. My thanks to Professor John Hunter (who generously answered my questions about British forensic procedure), Jill Salter Plump and Heather Stewart (who kindly helped me give dimension to Morag's professional and spiritual life), Ann Barbier (who gleefully helped shape Brian's work day), and Kit Ward (who patiently served as my first source of information on all things chelonian): any errors are of course my own. My best thanks and love to my husband, who did everything to support and encourage me through this (and every) project: words seem too small.

GRAVE
CONSEQUENCES

Chapter 1

I GRIPPED THE PHONE RECEIVER A LITTLE MORE TIGHTLY and tried, without much luck, to block out the airport noise around me. "You're sure there wasn't a message? Nothing?"

Because I love Brian more than anything on earth and none of this was even remotely his fault, I tried my best to be patient, but I was exhausted, I was short-tempered, and I smelled like I'd been cleaning up after the circus. It was June, but I couldn't plead working as a field archaeologist to excuse these shortcomings just at the moment.

My husband's voice was a torment; familiar and comforting, but 3,000 miles away. "Emma, I checked the machine; there was nothing there. Did you try calling Jane?"

"Yeah, a dozen times. No one's answering. I tried the university but they couldn't help me. Brian, they were supposed to be here almost two hours ago!" I wrapped the phone cable around my hand, worried and fresh out of ideas.

"Are you going to be okay? I can't think of what else to do and I'm already late—"

"No, it's fine, you get to your meeting. Thanks for checking, Brian."

"You call me when you get settled. I don't care what time it is."

"I will."

And even though there was nothing else that he could do, Brian still tried to reassure me. "Look, when I met Jane at the conference last year, she reminded me of you, okay? So I get the impression if she's not on time, there's a good reason for it. She didn't forget you, it's just traffic or the car or something unavoidable."

"I know, I'll sort something out. I just hate it when things don't go properly—"

"I know you do. I love you, Em."

"I love you, Brian. Take care, bye."

"Bye. Call me."

"I will; get to your meeting."

"Okay, I love you, bye."

"Bye."

I hung up reluctantly and was forced to come back to the grimy reality of London's Heathrow Airport. The place radiated unhygienic overuse—every surface was covered in fingerprints and smears, and the tang of disinfectant lingered impotently under the smells of the foodcourt and the persistent crush of human bodies—but I couldn't tell whether my own state of transatlantic grittiness and sleep deprivation was making the impression worse. People of every nation and color crowded past me at the exit gate for international flights. All of them seemed to be finding their rides, I thought resentfully. The noise of the airport was jarring: Announcements in several languages, including ubiquitous BBC-trained recordings in English, boomed over the loudspeaker, vying with the crowds of people who were greeting, kissing, arguing, crying, and parting. Weaving through the mass of humanity, battery-powered carts hauling luggage and more fragile passengers cruised by me, beeping insistently. Even the little squeaks of herds of identically wheeled black suitcases amplified my steadily growing despair.

I stood irresolutely, wondering what the hell to do next,

for no matter what Brian promised, I knew that Jane and Greg weren't going to show. I had to find my own way to the site.

I picked up my bag, thanking heaven that I'm as macha as I am about traveling with only one suitcase, a carryon backpack, and my purse, and wondered for the umpteenth time where the deuce my erstwhile friends Jane and Greg were. I walked toward the customer service desk again, trying to imagine that there'd be a message there for me *now*, but I was halted in my tracks by a familiar voice calling me.

I was thoroughly confused: it wasn't Jane's and it was American, although noticeably deep, precise, and cultured. I noticed a look of intense relief spread across the face of the woman behind the customer service desk as I turned away from her.

"Emma! I'm over here!"

My jaw dropped when I realized who the booming voice belonged to. Professor Dora Sarkes-Robinson is a colleague of mine from Caldwell College; she was in the Art History Department, just a few buildings over from my office in the Anthropology Department.

"Dora? What are you doing here? I thought you said you wouldn't be in England until—"

"I wasn't supposed to be here until August, but Addingham called and *begged* me to come and save them, and then in practically the same instant, Pooter called—"

I vaguely knew that Addingham was a prestigious study tour for students of the fine arts and material culture, but I hadn't a clue about who—or what—Pooter might be.

"—And said to stop by and look at his pictures and so things just simply *flew* together at the last minute and here I am. You're looking disreputable, Emma—"

I tuned out a moment, as used to Dora interrupting me as I was used to her blunt criticism. Neither meant a thing for long because Dora inevitably had more important things to think about. She and I shared a passion for our respective work, but there any similarity ended. Dora's built along generous lines that would make Caravaggio drool, while I flog myself mentally if I don't run five miles three times a week. She moves through social situations like a triumphant queen, but outside of academic circles, I always feel more like an observer than a participant. Dora's broad face is as dark as the skin of a hazelnut and her hair was woven into a thousand fine braids that formed a veritable crown, while my own auburn hair and pale skin immediately reveal that my heritage is sunk in the damp, cold peat of northern Europe. Dora, it was clear, had not traveled to London in the veal pens of coach class, and her stunning wine-colored Italian dress—I knew it was Italian only because everything she wore was Italian—looked as fresh as it had been the day the couturier had bestowed it upon her. My twin set and black jeans, which had looked so tidy and practical when I'd left Massachusetts, now looked, well, disreputable.

"—And so, no one's ever *really* convinced by the so-called slacker chic," Dora finished, all out of breath. "Where are you headed?"

I was tired enough to be annoyed. She and I had compared our summer schedules only a couple of weeks ago and Dora never forgot anything. "I'm supposed to be heading for Marchester, but I haven't got a clue how to get there. My ride is about two hours late—"

"It's not coming then," Dora concluded. She seized the handle of her wheeled tan patterned suitcase, one that even I could identify as expensive, and began to walk toward the exit. "I've a car; come with me."

"As if that settles it," I muttered under my breath, but I guess it really did settle it; I didn't have any other choice. I hurried after Dora. "Don't we need to pick up your luggage?"

She didn't bother to look back. "Don't be foolish, Emma."

I was impressed that Dora could fit everything she'd need into that one large case: I wouldn't have thought her capable of traveling light, not with her wardrobe. I struggled to get the strap of my suitcase, weighted down with lots of books, over my shoulder and caught up with Dora at the door that led to the outside. "The rental places are over that way," I said with a nod of my head.

Dora favored me with a raised, finely shaped eyebrow that echoed the sentiment of her last words and proceeded out the door.

I had just enough time to register the smells of diesel fuel and wet pavement outside—it had started to rain—and the rush of red double-decker buses and tiny cars whizzing past me in the wrong direction, when we heard a gruff voice call out.

"Professor! Over 'ere!"

I turned out of habit—nearly everyone I know, me included, has the first name "Professor"—but the call was, of course, for Dora. A tall, powerfully built man in a plain white shirt and black trousers raised an enormous hairy hand. His other hand was in his pocket jingling loose change—even that clanked in unfamiliar notes, I thought ruefully: I really was far from home. The hair on his head was brown, thinning, and unkempt, brushed toward his brow. His head was almost oblong, with a large mashed nose that didn't quite seem to sit square in the center of his ruddy face and dark eyes that were set back a bit under his brow, almost as if they were leery of revealing too much.

I'd hate to see the other guy, I thought when I realized his nose had been broken several times, and then followed Dora over to the man, who stood next to a sleek dark blue car.

"Ah, Palmer, excellent," she said, handing him her suitcase. "No problems, I trust?"

"Not in the least," Palmer responded. He effortlessly swung the heavy bag into the trunk of the car, which was almost filled to bursting with suitcases that matched the one Dora handed him.

Aha. This explained much: There was enough luggage to move an army; it should be just enough to get Dora through a month or so.

"Palmer, this is Dr. Emma Fielding, a dear friend of mine, who'll be joining us."

"Very good, Professor." Palmer extended a hand and I almost shook it before I realized that he was reaching for my suitcase.

"Oh, I've got it, thanks," I said, and wrestled my bag off my shoulder.

"Thank you, ma'am. It's not necessary." With that, Palmer took the bag away quite firmly, and as if it weighed no more than an empty pillowcase, placed it into the trunk with as much care as if he was arranging a shawl around the knees of his elderly mother. My black rip-stop nylon suitcase, with its many pockets and straps and technical design, of which I was so proud, looked ratty and juvenile compared to the orthogonal order of Dora's designer luggage. He slammed the trunk, and it was then that I recognized that I would be riding in a Bentley.

Holy snappers, I thought, as Palmer got the door for me. Dora slid in after me, and arranged herself comfortably. Palmer settled into the driver's seat on the right hand side of the car and soon we pulled away from the curb and began to navigate the gray maze of roads that led away from the airport.

"And how is Pooter? In the pink, I hope," Dora inquired of Palmer.

"His lordship is quite well, thank you, and looking forward to your visit."

Lord Pooter? I frowned; it simply wasn't possible. I ran my hand along the sleek leather of the seat; it was shockingly soft to the touch. The car moved silently and smoothly through traffic, and it wasn't until I noticed the speedometer showed around 120 kph that I realized how fast we were going. Nearly 70 miles an hour and nary a creak. I thought about my aging Honda Civic and Brian's pickup truck and decided that any comparisons were meaningless.

"And the dogs?"

"Quite well, thank you. Roxy had her pups last week. All five of the little hounds lived."

"Lovely. Things in town?"

"Much the same as usual. Although his lordship's been quite interested to observe the ongoing battle between some of the townsfolk and a developer who's eager to build a new supermarket on the banks—"

It was then that I began to doze. I couldn't help it, I was worn out with travel and worry about having been abandoned by Jane, and the interior of the car blocked out every sound save for Dora's conversation with the chauffeur. Occasionally, I rose near enough to the surface of wakefulness to catch snatches of Palmer's gossip.

"—Been gone missing for almost a week now—"

"—Complicated by the ever-so-uneasy relations between her and the, whatdoyoucallit, New Agers—"

I jerked fully awake, I couldn't say how much later, to the smell of smoke and a persistent crackling. Whipping my head back and forth in an effort to identify the source of the smoke, it took me a few seconds to remember where I was and what was happening. Palmer was smoking a cigar and Dora was just beginning to prepare her own.

"Welcome back, Emma. Everything catching all right up there, Palmer?"

"Yes, Professor, and I'm much obliged to you for the treat."

Dora sighed, leaned back, and pulled another cigar from her purse humidor. I barely suppressed an onrush of panic. She wasn't going to fill the back of this car, this masterpiece, with her foul cigar smoke?

Of course she was; she'd already bought Palmer's complicity in the matter. Rather than ask me if I minded, Dora offered me one of the enormous cigars. I shook my head and resigned myself to the fact that she was in charge now.

Her ritual had a hypnotic effect on me, who had always been an observer rather than a participant of this . . . well, there was no other word for it than *event*. The removal of the crinkly plastic, the examination and casual discard of the band. Dora dragged the *Romeo y Julieta* beneath her nose, sniffing carefully. Then after rolling it between her fingers, listening attentively for the sound of overdried leaves and hearing none, there was a flash of gold as she cut into the rounded business end with a wicked looking utensil made for the purpose. Quickly drawing each end into her mouth, slightly dampening the wrapper, she finally lit up. The first inhale was a prayer, she closed her eyes; the exhale was the answer.

"*Grazie a Dio!* That's better." She took another long drag and sighed with contentment. "The first step in overcoming the rigors of travel, Emma, is reclaiming the simple pleasures of one's everyday life. Are you sure you won't join me?"

"No thanks." Among other things, the simple pleasures of my day didn't include commandeering someone else's chauffeured Bentley. I looked around the car pointedly and frowned at her.

Dora sighed, this time as if in pain for me. "It is the little things, Emma, that make a life. Take Pooter, for instance. He's going to be delighted to meet you. When he finds out what your name is, he's going to simply squeal with glee, I assure you."

"I'm sure he won't be so rude," I said dryly. My name has been a sore spot between me and Dora since the first time we met.

"An archaeologist named Emma Fielding? I tell you, I don't know what your parents were thinking! It's too wonderful. One naturally is led to assume that you have an artist sister named Vita Brevis and a sociological cousin named Norma Loquendi."

"I do puns; it's not *that* good." But always on the lookout to connect the local money with the local scholars, I offered, "You should bring Poo—" I simply couldn't bring myself to say it—"er, his lordship to the site sometime, Dora. I'd be happy to show you both around. The dig at the abbey is going to be really interesting this year, from what I hear."

It was Dora's turn to wrinkle her nose. "I don't think we're either of us quite the . . . adventurer that you are. Dirt and . . . things." What "things" archaeology might represent for Dora—disease, alligators, or bandits—were left to her imagination alone. The other scholar shook her head definitely, rubbing her thumb against her fingers as if to rid them of imaginary filth.

"Dora, it's not like that! Research in the great outdoors? It's the best part of my job!"

Dora smiled pityingly and turned to watch the landscape as it rolled by, her head now wreathed in blue smoke.

Coughing a little, I was becoming increasingly dizzy. A glance at my watch revealed that it was now nearly one o'clock, an hour and a half since we'd begun our trek out of London and more than three and a half hours since Jane was supposed to pick me up. I began to worry again, but was then distracted by an overwhelming sense of déjà vu. A church tower stood above the other buildings in the town we were approaching. We crossed a bridge that spanned a wide, lazy-looking river and I shook my head: I'd never been here before, so why did it all seem so familiar?

Palmer answered my unspoken questions. "We're just coming to the outskirts of Marchester, this moment."

The townscape was familiar to me, I realized with a start, because I had been studying Jane's website in preparation for working on the dig. "Great! Mr. Palmer, the dig is over by the new church. Well, not really new new, but the replacement after the old abbey was burnt down in the sixteenth century. It's Church Street, that makes sense doesn't it? I guess that's where I'd better try to find Jane first."

Palmer drove along without paying much attention to me. "I know the town very well, ma'am. Never fear."

"So what is it you're looking for on this project?" Dora said. "Something unwholesome, I presume."

I frowned: Dora knew perfectly well what I was doing, we'd been over it all when we were trying to see whether our schedules in England would overlap. Her studied interest could only mean that she was planning something; I could practically hear the wheels turning within wheels. More machinations than a Detroit assembly line, more plots than a graveyard.

Nonetheless I was used to Dora, and more than that, I was presently grateful to her. So I indulged her, wondering what was hatching in that byzantine brain of hers.

"Jane Compton and I know each other from conferences and books—"

"Your books."

"And hers," I agreed. "We met just after I finished graduate school, years ago now; her work here in England tends to date earlier than mine in New England, but she is doing some fairly neat stuff with women's presence in the archaeological record, and that's how we connected. She and her husband Greg Ashford have been working on the site of Marchester Abbey, a Benedictine monastery that was built in the twelfth century. This is their second season. I thought I'd take a couple of weeks and see how things get done on this side of the puddle."

Dora looked sour and picked a tiny fleck of tobacco daintily from her tongue. "Don't be vulgar. What you really mean is that you wanted a vacation, but were too much of an obsessive actually to go somewhere warm with lots of rum. So you thought you'd take your spare time and do some more work. How typical of you, Emma."

"Not at all." I shifted a little in my seat. "Not entirely. I have other work in England, documentary research, that I need to get on to, for Fort Providence and my new research on the Chandler family. But I also thought I'd give myself a break by actually digging, for a change, rather than overseeing everyone else while they have all the fun. Being the director is great, but you never get to dig. And for your information, Brian and I are going on vacation, the last two weeks before classes start." So there, I thought.

Dora wasn't impressed. "Let me guess; you'll be tearing down more of that monstrosity of a house of yours?"

"No, we're taking a break from renovations." I had her now. "We're going away. Don't know where yet, he won't tell me. Anyway, Jane and Greg have been working on the burials this year, which will be fun for me. The rules about grave excavations are different in Britain than in the United States. It will be less complicated here anyway."

I noticed that Palmer was now studying me in the rearview as often as he could safely tear his eyes away from the road. I couldn't blame him because I was still as fascinated by archaeology as I had been when I started out in the field, almost twenty-five years ago, at the age of eight.

"The site is pretty close to the new church that was built after the abbey was destroyed. The abbey ruins are on the banks of that river we just crossed, so it should fill my requirements for working on really gorgeous sites. And I figure if the beer is as good as Jane keeps insisting, I may never go home."

"You know there was a student gone missing from that dig?" Palmer offered. "She's been missing since last Thursday."

"Did she go home?"

"Didn't say a word to anyone; she just vanished," he replied with ghoulish satisfaction.

"Students can get discouraged and take off," I said. "It happens, sometimes. Was there a fight or anything?"

"Nothing at all," Palmer said.

"Her parents must be going crazy."

"You might think so."

"Well, yeah, I'd think so," I said. "At home, a kid goes missing, the parents are all over the television, flyers plastered all over town—"

"Well," the driver said. "Twenty-two's hardly a kid, is it?"

"I really don't think there's that much difference—" I began, but it was then that I realized with a start that we were heading away from the church tower that I knew marked the site's approximate location. A few minutes passed, and it became clearer and clearer that we were not just navigating our way around the one-way streets, but were in fact heading for the outskirts of town, and directly away from the site. I began to worry.

"Dora, Palmer's overshot the site, I think," I said in a low voice. "The church tower back there—"

"He's not missed anything; he's taking us to Marchester-le-Grand. To see Pooter." Dora flicked an even inch of ash into the ashtray.

Panic rose in me. "What! Dora, Jane and Greg are going to get worried when I don't—"

"Jane and Greg should have picked you up hours ago if they were that worried," she mimicked back. "Emma, Pooter will be dying to meet you! He's never met an American archaeologist before and will be utterly charmed by you. It will only be for a moment or two, then I'll make sure that you're whisked back to your precious Jane and Greg."

I considered my grubby state and knew that I wasn't fit for meeting a lord of the realm. I was tired, worried, and plain pissed off with Dora for being exactly as she always was. "I'm not some sort of prize you can go parading around in front of your friends," I said tersely.

"Oh, my dear." Dora looked at me sympathetically; of course I was. "If Pooter's kind enough to offer you a lift, then you should be gracious enough to say thanks in person. Where are your manners?"

I eyed Dora sourly; Pooter didn't know I existed. I knew full well that she didn't buy all that Miss Manners nonsense and that she didn't really expect me to believe she did. She, however, knew that *I* believed in it and was using my ingrained pretentious Connecticut upbringing against me like a canny judo opponent. Anyone who treated other people's servants like her own, smoked Cuban stogies in other people's Bentleys, and generally ordered the universe to suit herself wasn't going to pay attention to my protests, no matter how logical, polite, or anything else. There was simply no gainsaying Dora, as I'd learned by hard experience back at home. So I settled back into the Bentley's upholstery and consoled myself that I could try calling Jane and Greg again when I got to Marchester-le-Grand, but deep in my heart, I knew I didn't have a choice at all.

"How's Brian?"

Since I knew Dora and Brian cordially loathe each other, it was obvious that the question was a distraction. The one thing I had been able to insist upon, early on in our relationship, was that she not criticize my husband to my face.

"Brian's fine. Busy," I said, not mollified by her overtures. I stared out the window.

"Good, good."

"Sure you wouldn't like to try one of the cigars, ma'am?" Palmer offered. "Might take the edge off you."

Great, now everyone thought I was edgy and unpleasant. I crossed my arms over my chest and continued to inspect Marchester as we drove away from it. The low, whitewashed shops and brick row houses gave way to low hills and fields separated by lines of trees. If you squinted, it wasn't so different from where I taught, in Maine, and where I lived, in rural Massachusetts.

Shortly thereafter, we turned down a long, tree-lined drive that led to a vast house of venerable gray masonry and darker sandstone details. I guessed that the main part of the house was sixteenth century, but it was clear to me that other, later additions had been built on through the years. The grounds were immaculately kept and I had to believe that the little folly that I could just make out on the horizon contained a piece of genuine classical statuary brought back for the purpose from someone's Grand Tour three hundred years ago.

The house was in good repair, and that, along with the Bentley, the grounds, and the driver, coupled with Dora's casual talk of "pictures," led me to believe that Lord . . . Pooter . . . was definitely not one of the growing fraternity of the titled impoverished.

We pulled up to the front of the house with a crunch of gravel. This time I waited until Palmer had opened my door for me, then got out and stretched. Dora headed right up to the front door as if she knew the way, and, once again, I was left to follow if I would.

"Perhaps you'd like to freshen up first, while I inform Lord Hyde-Spofford that you're here and get the tea?"

Hyde-Spofford makes much more sense than Pooter, I thought with relief, but why is the chauffeur getting the tea? "Yes, please, and if I could trouble you to use the phone? I'm sure my friends are quite worried—"

"Of course. Over there." Palmer led me to a curtained alcove that housed a modern touch-tone phone.

I dialed the number for Jane and Greg's house for the tenth time that day. This time I got an answer after the second *brrrr-brrrr.*

"Hello? Yes?" came the frantic answer. It was a male voice.

"Hello, er, this is Emma Fielding—"

"Oh, Emma, thank God!" Relief suffused the voice on the other end of the line. "This is Greg, Jane's husband. Where are you?"

"I'm in a house, Lord Hyde-Spofford's house, in Marchester-le-Grand. A friend gave me a lift."

"Oh?" There was a pause in which Greg was too polite to ask obvious questions. "Well, I'm glad you found your way this far. Things have been in a dreadful muddle here and when I ever realized that we'd left you stranded . . . Jane's almost in a state of nervous collapse—"

The worry in his voice was enough to infect me. "Is she all right? What's happened?"

"Jane's all right," Greg reassured me hurriedly. "Only she's had a dreadful shock. We unearthed something rather nasty and puzzling this morning, and since Julia's gone—"

I broke in before he could add any more confusion. "Greg, what did you find this morning?" I mentally ran down the list of possibilities: a broken sewer line or alarm system, contaminated groundwater, and old tannery or other early industrial waste site, any of which would require emergency attention.

"We . . . we found a skeleton."

That took me a minute. An instant urge to be sarcastic was replaced by a growing concern, and, hoping against hope that he didn't mean what I thought he did, I tried to keep the irony out of my words. "But Greg . . . it's an abbey *graveyard* you're working on . . ."

"Emma, this skellie isn't like the others." I could hear Greg swallow and, moisten his lips, and I knew I was correct. My heart sank.

"This one isn't right," he continued. "The orientation, the location, the depth . . . it doesn't look medieval. It's hard to tell, we've only just hit it and all, but it looks modern. Very modern. Too modern, actually. We called the police. They're still at the site. We're still trying to determine whether . . . whoever it is . . . died naturally."

Chapter 2

WHATEVER IT IS, I TOLD MYSELF FIRMLY, IT HAS nothing to do with me. It's not my problem, I don't know who it is; I wasn't even here when the skeleton was found.

"Emma? Are you there?"

"Yes, Greg, sorry, it's the jet lag. Umm, I'm not sure what to do. I'm not even really sure where I am, exactly—" I looked around, as if expecting to see a conveniently placed address plate inside the house. Outside the nook, the ever-helpful Palmer made a polite noise. I covered the receiver and stuck my head out from behind the curtain.

"Pardon me, Professor Fielding, but I'm sure Lord Hyde-Spofford would want me to offer you a lift after you've had a chance to catch your breath."

There at least was movement in the right direction: toward the dig. "That would be wonderful," I said with relief. I was pretty certain this place wasn't on a bus route. "Greg, I can find my way to you, but it will be an hour or so, while I—" What? Visit? *I* hadn't been invited. Pay my respects? I was certainly not some tenant shuffling in front of the great house, ready to drop eager curtsies to the laird. "—While I have tea," I finished.

Again, Greg's pause was full of politely unasked questions. "Well, if you can manage that, we can sort things out here, perhaps calm down a bit before you arrive. I'm most dreadfully sorry about all this—"

"No problem," I said. I was starting to develop the most appalling headache and wanted nothing more than to be left alone in the dark and quiet for a while, but that clearly wasn't in the cards, at least for the next few hours, at any rate. "Should I stop by the house or the dig? What would be easiest for you?"

"We live within walking distance of the site, so it might be better if you met us there." I heard another nervous swallow. "The police aren't entirely finished with us. Unless you'd like to go directly to your room—but, wait, no, you won't have a key, will you? I could meet you at the house, but, no I have to get—"

"Greg, I'll just come to the site. It will be simpler all around if I do that," I said firmly; clearly the morning's events were taking their toll on him. "I'll see you all shortly. Tell Jane I'm fine; I'm one less thing for you all to worry about."

"Right. Great. See you then." Greg rang off.

As I hung up, Palmer was again prepared. "Perhaps you'd like to freshen up a bit?"

My thoughts flew back to the airport and my hours incarcerated on the plane. "Ah, you've traveled, clearly. Yes, thanks."

Palmer pointed to a door just past the phone. "Not so's you'd notice, ma'am." His lips twitched. "Once to London, and several times to the Hackmoor, but apart from that, it's been back and forth from home to here, most my life. I don't hold with gallivanting to foreign parts."

I thanked him and then closed the door behind me with

relief. The bathroom was small and modern, the space obviously renovated from one of the original rooms. It was the first time in twelve hours that I'd had anything like privacy. I washed my face and hands, and buried my face in the towel. I didn't want to leave the bathroom; it was quiet, it was clean, it was very pretty. I didn't want to meet Lord Hyde-Spofford; if he was anything like the few other of Dora's art history colleagues I'd once encountered, he'd be horrible. They were all overdressed, arrogant, ironic, and dismissive, and I couldn't stand any of them. On the other hand, it was always fun to observe exotic creatures interacting in their native habitat. The plumage and pelts were spectacular, the mating dances complex, and the marking of territory aggressive. Since I am a much duller creature by comparison, I am generally ignored and left to watch in comparative safety, but there's a big difference between watching and interacting.

Just one more reason to dislike Lord Pooter, I decided, replacing the towel and opening the door. My irritation at Dora for this detour had quickly replaced gratitude; it overflowed effortlessly to engulf anyone else I thought was keeping me from the dig.

Especially when Jane and Greg had such troubles suddenly heaped upon them. The last thing they needed was to worry about me. It was imperative that I get to the site as soon as possible, to allay at least one of their concerns. I might even be able to take some of the burden of the dig from them while they worked with the police. I'd help with directing the crew, perhaps. It really was essential that I leave as soon as politely possible. They needed me.

When I returned to the entry hall, there was no one there, not even Palmer. Typical Dora, I thought, to leave me behind as casually as she'd picked me up, but then I realized that I could hear her voice farther down the hallway. Given Dora's capacity for projection, it wasn't difficult to follow her. Despite my earlier resolution to have my tea and leave quickly, however, I had to pause. This room, which might have been called the front hall or entryway if it had been in my house, was spectacular. I dug back through my memories of architectural research and lectures and decided that this would properly be called a hall or perhaps a communicating gallery. The fact that there were paintings and a tapestry hanging from the wall was incidental: this was not a place to loiter in, but a space to be walked through. It was made to make a grand first impression, but overall, it was an insignificant part of the whole establishment.

I glanced at the floor, which was polished marble covered with oriental carpets. They were Chinese, for the most part, I decided, and if they were real, the smallest red one would probably be worth about a year's worth of mortgage payments to me. I looked at the wainscoting that covered the walls—where there wasn't a painting covering it—and saw how the oak had aged, darkening over the course of centuries, had *been* aging since before the Pilgrims started shivering in their little shacks in salt-blown Plymouth Colony. Looking up, I could see that the ceiling was ornately carved into a complex pattern of lattice work and drops and had once been brilliantly painted, perhaps even gilded. Though the decoration had faded to near oblivion and there were cracks in the carving, it was astonishing still.

I found myself gaping like a baby bird waiting to be fed while I stared at the ceiling and forced myself to stop craning and move down the hallway toward the voices. It's just a front hall, Emma, I thought to myself. No boots scattered on the floor or coats hanging off the baluster or cat toys gathering dust in the corners, but it *is* a front hall. I thought of the Funny Farm, the nineteenth-century house with connected buildings that Brian and I had struggled to save for, had only bought just two years ago. I had prided myself on its age, its spaciousness, its architectural details, and, well, its style. It was larger than the Cape that most people can afford for their first house and far more interesting than the 1990s prefab McMansions my father had tried to convince me to buy—at a drastic discount, of course. It didn't matter to me that it was presently decorated in the height of early twenty-first-century Renovation Eclectic, with sawhorses and plywood stacked in the dining room, orange extension cords snaking along the floor between rooms, and a large hole in the kitchen wall where Brian had removed some water-cracked plaster.

It was my house and I loved it, but for all that pride, standing in this room, I was suddenly confronted with the knowledge, knowledge I'd really possessed since the first time I'd laid eyes on the Funny Farm, that my house was a spavined example of a Massachusetts farmhouse.

Pooter's house was a Stately Home.

I never felt so middle class, so small, so . . . *provincial* in my entire life.

That overwhelming sensation of being, simply and finally, outclassed shocked me into paralysis. Then something in me rallied and offered me comfort. Looking at it anthropologically, there was no way I could compete, should I have desired to, with Lord Hyde-Spofford. Any artillery I might have brought to bear—my advanced degrees, my supposed status as a college professor, all the things I had worked to earn—simply could not be compared with a hereditary title and its material appurtenances. Apples and oranges. So, even if I was the competitive type—which I certainly am not—I understood immediately that I just wasn't in the same league. That made me relax: the outcome of any social battle was a foregone conclusion.

Though I couldn't quite bring myself to believe that anyone whose front hall was worth my entire house, and then some, would be ordinary—common American snobbery ensured that—at least I could relax, be polite, and drink my tea.

Realizing I'd been dawdling too long, I hurried down the hall, only to be brought up short again. The paintings were all of Marchester, different views from various perspectives, ranging from the sixteenth to the nineteenth centuries. In most of the early ones, the original abbey tower could be seen only as a backdrop in various portraits of someone or other; in the later ones, particularly the romantic eighteenth- and nineteenth-century renderings, the landscape with the new church and the ruins of the abbey was the focus of the subject. I wondered if Jane had had a chance to study these: they would provide an invaluable record of how the site had changed over time. I took another quick look around before I headed for the room where I could hear Dora.

"You took your time, Emma," she called from across the parlor as soon as I entered.

I restrained myself from making a face. "I couldn't tear myself away from the views of the abbey in the hall. They make a nice history of the town."

"They're not bad, are they?" a man's voice said.

I turned to see my host for the first time. Subconsciously I suppose I had been expecting either an aged and jowly gentleman in the Hogarthian tradition or a refugee from a Brontë novel, talk, dark, brooding, and secretive. Like most preconceptions, this one was less than accurate. Lord Hyde-Spofford was probably in his forties, and although he was a little on the thickset side, he hadn't gone to jowls yet. His hair was light, short, with tight blond curls that were probably his mother's delight and a boy's worst nightmare growing up. His face had a babyish quality, round and full, that emphasized the cupidlike impression; his wide mouth and straight nose broke up the softness of his face. His eyes were alert, another thing that helped keep him from looking ridiculously immature. His lordship was dressed casually in dark trousers, a yellow shirt, and maroon cardigan, and I swear to God, he was actually wearing an ascot. Baby blue, to match his eyes. Even though all the colors clashed like crazy, it somehow seemed to work.

He offered his hand. "How do you do? I'm Jeremy Hyde-Spofford."

Oh, hell, there was yet another name to add to the mix of lordships and Pooters—what to call him? Well, I'd simply avoid the issue for the moment. I shook hands. "Emma Fielding. I'm very pleased to meet you."

"Emma's here to do something archaeological over at the abbey," Dora announced. She was draped comfortably, cup of tea in hand, across an antique chair with slender cabriole legs that looked scarcely sturdy enough to support her bulk.

He looked interested. "Is that so? Well, you must have a seat, and tell me about it. Can I interest you in a cup of tea?"

The gentleman gestured for me to take a seat in a chair that matched Dora's and I sat down tentatively on the edge of it, until I was sure it would bear my weight, and then settled back a little further.

"That would be lovely, thank you—" Here I paused, taking a deep enough breath to get both title and hyphenation out, but his lordship waved a hand and interrupted pleasantly.

"Oh, call me Jeremy. The rest of it makes too much of a mouthful. How do you take your tea?"

"Milk, no sugar, thanks, er, Jeremy."

Jeremy went to a small side table arranged with a porcelain and silver tea service that looked so much like the ones I'd studied in eighteenth-century paintings that I started. He handed me a delicate cup and saucer, so thin as to be translucent, and I was terrified that I might drop them.

Palmer came in with a tray full of sandwiches; his rough bearing and coarse demeanor stood out in this place of delicacy and refinement like a pig in a party dress, and yet he seemed to feel right at home in the house. Perhaps he was a sort of general dogsbody as well as driver?

Jeremy picked up one of the sandwiches, peeked under the bread hopefully, sighed in disappointment. "Perhaps cheese and pickle, just once, Palmer? Just for me?"

Palmer stood impassively, his eyes fixed on the ceiling.

"Palmer always makes cucumber," his lordship explained, "no matter how much I tell him I'd much rather have ham or cheese. They're very nice, though; please have one."

My stomach was just beginning to remind me that it was well past lunchtime and so I decided I'd better take him up on the offer. Jeremy turned to get me a small plate. While I still had one hand free, I automatically flipped my saucer over to examine its base.

"I'm pretty sure it's real, Emma," Dora said.

It wasn't until she'd opened her mouth that I realized my faux pas and blushed violently. I looked up in horror, first at Dora, who was positively delighted, and then at Jeremy, who had returned with my plate and was staring curiously at me.

"Uh, I . . . of course I know it's . . . er." I took a deep breath and tried to stop stammering. I will not apologize, I thought fiercely, I will not! I addressed Jeremy. "It's just this terrible habit I have of looking for the maker's marks on the bottom of dishes and things. Archaeologists learn so much about where and when the wares were made from the markings that I'm afraid I'm always embarrassing myself that way. I'm just happy that I didn't tip the cup over while it was full." I shrugged and smiled.

Jeremy was seriousness itself. "Well, if it's marks you're interested in, marks you shall have. I've a whole pantry full of 'em."

I began to blush again, but then realized he wasn't needling me when he continued.

"I'm afraid it's my fault you're here," he explained. "Dora knows I collect the little bits of things—pottery, glass, bones—that pop up when I'm gardening. I stash 'em in shoe boxes in my pantry. I mean, they belong with the house, don't they? I won't chuck them just because they were in my way." He handed me my plate, and I nodded my thanks. "Plenty of little marks on them. Perhaps sometime you'd stop back and have a look at them, tell me about whether I should hang onto them or no."

"I'd be happy to." I bit into a sandwich, pleased with myself. I surreptitiously gave Dora a little "so there" look, and she rolled her eyes back at me. "You should meet my friend, Jane Compton. It's her project I'll be working on at the abbey ruins, and I'm sure she'd be happy to show you around the site, if you're interested. And," I continued, somewhat boldly, "I'm sure she'd be very interested to see your paintings of Marchester—they'd be incredibly informative about the way the abbey's changed through time."

"Well then, she must come and see them." Jeremy took a sip of tea and looked thoughtful. "Jane Compton? Isn't she the one always causing all sorts of rumpus in town?"

I almost choked. "I beg your pardon?"

"It's in all the papers. Never seen so many people get so worked up over a little patch of damp ground, unless you consider Belgium during the war, of course."

I managed to swallow the rest of my tea, in spite of that last remark.

"Oh, she's got everyone simmering," Jeremy said. "I'm sure she's very nice, sterling, even, but how that little thing managed to annoy the town fathers and the shopping center folks who want to develop the waterfront property—what's that chappie's name, Palmer?"

"Whiting, sir. An 'orrible man, if I may say so."

"Nonsense, the man's ambitious, is all; a bit rough about the edges, but no worse than that. As I was saying, how she can annoy both parties on opposite sides of the debate *and* stir up the New Age types, I'll never know. Yes, I do; you simply can't mix ley lines with saints, is all."

Before I could ask him to explain that, he went on. "And apparently one of her students has gone missing to boot. Not that any of this is her fault, mind, but she does seem to be in the thick of it all."

I digested this all for a moment. "And now they've come up with a suspicious burial as well."

Jeremy put his cup and saucer down. "Suspicious? You mean a murder?"

I shrugged. "Something's not right on the site. Greg didn't tell me much about it, only that it appeared modern, and very fishy, and that the police were involved. Poor Jane."

"Poor Jane indeed. Well, perhaps—"

"Well, perhaps we'd be getting to look at that picture you've been teasing me with, Pooter," Dora interrupted. "My time here is too short to be worrying about poor Jane."

Jeremy shot Dora an exasperated look. "You are perfectly horrible, aren't you? Still, Mother's party is tomorrow and if you're going to see the thing before you bounce off to Italy, it had better be now. Perhaps Emma would also care to have a squint?"

Before I could open my mouth, Dora answered for me. "Emma's seen Raphaels before. She's got to be going, or so she's been telling me all along."

For once, I had to agree with Dora, although I would have given my eyeteeth to see a privately owned Raphael. "I'm afraid I really must be going—"

"I'll have Palmer bring you back to town, but you must promise to come back and look at my bits of things and we'll sneak you in to look at the picture while Mother's asleep. She's so deaf, dear thing, she'll never notice. Still, she's eighty tomorrow and that's something."

"Thank you so much for everything, Jeremy." I really hadn't expected, or wanted, to like him but I found myself charmed by his kind and frank manner. I set my teacup and plate aside with a smothered sigh of relief; despite my worst fears, they were still intact. It suddenly occurred to me that these were Jeremy's things, though; his household stuff. He lived with them every day.

We walked out to the hall and Jeremy and I shook hands again. "Here, now," he said suddenly. "You're very fit, aren't you?"

"Excuse me?"

"Fit. Healthy." He gave me an appraising look, up and down. "I suppose like so many Americans, you exercise like fury."

"Well, I run, but I—" I stammered, not knowing what was going on.

"Dear Pooter, always thinking of sport," Dora said.

I began to get really worried.

"Well, I'm sure you'll do fine," Jeremy announced. "You must come next hunt, you'll do splendidly."

"Ah . . . er . . ." I had no idea what was transpiring, but I wasn't at all convinced that I wanted any part of it. It sounded baroque and decadent and way out of my league. One heard stories about the jaded aristocracy, of course, but one never expected—

"We don't actually ride to the hounds, there are no horses, no guns, and we don't kill any foxes," his lordship said. "I could never stand the sight of the poor things struggling, long before the animal rights people came along and made it trendy. We don't even use a fox these days, we just send Palmer tearing off with a bit of burlap soaked in fox piss and then we just chase along, following after the dogs, baying like mad. The dogs, I mean, not us, but if you had the urge to bay, I'm sure no one would object. Dear, lovely things, the dogs, but not a spoonful of brains amongst fifty of them. It's really good fun, fresh air, brilliant food. Say you'll come."

I was so relieved to understand finally what he was going on about that I thought I would collapse. "I wouldn't miss it for the world." But no horses? Ma would be devastated when I told her that I was invited to a fox hunt by a sure-enough lord and there were no horses. Running after stinky burlap just doesn't play the same at the country club cocktail hour.

We made our farewells and I thanked Jeremy for his hospitality before Palmer escorted me back out to the car. As we left the parlor, I could hear Jeremy chewing Dora out.

"—The way you carry on sometimes, just a perfect duchess. I'm surprised you have any friends left at all."

"Oh, Pooter," Dora began, but by then we were too far away to hear the rest of it. It must have been funny, because I could hear them both crack up laughing.

As the car pulled back down the drive, with me the sole occupant in the backseat now, I felt a pang, wishing I could have spent a little more time at the house. It was another world, and this became increasingly clear as we pulled into town, where things seemed foreign to me, but were on a scale that I could relate to, at least.

I could see the tower of the new church growing as we approached the site and I was interrupted in my reflections by the gruff and polite clearing of Palmer's throat. "If I might offer a bit of advice?"

"Sure, Palmer." So easily I fell into the habits of those around me; where was the "Mr." now, Emma? But was Palmer his surname?

"I should be very careful about becoming involved in any of the goings on in the town. With the doings down the abbey."

I looked up, startled. "I'm not sure I—"

"It's local business, really," Palmer continued matter-of-factly, "and it's just we locals don't appreciate when outsiders try to come in and mess about with things. We're a close community, we don't want a lot of outsiders—like Jane Compton—mucking things up. See what I mean?"

Surely this wasn't some sort of threat? I thought, in a panic.

"I'm sure you understand. I wouldn't want you walking in on something you didn't belong in, what with your friend being in the thick of it and all, and especially seeing's his lordship has taken such a fancy to you. A word to the wise, eh?"

Palmer's words seemed quite friendly, but his eyes were cold as they regarded me in the rearview mirror. I noticed, for the first time, the web of scars that crisscrossed the chauffeur's large right hand as it gripped the steering wheel.

"Uh, sure. Thanks," I managed to stammer out.

"Ah, there you are, just to your left, Professor," Palmer called out, suddenly jolly. "The Prince of Wales."

"Where?" I whipped my head around, looking for my first sight of a royal.

"We're just coming up on it now. A very pleasant pub, and a very proper place for the ladies. You might sample the local bitter while you're here."

"I'll . . . I'll certainly make a point of it," I said. I frowned and rubbed my eyes. I was so tired that I could easily have been making too much of Palmer's warning, but it was certain that I'd landed in the middle of a real mess.

We turned down off the main street—the "high street," as Palmer called it, continuing his little tour of the local sites—and then one or two more side streets until the buildings fell away and I could see the sluggish river Mar again. We passed the new church and its tower, and as we approached the site of the ruined abbey about a half mile later, I could see a couple of police cars and the dig itself, partially cordoned off within the chain-linked enclosure.

It was the sight of blue and white police tape and backdirt piles that told me that, after a morning of adventures and seeing how the other half lived, I was back where I belonged.

Chapter 3

GETTING OUT OF THE CAR, I HEARD RAISED VOICES fifty or so feet away from the pavement. One of the police cars took off, leaving one left. A figure in a short dark green raincoat followed the remaining policeman back toward the car, not quite pleading, but certainly insistent.

Palmer set my bag on the sidewalk and shut the trunk with a solid-sounding *whomp*. "There you are, Professor. And, if I'm not mistaken, that should be la Compton over there, harrying the local constabulary—"

I might not buy into all of the niceties of class distinction here, or understand exactly what the social mores were, but I did know when it was time for me to speak up. "Mr. Palmer, Jane Compton is a good friend of mine. I don't appreciate your comments."

He stared at me, his grin fading instantly. "Of course, I beg your pardon," he said woodenly. "If there's nothing else, I'll be on my way."

"Well . . . thanks again," I said uncertainly.

He nodded and the car glided off; the people I saw were too busy arguing to pay it or me any attention. In the distance, I could see a crew working, digging neatly delineated squares and rectangles within the larger excavation, occasionally putting their finds into flat little trays, but then I started to look at the excavations like a digger and not a director, and realized I didn't see anyone using screens to sift their dirt. Filing this disturbing tidbit away for later consideration, I juggled my suitcase into a comfortable position, for what I hoped would be nearly the last time today, and began to walk over to the opened gate in the tall fence surrounding the entire site.

I admit it, I was tired and distracted by the day's events. That's why the car sneaking up on me from the right hand side had to honk suddenly, waking me up and forcing me back to the curb. I'd have to pay more attention to the traffic, if I didn't want to end up a smear on the road.

I stopped again, this time to readjust the strap of my backpack, and, just as Palmer had indicated, realized that it was Jane who was arguing with the policeman. I recognized her right away, in spite of her harassed expression. Perhaps it was because of this look; Jane has always struck me as being one of those efficient women, always right there with the answer, or a pencil, or a map, or a flashlight, or whatever happened to be needed at the moment. From conferences, I remembered that her nose was small and to the point, her mouth generally pursed, her brown eyes always focused on the task at hand, yet ever aware of what was going on in the periphery. The swing of her dark hair was almost impatient, and somehow she managed to make a chin-length blunt cut look elegant at the same time it was easy to maintain. There was something feline about her alertness, her focus, as if she were always waiting to pounce. She was the soul of organization, but now I could see there was little calm won from all of that productivity. I got the impression that even when she wasn't at work, Jane was always on red alert, and woe betide anyone who couldn't keep up with her.

After I looked both ways and crossed, I watched as Jane

threw up her hands. The policeman closed his notebook with finality, spoke again briefly, got into the last car, and left.

I noticed another man approach her; she didn't even look up when he put his hand on her shoulder and began to speak to her. He was wearing a dark green jacket identical to hers—in fact, they were both wearing jeans and rubber Wellington boots—but although he was of a similar height to Jane's, about medium for a man, his appearance was far less tidy. He had longish, wiry ginger hair that, when the wind blew, gave me the impression of ruffled fur, and his face was unremarkable, a domestic face, vaguely oval, nose a bit snub, eyes perhaps widened by glasses that gave the impression of being mildly interested and friendly. He slouched a bit, and when he went to pull a handkerchief out of his pocket, several other items fell out along with it. He retrieved them almost out of habit, and replaced his hand on Jane's shoulder, but she shrugged it off with annoyance, and I decided that I ought to make myself known before things got awkward.

I didn't quite make it. As I approached, I heard part of Jane's side of the conversation.

Her syllables were carefully pronounced and crisp to the point of staccato, like pebbles dropped in rapid succession onto gravel. "—Entirely well qualified to do my own excavating, thank you very much. Of all the fascist—"

The man interrupted casually. "You're making too much of it, Jane, it's nothing to do with you. It's entirely a matter of procedure, and when Andrew gets back—"

That confirmed it: I recognized the voice on the telephone from that morning. The man was Greg Ashford, Jane's husband. Jane interrupted him right back.

"*When* Andrew gets back?" she said bitterly. "Why isn't he here *now*? The last thing I need is for my staff to go wandering off, especially now. He should know better than that. This is the last straw, I promise you. Any more of these antics and I *will* kill him one day—"

More than time to make my presence known, I decided. "Umm. Hi, Jane?" I picked up my pace. "I finally made it!"

They turned to see me; I watched Jane's peaches and cream complexion go scarlet. The couple hurried over and Greg, reaching for my bag, said, "Here, please allow me."

"Oh, God, Emma! I can't tell you what a morning we've had!" Jane said. "I'm so sorry about missing you, but things have been an absolute shambles here! A complete nightmare. Still, I should have known you'd be all right— Emma's the sort who's always on top of things, Greg—but you shouldn't have had to find your own way."

I knew enough to anticipate Jane's kiss on my cheek—so much for British reserve—and I turned to shake hands with Greg.

"Welcome to Marchester Abbey," Greg said, a little lazier about his words than his wife, occasionally lopping the ends of them, blurring other letters together. He'd said "March'ster," while Jane had pronounced every bit of it; Jane was a geometry of angles and a mass of precisely directed energies, Greg was a little more blurred about the edges, more laid back. He hefted my bag. "The rest of your stuff going to follow?"

"No, this is everything," I said.

He exchanged a glance with his wife. "I see what you mean. Well, come have a look round. We're rather shorthanded at the moment—" here he exchanged another look with Jane—"But we should be able to give you a taste of how we do things."

"Bloody Andrew, pissing off like this!" Jane inserted vehemently, as though she'd forgotten that I was present. She gave every indication of resuming her tirade.

Greg looked horrified. "Er, Jane, surely . . . not in front of the . . . not in front of company."

Jane heaved a tremendous sigh. "Pardon my language, Emma, but our osteologist has done a runner. We've no idea where he's got to—"

Before I could stop myself, the incredulous words were out. "What? You've lost *another* one?"

Both Jane and Greg stopped dead to gape at me. "Well," I

said, shrugging uneasily, "Greg said 'Julia' to me on the phone, so I'm assuming that she's your student who's disappeared. Andrew must be someone else."

"I didn't say anything more . . . more than Julia was gone," Greg stammered.

Jane gave me a long look. "Gregory," she said slowly, "when I said that Emma was the sort who was always on top of things, I didn't actually mean clairvoyant, but apparently she's that too. How on earth did you find out—?"

"Oh, it's no trick," I assured her. "My friend Dora and Mr. Palmer were talking about town, and I heard a little of that, but then Jeremy filled some more for me."

"Jeremy?" Jane was puzzled and a little annoyed, I could tell, not to know immediately who I was talking about. Greg raised his eyebrows, which were just dark enough to give his face definition and the general appearance of good-natured curiosity.

"Or maybe you call him 'Pooter'? He's got a terrific collection of views of the abbey and said you should come have a look—"

"She's talking about Lord Hyde-Spofford," Greg said quietly to his wife. "I suspect 'Pooter' is an unfortunate relic of his school days."

Jane bristled. "I most certainly do *not* call him 'Pooter.' "

And then she was no longer addressing me, or even Greg, for that matter. "As for Julia, she's over twenty-one, she can do what she likes. Andrew, on the other hand, has a professional obligation to—"

Her husband interrupted mildly. "Julia had a professional obligation; Andrew's also over eighteen—"

"I'm not talking about an obligation to me, Greg," Jane said curtly, bright spots of color growing on her cheeks, "though I'm not convinced that isn't an issue. I'm talking about his responsibility to the police."

"What? How on earth was he supposed to know what we'd come across today?"

"He should have been here," Jane said stubbornly. "He

hasn't been on site since Friday morning and he's holding up work."

"We can work somewhere else and let the police get on—"

This was ridiculous, I thought, as I watched them go back and forth. "Perhaps I can help fill in for Andrew. Where was he supposed to be working?"

Jane remembered I was there again, and composed herself quickly. "He was supposed to be working on one of the burials," she explained, "but this is rather a dodgy case. It looks suspicious, you see. The shaft now appears to manifest itself too shallowly for a medieval burial—it's too near the modern surface and it's not terribly regular. There's a button that looks decidedly recent to me and the grave cuts through the edge of several other burials that are definitely known to be medieval, so stratigraphically, it *has* to be later, otherwise, it couldn't intrude into the burials that were already there. How much later, we can't say yet. It could be seventeenth- or eighteenth-century, or even—"

"Jane, I'm sure Emma understands this sort of thing," Greg said gently.

Jane sighed and rubbed at her eye. "Oh, Emma, I'm sorry. I've been behaving badly, haven't I?"

I was starting to feel a little impatient with her remedial lecture, but managed a smile. "You've had a rough day."

"Speaking of which." Greg gave Jane a meaningful look.

She turned to where the crew was working, some watching her expectantly. "Ah yes. Emma, could you oblige me with one of your absolutely excruciating whistles?"

I smiled for real this time, and put my pinkies to my lips just as Jane warned Greg to cover his ears. I let loose with a shrill whistle that got the attention of the entire crew.

"She did that at a conference once, when the person doing the slides was talking and didn't mind the focus," Jane told Greg. "I wish I could do that." She turned and called out to the crew of about fifteen or so, who looked up at this rude interruption. They gathered, a little warily, waiting for her announcement.

"Before you dig out your tea things, could I have your attention please?" she called to them. "This is Emma Fielding, PhD, of Caldwell College in Maine, in the United States—"

"Oh, so does that make you a maniac, then?" a youthful voice called out, in a Scots accent. There was playful shoving, and a young man with shaggy brown hair fell out of ranks, picked himself up, and waved at me, unapologetic. Although the rest of the crew was wearing the usual range of jeans or army surplus trousers, this student was wearing sweat pants, which were weighted down with caked mud and heading south, exposing an alarming proportion of some colorfully striped underpants.

Titters ran through the group and I saw Jane flush. Before she could say anything, I shot back, "No, I live in Massachusetts; that makes me a Masshole. Next question?"

There was a moment of quiet shock, followed by laughter; the crew relaxed noticeably. Jane continued.

"Now then, Gareth. Her postgraduate degrees are from Coolidge University and her work on early European–Native American contact sites took the ASAA dissertation prize. Those of you who had my material culture class will remember her articles on European pottery on early American colonial sites, others of you might have read her new monograph on the artifacts of Fort Providence. Recently she's been conducting work on several projects, including—"

God, I thought. Jane was really spreading it thick. I curbed my urge to stare at my shoes, smiling benignly as she continued to run down my résumé.

"—She's going to be working with us for the next fortnight or so, so please answer any questions she might have, and don't be afraid to make the most of her expertise while she's here. Perhaps she'll favor us with a lecture or two on her work?"

Jane raised her eyebrows enquiringly; we hadn't discussed this, but of course I'd brought some things along with me, just in case. "I've got the slides, if you've got the projector."

"And the beer?" A small brown-haired woman called.

Jane nodded, as much to acknowledge my favorable response as to the question. "Of course, of course. If we have an evening lecture, I wouldn't want it to cut into your valuable drinking time, Nicola—"

"I should think not," came the cheery response.

"Go get your tea, then." She dismissed them and I watched the crew amble over to a pile of backpacks from which they retrieved thermoses.

"Did you make any sarnies today, Jane?" This was the young Scot with a sense of humor.

"I'll get my rucksack, Gareth," she answered. "Back in a second, Emma."

Two voices piped up next to my elbow. "Could I get you to sign this for me, Professor?"

"And mine, please?"

Two of the students had pushed forward to me while the others were sorting through their bags. They both held copies of my Fort Providence book. This was still a relatively new thrill for me, so I was happy to oblige.

"And your name is . . . ?" I asked the red-haired lad with an embarrassing number of freckles.

"Will, please. Jane spent a lot of time on your work in class. I thought your book was brilliant."

"Jane's introduction was a bit much—" I began, a little put off by his bald flattery, and trying to concentrate on writing on the book with no surface to rest on.

"Oh, if Jane says something is so, it is. You can rely on it."

I handed him his book.

The young woman, the petite brunette with a pointy, foxy face, nodded in agreement, and held out hers. "I'm Nicola, with a C. Will's right, Jane always does her homework. There's always a reason for everything she says."

"I imagine she's a tough instructor," I said, scratching away on Nicola's book.

"Oh, well, yes, but, not . . . er—"

Will paused and I realized that he was trying not to say anything bad about Jane at the same time he was trying not to contradict me.

Nicola jumped in. "She is, she's very demanding, but she always knows how to explain something if you don't get it. That's the thing. You know, everyone has a different way of learning things and she always figures out where you're getting caught up and is able to explain it in a way that you'll understand. She asks a lot of us, but she's very patient that way, so we know it's well worth the effort. With Jane, you always know you'll learn something."

"Unless you're Bonnie," Will said.

Nicola snorted. "Bonnie's not a real archaeologist. She's an undergraduate who only signed up for an archaeology degree because she heard there were a lot of men. Thanks, Professor Fielding." She took her book back.

"You're welcome, but call me Emma, okay?"

Will just about wriggled. "Thanks, Emma."

"Yes, thanks." They hurried over to their tea, comparing what I'd written on their title pages. I'd written the same on both of them, "Pleased to meet you at Marchester Abbey, best wishes," etc. Not very imaginative, but at least personalized.

Jane returned, emptied rucksack in hand. "I hope Will hasn't been annoying you. He tends to be a bit of a creep, but he's not a bad sort. Have you eaten anything? I did actually bring extra for you today; I didn't plan on being a wretched hostess."

My stomach growled alarmingly. "I could do with a bite, but I don't want to keep you from work."

"Not a bit; we always have our tea break about this time. Have a sandwich, I made them in your honor." Greg brought over his backpack and a thermos. "Cup of tea?"

"Yes, please," I said, taking both the offered sandwich and the cup. My head was still feeling achy, but I attributed that to jet lag. I bit into the sandwich, and my surprise must have been evident on my face, because both Jane and Greg laughed.

"It's peanut butter and . . . what?" I said, crunching my mouthful cautiously.

"Cucumber. I thought you'd like a little taste of home," Jane said.

"It's very nice," I said, and it was, once I got used to the idea. It really wasn't bad, only curious and nothing I'd ever eaten in New England. I had been hoping for some of the much vaunted cheese sandwiches I'd recently heard about.

"Look, I'll show you around a bit today, and we'll meet up with everyone tonight at the pub, introduce you properly."

I could feel my shoulders sag. I couldn't face any more visiting today.

"It's just around the corner, very nice sort of place. Unless you're feeling tired," Greg guessed shrewdly.

Jane and Greg had looked so pleased with themselves and their plan that I hated to disappoint them. "Oh, that is so sweet of you, but I just can't. I'm beat and I honestly don't think that I would be very good company."

Greg turned to Jane, worried. "I thought you said that Emma drank beer?"

"Oh, I do, I'm definitely a fan!" I hastened to assure him. "But I just couldn't tonight."

I began to worry about etiquette; the way they were acting, an invitation to the pub sounded like an important gesture. I tried to staunch any social breach by suggesting tentatively, "Maybe tomorrow night? Would that be okay?"

My hosts exchanged a doubtful look. "Well, maybe this once," Jane said slowly.

Greg nodded more decisively. "No, no, we can do that." He took out a small pocket diary—along with a piece of flagging tape, which fluttered to the ground—and noted, "Tuesday, Emma, pub." He underlined the notation care-

fully, closed the calendar, and smiled broadly, as he tucked it
back into his pocket. "I'll make the necessary arrangements.
Nothing simpler." He stooped to pick up the flagging and returned it to its place as well.

Jane turned away and coughed, probably embarrassed
for me.

"I really appreciate it," I said, standing up and brushing
the crumbs from my lap. Jane and Greg watched me, puzzled.

"Er, the facilities are located just over there," Jane offered. "There's a porta-loo, if that's what you're looking
for."

Porta-loo? Probably British English for porta-potty.
"Maybe later; I was just finished with my sandwich and
thought we could get to work."

Jane looked at her watch. "There's another fifteen minutes, Emma, no rush."

My mouth twitched. It seemed a very loose way of running things, especially when there was daylight burning.
Everyone just lying around, drinking tea, eating the pile of
sandwiches that Jane had provided; my palms itched at the
thought of all those students lazing about. It wasn't right.

I surveyed the site. It was big for an urban site, nearly half
the size of a football field. Within the ten-foot-tall chain-link
fence it was open, save for a couple of stands of trees and the
low remains of a wall, less than half a meter high, by the
river's edge, suggesting the original location of the abbey.
The ground had been mechanically graded into a nearly
level, roughly rectangular shape, punctuated by neater, more
regular rectangles: the excavated burials.

Outside the fence were a few more trees and overgrown
weeds. Across the street I had come down were a few shops
and more houses, most of them in neat rows of dark gray
stone. I knew that the "new" church, a pretty but modest
structure built in 1520 after the destruction of the abbey, was
about a half mile to the west of us, obscured by the gentle
curve of the land and a few stands of trees. Across the river

Mar was the more commercial area of Marchester, which was still of a scale small enough to be human. All in all, it was a pretty spot; I thought it would have made a nice park, once the archaeologists had finished and decamped and someone spent a couple of weekends cleaning out the weeds and rubbish.

"Maybe I'll just take a walk around, have a look at things, stretch my legs until you're ready," I said.

"Well, I suppose we can oblige you there." Jane got up and dusted herself off. "Okay, follow me." She walked toward the water, talking and pointing very fast. "Right, then, the river is site south; the graves will generally be oriented east-west, according to your early Christian traditions—buried bodies face the east, so that they will be facing the proper direction at the last trump—so they will in most cases be running parallel to the river. I say in most cases, because excavations within the original confines of the abbey, where most of your important types tend to get buried, reveal that space was at a premium and your lesser gentry were getting bunged in any which way. No problem, really, because they were getting pretty well consecrated just by being within the abbey walls. You can see just the tiniest bit of the structure walls left—most of the ruins were knocked over during the war by a bomb's concussion—it doesn't look like anything actually hit the site here—and a lot of the rest of the stones were removed or robbed out after. Now, as for burial goods, we're not expecting much and we're not finding much—that's all in order. We are finding some personal adornment—fasteners, some leather, ornaments *very* rarely—and possibly the odd memento or two, men and women both—"

I knew from my reading that while Marchester Abbey was a female community, the wealthier and more important members of town—male and female alike—would be buried inside the abbey. I frowned.

"Why was Greg so concerned about having uncovered a man's skeleton, then?"

"Because we found it in what I believe, based on comparative data and remote sensing, was the sisters' graveyard. A man's burial would make more sense inside the abbey or outside where the rest of the town's parishioners could expect to be buried, as long as they hadn't done anything stupid, like killing themselves or someone else. In those cases, they were buried outside consecrated ground—not very desirable, in terms of salvation. Here we are."

Jane stopped and pulled back a large piece of green plastic. It covered a deep cut in the ground, in which a trench was cut about two meters long, about one wide, and about one deep.

"You can see here that it cuts into those other two burials that we'd begun to expose."

Sure enough, walking around to the other side, I could see where the more recent burial had been dug into the earlier ones. Luckily, it just nicked the edges and there wasn't too much mixing between the graves: the soil there was mottled where the pits intersected each other, and comparatively straight, clean edges existed where the burials had been left alone. This new shaft also contained more cobbles on the surface and in the wall profile.

"How old do you think this one is?" I said, squinting down into the shallow shaft. I could just make out the reddish-brown, soil-stained bones at the base of it. They'd barely been exposed.

"We've got one button, and I'm guessing it is no more than a hundred years old. You'd be better able to tell us, I suppose. Americans have the greater need to learn about much more recent artifacts." She said that with the faintly patronizing air I'd come to expect from European scholars used to sites with a much longer historical record.

"I'd be happy to look, but why isn't anyone working here now?"

"Because," Jane enunciated with reborn ire, "to start with, the bloody coppers have determined that I'm not fit to excavate my own site! And furthermore—"

"That can't be right—" I began, but Jane was on a tear.

"No, it's quite maddeningly correct! In this particular situation, where the burial is deemed to be suspicious, the police have to come in and investigate. They would like Andrew to have a look before they call the Home Office pathologist—Detective Chief Inspector Rhodes has used him as an expert before—"

"But he's nowhere to be found," I finished for her.

"So we must leave the grave, that whole area, in fact, alone, until his lordship thinks it meet and fit to grace us with his presence again." Jane's hands were knotted into fists so tight I thought she'd pop a knuckle out. Just as quickly, though, she regained command of herself and resumed our tour.

"I'm guessing you've done the reading I suggested, so I won't bore you with the details. Constructed in A.D. 1190 and destroyed by fire—a lightning strike, according to the chronicles—about 1504. Left a very nice little burn layer for us, helps show how far back in time we've gone when we dig. Benedictine pattern of building arrangement, I'm predicting, no great stretch there. While our main goals last year were to define the parameters of the abbey and nunnery, this year we're trying to determine the number and organization of the graves, interior and exterior. Looks to be quite a few; we've already identified twenty in ground, fully excavated seven of them. We should get a nice little population."

Jane stopped and looked at me. "Emma, are you feeling entirely well?"

I turned away from an odd sight—a line of paper plates that looked as though they'd been nailed to the grassy ground outside the perimeter of the excavation. Now that she mentioned it, I felt awful. My head was pounding and I kept feeling as though I were fading in and out of focus. "I think the time zone changes must be catching up with me. What time is it?"

"Nearly half four. Greg's got them closing up for the night."

Sure enough, I saw the crew going through the universally recognizable patterns of cleaning tools and storing them and covering units until work began again tomorrow morning.

"How about we get you home, into a hot bath, perhaps a glass of something, then dinner and bed for you? That sound like it would do the trick?"

"It sounds perfect," I said gratefully. A little food and a little quiet and rest would do me a world of good, particularly since my tummy was starting to feel queasy. Jane had a way of taking things in hand that was very soothing.

Jane was all concern, pushing her hair behind her ear. "Well, let's get going. It's not a long walk, just a few blocks, really—do you feel up for that? Just tired, not going to faint on us, are you?"

"No, I'll be fine after a good night's rest," I reassured her.

"Then we'll let Greg sort things out here and whisk you home, chez Ashford-Compton."

Jane took my big bag and her rucksack and I picked up my backpack; she called out, "Greg, we'll see you back there. You'll do the walk-through?" He waved. "I always like to take the crew around at the end of the day, make sure everyone gets an update on what's going on throughout the site."

We began to walk away from the river, through a little winding street crowded with homes and the odd corner store. It was a quiet part of a quiet little town, and had a very cozy, neighborly feel to it. I realized that the rowhouses were built with the same gray masonry as the new church; it must be a local stone. I noticed a lot of bicycles chained up in front yards and little window boxes filled with early summer blooms—people here obviously thought a lot of keeping their homes tidy. We went around a few more turns and down one more long street before we reached our destination.

"Here we are, 98 Liverpool Road," Jane said, pausing before the last door at the end of a block of rowhouses in a cul-de-sac. The building was three stories, and narrow, virtually identical to the other doors, but it was distinguished by a dark red doorway, outlined in white to match the window frames, and a row of pansies on the window ledge.

"We are lucky to have the last house on the end—much quieter than the others. Come in, I'll show you to the bath right away."

Jane gave me a spare key and then showed me to my room, a quiet space on the third floor, and then to the bath, on the second floor, which was narrow and a little old fashioned looking, but had a marvelous old white enameled tub.

"Take your time, fill it up, soak your cares away," she said, almost jolly, now that she was away from the dig. "I'll get to work on dinner and then we'll tuck you into bed."

"Sounds heavenly," I said. And it was. The water almost reached my chin and I steeped for what felt like hours, but when I checked my watch, it had only been about twenty minutes. Still, it was a luxury to me and I felt worlds better, despite my stomach. Odd, I thought. I have the constitution of a particularly tough rhino; it was unusual for me to feel ill.

The bath restored me in great part, and then I called Brian to let him know I'd made it all right. He sensed something was up immediately, and I finally told him about the missing student and the modern burial. I couldn't help saying that I was feeling a little haunted.

"It's nothing to do with you," he said immediately. "You're only there to dig and buy books and visit your friends, not necessarily in that order."

And with that, the subject changed, by mutual agreement, until we reluctantly said good-bye. When I finally found my way to the basement kitchen—painted a warm cream with green and orange accents—I discovered that Jane had kicked it up into high gear. A pot of tomato sauce was bubbling, filled with mushrooms, if the scent was any indication. Pasta was boiling on the tiny stove, and Jane was picking leaves off plants that grew in a row of pots near the basement window.

At first I was taken aback by that sight; her plants looked suspiciously like the illicit little set-up Kam and Brian had in their graduate school apartment, but then I realized that Jane was picking fresh basil. Next to a large terrarium tank with a light, she had an herb garden in the kitchen, all trained up and orderly.

"Anything I can help you with?" I asked.

"Yes, thanks. That chair at the table desperately needs to be held down, and that glass of wine needs to be emptied right away," Jane said. "Apart from that, I'm pretty well set: I've got the bread heating, a salad and dressing all done, Hildegard's fed—the tortoise is Greg's, the stupid thing—and there's a batch of little cheesy nibbles just ready . . . now." The instant she said "now," the oven timer chimed.

Jane continued as she pulled the tray from the oven; the most delicious smell of herbed cheese struck me. She nodded toward the tank. "When he told me he wanted a tortoise, I thought, great, a tortoise won't be any work at all. The perfect pet for the busy couple. When I ever found out how temperamental they are and how much care they need—diet, temperature, this, that, and the other—well, they're much more bother than a cat. And yet I've rather got attached to the bumpy little thing, I must say."

I sat obediently at a large oak farmhouse table and took a sip of my wine, overwhelmed by Jane's energy. She was already clean, somehow, and flushed with the steam of cooking food.

"Here, eat up while they're hot." She slid the hot canapés into a plate in front of me, then whirled back to the basil on the chopping board.

Greg came in and emptied his overstuffed pockets into a basket set on the counter for exactly that purpose. I was impressed by the range and amount of detritus that ended up in the basket.

"All right, Jane?" he said.

"Everything's just about set," she called over her shoulder as she chopped. "There's a paper by your chair; we didn't have the hands to fetch one on the way, but I dashed across the street while Emma was having her bath."

"Makes you dizzy to watch her, doesn't it?" Greg asked me fondly.

"I feel like a princess," I replied, "all looked after."

"Greg, if you'll grab those two bowls, I believe we are ready to begin."

Greg set the food on the table and Jane finally sat down, and it was as if I had been holding my breath the entire time. Jane's imitation of a whirlwind had exhausted me.

We dawdled over dinner, talking for a couple of hours; as curious as I was about the modern burial, I held off asking; Jane looked too relaxed to bring up work and, heaven knew, it would be there tomorrow. Even though we'd dined fairly early—just about six o'clock—I found myself almost sinking asleep into my plate by eight-thirty.

"Emma, don't try to fight it," Greg insisted. "We've all had one hell of a day and we'll be the better for it if we make an early night of it. We'll be down here for a while, but if you need anything, our room is on the second floor."

"Yes, do go up. Sleep well, Emma," Jane chimed in. She looked quite relaxed now, her knees drawn up, feet resting on another chair, cheeks flushed with food and wine.

"Thanks, I will. Dinner was wonderful, good night."

I had intended to go straight up to my room, but as I passed the parlor, I noticed the bookcases and couldn't resist a peek. You learn so much about people by their taste in books.

The wall by the door was covered in framed photos and bookcases. One bookshelf was for work, it seemed, full of titles by and about Chaucer, Christine de Pizan, and Hildegard of Bingen. There were some duplicates, probably where Jane and Greg's collections overlapped. On the next I saw lots of Orwell, lots of Lawrence and Woolf, followed by a whole row of Wodehouse. Right, I thought, those first will be Jane's and the next will be Greg's. When I snuck a look at the flyleaf of *The Inimitable Jeeves*, however, I saw Jane's decisive signature as well. Maybe Greg's were the collection of dog-eared Tom Clancys?

As I reached for the book, Greg came into the room. "Aha, I've caught you. Share Jane's addiction for spy novels, do you?"

"Not really. These are all hers?"

"Yeah, my taste runs more to nonfiction, architecture, natural history, that sort of thing. Nothing so psychological or technological. They're upstairs, if you're interested."

"Not really, I'm just being nosy. I was heading for the photos next."

"Oh, well, by all means, let me guide you. Here's a good one."

Greg pointed to a photo of him and Jane, he in a suit, Jane formal in academic robes adorned with the braid and fur I've always envied my European counterparts as well as the usual velvet hood and tam. She was beaming brighter than a thousand suns and I thought it was nicely appropriate that a scholar of medieval archaeology should be garbed in robes that had their origin in the Middle Ages.

"She'd just got her PhD. We went to the Lake District for a week after that, and spent most of the time hiking, drinking, or in bed."

"Sounds like fun."

"It was good. I finished the year after, and we went back to the same place, over here." In this picture, the pair of them were grinning cheesily for the camera, small peaks in the distance behind them. "I didn't go to the ceremony."

"Oh?"

"Well, honestly, I wasn't bothered. Some old man in muttering Latin over me wasn't going to turn me into an archaeologist, was he? Too much archaic ritual, for my taste."

"I suppose," I said. I wouldn't have missed my degree ceremony for the world.

He tapped the glass of the photo. "And besides, I would have felt ridiculous in the gown with all those bits of velvet and tassels and such. Jane thought I ought to, since I'd worked so hard, but really, she was the one who straightened me out, set me down to proper work. I might not have finished if left to my own devices."

I looked at him. "Did you really *want* to do the degree?"

Greg nodded soberly. "Yeah, I did, because I couldn't do the sort of work I want without one. I just found it hard to settle down to it. You see, it was the writing. The analysis and the reading were fine, but then there was the writing."

He shuddered. "Writing anything but a straight report gives me hives, and the thought of applying all that theory to my lovely, straightforward data stopped me cold. I found every excuse in the book to avoid it, but once Jane had finished, she took over. She did all the housework, looked after all the little things that can distract one. She taught me how to tackle the thesis so I wouldn't get overwhelmed by the enormity of it. She must have read my thesis thirty times, and her comments made it better, every time. I couldn't have done it without her."

I was impressed by the frankness of his admission, even as he colored at it. "What's this one? Who is this with you?" I could tell the picture had been taken a long time ago. Greg's hair was much longer, and therefore much frizzier, so that he resembled a dandelion going to seed. He must have been wearing contact lenses then. The other man's hair was dyed black and teased into New Wave tufts that must have required a fortune in styling gel to maintain. Both wore overlong black sweaters, narrowly cut trousers, and boots; both held half-empty beer glasses and wore the solemn smirks of new college students. Greg's friend, however, knew just how much makeup would give the best effect without hiding any of his good looks.

"Ah, that's Andrew Freeman and me." Greg grinned. "University in the eighties, when we were both so much younger and so much prettier. Well, I was as yet unlined, at least; Andrew's still pretty enough to suit his purposes."

"Works it, does he?" I asked, even though I knew the answer. The picture said it all; all that effort put into one's appearance told the story.

"Oh, women have always flocked to him and he's never minded it in the least. Nothing ever sticks, however, but that's just as well with him. His work comes first, always—Andrew's rather monomanic when it comes to his bones—though he does like to keep his hand in with the odd fling, every now and then. Can't blame him for it."

I brought my nose to within an inch of the photo, trying to make something out. "That's not eyeliner you're wearing, is it? Greg, you little Goth, you!"

"Ah, yes, I must cringingly admit that I was, a bit." Greg colored and shoved his glasses up his nose, but then considered the picture critically. "More of a Curehead, really, but we thought we were the coolest things going, all that bleak drama and all." He shook his head, smiling at his younger image, then turned back to me, mock-serious. "Mind you, *Andrew* always bought his own eyeliner and you will notice he's wearing nail varnish. *I* only ever borrowed Jane's eyeliner for parties, but nothing for working days, and nothing on the nails, you'll please notice."

I laughed. "You and Jane were dating then?"

"We'd just started. She took that picture, actually. Andrew wasn't thrilled about her joining us all the time, but eventually he came around, of course. Even flirted with her a bit, though of course Jane would have none of it. She tore him up one side and down the other. Later on, he apologized to me for being a bastard." Greg shrugged and grinned. "I knew he was really just flirting with her to make me feel good—I didn't date much, before Jane."

I didn't say anything. Plain, earnest, honest-looking Greg would have made the perfect foil for Andrew's glamour; I wondered whether there was anything deeper than that to his affection for Greg. As for innocent flirtation with Jane, when I looked at the picture again, I realized that Andrew was every bit as engaged with the photographer as Greg was. It didn't look the least bit innocent to me.

"Here's a nice one, of me and Gran and Aunty Mads." Greg pointed to another picture in a metallic gold frame, the surface glinting greenish with age. "That one's Gran, the smaller one, that's Auntie Mads Crawford. Well, I call her Auntie; she and Gran were great friends. They raised me after my parents died in a car crash."

I saw another even younger version of Greg, this time with shorter hair and heavily rimmed glasses and a navy blue leisure suit, flanked by two older women. A tall, stout woman with gingery hair, which although pinned into a large bun was clearly every bit as wiry as Greg's, was obviously his grandmother. The other woman was shorter, thinner, and thin-lipped, with lighter hair. Both women wore spring suits and hats that were dated, even for this photograph, with corsages and looks of well-satisfied pride. Young Greg, his head tilted down, smiled shyly for the camera.

Greg continued. "That was the day I left school. I thought they would bust, they were dead chuffed. Of course, they never said much about it to me—"

"But just look at them," I said.

"Absolutely. They worked very hard, the two of them, to pay my fees. I had a small grant but it didn't cover everything. I think back now to how hard that must have been for them, but they never said a word about it. They were tough old birds then, and Mads still is. I think it was the war, you know. They'd gone through so much then that I don't believe they ever believed anything less would ever stop them after that—"

"Greg? Where've you got to?" Jane called from downstairs. "I need to ask you about Bonnie's notes, and Emma needs to get to sleep."

Greg and I exchanged a smile and said good night again. I went up and washed at the little sink in my room—complete with a towel, herbal soap, and a clean "toothmug," as Jane had called it—and then fell gratefully into bed. I slept almost at once.

I don't know how long it was later, but it was still dark

when I abruptly woke up. Still groggy and blaming my confused circadian mechanism, I was about to roll over and try to get back to sleep when I realized that I had woken up for a reason. My door was opening.

At first, I thought it must be the fault of the door itself—the house was old, and the door frame was probably out of plumb—but then I saw a form in the faint light of a street-light shining through the hallway window. There was a man in the doorway.

Still uncertain that I wasn't dreaming, I couldn't find my voice for a second, but then I smelled the distinct sour smell of beery sweat and heard the man's harsh breath.

"Who—?" I managed to gasp out, but that was all. I summoned my breath for a scream, but then the stranger surprised me by speaking himself.

"You stubborn little bitch," he said in a low voice. "D'you have any idea what you've put me through?"

Shocked, I watched the stranger fumble for the light switch and then was blinded when the overhead light banished the darkness. When I was able to unscrew my eyes open, I realized that the stranger was in the same boat as I; he squinted back at me, disappointed and every bit as confused as I.

"Who the hell are you?" we demanded simultaneously.

Chapter 4

I GRABBED THE FLASHLIGHT FROM THE TOP OF MY nightstand, grateful that I'd brought the big metallic one that weighed about five pounds instead of the tiny one I use for taking notes in dark auditoriums. Its heft comforted me a little, but I couldn't decide what to do: I didn't want to get out from under the covers, but neither did I want to stay there, vulnerable, in bed. Then I saw how the man was barely able to stand without weaving and decided that I was okay for the moment.

"You first," I said, as assertively as I could. "Who are you? And I'd better like the answer, because I'm about two seconds away from screaming my head off."

"Oh, Christ. You're the . . . American, aren't you? I'd completely forgotten you were . . ." He waved his hand and almost tipped over. "Look, my apologies. . . I'll just be on my way—"

"I don't think so," I said. "Who are you?"

"Look . . . I live here, all right, friend of Greg's, so don't get your knickers in a knot. Honest mistake. I'm Freeman, Andrew Freeman."

"Bloody Andrew," I thought, but I must have said it out loud, because he snorted.

"I see that you've had Jane's opinion of me," he said. "I trus . . . trust you'll soon form your own."

"Yeah, and you're off to a roaring start," I said. A thought came to me. "Who did you expect was going to be here? Obviously not me."

"I thought you were . . ." His brow furrowed and he shook his head. "I don't even remember what I was thinking. As you can see,"—here he paused and licked his lips, and his tone and attitude shifted away from sarcasm—"I am more than a little worse for the drink, so if you don't mind, I'd like to get to bed. I do apologize, I can imagine how . . . startling this must be for you—"

"Startling's one way to look at it—"

"I know, I know. I'm so sorry. Let me take myself away from here; I won't trouble you further."

Without another word, he turned, stumbled against the door frame again, righted himself, and left. The door was left ajar, and although I knew I was probably safe enough, it took me a moment to push the covers off, get up, and close the door. I heard a door down the hall shut loudly as well.

As I scuttled back toward my bed, I realized that my head was still aching. I stopped just long enough to dig out and swallow a couple of aspirin, then leapt back into bed, my heart racing. I was shaken from the encounter.

Good aggression, Em, I thought ruefully to myself. Nice authority, with the comforter pulled up around your chin and a flashlight in your hand.

Well, what was I supposed to do? Ask him to wait while I pulled on my pants? Go for the throat? He was a mess, he didn't mean me any harm. It was just a stupid mistake.

But you didn't know that, my prudent self answered back. You can't rely on that.

I played the incident over and over in my head, left with an image of an ungainly man with brown hair and beard and a prominent nose, not dissimilar to the much younger picture I'd seen of him downstairs. Because I instinctively didn't believe his denials for one minute, I finally fell asleep wondering who the "stubborn little bitch" was.

It seemed like only a moment later that I heard a tapping on the door. I didn't answer at first; then I heard Greg's voice call out.

"Emma, time to get up. May I come in?"

What was it about this room? It seemed to be some kind of central thoroughfare.

"Uh, yeah, Greg." I sat up and tried to tidy myself a little—wipe a bit of drool from my chin, the sleep from my eyes, and realized that my head was pounding as though an enthusiastic blacksmith had taken up residency in it. I found I was entertaining thoughts of strangling Greg for adding to it with his knocking. What the hell was wrong with me?

Greg entered, holding a mug, looking abominably cheery for the hour of the day. "Prerogative of the gentleman of the house to bring morning tea. Milk, no sugar okay?"

"Fine. Thank you very much," I said, taking the mug from him. I took one sip and suddenly realized what was wrong. It was *tea*. It was very good tea, well-brewed and strong, with a nicely balanced flavor.

But I needed coffee.

I hadn't had a cup in nearly twenty-four hours. Hence the headache, hence the nausea. Hence my evil inclinations.

I was going through withdrawal.

Tea, I recalled, had more caffeine than coffee, but it came out in far smaller amounts when brewed. Assuming that some was better than none, I gulped down the entire mug.

Greg watched in silence. "Come downstairs when you've had a chance to wake up a bit. We'll have some breakfast and be off."

"Sounds good," I said, but my head was throbbing worse than ever.

"See you down there."

"Thanks, Greg."

I pulled on my digging clothes—jeans, layers of T-shirt, cotton workshirt, and sweater—and pulled on my boots. I realized that my hands were trembling and thought, if Jane's drinking coffee, I'll ask for some. Otherwise, there's bound to be a Starbucks or something around here. I'm not going to make a nuisance of myself the first morning, I told myself firmly.

What if there's no Starbucks?

Then I'll buy a bag of coffee and suck the grounds, I replied, gritting my teeth. I'm not going to be sidelined by some silly addiction compounding the early hour. I went downstairs.

Jane was whizzing around making another heap of sandwiches and calling out reminders to Greg, who was staring at his tortoise, which was out for a walk on the floor and slowly heading, with its snaky head outstretched and on little clawed elephant feet, toward where he stood in a patch of warm sunlight. I successfully resisted the urge to trip Jane, but not by much.

"Morning, Emma!" she called briskly.

"Morning, Jane."

"There's toast and muesli and more tea on the table—you do eat breakfast?—and I've got lunch packed up for you already. We've got a lot of work today—"

I picked up a triangle of toast and stared at it blankly as Jane listed the day's many goals. My eyes were almost watering with the pain in my head and I couldn't help but tune Jane out—it was as much for her safety as it was for my sanity. Nibbling at the cold, dry toast, I realized that Jane's speech was in fact a monologue. Greg was as silent as I. He had returned Hildegard to her tank, adjusted her lamp, and was now slowly feeding her. He picked up a kale leaf and arranged it at the other end of the terrarium, ostensibly to give Hildegard something to look forward to.

"—And Greg, will you leave that damned thing alone? I swear, you and Hildegard are two of a kind, poky and silent—"

The comment, which sounded like no more than an observation, caught me like a slap in the face. I noticed that Gregory slid a hurt glance toward his wife's back. She hadn't even looked up from the sandwich making.

"Jane, can I give you a hand with those?" I asked hurriedly.

"No, thanks, I'm all done," she said, turning and smiling at me. Then she realized what I was trying to do. "Oh, Emma, don't worry. It's just my way in the morning; Greg knows the claws aren't really out, don't you, dear?"

"Yes, of course. Claws not out, noted." He slid the top back over the terrarium and looked at me critically. "But I'm just wondering if our pet American isn't actually desperate for a cup of coffee? You're not one of those disgusting caffeine-crazed, can't-find-the-floor-in-the-morning-without-a-cup fiends, are you, Emma?"

"Oh, yes, God, yes," I said with relief. "I didn't want to ask, but is there a coffee shop or something I could run to real quick, before we get started? I won't take long, but it would be *really* good and I'm sure I'd be much more useful—"

My hosts exchanged a look and burst out laughing. I didn't even care, so long as the hope of coffee loomed.

"She's gibbering, Jane. I'll take her down the cafe, get her a fix, and meet you over there, shall I?"

"Yes, good, go, don't be late," Jane said, but she'd already turned back to sorting out her notes for the day.

"See you, pet."

She frowned at the notebooks, and when Greg went to buss her cheek, she made a vague kissing gesture about three inches off target, still engrossed in her paperwork.

Upstairs Gregory grabbed his green raincoat from a peg in the hall and led the way out onto the sunny high street. I followed, once again struck by the smell of exhaust that hadn't journeyed through a catalytic converter. The sun was still creeping up and the little town was waking up; a shop-keeper was setting out oranges in a bin, a newsstand vendor pored over a racing form, and a milk float whirred by, clinking empty bottles the only noise over the motor. Gregory walked along, waving to the folks who called good morning to him. He seemed to know everyone in town.

"Jane's preoccupied today," I ventured, hurrying to keep up.

"Jane's been preoccupied since, oh—" he looked at his watch "—about 1987. Someday she'll come back to us all."

At that moment, we arrived at a little shop front with a flyblown sign that simply said "Sandwiches" stuck in the window. Although the sign was faded and dog-eared, and the plastic tables and chairs lined along one wall looked to be about 1960s vintage, the rest of the place was spotless. On the counter was a glass case containing a variety of sandwiches and buns and a basket of candy bars. Behind the counter, pouring tea into six white mugs, was a diminutive old woman, wearing a gauzy purple triangle of a scarf tied under her chin and an apron that buttoned up the front over a quilted jacket; it would have been much too warm for me in the steamy little cafe. I recalled the image I'd seen of her in the photo and decided she'd probably lost something of her height and a lot of her mass since that time; she probably felt the cold more keenly now.

I looked around the rest of the room and saw a couple of patrons glancing back at me with the silent, wary curiosity of habitués sensing some potential disruption to their routine. One or two called over to Greg, who, instead of taking a seat at the last empty table, snuck up behind the old lady and grabbed her in a bear hug from behind.

"Good morning, Auntie Mads!"

"Ooooh!" came the shrill cry. "Aren't you awful, to give an old lady such a scare! And my poor heart being what it is!" She swatted at Greg, but smiled delightedly nonetheless. "What can I get for you, dear?"

"A coffee and a tea, please."

"Just a minute, then." She glanced over at me, then frowned. "Where's that wife of yours, who's too good to make my boy a cup of tea in the morning?"

Greg stopped smiling. "I won't have you talking about Jane like that, I've told you—"

She demurred hurriedly. "All right, all right, but you can't fault me for never thinking anyone would be good enough for my boy."

He gestured to me. "Auntie Mads, this is my friend Emma Fielding. She's helping us work on the abbey for a few weeks."

I wasn't there, for all she noticed me. "All that digging around in the nasty muck. Oh, I wish you'd leave off that, Gregory, and stick to teaching. It's much nicer."

Greg smiled again. "I *am* teaching, Auntie. I'm fine."

"I know you're fine, I just hate thinking of you with all them manky, dirty bones. Diseases, Gregory, there's awful diseases—" She stopped abruptly. "But as long as you're home again, I can stand anything." She gave him another hug, then went over to her kettle and mugs.

"Where'd you go, Greg?" I asked, as he sat down.

He grinned. "I made the mistake of leaving for university for three years, fifteen years ago, and she's never forgiven me for it. Fortunately for all concerned, I got the position at Marchester University after I finished my postgraduate degrees there—"

"Here's your tea, and your coffee." Auntie Mads had returned and set down mugs in front of us. She sighed tiredly, then thought of something. "Do you want me to fix you up a nice sandwich for your lunch?"

"No, thank you. Jane has me all taken care of."

The old lady waved her hand dismissively and returned to the counter. I didn't notice anything else after that, save for the mug in front of me. The coffee was only a shade or two darker than tan, not much darker than Greg's tea, and there was a faint greenish sheen swirling around on the surface. I sipped; it was hot and scorched and bitter and very, very strong. Coffee I would have avoided like a paper cut at home I now welcomed with surging relief. I felt the pain in my head recede at last.

"We should get going," I said guiltily, when I'd finished gulping. "It's almost quarter past."

"Oh." He glanced down at his watch. "We've got another forty-five minutes."

"You don't start until nine?" I was astonished. "But that's . . . practically noon."

"Are you complaining?"

"Oh, God, no. I'm not a morning person—"

"Really? I'd never have guessed. Still we should leave a bit early, to get you oriented. So you'll have time for another cup or two, before we get going."

He glanced over to the counter and frowned. "Aunty's not looking on top form today, I'm worried she's not been feeling well lately."

I looked over and saw Aunty chewing out a couple of the other patrons for bolting their food; they looked amused and did their best to reassure her that they'd taken their time and chewed properly. She looked okay to me, but then I saw her sigh again heavily, and wondered if Greg wasn't right.

On our way out, fifteen minutes later, Greg excused himself, pausing to speak with one of the men across the room. I decided to buy a candy bar, just in case my jet lag slowed me down later. Mads saw me pause in front of the small rack.

"So, you're here to work with Greg. You going to be here all summer, then?"

Her voice was as thin as she was, not high-pitched but a little unsteady.

"No, just a couple of weeks. I've got research to do in London and so I'm combining it with a visit to Jane and Greg."

"And you're an archaeologist too?"

"That's right."

Mads rubbed a cloth over the cash register. "Are you married?"

Ah, that's it; she's worried I'm poaching on Greg. "Yes, I am. Brian's at home."

"What's he think of you gallivanting all over the place?" She looked at me sharply.

"Well, he misses me, but he knows it's for work, and it won't be forever. He has to do the same sometimes, so we just try to make the best of it."

"Hmm." Apparently satisfied that I wasn't going to disrupt things too much, she relented. "You want one of them candy bars?"

"I'm trying to decide which one would be good. Any suggestions?"

"I'm not supposed to eat sweets—they do awful things to my dentals—but . . ." She lowered her voice to a whistling whisper. "I do like one of them Double Deckers, every so often."

"Okay, I'll take one of them."

Auntie Mads beamed approval as I picked a hideously colored one in a bright purple and orange wrapper and paid.

Greg came up to us. "All right, then, Emma?"

"All set." I pocketed my candy bar.

"Good-bye, Auntie. You be good today."

Mads kissed him on the cheek again. "Well, Greg, when I'm not good, I'm careful not to get caught. You mind yourself."

If I'd known what would be waiting for me at the site, I would have had a fourth cup of coffee, and maybe a fifth. As we approached the dig, I could see Jane chewing out Andrew. Even though I couldn't hear what she was saying, I could see the tension in her body and how the sharp, jabbing movements of her hands as she gestured were echoed by the way her hair swung in short, uniform arcs as she moved her head. There were students already at work, removing the covering from their units, putting out tools and notebooks.

They didn't seem fazed by Jane's tirade; in fact, I noticed with a frown, they had a radio on and I could hear the faint sounds of reggae music.

"Let's rescue Andrew, before Jane goes in for a spot of GBH, shall we?" Greg whispered to me.

"GBH?" I didn't think he was referring to the Boston public television station.

"Grievous bodily harm. I suspect he'll be his own worst punishment today, if history is any indication."

Before I could ask about that history, Greg picked up his pace; this caused us to hear the last of Jane's words to Andrew.

"—Don't you forget your arsing about reflects on me as well—"

Andrew uttered a short laugh. "And God forbid anything should tarnish your reputation."

Two bright spots of colors enflamed Jane's cheeks. "Don't you even think of diminishing how angry I am or what I will do to protect my position! Any more of this nonsense—"

"Spare me, Jane," Andrew said. "Why not make it easier on yourself and sack me now?"

I almost chalked it up to imagination or a trick of the light through the clouds, but I could have sworn I saw an expression like eagerness flit across Andrew's face. An instant later, there was nothing but the boredom that had been present before.

"Because I need you, you know that, and you don't really want to leave, in spite of your stupid antics. So pull yourself together, friend." Jane pursed her lips, looking as though she wanted to shake Andrew; then she looked up, saw us, and waved us over. Her demeanor totally changed: there was no trace of her former anger now.

"Emma, this is Andrew Freeman, our osteologist. Andrew, this is Emma Fielding, who'll be working with us the next couple of weeks."

Since Andrew didn't speak up, I decided not to volunteer anything about our early morning meeting. "How do you do, Andrew?"

I could see full well how he did, however: his skin was almost gray, lines ran deeply around bloodshot eyes, and his brown hair was matted down, presumably still wet from a shower that hadn't done much to revive him. He was wearing a blue workshirt untucked over baggy green khaki fatigues and a gray army surplus anorak that looked as though it had been dragged behind a Jeep for a year. This quite apart, I had to admit that Andrew—in the light of day and not reeling drunk—was not bad looking. His long face and high cheekbones—particularly with the beard that came down to a little point just at his chin—looked as though they ought to have been the carving on the top of a medieval crypt, a knight with his shield laid out over his body. In fact, the more I looked, the more the mournful quality of his face and sad eyes seemed downright attractive in the he's-been-hurt-I-can-help-him-smile-again way that is the foundation of so many impetuous decisions and bad relationships.

Damn.

"I'm really pleased to meet you, Emma." He clasped my hand warmly, with both of his own. "Jane's told me a lot about you—and your work."

Okay, so it was clear that he really didn't want me saying anything about our previous encounter. I decided to smile back. "I'm really looking forward to working on the site with, uh, everyone."

Jane beamed upon us both. "Since you're both going to be housemates—Andrew's just down the hall from you, Emma, did I mention it in all the excitement yesterday?— you might as well get to know one another straight off. Emma, why don't you help Andrew work on this skellie? That way, he can show you the ropes here, you can have a look at the button I mentioned—if that will satisfy proper police procedure, Andrew?" she asked, mockingly.

He shrugged almost apologetically. "It should be fine, Jane, at least until I get something conclusive."

"Then we'll leave you to it; come on, Greg, let's look at burial nineteen." Jane took her husband's arm and marched off. Andrew watched them leave.

"I've got my tools right here," I said, holding up my backpack. "Where shall I begin?"

He started rummaging through his own large canvas backpack. "Nowhere, actually. You don't use anything on one of my burials that I don't first approve."

I raised one eyebrow. His burials? Andrew didn't notice, but handed me a three-ring notebook. "Here's the recording system for the site. Why don't you get familiar with it while I start a separate set for the police? They have different set of requirements than archaeologists do, to maintain the chain of custody for artifacts and the like."

"I *have* worked with human remains before," I said, as matter-of-factly as I could, flipping through the sheets. "I think I've got a good idea—"

Without looking up, the osteologist rubbed his hand over his face and head. "Look, I am in the throes of a spectacular hangover, so if you could keep the chat down to a minimum, I would be eternally grateful." He turned and smiled again, a little too late to make up for the edge in his voice.

I shrugged. "I could just squat down over here silently and hand you things when you need them, how about that? Fetch you coffee and sandwiches, maybe? Wipe your fevered brow?"

"It would make my life easier." He turned back to his bag and pulled out a mechanical pencil. "Sounds good to me."

"Good, but also unlikely, I fear. Look, if you're not in the mood for company, I'll ask Jane for another job."

"And I don't need Jane on my neck, again, do I?" He smiled ruefully.

Again I was struck by Andrew's appeal, but I wasn't going to forgive him just because he'd smiled. "It doesn't matter to me."

The osteologist cocked his head, sizing me up, and then nodded. "Fine. Once you've gone over the sheets, there is a second set of bamboo probes, brushes, and a proper small trowel in my kit—Americans always use such whacking great things. You may take them and finish exposing the rest of the phalanges—you know, finger bones?—on the right hand. There won't be too much trouble for you to get into."

I nodded and bent over Andrew's bag to find the tools. Behind me, I heard a familiar mechanical click, followed by a low chuckle.

"Piss off, Avery," Andrew said. I glanced behind me and saw a thickset man with greasy dark hair, an expensive German camera in his hands. If his stance was any indication, he'd just taken a picture of me. Bending over.

"You're not wanted, Avery. I'll call you when we're ready to shoot our friend here."

The camera man didn't answer, but chuckled again and scurried away, rolling from side to side, badgerlike, toward Jane and Greg, who were huddled in conversation. I turned to Andrew for an explanation.

He sighed. "Site photographer. Very good at what he does, but a remarkable specimen of saddle sniffer."

I raised my eyebrows. "I beg your pardon?"

"Dean Avery is a pervert. Waits for young women to find themselves in some ungainly position, and then shoots candid pictures of them. He's got them plastered all over his rooms; I had the misfortune to see his lair once and it imbued in me a desire never to return. I'd watch how I squat, if I were you. Archaeology is like a luncheon buffet for his sort."

I digested that in silence; like every dig, this one certainly was replete with characters. I paused, then looked down at the burial before me. The skeleton was on its left side, in a crouched position, with the head pointing south, toward the river. Most of the soil-stained bones that were present were now at least partially exposed, save for the last bones in the fingers, and the solid look of the bones' surfaces suggested that they were in good shape.

"He—it is a he?—wasn't buried in a coffin," I observed.

Andrew hunkered down beside me. "Bright girl. Yes, it is a he, and no, he wasn't buried in a coffin."

"That's not unusual for burials, right into the nineteenth century," I mused. "But the pelvis isn't fully exposed and the long bones aren't all that long. How do you know for sure it's male?"

"I just do, that's all."

I looked at Andrew askance. He scratched at his beard. "I'm sorry, I'm not being obstructionist, it's just that once you've handled as many skeletons as I have, you have an instinct before you have the reason. As for this one here, it's just a very strong hunch, based on what I can see of the mandible and pronounced occipital ridge. Also, the femur is pretty robust."

Okay, so whoever it is is on the large side. "So it probably isn't the missing student, who is a woman, right? The bones look like they've been there for years, not days."

Andrew looked startled. "Julia will turn up. Trust me."

I watched him struggle to find something to explain that.

"She's a very reliable girl. Something's probably . . . just come up, that's all."

I shrugged again and then examined the ends of the long bones and the sutures in the skull. "Looks like the epiphyses are pretty well fused, too."

He jotted down a few notes, then got up, stood back, and appraised the burial and nodded. "Yes, I'd say that we're looking at an adult, fully mature but not too old. There's only a moderate amount of wear on the teeth, if you look over here. I wonder if we'll see evidence of modern dentistry, fillings or some such, once we are able to pull the skull."

I looked; the exposed teeth were worn, but not to the extent that you would find on an older adult. "Hey, what's up with those foot bones? They look deformed to me, or am I just seeing things?"

Andrew knelt down. "No, you're right. I'll get a better look at them in the lab, but whoever it was would have had quite a limp." He smiled, this time genuinely. "It's nice to have an informed audience."

I found it very hard to resist returning his smile, so I didn't bother. "Jane said you found a button? Mind if I have a look?"

"Certainly. I expect we'll find more buttons as we expose more of the bones. Probably fell off the coat as it deteriorated." Andrew reached into a deep tray, removed a small, plastic bag, and handed it to me.

It was very dirty, and stained yellowish with age, perhaps, or the same chemicals in the ground that had stained the bones. Flat, with four holes punched through it. I could see a faint ridge around the rim of it.

"It's pretty recent," I said. "It looks like bakelite to me."

"That so?" I got the impression that he was assessing me again.

"It's an early form of plastic," I continued. "It was invented at the very beginning of the twentieth century."

"Yes, yes, I know what bakelite is." Andrew snorted. "Even though I cut my teeth on the neolithic and they didn't have mass-manufactured buttons . . . but this modern medieval shit is overburden as far as I'm concerned."

I handed the bag back to him. "Then why are you here?"

"Greg needed someone to do the bones." He tossed the button into the tray impatiently. "Look, why don't you just get started digging? See if you can't find those phalanges."

I got a small dustpan and bucket, but looked around. "Why isn't everyone using a screen?" Andrew was the only one with a tiny hand screen; none of the students had one.

He was amused. "We don't generally use sifters, if that's what you mean. You should be able to find everything by trowling. They dump their soil over there." He indicated the backdirt pile with a nod of his head.

"They'll lose a lot of data that way," I muttered, hunkering down.

"Jane's the boss here," Andrew replied. "Now I need to concentrate on taking some measurements."

I was glad to start work and leave my changeable colleague to his. The soil was only moderately heavy, silty loam. It pulled back nicely, though, and even working carefully, I was quickly able to uncover several of the end bones to the fingers of the left hand. I left them in place on little pedestals of earth, not wanting to remove them before they'd been recorded and not wanting to dig any deeper.

I turned to the burial where the right hand was raised slightly, closer to the head than the left hand was, finger bones fanned out in an arrangement that was in its own way graceful. I worked for a few moments, enjoying the feel of the fussy work, alternating use of the small trowel with a pointy piece of bamboo and a fine sable brush, being careful lest I damage the bone.

Everything went smoothly, but then I realized that I was missing a bone—three bones, actually. I frowned, then scraped away a bit more soil, but to no avail. They simply weren't where they should be.

"Andrew? I've got something—or rather, I don't have something."

He looked up. "What's that?"

"There's nice preservation—no rodent disturbance, the soil's not too acidic, and it looks like he was covered up pretty quick, not left exposed to the elements. I've got everything, even the small bones from the pinkie, but the middle finger of the right hand seems to be missing altogether. I just don't think it's here."

The osteologist considered and began speaking, almost as if to himself. "The presence of the other small bones, in situ, suggests that this was a rapid deposit, not left open to taphonomic forces, you know, wind, water, animals, anything that would have scattered the smaller bits postdeposition—"

I nodded and tried not to roll my eyes; yes, I knew.

Andrew stared at the hand a moment. "No chance it's lying at an odd angle? You couldn't have missed them, otherwise."

"I don't think so," I said. "Do you mind if I take a closer look at something? One of the metacarpals is sitting right on top of the soil—"

"Go ahead."

Leaving my trowel to mark the location, I picked up what would have been the last bone in the hand proper and looked at it carefully. It was cool and a little damp from the soil, a little lighter than I thought it would be. The edge was imperfect, though not because of some trick of preservation.

"Butchery marks," I said, holding it up to him. "Not that someone was trying to eat this guy, but it looks like that middle finger was cut off. See, you can see where this bone was nicked. It happened shortly before death, I guess, there's no sign of healing—"

Andrew stared at the bone, a startled expression on his face. "My God, you're right." Then he dropped down beside me and I couldn't help but notice how nicely male he smelled, some kind of herbal soap or aftershave under clean sweat. "But I think our friend here had worse things to worry about. Look there, the proximal sternum, near the top of the corpus sterni."

I followed where he was pointing, to the top of the long part of the breastbone. I had to strain to see it, and finally, in spite of my worries about becoming the unwilling target of the photographer, I bent over and brought my face to within two inches of the remains. At first, I couldn't see anything as my shadow obscured it all, but then, as my eyes adjusted, I realized that there was a hairline crack in the bone, a crack that widened almost imperceptibly as my gaze followed it. Where it stopped, close to the center of the sternum, I could see the faintest discoloration showing against the discolored bone. Rust.

"There's a piece of iron in there," I announced, rocking back on my heels, a little dizzy as I realized what this meant.

"Got it in one, full marks." Andrew clapped his hands together, almost jolly. "He didn't die of old age, that's for certain. Someone tried to bone our friend here like a frying chicken and pretty well succeeded."

Chapter 5

"TCH, TCH, ANDREW. THAT'S A BIT COLD, EVEN FOR you, don't you think?"

We both looked up. I squinted, the sun in my eyes, and saw a short, sturdy wavy-haired blonde in a cardigan and dark trousers, her head cocked to one side, surveying our work doubtfully.

Andrew's face fell. "Brilliant. I was just thinking, Sabine, that I needed another brainy female to have a go at my work." I was surprised at how suddenly, openly antagonistic he became.

"Ah, but we girly swots have always been rather a bit of a specialty of yours, haven't we, Andrew—"

Andrew went scarlet.

The woman continued, not noticing or not caring about his discomfort. "—But, in any case, I do think a little more respect for the dead is in order. Particularly this poor soul."

"You would, wouldn't you?"

It was at that point I realized that the woman was wearing a clerical collar. She was quite plain and it was only by the grace of strong cheekbones and alert green eyes that kept her face from looking a blank oval: when she pursed her lips, as she did at Andrew's retort, her mouth seemed to vanish. She also had a pale scar along her right eyebrow that gave her a look of skepticism even when there was none expressed. She stared down at the skeleton.

"You'll be talking to Detective Rhodes, won't you?" the woman asked.

"Already am." Andrew was almost petulant.

She pointed to the burial. "This isn't recent, though, is it? I mean, judging by that stratigraphy—"

I looked up, startled. It was usual for me to hear a civilian so casually discussing the layers of soil we studied.

"Yes, yes, smartyboots." Andrew struck me as being unusually irritated.

She turned, offered her hand to me, and indicated the way toward a church down the way from where we were working.

"I'm Sabine Jones. I'm the vicar down at St. Alban's. Or perhaps I should say, up at St. Alban's, depending on how you look at things."

I noticed she pronounced her name "Sah-*bee*-nah," whereas Andrew had called her "*Say*-bine." Obviously, theirs was a longtime relationship and there wasn't much love lost between them: Sabine took his rudeness in stride.

I dusted off my hand and shook hers. "Emma Fielding. I'm a friend of Jane's, helping out for a couple of weeks."

"Ah, yes, the long-awaited American visitor. Welcome to Marchester. We're all excited about the work Jane's doing here."

I recalled the comments that both Pooter and Palmer had made. Sabine nodded, conceding this unspoken point. "Well, perhaps 'everyone who matters' is a better way of putting it. One of the local contractors wants to put a supermarket in here. Although the land rights are somewhat at question, he'd prefer Jane not find anything terribly interesting, but it's too late for that, I think."

"It would be a shame to put a supermarket in here, it's such a nice view," I said.

Sabine shook her head. "That's as may be, but it would make it easier for the older folk on this side to get their shopping done. There's sure to be some compromise, though. And then there's Morag . . . oh, dear. Literally, there's Morag. She's late getting to work today."

She pointed to the field just beyond the area of the dig, where a tall woman in gauzy black skirts was engrossed, walking back and forth across the grass, sometimes pausing with her hands outstretched. If I hadn't known better, I'd have guessed that she was field walking, looking for artifacts that had washed out of the soil in the rain, or looking for variations in the ground level that might indicate the presence of subsurface features. I wasn't certain, but I thought I heard the faint tinkling of tiny bells on the wind as she moved across the grass.

Andrew twisted around to see where she was pointing. "Now you're talking. Morag the Moonbeam is more my speed, right now. Thick as two short planks, that one."

"Well, I think she's available," the vicar replied.

Andrew ignored the remark, scanning the site for something else. "Jane will be foaming, about now. There's nothing she can do about it either. Lovely."

"What's the problem?" I asked, twisting around and craning my neck. Just as Andrew predicted, Jane had taken a few steps toward the edge of the site, then stopped. She had the same tense expression as she had this morning, when she was yelling at Andrew, or last night, when she was arguing with the police officer. Jane spent a lot of time being tense, I noticed.

"Ley lines," Sabine said, as if that explained everything. "According to Morag, the place is thick with 'em. A convergence spot, I think she called it."

I dragged my attention away from the little drama across the site. "Lay lines? Is that something to do with the church, you know, laity? Poo—Jeremy Hyde-Spofford used the same word yesterday, I think."

"No, L-E-Y. Ley lines are . . . well, they're supposed to be lines of cosmic power that course through the earth. A person's power is supposed to be enhanced when in their vicinity. Pagan, neopagan thought, really."

"Load of shit, really," Andrew muttered to himself.

"Now, now, Andrew," Sabine murmured. "There are places that are considered powerfully holy in our religion too—"

"It's *not* my religion. I don't believe in that rubbish, either." He looked up at Sabine hopefully.

"Nice try, Andrew, but I simply won't rise to it." She turned back to me. "Morag claims, as do quite a lot of others, that there is a particularly strong ley line running into a convergence in this area. Probably right through the old site of the abbey. Draws a lot of attention from the local neopagan crowd."

"Oh?" I said.

"Well, I don't know how they determine where the ley lines are," she explained, "but oftentimes churches were built on the sites of pagan shrines, to try and convert the heathen, so that may be what inspired that notion."

"Don't forget Saint Whatshername," Andrew piped up.

Sabine finally looked pained, much to Andrew's delight. "The abbess was a particularly holy woman named Mother Beatrice. Lived about 1437 to about 1472, or thereabouts," she explained to me. "She's actually been considered for canonization, but although she was supposed to have seen visions, she came up a little short in the miracles department. The Wiccans have decided, probably for the former reason, that she was a secret worshiper of the Mother Goddess, as they call her, and have claimed her as one of their own."

"And that narks you no end, doesn't it?" Andrew grinned unpleasantly.

She shrugged. "I'm not one to question someone else's religion, but when it comes to earthly matters—people, for example—I like to work with the evidence at hand—"

"Which is, of course, why you dropped geology to become a priest, isn't it, Sabine?"

She finally lost her patience and I was glad that she wasn't mad at me. She stepped toward Andrew, and I involuntarily stepped back a pace. "Andrew, if you ever stopped to listen to yourself—"

I decided to jump in.

"What do you think was important about Beatrice, Sabine?" My question had the effect of drawing Sabine onto a more interesting topic and disappointing Andrew.

"I don't know, I'm not much for history, but I think we ought to consider her example. She was responsible for supporting a large number of poor through some difficult times, if the church records are any indication. She looked after her townsfolk, even to the point of political conflict with the bishop, but she won out in the end and continued her work. That's what I think is important about her. *That's* the point."

Her lecture over, she glanced at her watch. "I must run. Very nice meeting you, Emma. If you'd like, sometime, I'd be happy to show you the view from our bell tower. It's a nice way to see Marchester and it has a good view of the site. And of course, you're always welcome to join us on Sunday."

"Thanks for the offer. Nice to meet you, too."

"Good-bye, Andrew."

"Go away, Sabine." He didn't look up.

She paused, said a little prayer over the skeleton, shook her head again at Andrew, and then left, but just a few steps away, Sabine paused, looked around, and took out two items from her cardigan pocket. She took out a piece of rolling paper, and quickly rolled herself a cigarette from a little block of tobacco. She lit up with something like the same reverence I saw on Dora's face when she smoked her cigar.

"Doesn't want her parishioners to catch her with her

filthy rollies," Andrew said with relish. "Not quite a holy enough image, you see, for all it is a sound socialist practice." He shook himself. "Oh, don't mind me. Sabine's all right; we just get up each other's noses. It's nothing, really, just a long-standing habit."

I had to wonder what had engendered the sparring in the first place. I decided to change the subject. "So those plates I see over there, they're marking the ley line? Sometimes we use plates to mark postholes for aerial photography."

"They will mark the line until someone gets annoyed enough to rip them off. Then Morag'll put them back again. Jane claims she's not the one doing it, but my money's on her anyway. She and Morag don't see eye to eye on much of anything and Morag doesn't think twice about wandering around the site, trying to get others to feel the vibe, or whatever. I swear, you can almost see Jane's blood pressure shoot up when she's around."

"Oh. What should I do next?"

"Write up your observations on the recording sheets. I'll call the police and they'll initiate a proper investigation. I'm afraid that's it for you working here, though, once we help Avery get his pictures taken."

I shivered at the thought; that guy Avery gave me the creeps. Andrew left and I soon finished with my few notes, so I decided to get a head start on preparing for the record photographs. I carefully started cleaning the dirt that had dried into little pills away from the bones I had exposed, then began to work my way across the rest of the skeleton. I didn't get far when—

"Oh, God! Wait! Look, what is it you're doing?" Andrew had returned from making his call and was almost hopping, torn between getting me to stop and trying to do it nicely. "Hold off, half a tic—"

I stopped, wondering what he was getting so excited about. "We're done here; I'm cleaning off the surface so we can get some pictures."

He tried to compose himself. "Right, yes, but . . . there

are certain things we need to look out for, especially now that we know it's a recent crime scene. Comparatively recent crime scene. First we call Avery over, so he can start setting up. Then I'll draw in those last three bones onto my plan, *then* I will clean it off."

"Hey, okay, it's okay!" I got the impression that one more minute, and Andrew might have snatched the trowel from my hand. "I'm not going to hurt anything."

He made small, rigid chopping motions with both hands, as if he were measuring out each word carefully. "Emma, I know you're not going to hurt anything, but I just want you to—"

I was tired of being lectured to by one and all. "Look, I know enough to hang onto any insect parts I find, note unusual soil stains, or anything like that. I know we need to be careful. I know anything I find might impact the police investigation."

Andrew took a deep breath. "I know, I know, but it's not like it is in America, this kind of burial is strictly the purview of the Home Office forensic pathologist. We wait on the police in these matters, let them dictate what they want done and how. It's not that I doubt your skills—" here he let loose with a knee-melting smile, "—but it's just, some of these students . . . well, let's just say that there's a wildly diverse range of abilities at work on this site. It's easy to forget there are some real professionals here. I am a bit of a perfectionist, but it really does matter, particularly in this situation." He examined my handiwork. "But there's no harm done."

I could feel my face burning. "I'm sorry, I shouldn't have jumped the gun like that. Really, I thought it would be all right. I should have asked." I grinned to myself when I thought, but *I'm* the one digging; he should know he has nothing to worry about. Whatever else there was about Andrew Freeman, he was manifestly concerned with how work on "his" skeletons was undertaken.

Andrew called for the photographer, then took out a plan

that was almost complete and hastily drew in the last of the bones. I glanced over his shoulder; it was beautiful work, done with a minimum of fuss in the measuring.

Trying to make up for my gaffe, I said, "Do you want to get an elevation on the bones I exposed?"

He nodded. "I'll get the rod now."

We measured the depth of the finger bones and then Andrew called the photographer over. I tried to be as helpful as I could, putting together sign boards and clipping roots on the edge of the unit so they didn't cast shadows, but I noticed that Dean Avery, the photographer, would look up from his work almost every time I glanced at him. Andrew and he pulled aside to discuss whether more shots were needed.

Suddenly, I noticed that all the rest of the crew was walking away from the site. Jane appeared by my side.

"What's going on?" I asked in alarm.

Jane furrowed her brow and looked around. "What do you mean?"

"Where's everyone going?"

"Oh." She looked at her watch and her face cleared. "Ten-thirty already?"

"What's at ten-thirty?" I relaxed a little. At least whatever was going on was an expected occurrence.

"Morning coffee; half hour break."

"But we just started at nine," I protested. "How can you get anything done with a break in the middle of the morning?"

"It's a proper workday," Jane said defensively. "Start at nine, morning coffee at half ten, lunch from noon to one—"

I was aghast. "You take a whole hour for lunch?"

"—Then tea at three-thirty and off site by five pip emma. Why, what do you do?"

"Start at eight-thirty, thirty minutes at noon, wrap up at four-thirty."

"My God, you're a slave driver!" She mulled it over and shook her head finally. "You don't stop for any breaks?"

Now it was my turn to be amused. "No, not really. I usually just make sure everyone drinks enough water, if it's hot out."

"Water?" Jane's face now registered as much confusion as mine had: How could any crew manage on just water? she seemed to ask.

"It's pretty standard. Actually, I'm considered a kind and beneficent director."

"Uncivilized." Jane was having a hard time grasping the Yankee work ethic. "Are you saying that you don't want coffee now? I'd've thought you'd be glad, after this morning . . ."

"Actually, I'm floating. Maybe just a quick trip to the . . . what was it you called it? Porta-loo?"

"Yes, just over there. And when you get back—" She paused indecisively.

"Yes?"

"Well, I'm not stopping at the moment either. Perhaps we could discuss where to put you next."

She must have seen Andrew hopping around. "Look, I'm sorry about how things went with Andrew, but I don't think he can use me anymore—"

"I thought you did splendidly with Andrew," she interrupted evenly. "He hasn't complained about you and you haven't cut his throat. He can be a charmer, when he chooses, and when he doesn't choose, he can be something considerably less appealing. It's just that you can't work there any longer and we can use you better elsewhere in the meantime."

I nodded. "I'll just be a moment then."

When I returned from my mission—and despite the different name, the British version of the outdoor convenience was no more appealing than its American counterpart—I idly followed the line of paper plates over to the edge of the site. They seemed to point directly to the center of the site, where I now saw Jane standing, waving me over to where she and Greg had been talking earlier that morning.

Jane was uncharacteristically hesitant when I arrived. She

stood beside a wide excavation area that was described by
twelve nails that marked out the corners of six one-meter
squares, three units over three. I noticed a faint, darker stain
in the soil, about six feet by two, located just to the south of
the middle set of nails. It was another burial.

"I'd like you to work here," Jane said abruptly. "It's rather
sensitive and . . . I think you're the person I'd trust most
with it."

I frowned. "What about you or Greg? What about Andrew? The rest of your crew have been here longer than I—"

"I can't do it myself, obviously, and oversee the rest of
the site. I wish I could. Greg can't, because he has to help
me and supervise the lab work as well. Andrew can't because generally he doesn't focus on just one burial—the one
you were working on was special, because it looks like it is
a crime scene. He has to help with that as well as keep an
eye on all the other skeletons that are exposed. Julia would
have been the one . . . but she's not to be found and I can't
wait any longer. This is burial nineteen . . . and it's important. It's important to Marchester and it's important to me,
personally, truth be told."

We were much closer to the last remaining wall of the
abbey, closer to the river itself. I looked up and down the
site, orienting myself, and guessed that we were well within
the confines of the old abbey. The students were a ways off,
definitely outside the building itself. If what I knew from my
reading held true—

"You think this is where the abbess, Beatrice, might have
been buried, don't you?" I said.

Relief washed over Jane's face. "Yes. The rest of the
crew . . . well, they're nowhere near as experienced as you,
of course. Some of them I don't want near it simply because
I'm afraid that they are more susceptible to some of the new
agey rubbish that some people have been propagating
around town."

I nodded slowly, understanding. "You mean Morag."

Jane was amazed. "How do you know about her?"

"Andrew and Sabine—the vicar?—told me a little when she stopped by."

My friend chewed her bottom lip. "I'm sorry to have missed Sabine, but I wasn't about to take my eyes off that Morag. Well, yes, in any case, the more experienced ones are where I need them to be, and putting you here keeps them from being jealous of a fellow student getting the honor. And the less experienced ones just don't get to cut their teeth on Beatrice."

"What is her story?"

"She was a wealthy widow when she came to Marchester, where she had family connections. It wasn't all that unusual for widows or young women to become vowesses—living a religious life of poverty and chastity without taking vows—but she actually became a nun. In a few years, she rose to the rank of abbess; this might have been because she was particularly holy, it might have been because her family in Marchester were powerful and able to exert a good deal of influence in the Church, or it might have been because it was her money that got the abbey out of debt and in good running order, through some rough times."

Jane smiled. "I, of course, like to think it was a combination of things, and it helps if you look at the historical context as well. It's disputed, of course, but thinking these days suggests that the late medieval Church offered responsibilities and freedoms to women that they couldn't get in secular life, especially since there was supposed to be a special kind of piety in women who were consecrated as the brides of Christ. I think Beatrice was an ambitious woman who saw an opportunity to be someone of power, of consequence, and took that opportunity."

I nodded. "Do you have any of her personal records? Is that what they suggest?"

"No, we just have a fragment of a set of instructions, informing her community that she wanted to be buried within the abbey—near this spot—and that she did not want an elaborate coffin. She saw no reason to lavish money on housing the empty shell of her body when it could be better used in charity or in fixing the sisters' leaking roofs.

"I'm sure I'll turn up more as I continue the search. The anomalies from the remote sensing suggest that this is the right place within the east end of the church and I'm betting that even if she wasn't the founder of the house, Mother Beatrice's money would have gone a long way in assuring her wishes were carried out. And since you've got the credentials and the experience and you've nothing to do with any of the foo-faraw, you're going to be the one to find out. I don't think I could make a fairer choice than that."

What Jane didn't say, and what was immediately clear to me was that by placing me here, she was thrusting me into the middle of everything Palmer had warned me against.

When I didn't say anything right away, Jane said, "You can handle it anyway you like, of course, just run it past me first."

"If you really mean that, I'd like to find a screen and sift what I excavate, then," I said quickly. "I just wouldn't want to risk losing any of the data from such an important burial."

"Of course," Jane agreed, "if you like, though I honestly think your eye will be enough. Tell me what you need, and I'll have Greg or one of the students pick it up from the DIY—the 'do-it-yourself' building center—tonight."

"Just a couple of two-by-fours and some wire screening, two pieces, each about two feet square, one quarter-inch, the other, eighth-inch. I'll put them together myself."

"Fine." Jane nodded. "For the moment, I think you've probably got a good bit of depth to go before you see the burial proper, so perhaps you could work on bringing that down?"

"Sure, but—" I frowned. "Shouldn't there be paving, stones or brick, or something, though, for the floor of the abbey? Over the graves?"

"There would have been, but the worked stone was robbed out over the centuries. If you're all set, I'll be off."

I began a recording sheet of my own on a beat-up clipboard and started work just as the rest of the crew reappeared. Not too much later, I heard Jane announce the lunch hour. I was getting annoyed with all these disruptions.

"Off you go," she called to the departing students, "but no more than an hour. If I have to come down the pub to find you again, it'll be off limits at lunch!"

She came over with Greg to fetch me. "How's it going?" She peered down at my work eagerly.

I put my notebook under a bucket, lest it blow away or the weather turn bad. "Pretty well, I think." I tried to restrain myself, but then blurted out, "You let them *drink* at lunchtime? And you let them play a radio?"

She looked puzzled. "Of course. Why not?"

"I just . . . never mind. What shall we do?"

"I say we pull up a couple of trees and eat. I'm ravenous."

We ate the sandwiches Jane had made, and I listened while she and Greg went over the day's progress. It sounded remarkably like what I was used to: some students who were on top of things, others who needed some help to do a good job, and a few who were just not able.

"—And Nicola's doing okay, as long as I keep at her," Greg said, around mouthfuls of egg salad—egg mayonaise, he'd called it. "She's not as good as Julia, of course—"

"Oh, no, no one's ever as good as *Julia*," Jane said, uncharacteristically sarcastic.

I turned, all attention at this surprising vehemence, but Greg paid no attention. "—But she's coming down cleanly enough. But unfortunately, Bonnie is not improving and Trevor is still making a mess of things, no matter where we put him. I wonder sometimes if it isn't intentional."

I recalled that I'd seen Bonnie busily at work that morning. At one point, she picked up a stone, troweled beneath it, and then replaced the rock, when she should either have removed the rock, if she'd judged it unimportant, or just left it be. No way do you mess around with context as she had. I'd been too shocked to say anything before Greg caught her at it.

After about fifty-five minutes, students began to come back in groups of threes and fours, some eager to return to work, others making the most of their break. Jane, Greg, and I discussed strategy and students for another twenty minutes.

"Bonnie's a disaster and Trevor's been flirting with disaster since we started here," Jane said impatiently.

"He's gone well beyond flirting with disaster; he's gotten a leg over some time ago," Greg replied.

"Just keep on him, I guess," Jane said with resignation. "Keep him where he'll do the least harm." It was time for us to think about getting back to work too.

"Oh, God, here he comes. Greg, I simply can't bear the sight of him right now. Would you mind—?"

"No, no, off you go."

Jane made a hasty retreat as a bulky young man in what looked like untidy secondhand clothes sauntered toward us, a full ten minutes after everyone else had been back to work. He was fishing the last of a few french fries from out of the bottom of a McDonald's container, ketchup and salt smeared over his fingers and mouth. In fact, although Greg was a bit dusty and rumpled from his morning's work, Trevor looked as though he hadn't changed his clothes in a month. The change the sight of this guy made in Greg was unbelievable; one of the quietest, kindest people I knew was now tightlipped with anger.

"Ah, we see our Trevor arriving now," he said with mock welcome. "Good evening, Trev. Nice of you to join us at long last."

Trevor pretended to be surprised by this reception and it instantly made *me* want to smack him. "Wot? I had to eat." I noticed that Trevor's pronunciation of vowels was longer, flatter, and more heavily accented than the others; he was not from around here.

"And yet everyone else seemed able to find their way through lunch and be back here on time," Greg replied. "Why is it that you can't, I wonder?"

Trevor ignored Greg and turned to me. "You the American?"

Greg went scarlet. "Hey, I'm *talking* to you—"

The student stuck another french fry in his mouth and chewed noisily. "I hate Americans. Fucking awful."

I barely suppressed a laugh at this adolescent behavior. "I'm so sorry to hear it."

Greg wasn't nearly as amused as I was and advanced a step on Trevor. "You watch your goddamned mouth!"

Trevor shrugged helplessly and licked the tips of his fingers. "Sorry, but it's true. I just can't bring myself to be a hypocrite. I have to speak my mind."

"How about this? How about you stop stuffing your stupid face and get to work?"

Trevor yawned. "Why? It's not like I'm anywhere near anything interesting. Why bother?"

"Because as much as I have no desire to endure your odious presence any longer than absolutely required, I will not pass you simply for being the bone-idle, nasty little toe-rag that you are." Greg's voice was low and steeped with menace. "You will put in at least what looks like an honest effort to show a minimal competence or I will not sign off. I can't just kick you out, but neither do I want you back here. Therefore, upon learning that you will return next year, for yet another final year, I will undertake to make your life miserable until you leave on your own. So I suggest you get to work and endeavor to meet the low level of achievement I have set for you, lest you cause me to start considering how best to ruin your life."

Trevor paused, as impressed as I.

"But . . . Jane won't like it," he replied, rallying. "She won't let you."

Greg nodded. "But the problem is, Jane is a just person. She sees injustice in the world and is determined not to contribute to it. I, on the other hand, see that there is injustice in the world and reason that a spot more—carefully localized—will harm no one it's not meant to and may in fact do a bit of good."

Greg's vehemence and willingness to threaten the student surprised me and Trevor too, it seemed. He actually stopped chewing for a moment, then looking Greg straight in the eye, deliberately dropped the bright red cardboard box at his instructor's feet. "I'm done, anyway," he announced, shuffling off toward his area.

Greg looked like he would cheerfully have pounded Trevor into the ground as he watched him leave. He shrugged off his anger and then smiled at me. "I'm sorry. I thought, for some stupid reason, that calling him out in front of a stranger might actually make an impact on the lout."

"Well, you convinced me, anyway," I said. "I'll behave from now on."

Greg smiled wryly. "He knows I am capable of torture; I went to public school."

I translated "public school," British for "private school," and remembered some of the horror stories of schoolboy torture with which my friend Kam had regaled me. I thought of stories—stories I just *knew* were carefully edited—about thin mattresses folded and taped around hapless sleepers into an "apple pie," "pranks" involving homemade black powder, and horrors with snapped wet towels. Greg was right; he'd had training in how to make someone miserable, all right. "Which school? You didn't mention the other night. A friend of mine went to Winchester."

At first, I thought he wasn't going to answer me. Then, "Nice quiet little place, close to London."

"Which one is that?" I picked up my notes.

I caught sight of an irritated grimace before Greg turned away and I realized I'd missed something. Finally, staring across the site, he said, "Harrow."

Although I'd heard of it, I couldn't understand his reticence. As Greg stooped to tie his shoelace, I saw something of a conflict manifesting itself across his features. His next words made it clear to me that pride had won out over—what? Self restraint? A desire not to seem boastful? "Mind you, Winchester might be older, but Harrow has certainly produced its share of prime ministers."

Nothing brash, nothing overt, but apparently Old Harrovians were no less willing to stand up for their alma mater or get their digs in on a competing school than graduates of any other all male institution. I made a note to pay more attention to this subtle kind of behavior.

"Things should be quiet until tea," Greg said. "I'll just run out and get the timber for your sifter."

"That would be great," I said. "I'll just carry on here, then."

As the afternoon wore on, and the tea-break came, I noticed that a police car pulled up to the site, soon to be joined by several other civilian vehicles. A police officer in plain clothes got out of the car, shook hands with the other men who joined him, and then began to talk to Andrew, with whom he seemed very familiar, both of them looking at the burial. At one point, as Andrew showed the cop the button, they both looked over at me. Fortunately, they left me alone, and I was very pleased about that. I had absolutely no desire to become embroiled either in whatever had transpired here a hundred years ago or in what was going on in the immediate present. No desire whatsoever. They began to work on recording and then removing the skeleton with the efficiency of long practice, occasionally consulting with Andrew.

I also noticed that with as many breaks as Jane allowed, she never left the site herself. I recognized the instinct to look after the tools and the equipment myself, but I wondered what else she might be worrying about. Now she went over to the modern burial and was listening in on the discussion between Andrew and the officer in charge, whose body language suggested that she was only tolerated there.

After the last of the cars pulled away, I got up to stretch my legs and asked Andrew what had been found. I told myself it was purely a professional interest and that Andrew's looks were merely a nice fringe benefit.

"A few more buttons, that's all," he said shortly, fiddling with his clipboard. "I'd rather not draw any more conclusions at this point. And now if you don't mind—"

"But . . . I was wondering, did you find any other marks on the ribs? Stab marks, or other indications of what happened?"

Andrew didn't look up at all, but merely stroked his beard. "I assure you, Doctor Fielding, I will do a thorough examination." He sat down and continued to write.

"Can I have a look at the police report? It's just curiosity, but I'd like to, if I could."

"We'll see." He didn't even look up.

I stared at his back: Okay. As I walked back to my unit, I decided that when the charm wasn't turned on or the professional connection wasn't established, looks aside, there wasn't really much left to recommend Mr Freeman as a person.

By late afternoon, I'd made good progress on my work. I took an elevation to establish how far down I'd dug and determined that based on what the others were finding in their burials, I should hit mine soon. The stain persisted, even grew a little darker, the outline a little more distinct, so that I knew I definitely had a grave. I'd found no artifacts, but that only meant that no one had disturbed any earlier material when they'd dug the grave hundreds of years ago, and they hadn't dropped anything into it, either.

Two very interesting things occurred at the end of the day. The first was a curious ritual I'd never seen on any dig in twenty-five-odd years. I watched the students pause at Andrew's unit after they put their tools away but before they left the site. I began to realize that each one of them had a paper bag or a Styrofoam coffee cup or something and each was dumping something brown into a small plastic bag that Andrew kept with him. He thanked each of the students gravely, with a bow; most of the young women giggled.

I caught the eye of a baby-faced blonde with bangs as she went past. "Excuse, me but what's going on over there, er—?"

"I'm Lucy." She nodded over at Andrew. "That? It's worm day."

"Come again?"

She giggled. "Andrew found out that Hildegard—you know, Greg's tortoise—eats worms occasionally, so every once and a while he'll collect the earthworms that we dig up for her. Isn't that sweet?"

"Um, sure."

Lucy leaned in conspiratorially. "You mustn't say anything, of course, but we all fancy him like mad. So smart, so dishy, and so . . . oh, I don't know. Rather mysterious. Don't you think he's scrummy?"

I thought Andrew's charm was entirely a matter of his own convenience, and his scrumminess, while undeniable, was something he exploited on an epic scale. "I guess he's not my type. Was Hildegard Greg's grandmother's name or something?"

"Oh, no, I don't know what that was. Hildegard was named for Hildegard of Bingen, wasn't she?" She caught my blank look. "You know, the saint? Lived from 1098 to 1179 in Germany? Known for her theological studies and her church music?"

"Oh. So the turtle sings?" I grinned; my students thought I was a riot.

"No, not that I know of." Lucy gave me a strange look, as if she were afraid that I might be serious. "Jane sings though. Like a dream. And she's a tortoise, not a turtle, a Russian or Horsfield's, I think. Hildegard, I mean, not Professor Compton. Well, I've got to be going. It's time for the walk-around."

I soon found out what that was. It was obvious enough: Jane took the entire crew around the site and reviewed what each had done over the day. The thing that I really found fas-

cinating, though, was what she managed to accomplish with
it. It was in part a review of what to expect, what to look for
when encountering a burial. It was also a way for Jane to
praise or encourage the students publicly, which left everyone feeling pleased with himself and visibly built up morale
in the crew. Even Bonnie, who was obviously trying, in spite
of Will's and Nicola's harsh observations, looked like she
was ready to try again tomorrow. Jane simply summarized
Trevor's work and no one seemed to think any less of her for
not struggling bravely to find a few charitable words.

I did notice that Jane's criticism became more particular
and her praise harder to win when she was examining the
work of the more advanced graduate students. I could almost tell by the way she questioned them who was close to
completing a degree: The more advanced they were, the
harder she pushed them. None of them seemed to mind her
exacting comments, though; indeed, they reacted as if they
had earned the right to sharper scrutiny and would have
found any ordinary encouragement debased currency. The
younger or less experienced ones, though markedly pleased
with her attention to them, seemed to think that level of ex-
pectation was something to aim for. It was an impressive
display of team-building, something that most directors aim
for but seldom achieve with quite as much artistry as Jane.
Spirits were quite high when she dismissed them.

"Ready for a pint?" Greg asked, when we finished, about
five o'clock. Jane was with him.

I nodded. "I felt a little lagged, earlier in the afternoon,
but I've got a second wind now."

"They won't mind us in our work clothes," Jane said, "so
we'll just go straight there, once we've closed up for the
night." She looked up at the sky to gauge the weather.

Like most crews, this one was speeded along by the
promise of a beer, and as we departed, they were hastily covering their work with plywood and tarps. Jane, Greg, and I
walked down the street toward the Prince of Wales.

"You been keeping up with your running, Emma?" Jane inquired. She and I often found each other in the gym at conference hotels.

What was this fascination with my exercise habits? I wondered. First Pooter, now Jane. "Yes."

"Well, I go to the university athletics club a couple of times a week and I'm going tomorrow before work. I didn't know whether you'd care to join me?"

"I don't usually bother when I'm in the field," I said, "but it would probably do me good. Clear out the cobwebs. Thanks."

"And we'll stop by the cafe on our way," Jane promised.

The last little bit of hesitation melted away from me. "Better and better."

"Here we are," Greg announced, and held the door open for us.

I hadn't even had time to adjust my eyes to the dim light when I heard a voice greet my friends. "Missed you last night, Professors! Wasn't the same without you. Usual for you both?"

"Yes, please, Ian," Greg answered. "And for you, Emma?"

"Whatever you're having," I said, a little confused. I'd had the impression that the pub was a treat, a big deal for Jane and Greg. They looked at me, barely suppressing their mirth.

"And another bitter, as well, Ian." Greg looked at his wife, who nodded. "Pint, please. And one for yourself."

"Ta very much. I'll bring them right over."

We'd no sooner sat down then the bartender brought over our drinks. "Kev got his new guitar today," he said to Jane.

"Good for him! He's had his eye on it forever—"

But the bartender cut her off, other plans on his mind. "He said he'll try it out for us, if you promise to sing."

"Oh, I don't think—" Jane began, but the bartender waved her off.

"Course you will. And the next round's on me, to seal the bargain." And he was off before she could reply.

"What do I owe you?" I asked Greg.

"My round," he said, shaking his head.

I wasn't quite certain what that meant, but said, "Thanks," and raised my glass.

Greg and Jane beat me to it. "Cheers," they both said.

And with that, they drained off more than half their respective drinks in a single draught. I blinked; clearly I was in the company of heavyweights and any talk about the pub as an event was utter leg-pulling. I did my best to catch up.

The students came in and waved to us. I moved over instinctively to make room for them, but they congregated at a table just out of earshot of our own. Jane caught the eye of the bartender, who nodded, and after a moment, brought a tray of foaming beer glasses over for the students, who in turn, thanked her. Andrew then entered, and without a word, pushed a low stool over from the next table with his foot and joined us. Without even asking us, he called out, "Same again, here, Ian," to the bartender, busy now with the growing crowd of after-work drinkers.

"You'd better drink up, Emma," Jane said, finishing her glass.

I suddenly realized what was going on. If each drinker at our table took a turn buying a round, as seemed to be the custom, by the end of the evening, I would have consumed four pints, well beyond my usual weeknight's consumption. Five, if the bartender kept his word. Six, if I were to buy a round as well, as it seemed I ought. How could I honorably refuse so many drinks?

I was in deep, deep trouble here.

We drank off the next beer, now shouting a little to be heard over the noise, but it was clear that drinking and not conversation was the real order of the day. Suddenly, the bartender brought over the promised round and said, "You're on, Jane, Kevin's ready. Time to sing for your supper."

The change that came over Jane—indeed, the rest of the pub—was remarkable. Suddenly, all was quiet, except for a few calls of "Now, then, Kev," and "Quiet, Jane Compton's going to sing." Jane conferred with Kevin, a young kid who'd been working behind the bar washing glasses, as he pulled out a beautiful acoustic guitar from a brand new case and began to tune it reverently. She nodded, and I could hear her say, "Rockville." As Kevin began to play the introduction—a rock tune with country overtones—the crowd quieted instantly. All the tension drained out of Jane's face, her shoulders relaxed for the first time since I'd seen her, and then she began to sing.

Her voice was not sweet, but rather aching with soul and remorse. I don't listen to modern rock, but I recognized the tune from the REM tapes I had stolen from my sister's collection and soon I realized that she was blowing the doors off the way the song had originally been sung. Her voice was clean and controlled and she worked it—and the crowd—for everything it was worth. I'd never seen Jane like that before, passionate, relaxed, and effortlessly powerful: I'd never suspected she was capable of that range of emotion and mastery.

She and Kevin didn't even notice the applause at the end of the song, but, so eager to begin again, started right in on the next one. I recognized this one right away; Annie Lennox's "Why." The guitar player was very good, easily translating the super-orchestrated ballad into a simple guitar solo, but we hardly noticed because Jane was singing.

I looked around, amazed, and saw that the others were equally transfixed: Greg had a look of unparalleled adoration on his face, as if recognizing the girl he married for the first time in a long time; the snotty Trevor was awestruck, I thought, perhaps perceiving that this was something that he would never be able to imagine, never be able convey to another mortal soul; the rest of the crew was rapt, some with concentration, some with wonder. This was how she bound them together, I realized; her focus, her ardor, sometimes slipping beneath the surface of her all-too-present nerves, were crystal clear at the moment. She set high standards that she expected them to achieve because she met the high standards she set for herself, and they knew it. The only one who wasn't entirely focused on Jane was Andrew.

Through each song he stared straight into the thin foam that remained on the top of his half-emptied beer. His hand was clenched around the glass so tightly that I thought he would shatter it. Finally, even before the song was finished, I watched him slip silently out of the pub, unremarked by anyone else, closing the door silently behind him.

The applause as she finished was exuberant. Jane, flushed with effort and pride, launched into a Billie Holiday lament. She finished that to utter silence, followed by immediate cries for more. People were pressing her to go on, to sing another song, when the door opened again and slammed against the opposite wall, and this time everyone was aware of it.

A young man barged in. "They've just found Julia Whiting!"

Instantly the mood of the pub altered to disbelief. The blood drained utterly from Jane's face.

"My God, where is she?" was the variation of the question everyone was asking.

"They found her in a skip on the construction site, the new block of flats on Leather Street—!"

"What's a skip?" I whispered to Greg, who'd gone white.

"A waste container, a—what do you call them? Dumpster."

"Is she okay?" someone called.

"She's dead!"

And for some reason, every pair of eyes returned to fix on the ashen face of my friend Jane.

Chapter 6

I AWOKE WITH A JOLT THE NEXT MORNING. I GLANCED at my watch, and with a heavy sigh, slumped back into my pillow: it was just seven o'clock. There was plenty of time to consider the events of the previous evening before it was time to get ready for work. But . . . maybe just another half hour of sleep first. Ten minutes, even. I was in no way ready to go out and face all that I knew was out there.

Just as I'd scrunched back down under the covers and achieved the optimum balance of warmth and darkness, with a little tunnel for fresh air, there was a brisk rap at the door. For nearly ten seconds, I managed to convince myself that the knocking was on someone else's door, Andrew's, maybe, but then was forced back to reality by Jane's voice, crisply calling, "Morning, Emma! You up yet?"

"No," I said into the pillow. Then, louder, "Yes, I'm up."

Taking that as an invitation, Jane came in. She was dressed in a smart gray tracksuit and had a bag over her shoulder. "Still up for that run?"

I sat up and looked at her in disbelief. "Well, I just thought that since—"

"If you're too tired, I'll understand," she said, a concerned look on her face. "Actually, we got to bed pretty late last night, maybe you should just have a lie in, today."

"I'm fine," I said, annoyed. I swung my legs to the floor and rubbed my face. "Just give me a minute."

"Great! I'll see you downstairs." Jane banged the door shut and I could hear her bounce down the stairs with far too much enthusiasm. If anyone should have been in need of a lie in, especially after last night, shouldn't it have been Jane?

I dug through my suitcase, found my running stuff, and pulled myself together. Down in the kitchen, I saw Greg feeding Hildegard, his morning ritual. His face was haggard and he was preoccupied—or pretended to be so—and barely looked up as Jane said good-bye and we left.

True to Jane's promise, we stopped for a coffee at the cafe. Aunty Mads brightened at our arrival, then, when she saw that Greg wasn't with us, her face fell and she became almost sulky. I wasn't surprised when Jane asked if we couldn't please have our drinks to go.

"I was trying to figure out by the buildings," I said, when Aunty Mads handed us our coffee, "which side of town was older. I'm having a hard time deciding because everything on both sides of the river looks like pretty new construction."

"That's the war," Mads said. "Both sides got hit hard during the bombings, because of the factory, so it was all rebuilt after. But across the river is older; the abbey was built because there wasn't any room on the other side, and then the town spread around it, see."

"Sounds like you've got an interest in local history," I said, lapping up the extra coffee that had spilled onto the lid of the paper cup.

"Well, now, I wouldn't say that. No, I wouldn't say that at all," Mads objected. "That's what they told us in school, about the abbey and the town, and it stuck with me. I never open a book, if I can help it, except for biographical ones about film stars. And as far as history goes, I think it ought to be let lie." With a pointed look at Jane, Mads turned to the case full of sandwiches and began to reorganize them into neat rows with some asperity.

Jane shot me a look that said, "Thanks for bringing *that* up," and we left.

Walking down the street, the coffee, burnt as it was, convinced me that the world wasn't really such a bad place, I tried my hand at more serious conversation. It wasn't as hard as I thought it would be: all it took was caffeine. I've often thought that if chimpanzees had discovered coffee, they'd also have worked out speech too.

"Greg seemed pretty quiet this morning," I offered. It was my way of bringing up last night's revelations.

"Umm. Yes, he was a bit." Jane's lips compressed as she strode down the street. We traveled the next several blocks to the gym in silence, me with the growing concern that Jane was avoiding something.

The University Athletics Club was modern, nicely appointed, and relatively—by American standards—empty for this time of morning. Just two other hardy souls working with weight machines, and, if their faces were anything to judge by, they were considering the mammalian qualities of the breakfast blonde on the television on the wall. Jane and I dropped off our bags in the locker room and found a couple of treadmills side by side. It took me a minute to sort out the unfamiliar controls but soon we were warming up. After a few moments, I increased my speed to a fast jog. Jane followed suit.

"Pretty dramatic last night," Jane announced at last. "Bound to complicate work at the site today."

I thought about the crowd at the pub after the announcement. After the initial shock wore off, the place was abuzz with the news of Julia Whiting's death. We'd left soon after, all the calm attending Jane's singing irreparably shattered. I was actually surprised that she should bring it up. "I suppose so," I said slowly. "Lots of curiosity seekers."

"Bloody ghouls. Even if it was too late for the morning paper, it's odds on everyone in Marchester already knows.

Poor Julia; I hate that she's become gossip fodder; it makes her death all the more appalling. That's what I hate about these small towns. You can't *move* without the news of it racing around the pub, *and* the market, *and* the post office."

The ferocity of Jane's words surprised me. "Why not move?"

Jane looked grimly determined. "The job, of course. I'm not about to give that up."

"There are other jobs," I pointed out. "It's a good market at the moment."

"Not when I've worked so hard to secure this one. I've got tenure, and they're not about to shake me off now. And of course, there's the house. It's Greg's, you know."

I hadn't known.

"His grandmother left it to him. It's why we decided on Marchester when the job offers came; just one less thing to worry about, financially." She sounded resentful, though I couldn't tell whether it was because Greg removed some worry or the simple fact of his grandmother's bequest.

"Well, it can hardly be worth it, if you're so unhappy—"

"Who's unhappy?" Jane jogged along, her face set. "I'm perfectly happy. I'm exactly where I want to be. My job isn't perfect, but I'm carving into something that will be, someday. I've just been allocated new lab space. The site is shaping up. I'm doing precisely what I've always wanted. Starting to make quite a nice little reputation for myself."

I thought about this as I trotted alongside Jane, comparing her overly upbeat words with what I'd heard about her reputation in the town, the tension between her and what seemed to be everyone else. Hardly ideal. But on the other hand, Jane spoke of her reputation as if it was a new thing, whereas, as far as everyone I knew was concerned, she was one of the top people in her field. It just didn't make sense to me.

I noticed that the faster Jane ran, the more voluble she became. I increased the speed of my treadmill again, building up a nice, steady rhythm.

She continued. "And I've got more students doing advanced work than I ever have had before."

"Julia was one of them?"

Suddenly, Jane's face turned stony. "Yes, she was. And she nearly drove me round the twist, that girl."

"How's that?" The change in my friend was startling.

"Oh, well," she said. "Well, when Julia started the postgraduate program, she was very quiet, almost withdrawn, and her work was only solidly average. But she responded to the least little encouragement and about midway through the first half of the term, something turned on a lightbulb for her and she took off like a shot—"

Based on what I'd heard from her other students, I thought it was very likely that it was Jane's instruction that had so completely awakened Julia.

"She ate it all up. Devoured any book you cared to suggest and began working at a level that you usually expect of much more advanced students, but with equally big holes in her learning. She really just didn't have the experience to back up what she was studying out of books."

"Jane, that's easily fixed. She sounds like she was having a great time of it."

"Well, she was, but she kept haring on ahead of everyone else. Made it dreadfully difficult to conduct a seminar when it was just her and me arguing about theory. The other students always felt a bit left out and I felt compelled to rein her in a bit, for their sakes."

"Jeez, I'd kill for a student like that."

"Ah, well, you say so, but she never seemed to give my lectures any credence. She was always questioning me," Jane puffed, her brow creased with concentration and memory. "Don't get me wrong. I like to encourage bright students, especially the women—have to create a support system within the hegemony, don't we? But her precocity did wear thin, that I can promise you."

I set the speed for my usual fastest pace now, and noticed that Jane was monitoring my speed too: as soon as I increased my pace, she did the same, or even went a tenth or two faster. I rolled my eyes inwardly; fine, Jane, whatever. You win.

Perhaps Jane thought her words sounded too harsh; she seemed to reconsider. "I mean to say, her work was first rate. Really excellent . . . if a little erratic. Just a bit off the mark, simply because she hadn't bothered to master the basics." She was breathing heavily between sentences. "Built a foundation first. I felt like I was always trying to slow her down. For the sake of her future work. You must crawl before you can walk."

I was becoming uncomfortable; Jane hadn't been much of a crawler herself. There was something a little creepy going on here and I wondered if it wasn't time to change the subject. "Apart from work, though, you've got Greg, of course."

Jane's face, lightly filmed with perspiration, was now carefully neutral. "Well, yes, of course." She ran a few more steps. "Though that's not entirely Edenic at the moment."

"Oh?" I took a sip from my water bottle and returned it to the holder.

Jane nodded. "We're just at one of those dreadful crossroads, you see. Greg wants to start a family and I'm simply not ready. Still too many things to sort out first."

I frowned. "But do you want children?"

"Yes, of course. More important, I want his children. But I'm so newly established that I don't want to jeopardize things."

"And Greg doesn't see it that way?" I knew *I* didn't see it that way; as far as I was concerned, Jane was in the catbird seat and perfectly situated to start a family.

"No. We had the most frightful row over it, just Friday night. It was . . . hell, it was my birthday dinner. I hate the fact that I'm thirty-four. I feel ancient. I feel exhausted . . . and there's so much more work to be done. Anyway, we went out to this place—it was far too expensive, I said, but Greg insisted—and were becoming rather twining and romantic when he brought it up again. I'm afraid I lost patience."

We ran on in silence for a few moments, just the sound of our pounding feet, rhythmic breathing, and the television morning show in the corner. There wasn't another soul around now.

Jane wasn't done yet. She took a deep breath, held it for a few paces, and let it out. "The long and short of it was, I left before dessert. Stormed out, actually. I mean, honestly. He of all people should understand what I'm going through. He's been very supportive, but it's only a few more years. I just want to get caught up on my reports, and get one or two more juicy articles out before we start talking about bairns."

There is no perfect moment, I thought, never a real stopping point. There'll always be one more thing. And a couple of years puts one rather close to the biologically decisive age of forty, but there was no way I'd say that out loud to Jane. Especially since I hadn't ever been able to shed the "just one more book/project/conference and I'll relax" theory myself. Yet.

"And as for last night, well. All he wanted to do was talk about Julia and I . . . just couldn't. It's still so fresh, it's so awful, I just needed some space to get past the shock. Some people can do that by going on and on about it, till it doesn't smart anymore, but some just need to hide themselves away. I need some time to take it in, is all."

As if aware she might have revealed too much, Jane suddenly sped up into a sprint and, deciding that I was feeling pretty good myself, I matched her speed.

"How about a race?" she panted after a bit. "First one to finish the next half mile buys breakfast?"

"No, thanks, I hate races," I said, breathing heavily myself. "I like it being just me and the road."

"Suit yourself," Jane said.

After another fifteen seconds, I decided that I wasn't actually straining and picked up the pace a little bit. My friend noticed this and again raised her own speed.

For God's sake, I thought. Fine, she wants a race, I'll give her a race. I jabbed at the touch pad accordingly.

This went on for the next few minutes, both of us pounding away, sweating rivers, neither saying a word over the mechanical rhythm of the treadmills. Then a timer beeped, announcing a cool-down period. We slowed to a fast walk, still not able to talk after the last hard push. It was then that I realized something from the way that Jane dealt with her advanced students, what she'd said about Julia, how she behaved with me. She was perfectly fine with people who were students, who were somewhere beneath her level, academically speaking, but when they started to approach that, she became nervous and pushed them harder because she was intimidated. The irony of it all was, the more Jane pushed, the better they generally became, so that she was surrounding herself with excellent students, who in turn, drove her to surpass herself.

"Nice job," Jane gasped out after a bit. "Not bad after a late night."

"You too." I nodded. "You got a tenth farther along than I did."

"Ah, well," she replied, pleased with herself. "You've been jet lagged. Besides, we weren't racing,"

"No, 'course not," I said. "I hate competitions."

On the way back to the locker room, however, I happened to notice that I got my breath back a whole lot sooner than Jane did.

There was a nasty surprise waiting for us when we returned to the house, a message asking Jane to come down to the police station to be interviewed by the Marchester constabulary. Greg was pacing, waiting for Jane's arrival.

I watched her face go from curiosity to concern to alarm to . . . boredom. "God, how tedious," she said, after she'd read the note. "Well, maybe during morning coffee I'll nip down and take care of this—"

I thought it was a classic example of covering, but apparently Greg didn't see that; Jane seemed to be pretty good at it. "They're serious, Jane!" Greg said. "They mean first thing, *not* at your convenience. It's not just one more thing to be shoved aside to await your leisure."

Ouch, I thought. That bit.

Both Jane and I looked up at him. Although his voice was level, his words were angry. I thought about what Jane had told me about their present marital difficulties and how they'd left things last night.

"No need to take my head off," Jane snapped, nerves fraying past masking. "I only thought—"

"Jane, this is serious. Julia has *died*—"

"Greg, I—" Jane was now visibly rocked, but it came too late for Greg to notice, and I wished myself anywhere but there.

"Only sometimes, I wonder if you have any sense of the importance of anything besides your job. I wonder if anything else matters. It colors everything you do. Even your relationship with Julia was poisoned because *you* were *threatened* by her—"

"I think you'd better leave off there," Jane said, quite coldly. "I have to change. I have to see the police, and I wouldn't want to keep them waiting."

"Fine," Greg said stiffly. "I'll see to things at the site."

"Fine."

And with that it was over, even before I could figure out how to sneak away and give them a little privacy. Greg banged out the door and Jane turned to me, all business.

"Sorry. Emma, if you think you can manage, I'm going to be away for a bit. But if you have any questions, just pass them on to Greg, okay? If you don't mind, I'll take the tub first, okay? Brilliant, thanks."

As if I hadn't been there to see any of their fight. Whatever doubts I'd had as to the existence of the unflappable British exterior during the argument were slammed back into place by Jane's behavior afterward. It happened so quickly, so much compressed emotion forcibly released, that it was like being stunned in the aftermath of an explosion.

Soon after Jane left, I washed up and trotted out to the site, where everyone was just starting work. Everyone, that is, except Andrew, I noticed. He was nowhere to be seen. Then I frowned. Trevor the Odious was also missing; it wasn't so much his absence that I noticed, it was the lack of complaint coming from his area. I began to head out to the center of the site, but was halted by Greg's call. I joined him by the work desk, where I saw a pile of lumber and tools.

"The materials I picked up from the DIY yesterday," he explained, and I recalled that we'd discussed getting the materials to make me some screens. Wasn't that like Greg to remember, even after last night?

"No one was in any state to start anything . . . last night," he continued, apologetically and a little embarassed.

"No, naturally not," I said, thinking at last someone would be willing to talk to me about it. "Everyone was in a state of shock."

"Dreadful. I offered to let some of the students off for the day or two—those who knew Julia best, that is, but no one was really very close to her," he said hesitantly. "Everyone seemed to want the security of a normal day, what with all the uncertainty about. I think they are looking to Jane for some guidance, but she's only going to find solace in work."

"Everyone except for Trevor?" I said.

Greg sighed. "I don't know where the little pillock has got himself off to, but it wasn't with any of my leave. I'd just as soon he kept himself out of my sight, to be quite honest with you. And," he said, anticipating my next question, "I haven't the faintest notion of where Andrew is. I don't believe he ever came home last night. The man might have had the sense to help out, today of all days, but there you are." Greg finally seemed to be losing patience with his unreliable friend.

I shrugged. "What about the modern skeleton? Has he finished working on that in the lab yet?"

"I leave that up to Andrew; no matter what, he'll meet his

work obligations—in his own time, mind you. But we do tend to leave our specialists to their own devices in England; it's not so hands-on for the directors in England as it is in the States."

Greg then rubbed his hands together, shaking off these unpleasant thoughts and effectively squelching any more of my questions. "But let's get you set up. As you can see, I got the timber you wanted. Took a bit of doing, but it's all just as you ordered. Good English oak," Greg pointed out with satisfaction. "We'll get you sifting away in no time."

I looked down at the pile of lumber stock, nails, and screening and frowned. Something wasn't quite right; the lengths of wood were absolutely enormous. The stock was thick, like beams for a house, it seemed.

"You got two-by-fours," I said uncertainly.

"Yes. Had to have them ripped to specification, of course, as timber on this side of the water is in metric and in different standard heights and widths. I'm very interested to see how you put this all together."

And so was I, I thought. The problem was, there isn't a two-by-four in America that is actually two inches by four inches; it's just a handy approximation. Everything's actually a bit smaller than that and, for my purposes, much better suited to comfortable use. But I told Greg that everything looked fine and in a little less than an hour, we'd got things into roughly the right shape. It would sift dirt, certainly, but it wasn't portable by any stretch of the imagination.

"Well, that's not going anywhere," Greg announced, beads of sweat running. "Make it through the next ice age, I shouldn't wonder."

He was right. What one generally ended up with, in my experience, was a shallow box with a screen bottom, the long sides of which extended out into a pair of handles with the opposite end supported on the bottom by a hinged set of legs. It took a bit of balancing, but ordinarily what you'd end up with was a screen that folded neatly onto its legs and was fairly portable. This one was similar but on a larger, bulkier scale, portable the same way the Empire State Building was portable. With that in mind, I silently dubbed my new screen Kong.

"Is this really what you use on your digs?" Greg asked, a little confused. "It's enormous."

"I guess I got the measurements off," I said. After all his trouble in getting the materials, I wasn't about to tell him that it wouldn't do. "I'll cut down the handles a bit, so that they'll be a bit more manageable."

We both struggled to get Kong out to my burial, and then I began work. The day was pleasant enough, but the first break came and went without any sign of Jane. I tried to put it out of my mind, but found myself unable to concentrate properly. I kept looking up for her arrival, and kept being surprised when she didn't come. I was starting to get worried about my friend, and it reflected in my work. Rather than bringing the entire length of the stain down in one even level, I got into a sort of downward spiral, where I would get one corner sorted out, only to find that the other three were still too high. Every time I tried to bring things level, I realized that I had gone too far.

At lunch I finally gave up trying. The crew was unusually subdued and Greg, so far from his usual pleasant efficient self, was snappish, particularly after a small red car pulled up to the site and a man got out, asking for a moment of his time. When Greg returned, his face was a torment. I didn't dare to ask him what he'd learned.

We continued to eat in silence, but before the bulk of the crew returned from their pub run, I heard Greg sigh yet again. Knowing that personal conversation wasn't his favorite thing, I decided to risk it, on the off chance that he might relax a little.

"You're worried about Jane," I said.

"I was hoping she'd be done by now," he said abruptly. "I . . . I assumed that it would just be the same as before, when Julia was first reported missing. The police simply took statements from everyone, right here on the site. But this is different. I don't know why and I don't like it."

That having been said, there was little I could say to comfort him. I stuck with the commonplaces, which were as ever horribly insufficient. "I'm sure they're just asking about Julia's behavior on site, who she knew, that sort of thing. I'm sure it's nothing."

Greg looked at me with impatience. "I'm absolutely certain it's not nothing. I was just told that she probably won't be back to work today, but that I should continue on here. There's a student dead, and my wife quite well known for disliking her, and *she* wants me to keep working. How could anyone—?"

Then his face almost crumpled. He mastered himself before he'd even allowed himself the emotion. "Oh, God, Emma, I apologize. It's . . . there's no excuse. I'm dreadfully sorry."

"Don't worry about it," I said hastily. "Please."

Greg said nothing, but only kept shaking his head and staring at the tops of his rubber work boots.

I hated seeing him like this. "Look, I'm going to straighten out the mess in my unit. I'm keeping you from looking in on the others when I'm supposed to be a bigger help."

"Right, and we wouldn't want Jane to come back and find us slacking off, would we?" he said with a faint smile. "I'll stop by later." He fled.

It took most of the rest of the afternoon, but at last I got my unit to a respectable state: corners square, floor level, extraneous dirt removed. Rather than follow the others for tea, or bother Greg, who had found refuge deep in a notebook with the intent of ignoring what was going on, I stayed by my unit, squatting on an upturned bucket, scribbling notes. Truth to tell, there wasn't much to write, only that the feature of the burial was becoming more and better defined, and that based on the depth I would probably start to uncover any skeletal remains shortly. There was a light breeze com-

ing off the river, and off in the distance I heard the faint tinkling of wind chimes; I pulled the shell of my barn coat
closer around me, wondering when spring really started in
around here. I found myself doodling names—Jane, Julia,
Palmer, Andrew—but none of them meant anything to me in
relation to the others. I tried to dig back through my memories, reexamine everything of context that everyone had
mentioned to me since I'd been here; there seemed to be
connections, but nothing clear. I knew so little that it was
meaningless. Add to that the presence of a relatively recent
skeleton that showed every indication of having been murdered, and a less suspicious nature than mine would be concerned. As Jane was embroiled in this, innocent though I
knew she must be, I decided suddenly I was going to make it
my business to find out exactly what those connections rep-
resented. After all, I was on vacation, I could afford to nose
about, and I simply couldn't stand idly by . . .

One tiny little something did surface, however, from all
my mental sieving that I began to wonder about. Julia's body
had been found on a construction site, in a Dumpster or skip,
to be precise. I recalled Palmer's comments that Jane was at
odds with one of the local builders. That struck me as something worth investigating.

At that moment, a chill stole over me. At first I thought
the sun had gone behind a cloud, but after I hurriedly jotted
down my last notes, I realized that someone was standing
behind me. I covered over my notes. It wasn't Greg, it
wasn't one of the students—twisting around awkwardly, I
knew that none of them would be wearing a long black skirt.
The tinkling I'd heard earlier was closer now, and I now
knew that it came from two rows of tiny bells sewn into the
skirt. As I looked up, the first thing that caught my eye was a
pale white hand, with what at first I thought was a complex
bracelet draped over it. Then that little part of my brain that
is so good at recognizing patterns identified the bracelet as a
tattoo, a complex trailing green vine that wrapped around

the woman's middle finger and curled up round her wrist and presumably up the rest of her arm. I swung all the way around to look up into the stranger's face.

"Brightest blessings," said the woman, smiling warmly, though there was a guarded look in her eyes.

I sighed. Oh, puh-lease.

"You know, I don't think you're supposed to be here," I said.

"Oh, but you're wrong there," she replied with an accent that was coarser and less precise than either Jane's or Greg's: I knew that I was talking to Morag. "I think we'll both find, at the end, that I'm exactly where I'm meant to be, in the midst of all these lines and triangles. But judging by the look on your face, I wonder: Can you say the same for yourself?"

Chapter 7

"A CTUALLY," I SAID WITH SOME ASPERITY, "I CAN say why I'm meant to be here, but why don't we discuss that outside the dig parameters?" I noticed distantly that I sounded a bit like Jane.

"Certainly, but I don't see what harm I'm doing here," Morag replied haughtily. "Simply standing here, not touching anything. My mere presence isn't going to pollute your work."

Her tone struck me as the same used by teenagers at times, confrontational and defensive all at once. Her stance was very much the same: arms crossed over her plump little pot belly, head tilted backward, so that her tangle of red hair was thrown dramatically back, exposing a silver pentacle pendant snagged on the laces of her blouse. Morag was a nice study in contrasts: the round face I might expect to see across the bakery counter and the clothing—all black, save for a bit of gold and red trim—that made me think of first-year art students.

"No, of course not," I said as I got up out of my crouch

with a crack of my knees. "But there are issues of safety and security that I need to attend to."

"Fine, but—" Morag turned, a little cascade of single notes following the abrupt motion of her skirt. "Just one thing."

Unless I was going to frog-march her off the site, I had to listen. For now. I always wondered whether I could effectively frog-march someone.

"Can I see one of the relics? From that area where you're working? Right here?"

"There isn't much," I said, "not from a—"

She nodded impatiently. "From a grave shaft, yes I know. But 'not much' doesn't mean 'nothing,' does it?"

"Let's take it with us, shall we?" I suggested. I bent over and pulled something from a plastic bag in the tray. "There's a nice bit of sunny patch over beyond the barrier, and I'd like to warm up a bit."

"I'm really not going to hurt anything," she said; again, half-ironic, half-defensive.

"No one said you would. Shall we?" I held out my hand in invitation toward the gate.

Once we were off the actual site, I decided to reestablish things on my terms. I stuck out my hand. "Hi, I'm Emma Fielding."

"Morag Traeger." She shook my hand.

"Now, what can I do for you?"

"May I see the relic?"

I hesitated, knowing what she was going to do, but not quite certain why. "The word 'relic' is probably a bit of an overstatement; you're probably closer to the mark with 'artifact.' I consider anything a relic to be religious object, properly associated with a saint."

Morag smiled patronizingly. "Don't you consider Mother Beatrice a saint? I think she was a holy person, not a Christian, but a worshiper of the Old Religion."

I shrugged. "I guess if the Church doesn't think her a

saint, then I don't. I don't know her story that well. Besides,
I'm pretty sure this never belonged to her. I don't even know
if I'm actually working on her grave." I realized that she
couldn't know that I might be working on Mother Beatrice;
I must have just looked like fresh meat she could get around.

I handed Morag the sherd I was carrying, and she scruti-
nized it carefully. Then she closed her eyes and held the
lowly bit of pottery up to her forehead reverently. I watched,
a little curious, a little annoyed, a little uncomfortable.

"No," she said finally, opening her eyes, and handing
back the sherd to me. "It was never hers, but it did belong to
some troubled soul—"

I noticed that she didn't actually identify the piece of
stoneware for me; it was from a ceramic mug, probably several centuries later than Mother Beatrice's period. "Just
someone picnicking in the graveyard," I said, "maybe a
gravedigger had a drink of something, and this got kicked
around for a couple of centuries. It was from just above the
shaft. No way to tell if he—or she—was troubled or not."

"Of course there is," she said. *"There are more things in
heaven and earth than are dreamed of in your philosophies—"*

Mentally I corrected her: dreamt, not dreamed; philoso-
phy, not philosophies. Easy enough mistakes, but she left
out poor Horatio altogether.

"Besides. You were trying to trick me. It's not from the
grave itself."

"No, I did just what you asked," I replied. "I even told
you. You asked to see an artifact from where I was working.
Besides, nothing I might find there is going to have been put
there by Mother Beatrice. Once you're dead, you have very
little say in what people put in the ground with you."

Morag shook her head sadly and I caught a strong scent
of some heavy incense. "I will tell you, Emma, that I feel
lots of hostility from the people working on this site. I
deeply resent the fact that this important part of history—

local and spiritual—is being co-opted, dominated by a select few. It seems wrong that history should be hoarded, perverted to serve the interests of the governing."

Problem was, I agreed with her—in principle, just not in this specific case. "I'm sorry you feel threatened—"

"Not *threatened*," she said. "I didn't say *threatened*, I said I feel hostility, which is very—"

"—But maybe what you are sensing is the anger of people who feel you don't respect their work or their rules. The fences are up there to help protect the site—which, you're right, does belong to everyone, in a sense—and to protect the public. I've seen unwary visitors break ankles by falling into working units because they weren't looking where they were going. Jane would be blamed if anyone got hurt. I'm sure you wouldn't want that."

"No, I wish no one to be hurt, or blamed. I just question her right to be on this site, when so many others are denied. From where does her privilege come, to pick and chose who might be here?"

My shoulders heaved; this drama was tiring. It was the oldest story in the book, the rights of scientists versus the rights of everyone else—to history, to be on a particular bit of land, to dig, even.

"It's not fair," I said. "But it's the best solution. By letting people who are trained excavate a site, you have the best chance of preserving all the data—for everyone. On the other hand, Jane and Greg, and even the students, have trained for years, so it's not without some sacrifice on their part, this privilege. And it's not random: They had to prove their ability to be here, had to get a license from the Home Office to work on the human remains."

"Still and all, I wish that you scientists would be a little more open-minded," Morag persisted. "I think that Mother Beatrice was something special, someone important, and I think she's not been granted her due. She was tied into this place—a place of real power, mind you—in a way that I think is truly important. She had visions and I know, just know, she was one of us. I'm just trying to see that justice is done, that her story is given as much prominence as it deserves, as much as any Christian's. As much as any man's."

Again I found myself agreeing with her, but only halfway. I also felt a headache coming on. "Look, like I said, I don't know the story all that well, but I find it pretty amusing that you should lump Jane with the establishment. As far as I can tell, Jane's in everyone's bad graces here, and as far as feminist interpretations go, you've got a better chance with Jane than most." Morag really wasn't all that politically astute, that was for sure.

"I can see I won't get anywhere with you." The other woman gestured grandly, again to the sound of tinkling bells. "You're as shut off as the rest of them—"

Now, if you want to get me angry, just tell me how narrow-minded I am. I've spent my life training myself not only to see patterns, to make logical leaps, to pay attention, but also to follow my instincts as much as my intellect. I could feel my jaw muscles tighten.

"Look, Ms. Traeger. Why don't you tell me what evidence you have for Mother Beatrice's spiritual—pagan—importance, and I'll consider it. Next time you visit the site—just wait at the fence—I'll tell you what I think."

There, I thought, she'll say I'm not considering the spiritual side of things, that I'll only consider the ordinary, material world that anyone can look at. Then she'll leave and I can get back to work.

To my surprise, however, Morag nodded, and pulled out a file from the large bag on her shoulder. "Here, take it. I've made copies. Take my card, too. Come and chat, if you like. I'd be very interested to hear your point of view."

More than surprised, I took the folder and the card, which read, "Marchester Interactive, Web Site Design and Construction, Morag Traeger, Creative Lead/ Co-Founder" with a telephone number, Web site address, and a Fitzwilliam Street address.

"I'll be sure to have a look," I said. I was very curious to see what she'd collected.

"I wonder. Still, it was nice to meet you Emma. I get a good feeling from you." She looked around the site, and shook her head sadly. "And that's a relief, in the midst of all this pain, all of those triangles." And with that, she walked off, the self-assured sway of her hips causing the little bells to jingle madly.

Greg came over as Morag left. "Well, that was unusually quiet."

"Huh?" With all of the bells, the garish trim, the smell of incense, and Morag's insistent defensiveness, her theatrical choice of words, I couldn't imagine anything less quiet. She overwhelmed every one of the senses.

"Usually, Jane ends up in a slanging match with her."

"Well, that never works with her sort of people. Morag's, I mean. People who are stuck on one idea."

"Oh, and don't I know it. Jane knows it too, but she just can't stand that Morag is so . . ."

"So very . . ."

"That's it, exactly," Greg agreed. He pulled a handkerchief from his pocket and rubbed his glasses with it. The usual confetti of odds and ends landed on the ground, and he retrieved them after he'd replaced his glasses. "What'd she want this time? I've worked on sites where the visitors wanted to come in and lie on one of the graves. Get the vibe."

I shivered; the idea wasn't so much spooky as it was just weird. "No. She wanted to hold one of the artifacts. I let her and she said it belonged to some tortured soul."

He smiled faintly. "Well, it's no fun if no one's tortured. Anyway, I was going to suggest—"

Suddenly Greg was interrupted by a loud honking. He frowned at this infraction of common decency and we both turned to see what the matter was. I should have suspected: the matter, as it was so often, was Dora.

"Emma! I'm over here, Emma! Emma!" Dora was calling out of the car window as though we were on separate alpine peaks, or as if she were on a sinking ship and I had the lifeboat. Jeremy Hyde-Spofford was seated next to her, and Palmer, scowling all the while, hopped from the driver's seat to open the door for them. It wasn't the Bentley this time, but a huge Land Rover that actually looked as though it did estate work.

Palmer had just enough time to shoot me one truly poisonous look, reminding me of his implied threats to me, before he opened the door and Dora emerged, still hallooing. I sighed, realizing that, as always, I couldn't just wave from where I was: Dora required my full attention. I wiped the dirt off my trowel and went to meet them at the gate.

"Hello, Dora, Jeremy." I turned and smiled sweetly at Palmer, in memory of our last, rather hostile encounter. "Mr. Palmer."

"Good afternoon, Emma," Jeremy replied. He was wearing a green jacket similar to Greg's and a truly horrible silk scarf—so crammed with electric yellow paisleys that the thing appeared to be alive and crawling. "I hope that we're not interrupt—"

"We haven't got time to stop, Emma," Dora trumpeted, by way of greeting. "I'm on my way to the airport, off to Florence."

"I thought you were supposed to be there already," I said.

"Well, you know how it is. One gets caught up where one is. They won't mind, once I get there," Dora responded, waving a hand airily.

"But I did want to take the opportunity to renew my invitation for this weekend," Pooter said, firmly stanching any further philosophizing on Dora's part. "And to ask your friends too, if they'd like. The more the merrier."

So Dora wouldn't be at the faux fox hunt. That would have been worth seeing. "I'm afraid Jane's not here at the moment," I said. I turned and found I couldn't keep my eyes off Palmer, who, although seeming to pay close attention to rubbing some dirt off the front headlight, was, I was sure, paying deepest attention. "But Greg is."

"I'm what?" Greg asked, joining us. I made the introductions and Jeremy repeated his invitation to Greg, who looked uneasy, his wavy ginger hair blown about by the light breeze.

"Thanks all the same, but I'm afraid you'd better not count on us. I'm sure you've heard the sad news about Julia Whiting and our troubles here, and I wouldn't want to accept your offer without checking with my wife first."

"I understand completely," Jeremy said. "In fact, I almost canceled, out of respect to George and Ellen Whiting, but George insisted we carry on the yearly tradition. Quite adamant on that account. So, please, if you find yourselves free, don't hesitate to join us. Emma, if your friends can't make it, I'll send Palmer to fetch you."

Palmer looked carefully blank, and I tried to squash the butterflies in my stomach. "That's very kind of you."

"Pooter! We must leave immediately," Dora announced. "Signor Bravatelli won't wait another instant."

Jeremy made a studied attempt to ignore her. "I'm sorry to have to dash off, Ashford."

"Perhaps you'll join us again when I can give you a tour of the site," Greg said.

"Delighted to. Emma, until this weekend."

"Good-bye. Bye, Dora. Have a good time in Florence."

My colleague slid back into the vehicle. "I'm going to seize, remove, and totally reconstruct the idea of Raphael for a generation of scholars. I shall not have a good time, but it shall be worthwhile and they shall thank me after. It is not easy, revising hundreds of years of erroneous academic consideration, but I shall persevere."

Greg watched thoughtfully as the Land Rover tore away. My pounding headache worsened, and I suddenly decided I needed a break. "Greg, can you spare me for an hour or so?"

"Of course. We're getting ready to close up, you don't need to be here for that."

"Well, I'm caught up on my paperwork, so I just thought I'd go have a look at the church. Sabine, ah, Reverend Jones, offered to show me the tower, and I'd like to go."

"No problem. We'll have dinner when you get back. With any luck, Jane'll be home by then." Although he'd been trying to maintain his composure all day, Greg was morose at the very thought of his wife's absence. But I noticed that he didn't seem *worried* for Jane, somehow.

"See you then." I waved, crossed the site, and found the path that was just below the top of the bank. I started hiking along the riverbank toward the "new" church. My head was pounding and I thought, still no sign of Trevor. While it was very nice to have the break from him and his attitude, which hung over the site like a miasma, I wondered where he'd gotten himself to. Jane didn't need another missing student, that was for sure.

Tall grass and weeds grabbed at my boots as I clumped down on the hard packed dirt path. Down about ten feet below me, the river Mar was dull gray-blue and sluggish, nearly indistinguishable from the smoothed stones along the bank, but just the quiet and the smell of wet mud and plants was soothing after my frustrating day; I couldn't even see the road from down here. The air was still chilly and there was a little breeze that occasionally moved the clouds away from the sun.

About ten minutes later, voices, or rather, a single, shouting voice, intruded upon the tranquility of the path. I found myself at the edge of a mowed grassy space between the riverbank and the back of the church—too small to be a field, too large to be a yard—and saw the source of all the noise.

To my amazement, Sabine Jones, garbed in shorts, a sweatshirt, athletic socks, and cleats, was expertly dribbling a soccer ball, charging toward a makeshift goal and the skinny, rather nervous looking boy with dark curly hair who was defending it. Her blond hair was frizzing from perspiration, combs falling out and tangled.

"Anticipate, anticipate! Come on, come on, Teddy! Not just the eyes, not just the body language, anticipate where I'm going to go!"

As I watched, she faked left, then dove right, and attempted to drive the ball between the two battered orange pylons. Teddy was fooled for a moment, but at the last second lunged at the ball, just barely brushing it away from the goal with the tips of his fingers.

"And Jones is denied, with a brilliant save by Tedman!" The vicar ran around in a tight circle, celebrating his save herself, as the goalie watched with embarrassed pride. Then she composed herself, collected the ball, and addressed her companion in a stern voice.

"And now, Mr. Tedman, what's going to happen?"

"I'm going to go home and study my maths," the boy replied, as if by rote.

"And then?"

"And then I'm going to pass the exam with a better than average score."

"Whereupon?"

"I'll be allowed to play against St. John's parish on Saturday."

"And the result of that shall be?"

"That we ev . . . eviscerate their side!"

"Good lad. Now go home, and don't let the xs and ys fool you; they're only code names. Geometry is crucial to aspiring footballers." Sabine handed the boy a pile of schoolbooks, and then she noticed me. "And be nice to your mother," she called after the boy as he tore off around the church.

"Hello," I said, drawing nearer. "Hope I didn't interrupt anything."

"Not a bit. Young Tedman has been coming for some extra help with his schoolwork, spurred on by the fact that I coach St. Alban's football. The boys can't play if they don't keep their grades up, and while none of them will ever play for Arsenal, if it keeps them slogging through plane geometry, I don't mind using the carrot."

"Sounds like a good idea." I bit my lip, uncertain of what I was here for. "Have you got a minute?"

"Yes, certainly." Sabine grabbed a towel and wiped off her face, then replaced the combs that were tangled loosely in her hair.

"You mentioned the tower before. I just thought, maybe, if it wouldn't be any trouble, you could show me the view from the tower?"

"No trouble at all. Follow me."

She led the way from the back lot round to the front doors and into the church itself.

"You should have a look at the church proper, before we head up to the tower. It's rather ordinary but a pleasant enough place."

We stepped into the main section of the church. The gray stone was cool and the interior was dark; our footsteps echoed through the building. Dog-eared hymnals sat on the wooden pews and the gloom was broken periodically along the walls by stained glass windows the color of rich jewels and at the far end, where the altar, dazzlingly lit from above, was bedecked with flowers and bright brass candlesticks.

"It's not quite so grim when the pews are full," Sabine said. "Bodies damp down the echoes, but the choir still sounds respectable."

"I don't think it's grim at all," I replied. "I like the emptiness."

"Well, like I said." She waved around, indicating the interior. "Nothing special, in terms of the construction—not really my bag anyway—finished building around 1520, after the abbey was destroyed, lots of bits added on after that. I'm not sure how much of the original is still standing by now or covered by later additions. The stained glass over the altar was done by a local master—forget his name—in the 1700s or something, but it was all bombed out during the war. Fortunately, some clear thinking parishioner saved all the fragments, and while they weren't able to repair the window, a very good copy was made." Sabine looked around in approval at the windows, but then looked at me and frowned.

"But I don't think you're interested in my small store of architectural knowledge, are you?"

I protested feebly; Sabine shook her head. "Follow me."

She took a key ring out of her pocket and opened a heavy old-fashioned wooden door. We started climbing the stairs that twisted tightly; the steps were steep and badly spaced.

"Speaking of which, a little more geometry would have been in order here," the vicar said. "Watch that next step, it's a little worn and slick."

Too late; I slipped a little but caught myself before I actually fell forward.

"Here we are." She opened another door and led the way out to a room that had once housed the bells. I looked above me and could see the place where they would have been. Now the tower was merely a room open to the elements, a haven for nesting birds, if the droppings and fallen twigs were anything to go by. I could hear the shuffling and throaty muttering of birds overhead.

"Again, the bells were lost during the war. The tower was rebuilt, with the hope that the bells would be replaced someday. Not this year, the account books always tell us. Still, I'd be happy just to get these windows screened up. The birds do a tremendous amount of damage. But then I wouldn't be able to hide out up here and enjoy my view."

I looked out from the tower and saw what she meant. Ahead of us, in the distance beyond the churchyard cemetery and the makeshift football field and the trees, I could see the site and the crew packing up for the evening. To our right was the business district and the center of town, to our left, the residential section.

"Nice, isn't it?" the vicar asked. I noticed that she wasn't so besotted by the panorama that she couldn't roll another cigarette. Presumably, no one could see—or cared—whether she smoked up here. I also noticed that there was a large can filled with sand and the ends of little rolled-up cigarettes.

I stared out at the site a moment longer. "Far above it all," I answered absently. "No racket, no people here."

Sabine guffawed loudly. "Just us chickens." She picked a loose piece of tobacco from her teeth and grinned broadly.

"I'm sorry." I shrugged. "You know what I mean. You especially, I imagine. Up to your hip boots in them. People, I mean."

"Yes. That's why I stuck with the C of E, because of the community work, the social action. It's important to me."

I realized that she probably wouldn't understand my antisocial feelings, so I decided to drop it.

Sabine was watching me closely. "We're in similar fields, really, you and I. We get a different perspective on things than most people."

"I suppose so." I suppressed a flicker of annoyance. "Morag stopped by the site again today. Came right in and made herself at home."

"Oh, yes?"

"Gave me some reading, about Mother Beatrice, I guess."

"Ah, yes, the supposed martyr for the pagan cause. I wonder why the idea of persecution automatically gives someone credibility. As far as local historians can tell, she died of natural causes, of old age or disease, at forty-five or so."

"Well, I told her I would read it." I watched as the students on the site made a last sweep, checking for lost tools and notebooks. "There's something about Morag, though. I mean, she really sort of batters one—the bells, the tattoos, the incense, her insistent questions—and yet—"

"Yet?"

"There's something guarded about her. She's protecting something, or . . . hiding something."

There was a pause while Sabine smoked thoughtfully. "In

my experience," she said, "loss leaves a void, a silence. Some people try to fill that up themselves. In this case, literally."

Which told me exactly nothing. I tried again. "She also made an interesting comment. A couple of them, really. She said that there were all sorts of lines on the site, by which I guess she meant the ley lines. She also said that there were triangles, and that's what I didn't understand. Was she talking about personal relationships? Was she talking about some other new-agey thing? Do you know?"

Sabine's face was blank. "Did you ask *her*?"

"No, but we were talking about so many things that I could hardly keep up with her." I ran my hands along the cool stone of the wall, then brushed the damp and crumbly mortar from my fingers. "I wonder if she wasn't talking about some of the other things Jane seems to be tangled up in, whether it wasn't something about Julia—"

"I can't imagine why you're interested."

The words came so sharply, the tone so thoroughly meant to end a conversation, that for a moment I was shocked into speechlessness. What had I done? I turned; Sabine was looking away, smoking furiously.

I spread my hands helplessly. "I . . . my friend's being questioned by the police about a murder. She . . . she may even be accused of that murder. I want to help."

Reverend Jones stubbed out her poor little cigarette with far more violence than I thought necessary to do the job. "Well, that's taken care of, isn't it? The police are the ones to help. They're paid to do it. They're sanctioned to do it. They're part of the community, they know people."

She let the implications settle upon me.

What was going on here? "I *need* to do something. I need to help."

She waved toward the dig. "Isn't working on the site a help? Isn't being there for your friends a help?"

"It's not enough. I think . . . I can do more. If you'll help me."

There was a long silence, so long that I thought that the

conversation really was over. Fine, I thought, I'll find out what I need to know from someone else.

I looked out over the river, then toward the site, now abandoned. Everyone will be down in the pub now, I thought. I could see the lights of the businesses on one side of the river dimming down, those on the other side, in the houses, just starting to wink on. Not because it was dark yet, but more to keep the shadows at bay. Five hundred years ago, even two hundred years ago, there wouldn't be this division between work and home, everything would have taken place at home. I could see shadows creeping across the churchyard cemetery and backlot, across to the dig, even, where the subtle changes in the surface of the site hinted at what might lie beneath. Weeds grew over soil that had been disturbed by plowing or by digging graves, mixed in with the long grass, so that up close, you might not notice the differences, but with a little distance, you could see these variations. All it took was a different perspective, a little removal, and you could almost imagine that you could see beneath the earth's surface, just like Superman.

Sabine had rolled up another cigarette while I was busy with my thoughts. I heard the match flare up and then smelled the acrid odor as she extinguished it. I heard her inhale impatiently, as though the cigarette wasn't giving her the responses she wanted, either. I turned to look at her, and after three more puffs, she ground that cigarette out too. She'd come to some sort of decision. I waited, holding my breath.

"I'm not going to tell you anything that isn't common knowledge," she said, as though she was trying to convince herself. "I'm not going to betray any trusts. I'm not going to let you in just because you've asked—I'm not at all certain you have an understanding of what you're asking, of what you're doing and why, and I certainly think that you need to consider that. Confront that. But I'll tell you a bit, and maybe this will give you something to think about. Maybe that will lead you in the right direction."

I mentally discarded all that dross about me confronting things—I mean, honestly! That seemed to be all I ever did, these days—and polished that little nugget that was buried in it. Sabine was going to tell me why the site seemed to be so bedeviled.

Chapter 8

WE SAT THERE AT THE TOP OF THE BELL TOWER, AR-chaeologist and vicar, staring at each other, each waiting for the other to start.

"Well?" Sabine said impatiently. "What is it you want to know?"

There was so much . . . "Let's start with what Morag said about the lines and triangles. Was she talking about the ley lines?"

"I assume so, yes, which is pretty straight forward. I suspect she could also have been referring to lines drawn within the community, or rather, between the town and the dig. Most people are very excited about the project, as you might expect. Lots of interest in local history, and many people even take an A level in archaeology, even if they have no intention of pursuing it as a career—"

"A level?"

"Advanced exams for teenagers; I guess you would call them high school-aged. Anyway, the problem is with those who want to modernize Marchester at a faster pace, you know, the developers, certain members of the city corporation, the most vocal of whom is George Whiting. He's a sharp man, a hard man, maybe, with few social skills, so he manages to put the back up of almost everyone he meets, which is a shame, because he really tries to do a lot of good for the town, in his way."

She hesitated, trying to find the right words to explain. "I think he wants to make money, which he is good at, and that he may have a plan for Marchester, bringing it into the twenty-first century, is how it is so often put. Since we've only just barely made it into the twentieth, I prefer a slower pace, myself. He wants to make a name for himself, too, doesn't he? But he doesn't stop to think how people feel, just how to get things done most efficiently, and that's where he and Jane have crossed swords."

"Oh?"

"He hired her to evaluate a site that he was planning on developing, and he . . . well, he thought they had an understanding. That it would be very unfortunate to find anything important on that area, because a lot of people would be denied a shopping district. Well, Jane did find something, some pottery manufactory or something, and she wasn't about to roll over and say she didn't. Things got very ugly."

"What happened?"

"The shops were put in—eventually. It took another two years, with a full mitigation of the site, and only after several very ugly council meetings. George lost a lot of money, though, of course, he's made it all back now, I'm sure of it. Then later, after, Jane jumped in and actually did prevent him from putting in a launderette where he wanted, kept him from tearing down an old house that was important."

"Well, that's part of her job," I interjected, "looking after sites like that."

Sabine disagreed, shaking her head emphatically. "It was foolish on her part; she was just showing him that he couldn't mess with her, and it was a bad battle to chose. So they're at guns drawn, and it's worse since Julia—George and Ellen's daughter—started at university for archaeology.

With Jane. That family's got enough problems of their own—God knows I've spent enough time with—"

Sabine stopped and pursed her lips. Then she began on what I knew was a completely different track than she had been about to go down. "At any rate, George has managed to put all of the blame for his problems with Julia on Jane. God knows what possessed her to do it—Julia, I mean. The rows at home must have been awful."

I worried my bottom lip. "You said it might be that. What else might it be?"

"I think that Morag really feels like the archaeology is just another way of persecuting her people, pagans, Wiccans, what have you. She finds it terribly easy to feel conspired against, if you know what I mean, which isn't made any easier by the fact that she approached the council trying to get the work stopped at one point, to make it a monument to Mother Beatrice's supposed pagan persecution. They want it left alone so they can pick up on the ley lines, or something; it's all very vague. I don't see why the archaeology will bother the ley lines, and frankly, Jane is only going to do everything that Morag could want in terms of bringing Beatrice's history to life, but Morag seems to think that anything not done precisely her way is a slap in her face. Too bad, really, she's not a bad sort. Just a bit . . . out there."

I nodded slowly. "You said Morag'd been bereaved?"

Sabine nodded. "Her parents died several years ago, within a year of each other, both from cancer. Morag'd always been a bit of a hippy, but she really started in on the pagan stuff about that time. I did what I could, of course, her people have been part of the parish for donkey's years—her grandfather or great uncle or something was a deacon, I think, during the war, I think—but it wasn't M's cup of tea. There are far less benign things she could have turned to, and I'm glad her beliefs have helped her, but the way she goes about things now . . . well. I just think she's putting up more walls between her and other people, when that needn't be the case. She was very close to her parents and she felt the loss keenly. Still feels it; I'm not sure she's thought about just how much that grief has done to her."

I digested that. "And the triangles?"

Sabine gave me another one of her irritated looks. "You do know these *are* people we're discussing? I'm really not interested in feeding some prurient instinct of yours to gossip."

And what was that she was telling me before, if not gossip? I worried the inside of my lip. "Why do you assume the worst of me?"

She shrugged, crossed her arms. "I have to look out for people."

I was getting really irritated with the on-again, off-again British personality disconnect, unbelievably frank one moment, unbelievably distant the next. Was it because I was American? Why was she so changeable? I just didn't understand it, I couldn't follow what was going on.

I sighed. "I can tell you this: When I heard that Jane was having some problems at the site and that there was a modern burial involved, I wanted to run and hide." I tried to flatten the curled-up hem of my untucked shirt tail. "There's . . . been too much of that in my life lately. But I couldn't leave her in the lurch, and so I came. And now that she's in trouble, I'm trying to help." And that's all there is to it; you can like it or lump it.

The vicar stubbed out her cigarette with a jab. "Come back another time, when you really want to talk."

This time I didn't bother with diplomacy; my feelings were a little hurt. "What is it you want from me? What is it you want me to talk about?"

"I want to talk with you about why it is you're really interested in all this." There was another abrupt change in Sabine's demeanor, but this was clearly recognizable as a shift of topic. She smoothed her hands down her sweatshirt. "Now, I've got a meeting I must get to. There's been someone sleeping rough in the churchyard, but whoever it is hasn't been around for a while and I'm starting to fear the worst."

I thought of the very recent burial in the abbey graveyard and swallowed. But the buttons were bakelite and struck me as decades old at least—did that preclude a much more recent death? I wasn't at all certain of that.

"I wanted to talk with the local shelters about it—to make sure one of their clients hasn't run off and not brought his meds." A thought struck her. "Although it's possible it's—" Sabine broke off and simply finished, "I'd hate to think someone slipped through our net here."

I realized that there was no way to tell the date of the bones until there was further study, so I didn't bring it up. But I was starting to fear the worst as well.

Sabine led the way back down to the ground floor. "I'm hoping that they've found some place more hospitable, but it seldom ends up that well, unfortunately. Good-bye."

I heard a door behind me and found myself dismissed. Even if I'd had the energy to protest again my reasons for being interested, I wasn't going to have the opportunity.

I walked slowly back to the site along the river—it was strange to see it empty and abandoned. It surprises me to remember, sometimes, just how much fieldwork—and the past, for that matter—is made up of the people I'm working with. I navigated back to Liverpool Road from there. Any hopes I might have had that Jane was already home were dashed as soon as I opened the door and heard Greg's voice call out, "Jane?"

"No, it's me, Emma."

"Oh." The disappointment in his voice was profound, but there was something else that was a little more desperate. "Well, come downstairs and have your tea."

I was starving, a bad complement to the headache that had just returned. I dropped my backpack in the front hall.

"Why don't I take you out for dinner?" I called as I took off my coat, then quickly altered my proposal as I trotted through the hallway and down the stairs. "No, you'll want to wait here if Jane should call or come back. How about if I get some take-out?"

"No need for take-away," Greg said. "I stopped by the chippy on my way from the pub with the crew; it was Gareth's birthday, so there was a couple of rounds of whiskey tonight in honor of it. I brought you back a cod and large chips. How about a drink?"

I emerged from the stairway into the kitchen, after hitting that creaky bottom stair dead on. "Water would be great, thanks. I'm parched; the wind really takes it out of you."

Greg sat at the kitchen table, still dressed in his dirty field clothing. The table was littered with white paper, the sort I usually associate with sub sandwiches, and the messy remains of a fish and chips dinner. A few of the chips had gotten away, and were mashed into greasy smears on the floor under the big country table. Two other white-wrapped packages sat on the table, still neatly taped together, along with a bottle of red wine, about two-thirds empty. But then I noticed that there were also two corks, both of which were freshly damp from the bottle. Apparently there was another recently emptied bottle somewhere nearby.

"No, I mean a proper drink," Greg said. "Wait, I'll get you a glass."

Before I could refuse again, he pushed back his chair and stumbled over to the cabinets, where he rummaged noisily with the ominous clink of glasses. I sat down slowly, not liking any of this. I did a little calculation and the result was disturbing: a couple of whiskeys, followed by more than a bottle and a half wine on his own? I was surprised that Greg could stand and speak.

"Here we are." He returned with a stemmed glass and set it down hard on the table, filling it by tipping the bottle almost completely vertical. The wine glugged out of the bottle and some splashed onto the table. "Plenty of . . . aeration," Greg announced. "Must let a wine breathe. Must give it space to develop, mustn't crowd it. Here, give it a try, it's not a bad little bottle."

He slid the almost full glass across the table to me and it hit an irregularity in the big oak table. The dark red, almost purple, wine sloshed over the edge.

I shook my head tiredly; I really wasn't up to this. "No, thanks. My head is really killing me and I think I'll—"

"Oh, for fuck's sake! Would it kill you to simply drink the bloody wine?"

He slammed the bottle down so hard that I jumped. I looked closely at Greg and wished I hadn't. He looked like a zombie, face slack and movements jerky, and his frizzy hair was weighted down with sweat and dust. He kept blinking his eyes slowly, like he was trying hard not to see something, and while his teeth were clenched hard, his lips couldn't quite stay closed together.

Still watching him, I took a small sip. "It is nice," I agreed carefully, afraid to say more but also wondering whether I should call him on it.

"See? I knew you'd like it. And it didn't hurt a bit, did it? Me being right?" His tone was still scary, belligerent, all the more so because this was nothing of what I'd come to expect from Greg. "I always knew someday I'd be right and it wouldn't hurt a soul."

I paused, then slowly began to open one of the wrapped parcels; it was stone cold from sitting there for so long and the sharp scent of vinegar on the cold grease hit me. "Well, I haven't seen you be wrong about anything yet, Greg. Not since I've been here."

I had been hoping that my deliberate tone would calm him down, but I was unprepared for what happened next. Greg's eyes began to fill, and he slumped forward, all the hostility gone. "Oh, God, Emma, I'm afraid I was wrong about Jane. So wrong. She'll never come back to me now."

I froze; that was a bit extreme. Did he mean never come back from the police station, or never come back to him ever? "What do you mean? Have you heard from her?"

"No, not a word. I called the station after I left the site, and they said she'd left, ages ago. And she hasn't been home, hasn't called, nothing. She just doesn't need me. She's never needed me and now she's decided she's had enough."

"I'm sure that she's just thinking . . . or something," I said, but the truth was, I couldn't imagine what would keep Jane from coming home, after the day I supposed she'd had. "Maybe she just needs some time to get her head together."

"When is her head not together? Have you ever seen any-one who wasn't more on top of things?"

"Not often." Neither of us brought up the fact that Jane felt she could concentrate better away from her home and husband.

Greg wiped his nose with the back of his hand. "We had a dreadful row, the night just before you got here. We were out at dinner, for Jane's birthday, at a marvelous place. But Jane was exhausted, she wasn't enjoying it the way I thought she should. She kept talking about how old she was, how old she felt. God almighty."

He poured another glass for himself and drank deeply. "I mean, the first several times she announces that she'll sleep when she's dead, it's amusing, in a grim way. After a while . . . it starts to sound like a wish. Do you have any idea what it does to a man to hear the woman he loves more than anything, more than reason, talk about how *mortally* tired she is?"

It wasn't meant to be answered. Greg kept right on talk-ing, oblivious to me now. I hadn't got this part of the story from Jane, not like this. Not this kind of raw, unexpected emotion.

Greg picked up one of the corks and set it on one end, then began to turn it over and over, setting on its end each time, concentrating very hard on it. "I finally suggested that she should pull back a little, not spread herself so thin. She's got what she wanted now—and Jane's always known what she's wanted. I knew that from day one. That's why I love her so much. Well, I pointed out to her, Jane, you've got the job, you've got the everything. Time to enjoy yourself, enjoy us, for a change. Why not cut back, take a holiday, a sabbatical, anything. She said she couldn't, not with all the Julias in the world."

I caught my breath; it was such an ugly idea, and Julia at the heart of it. "What did she mean?"

He pushed the cork over and it rolled away from him. "She couldn't stop now, because of all the ambitious young turks right behind her, waiting to steal it all from her. I told her she was silly, she got angry. I got angry. Of course I did."

He drank again and finished his wine. "I want a family more than anything—I grew up with no one but my Gran and Mads—and I know she wants one too. And now she was saying that she didn't feel like she could stop because of the Julias. She left, and I left. It was horrible. But I was absolutely determined to have it out, to sort this all out for once and all."

I had an appalling image of ranks upon ranks of young women marching on Jane. But Greg caught my attention: the more he spoke, the faster he spoke, as if releasing something that had been trapped inside of him. He didn't slur his words much and seldom paused. This had been building awhile, I guessed.

"I had tried, you know, to do without her, to give her all the space she seems to want, but I couldn't do it. I just couldn't stay away from her, no matter how much I tried, how much I tried not to think about her. I don't like to think about how I tried. But I couldn't do it, and I came to the realization that we would have this out or we would be over. But I can't make her see . . ."

"Jane's a bright girl," I said, picking at the chips that were limp on the wrapping paper. "She'll sort something—"

"You know, everyone is always talking about how *brilliant* Jane is, how much *energy* she has," Greg interjected. "I love hearing that, you know. But every once in a while, I get the undertone, sometimes the edge of a conversation, that people don't think I'm up to her level. But would someone that bright be willing to hang around with a complete duffer? I think anyone with a bit of sense would realize that Jane wouldn't pick someone who wasn't on the ball. If she's so bloody marvelous, then there should be something to me, wouldn't it follow? But she is marvelous, I'd do anything for her, I love her, I just want her to come *home*—"

The phone rang, effectively cutting off this unwelcome outpouring. I sagged with relief and embarrassment but noticed that Greg's eyes were red but he didn't shed a tear. Something in him was keeping him from that, even in the state he was presently in. Greg shook his head, trying to clear it, and sprang for the phone.

"Jane, where are—? Oh. Oh yes, of course. I'll put her right on." He held the receiver up. "It's your husband, Brian. Why don't you take it upstairs, in the parlor."

"Are you sure?"

"It will give me a chance to clear up down here."

As I hurried up the stairs, I realized that it was astonishing to me how Greg's personality had done a complete turnabout. It was as if the rest of the evening hadn't happened. Was it just that he needed a bit of catharsis, and now that he'd had it, it switched off what had been driving him before? Or was it something else?

I didn't have time to wonder. I found the phone in the parlor—a cozy, decadent little room decorated in what might be called pre-Raphaelite Turkish—settled down into a deeply cushioned couch, and answered.

"Brian!" I heard the click of the phone downstairs being hung up.

"Hey, babe. How are you?" I could hear the hum of the lab outside his office.

"I'm good, fine."

"Emma, what's wrong?" came the immediate reply, concerned and urgent.

I thought about how I could hear the sounds of clearing up downstairs—had they become a little fainter, a little slower?—and realized I didn't want to tell Brian what was going on and let Greg hear. Was that the squeaky bottom stair outside the kitchen? Was Greg listening to our conversation? Would he? "I can't really say . . ."

"Oh, man. It's the student, isn't it? The missing one?"

"Yes."

"It's bad, right? She's been . . . found?"

"Yes."

"And things are . . . getting worse?" Although there was no need for Brian, he'd lowered his voice too.

"Yes."

"Oh, man, I'm sorry to hear that. Are you going to be okay?"

"Oh, yes, fine. I'm great."

"Hmmm."

"Really."

"Well, be careful, okay? And call me tomorrow when you can talk."

"Okay."

"I mean it." His tone suggested that he knew I'd already started looking into things in that casual way that's gotten me into so much trouble in the past. He didn't tell me not to, I noticed, which wouldn't have worked anyway. "Now. Er. How did you feel about that green pillow on the couch? The one with the tassels?"

Alarm bells went off and I was temporarily distracted. "Oh, no. Don't tell me Quasi—?"

"It looks like he took a sudden aversion to it. Dragged it out to the garden and savaged it. I've been picking stuffing off the baby tomato plants since yesterday night."

"I loved that pillow!" I said. "It was going to be perfect, when we got the living room done and a new couch and curtains and—"

"Well, we can get a new one, right?"

I stared at the bookcases opposite me and swore under my breath. "That pillow weighed almost three pounds! How the hell did he do it? And what is it about that cat? I wasn't even there, I couldn't have aroused his wrath long-distance, could I?"

"Maybe he misses you."

"Ha!" Quasimodo was a belligerent stray that Brian had taken in, named for his unappetizing appearance and his anti-social behavior. He was devoted to Brian, who'd never had a cat, and a terror to everyone else. He tolerated me when Brian was there or when I had a food bowl in my hands, but other than those two cases, it was gloves off, claws-unsheathed loathing between us. And I like cats.

Brian continued. "The bell seems to be working, though—"

Ah, that was it: revenge for the bell. Quasi was a formidable hunter and the bird song outside my window had diminished considerably since Brian had rescued him and brought him home from work. The cat only seemed to get the interesting ones, never grackles or sparrows, though he did bring home an inordinate number of seagulls. So shortly before I'd left, I had proposed the bell and, presumably, signed the death warrant of the pillow.

"—He's only gotten two since you've been gone."

"That's better, but someday he'll bring home a wild turkey, and then I'm moving out."

"I checked that your office was still locked up tight, just in case, anyway. I don't want any more 'accidents.' How's work going?"

Back to the world I'd so happily escaped for a few moments. "Um, apart from the obvious, my work is going along pretty well, I guess. Not a great day today, though. I couldn't seem to find my groove."

"You'll get it back tomorrow." Brian seemed to sense that I needed to change the topic. "I'm doing real good, though. My new vacuum flasks came in—"

"Are they beautiful?"

"Gorgeous. And work is going really well. I did a Stille coupling *and* I dodged a meeting this morning."

I fiddled with the phone cord. "Well, I'm glad to hear someone's doing okay. You are pining for me, though, aren't you? New flasks and Stille couplings aside, you're absolutely miserable, right? Can't wait for me to come home?"

"Of course," Brian said cheerfully. "I can't believe it's only been three days."

"Me either." I heard the door slam and watched as Jane blurred past the parlor doorway, rushing down the stairs to the kitchen. "Brian, Jane's home. I've got to see how she is."

"Okay, but call me later tomorrow, okay? I'm worried about you."

"I'm fine. It's nothing to do with me." But Jane was being questioned and Greg was revealing unsuspected depths of unhappy emotion; how could it not affect me?

"And yet it always seems to become something to do with you."

"Brian, I'll be careful. I love you."

"I love you too. And so does Quasi, in his own way."

"Please. Bye, hon."

"Bye."

The voices had already become raised by the time I hung up. I couldn't hear everything that was being said, but enough to know that my presence would be unwelcome and superfluous. Jane was pleading, Greg was furious, and I was wondering why I'd come here in the first place.

"—Don't know. Walking, thinking. Please, Greg, I'm—"

"Jane, don't you dare shut me out again! You need me now, especially now! After all we've been through, after all I've done for you—"

"Will you keep your voice down! You've no business—"

It was at that point that I decided that I had to go up to my room. I picked up my backpack out of the front hall and climbed the stairs as quietly as I could. I admit that I thought about listening to my friends—I was desperate to know what was going on. But somehow, this seemed wrong, like taking advantage of the situation. I locked my door and thought about what Sabine had said in the bell tower, about prurience and my habit of getting into the middle of matters. I was saturated by the emotion around me, expressed and unexpressed.

My stomach was now growling—I'd had nothing to eat but a few cold, soggy chips and a mouthful of wine. I wasn't about to go downstairs again, though, not for something as unnecessary as food. Then I remembered the candy bar I'd bought at the cafe that first day and thanking my provident stars, tore the purple and orange wrapper off it. It was melted and very sweet, but I wolfed it down and then washed up and got into bed, trying desperately to get to sleep before my belly realized it was getting nothing else tonight and my brain started to consider all it had been force-fed.

Chapter 9

I WAS RELIEVED TO WAKE UP THE NEXT MORNING, ONCE I realized that I was no longer asleep and had been dreaming. My dreams were disturbing, unfocused save for the omnipresent thought that no matter where I turned, I was unwanted. Then a long line of gray, twisted people, straight out of a Hieronymous Bosch painting, followed me, claiming me for one of their own. The emotional content was high, and I was left uneasy and sweating when I awoke.

Even the relief at being awake didn't last for long. The memory of the previous night's scene with Greg and the row that followed Jane's arrival home soured my still clamoring stomach. I'd have to go downstairs and find out what had developed, if I wanted to get any coffee or food, the only things that were going to take the ugly edge off my mood.

I washed up and on my way out of the bathroom, noticed that the door to Andrew's room was closed tight; there was still no sign that he'd been home since Tuesday or worked any further on the report on the modern skeleton for all I knew. I dressed, sighed, gathered together my courage, which was more than bolstered by curiosity about where

Jane had been after she'd left the police, and went downstairs.

Greg was nowhere to be seen and Jane . . . well, Jane looked as though she hadn't slept a wink all night. She probably hadn't. Her face was drawn, her eyes were swollen and red, and I'd have bet my hope of coffee that she'd just finished crying. Her hair was still damp, her clothing wrinkled and untucked, and it suddenly struck me that Jane usually ironed her work clothes. I never ironed anything at all, if I could help it, much less clothes for fieldwork. She sat at the table, now cleared of the disastrous fish and chips feast, twisting the plain gold wedding band on her left hand. It made me nervous just to see her; strange how uneasy you feel when someone you think of as invulnerable suddenly isn't.

"I was just waiting for you," she said, but the false brightness in her voice didn't even convince her. She wrung her hands plaintively. "Oh, God, Emma. I'm in shambles. I don't know what to do. I can't even think properly. It was all I could do to get dressed."

"Yesterday must have been horrible for you," I said.

She shrugged listlessly. "I had a case of nerves while I was waiting to be interviewed by the police, but after that, it was just boring, for the most part, sitting in that horrid, institutional little room. It was only at the end, when they started asking about who knows whom on the site, how everyone interacts, that I felt really upset. I realized . . . too many things. The worst of which is that the police actually think that someone Julia knew did this to her."

She fell silent, resisting that idea. "I can't even imagine this. I don't know the crew well—as long as they do their work, I don't have much to do with them, outside of class, I mean—but to think that someone I know might be a killer. It's just too much. No sooner had they started in with all these questions, than they stopped . . . made me a cup of tea, sent me on my way. I was so . . . so thrown by it all, that I just left, just started walking. It was hours later that I finally snapped out of it."

I nodded, but still wasn't convinced; her story didn't really strike all the right chords with me, and Jane herself seemed to be reciting rather than telling her story. "You just walked around? Didn't talk to anyone, didn't stop for a bite to eat?"

Jane had paused long enough before answering me to make me wonder whether she wasn't lying to me, covering something up. "No, not at all. I found myself almost at the far edge of town by the time I woke up."

Could it be true? Why she hadn't come home, or at least found Greg at the site, if she was so overwrought?

She must have read my mind, or maybe some facial clue gave me away, because she looked at me sharply. "I have a tendency to hide myself away to lick my wounds. I'm afraid it's not sitting very well with Greg at the moment." She dug a handkerchief from her pocket and sighed. "He's been acting so strangely lately. We've been fighting so much . . ."

I almost thought she'd finished when she added, "We've been fighting so much that I wonder if we're not coming to the end of things."

I let out a breath. "If you think so, you'd better start talking to him about it. That's the only way to fix it or find out."

She shook her head with a quick, jerky movement, overwhelmed. "I just don't know how. I just need to get through today. I'm sure you must have heard us last night, I do apologize."

I waved it away. "Things have been very hard lately. Don't worry about it."

"But it's so much worse than I thought—" she blurted out. And then started crying.

I looked around desperately. I got up and brought over a box of tissues, even though Jane had her own already. Jane was not the sort to be hugged and comforted, but I couldn't sit and do nothing. "Look," I said, "I'll help you get through today. Then you'll feel a little more like handling everything else, okay?"

She sniffed. "Thank you, Emma. You can't know how that helps."

I smiled ruefully. "Well, just don't resent me for it too much, later."

That took Jane aback, and she had a look of comic confusion and horror on her face at my bald statement. Then she laughed, and blew her nose.

"Come on. I'll buy you one of those really disgusting breakfasts down at the cafe," I offered. "Nothing left unfried: eggs, beans, tomatoes, mushrooms, sausage. Fried bread, yum. There won't be a piece of fruit, a flake of oatmeal in sight."

"You just want the excuse for one yourself," Jane answered back. She looked better now, a little relieved, and she sounded better too.

"Yep, that's my plan."

She got up, then paused. "Just a minute, Emma." She went to the fridge and got out some carrot peelings and dandelion greens and put them in the tortoise's tank and changed the water in the shallow little dish. "I think Greg forgot to feed Hildegard this morning."

After the promised fry-up breakfast, served by a waitress I'd never seen before and washed down with enough coffee to fuel a fighter jet, we got to the site. Greg was already there, and barely greeted Jane; every comment addressed to her was carefully neutral and directly related to the running of the project. There still was no sign of Andrew—he hadn't been at work since Tuesday. Needless to say, nothing was being done about the area from where the modern skeleton had been removed, though Jane badly wanted to have a chance to study the stratigraphy—the changes in soil levels—particularly as it cut through the two earlier burials that were definitely medieval. It was some indication of just how depressed she was that she hardly spared a curse for the absent Andrew, and when I asked about the police report on the modern skeleton with the iron in its sternum, she only shrugged.

"I probably won't ever see that; he'll write something up for me. That's all I'm really concerned about. As long as the police are off my back for that, I don't care what he does."

I found that hard to believe. "Is he always this unreliable?" I said. Or is he dragging his feet for some reason? I wondered.

"His work is first rate and he meets his deadlines," Jane said. "That's all I care about."

"Yeah, but Jane," I said, "aren't you the least little bit curious about the skeleton?"

"Of course I am, it is an odd situation, but I can hardly do anything about it until Andrew formulates his opinion, can I, Emma?" she replied reasonably. "It has no direct bearing on my work and I am in no position to push forward with the report: that is Andrew's job. It's entirely under control, trust me."

This sorry state of affairs continued through all of Thursday and into Friday morning. The tension at the house was almost unbearable, and worse since it was so obvious that Jane and Greg were struggling to act normally in front of me. At least at the site, I was able to bury my own unease as I worked, but the crew was unusually quiet, as if they sensed the friction between their directors. We were all relieved when a local school group stopped by for a tour of the site Friday morning. A horde of ten-year-olds in dark blue pullovers and gray trousers and skirts were barely kept in check by the half dozen or so teachers who tried, with limited success, to keep everyone's attention on the talk Jane was giving. Head down over my work, I smiled to myself as I heard the kids' comments: "Sir, are they going to dig up an ancient toilet?" "Sir, Stuart said he's going to steal one of the skellies!" "Sir, will this be on the exams?"

But Jane soon got their attention by telling them what

could be learned from studying whole groups of burials—about age indicators and the sexual differences that can be seen in the skeletons, as well as information about diet and disease, which fascinated them—and asking them what future archaeologists might say about their skeletons. The hands shot up and a chorus of "ooh, miss, please!" followed as each student tried to get Jane to pick her. The teachers settled back in a clump to smoke long-awaited cigarettes, a fog of smoke around them. After about an hour, Jane finished and the group left, caroling good-byes and thanks, and a sort of tranquility reigned again.

Jane, faintly flushed, and pleased with her success, came over to see how my work was progressing on burial nineteen.

"Got a few converts there," I said.

"Could be," she said. "I'm past due for looking in on my students, though, and—oh, blast!" She looked around her, searching for someone. Her shoulders slumped again when she had no luck. "I suppose Avery's already gone on his supply run? I'm assuming that he's finished developing the pics he took of the ringer skellie already. They're probably in the darkroom—"

Just then, Bonnie, the singularly untalented student, approached. "Pardon me, Dr. Compton? You told me to come get you when I thought I was getting near the surface of the burial, and I think I've got there."

Jane raised an eyebrow skeptically. "You've got a soil change?"

The student nodded. "Yes, though that was a bit ago. And this is a bone, right?"

Bonnie held up what was—or, at least, should have been—to all eyes, a very nicely preserved human metatarsal or foot bone, ripped untimely from its place in situ. My grandfather Oscar used to call such a find, taken out of the ground before it could be properly measured or photographed and waved around for all to see, "aerial archaeology." It was a very bad thing. I was just glad that she hadn't done this in front of the school group and that Andrew wasn't also there to see this. Seeing how Bonnie was mishandling the skeletal remains, he might have gone in for a spot of GBH.

I looked anxiously at Jane, who had closed her eyes, apparently in silent prayer for strength. She opened her eyes but nothing came when she tried to speak. Before words she might later regret did come out of her mouth, I spoke up quickly.

"Why don't you go over and help Bonnie and I'll run to the darkroom and get the photos you need? Just tell me what and where."

When Jane could bring herself to speak, her words were careful and measured. "Thank you, Emma. The darkroom is back at the house, a little addition right off the kitchen's garden door. Here's the key to it. If you would bring back anything that has been dried and pertaining to the modern burial you worked on the first day, I would be eternally grateful. It should be on the right hand side. I hope Avery hasn't moved things around too much; I haven't been in the darkroom since we hired him." She pulled out a key chain and unhooked one and gave it to me. Then Jane turned back to Bonnie and crooked a finger, her face grim.

"Come, miss. Let us have a look at this 'possible grave' you've uncovered."

I scurried off, lest I be caught as collateral damage when Jane saw just what kind of havoc Bonnie had wrought. The sky was clouding over and the threat of rain also hurried me along the streets back to the house.

It was odd to be in the house by myself. The quiet seemed to warn me against making too much noise, and I found myself treading as silently as I could, avoiding the last squeaky step. The kitchen was as clean as it had been earlier, but the room seemed almost to hum with the high emotions that had been generated here last night, barely contained by the mere material things. I passed through to the back of the room quickly. Just as Jane had said, ahead of me there was a door; this led to a small mudroom with two doors. One led out to the *garden,* Greg would have called it—a *yard,* he had explained patiently to me, was a nasty place where garbage was kept and animals stalled—and another, newer one that led into a small shed addition on the left. I knocked, then, feeling silly, noticed the brand-new padlock on the door. There would be no one working in there with that on. I used the key and let myself in.

I couldn't see a thing and paused: a heavy curtain brushed my outstretched hand and barred my way. Reasoning that I wouldn't be able to find anything without turning a light on, and that nothing should have been left unfinished in the developing baths, I reached out my left hand, located the edge of the curtain, and instinctively felt for a switch. The cool dryness of the wall reassured me—I had automatically suspected cobwebs, but there were none—and hit the switch. Around the curtain I could see a dim light flicker on; and I pushed the curtain aside and stepped into the room.

The room was small and very tidy—on the counter surfaces. The floor, however, was littered with all sorts of odds and ends: bits of paper, clips, empty coffee cups, and empty chemical bottles. A small sink was on the wall shared with the kitchen—the easier for plumbing, I assumed—and an enlarger on a table on the wall off that one. A large metal table was in the center of the room, and a string for drying prints ran over that. On the last wall was a tall cabinet for drying negatives of 35mm film, which were hanging like wilted party streamers, a rack of chemicals, and a lightbox. The room smelled like ashtray and astringent chemicals. I found a tray marked "finished prints" and recognized the number of the burial I'd been working on with Andrew. I didn't dare rely on looks alone: one set of bones could easily look like another. I scooped out the photos and put them into an envelope after scrutinizing them: I still couldn't identify what was bothering me about the stratigraphy. I turned to leave and slipped on a candy wrapper.

If I hadn't slipped, I would never have seen the photos tacked to the far side of the cabinet. Pictures of women. Not just the usual Dean Avery–the-site-pervert bum pictures, but quite beautiful shots, taken candidly on the site. Then I realized that the photos were of just one woman. There were nearly two dozen of them.

And they were all of Jane.

I was so shocked by this realization that it took me a minute to realize that they weren't of Jane at all. Picking a close-up shot, I pulled it and the adhesive gum that held it to the cabinet away to stare at it under the center light. This was a much younger woman, but the superficial resemblance was quite striking in the dim light of the shadowed side of the cabinet. She was dark haired, with a pointed nose and unsmiling demeanor that defied you to call her pretty. I had never seen this young woman before. It was her intensity, the set of her face, that reminded me of my friend.

I hurriedly replaced it and was glad I did; I could hear steps outside the darkroom, followed by a pause and then a brief curse. I came around from the cabinet to the out-box just as Dean Avery pushed past the curtain, carrying a box full of papers and chemicals. For a fat man, he moved very smoothly indeed.

"Are you looking for me?" he said suggestively. His voice was higher pitched than I expected, and the squeaky cartoon animal sound made his attitude all the more loathsome. Avery put the box down on the table and stepped toward me. His unwashed hair reflected the low light readily.

"No, Jane couldn't find you. She needed some photos," I said.

"Look at us here, all on our lonesome. We could get acquainted, you and me. I don't like people messing about in here, this is my place. But so long as you're here . . ." He took another step forward.

I backed up again, swearing to myself. This was exactly what this jerk wanted. "Maybe another time. I've got to get back."

"What's your hurry?"

"Jane wanted these right away and you weren't there, and she's got a lot on her plate—"

By now I'd backed up all the way around the table until I felt the coarse fabric of the curtain over the door. Avery had followed, slowly, inevitably.

"Jane doesn't get away with bossing everyone around, you know," he said.

I stopped abruptly, which disconcerted the photographer. "She's not bossing me, and no one else is, either. I do exactly what I like, so maybe we can chat later, okay? I'm going to get back now."

"Whatever you like."

I turned, swept my way past the curtain, hoping that my heart couldn't be heard to beat as loudly as I thought it did. The air in the hallway outside the darkroom was wonderfully cool, and I sucked in a lungful gratefully. I kept moving through to the kitchen and out the door. Half my instinct told me to make sure that the creep didn't loiter around Jane and Greg's house—my house, too, for the time being—the other half didn't want me to wait around for him to finish. A walk back to the site with him? No, thank you.

As I walked slowly back to the site, I pondered the pictures I'd seen. Even in the dim light they'd made an impression, and I didn't believe that was entirely due to Avery's acknowledged talents as a photographer. The young woman in the shots was striking, and obviously she had captured his attention as well. I would have to scrutinize the dozen or so students once I returned to the dig; I have to admit, I had rather relegated them to the background, so preoccupied had I been with the senior staff.

But as it happened, her identity was discovered long before my walk was over. I looked up from my reflections to see the same young woman from the photographs staring down at me—from another photograph. I was in front of the newstand down the street from Jane and Greg's, and the morning edition of the paper was out. The headline read: "POLICE CONTINUE SEARCH FOR STUDENT'S KILLER." Just beneath it was a picture of the young woman, who was, according to the caption, Julia Whiting.

Holy crow.

I pulled some change from my pocket, carefully sorted out the unfamiliar coins, and handed the news dealer the proper amount. He said something in an accent so quick and blurred that I couldn't catch a word of it.

"I beg your pardon?"

"Oh, you're American. Thought you might be, but your clothes . . ."

He shrugged as if to say, "What can one say about them?" At home, whenever I ventured off the site on an errand, it always took me a moment to remember that I wasn't dressed like other women. The boots and work pants would have been enough, but the dirt and clank of small tools stuffed into my pockets was quite another thing.

"I said," he continued, enunciating carefully and loudly so I would understand, "shame about that poor girl, isn't it? Ending up in a . . . like that? Terrible thing."

"Yes, it is. I'm working on the site where she had been working."

He clucked. "Now, I say that's too bad for her family as well. Local people, been here for years."

I remembered my conversation with Palmer during the drive into town, about how Julia's parents hadn't raised the alarm when she'd first gone missing, and mentioned it to the news dealer.

"Oh, yes, Mr. Whiting took out an ad, as I recall. Must have cost him a penny or two."

That didn't seem like enough to me. "But her mother—Ellen, is it? Nothing from her?"

The news dealer seemed to consider. "Not that I recall, but I'm sure the poor lady was distraught, wasn't she? Terrible thing, when a young person goes and gets killed like that, with no reason."

"I suppose." Her daughter was only missing at that point, I thought, the wife of a man prominent in town, you'd think she'd be using all her resources, all her connections, to find Julia.

"—No reason at all for it, know what I mean?"

The news dealer was unaware that I'd been focusing on my own thoughts for a moment. "Oh?"

"Well, she was a bit of a swot, wasn't she? Head down in the books, she was at school with my girl. So it wasn't the drugs, was it? Smart as a whip, Julia was—and her brother too, gone off to university last year. Awful, a nice, quiet girl like that." He reached up and scratched under his cap.

"I hope they catch whoever it was soon," I said.

"Amen to that."

"You take care now," I said.

"Righto."

I walked around the corner, but stopped a bit shy of crossing the street. If the woman in the pictures was indeed Julia Whiting, then what did that say about Avery? What was the relationship there? There had to be some way of finding out, besides simply asking outright.

I sat down on a bench and read the article, which was a continuation of the one that had been out yesterday that we'd missed. None of the furor had diminished, however, and it must have been doubly exciting for a town as small as Marchester, never mind that she was local and the daughter of a prominent citizen.

Police are still investigating the disappearance and murder of a Marchester woman. Miss Julia Whiting, 22, a postgraduate student at Marchester University, was last seen on June ____. Her body was recovered two days ago, from a skip on the Leather Street construction site. The site is the location of a new block of luxury flats being built by G. Whiting Contractors. George Whiting, the firm's founder and owner, is the victim's father. He and his wife, Ellen Whiting, who reside at 375 Green Cross Road, were unavailable for comment.

Police sources, in the early stages of the investigation, state that they have not ruled out the possibility of a connection to Mr. Whiting's business—

Whoa! I thought. It was her *father's* Dumpster? My skin crawled and I looked around me apprehensively. At just that moment, Dean Avery came around the corner, heading back to the site. I froze, hoping that the breeze wouldn't rattle the newspaper, even though I wasn't entirely certain why I didn't want him to see me. He didn't look down the street to where my bench was, and I watched him walk directly to the site.

I turned back to the article, but things were still very sketchy. No details were being released from the autopsy pending conclusive results, etc., but the cause of Julia's death had been suffocation. The only thing that had been positively ruled out was suicide; her wallet was missing, suggesting the possibility of a mugging.

The lack of details was infuriating. Ordinarily, I wouldn't have paid so much attention to the death of a stranger, but I wanted to help Jane. It was only the last paragraph, a plea for information on behalf of the police, that gave me anything substantial to think about:

Miss Whiting was believed to have left her work on the Church Street archaeological site at five o'clock the evening before her death: she did not return to it. Saturday, she is reported to have visited her parents at Green Cross Road and told them that she intended to visit the Grub and Cabbage Pub. She was seen leaving the public house, but her whereabouts from then until the time of her death are unknown. She was last seen wearing black jeans and a red jumper. Anyone with information should contact Detective Chief Inspector Rhodes at Hewett Street—

I folded up the newspaper quickly and stuffed it into my back pocket. I'd been away from the site too long already, but I dawdled heading back. It seemed impossible that this was just an accident, a chance mugging; there were just too many connections close to home. And suffocation? That was by no means an impersonal mugger. Julia had died, practically on her own doorstep, metaphysically speaking, and that must be where the police were going to focus their efforts. I thought briefly about contacting Dave Stannard, but dismissed that idea quickly: he hated when I got involved in these sorts of investigations. Besides, the sheriff of a small Maine county would have no influence with the police here.

The other thing that kept me from walking quickly back to the site was the thought of all the sudden connections there to Julia. But wait—what if the intended victim had been Jane, and not Julia? Given their similarities of appearance and manner, mightn't it be possible that the murderer had mistaken student for professor?

I shivered, slowed even more, then finally stopped. Given the disappearance of Trevor and the photographs of Julia in the darkroom—and, I had to admit, the impenetrable wall between Greg and Jane—it was just possible that there were some undercurrents that wouldn't bear too much scrutiny. But that was exactly what I had to do: explore those possibilities. And the best way to do that, I decided, was to start with the crew. At the pub. That evening.

I glanced at my watch: I had been gone for almost an hour. Jane would be in a state, I decided; she wasn't looking very well when I left. I had at first thought I would sidle over to my work area and stash the newspaper in my backpack. No sense dragging unpleasant reminders into the maelstrom of the working day, I reasoned.

But then I saw something peculiar happen. A Jaguar roared past the site, then suddenly stopped and reversed, back up the street to the site, almost as quickly as it had passed. A short, slight man got out and homed in on Jane like a heat-seeking missile. He began shouting almost as soon as he reached the gate, and soon she was shouting too.

I didn't recognize him, and since the rest of the crew was sitting aside having their morning tea-break, they were not aware of what was going on. Greg was working on his notes by the wall. Jane looked uncharacteristically scared. I pulled my coat over the top of the newspaper to conceal it, and hurried over.

The man was short, compact, and trembling with energy, every angry bit of which was directed at Jane. His gray hair was in a crew cut and had a bristly look that suggested a cock's comb. His voice was harsh, his accent unschooled, and I caught only the end of the sentence:

"—All your fault, and I hold you personally responsible for what's happened!"

"As if anything I said or did would ever make that kind of impression on her!" Jane was nearly pleading. "She had a mind of her own!" She seemed to be trying to convince herself as well.

"Don't underestimate yourself, you bloody woman!" He mimicked a girl's voice cruelly. "Jane said *this,* Jane said *that!* That's all we ever heard, when she bothered to come home. If she bothered to come home. No, no, Dr. Compton, taking out your hostility against me on her, that's despicable! Why couldn't you have left her alone, you bloody . . . *murderer!*"

The stranger—who I now suspected was Julia's father, George Whiting—was in a state of angry shock. Grief had left his face a blank canvas for the rage that was there now, but apparently he wasn't the sort to keep his thoughts to himself, and he wasn't the sort to grieve quietly. His short, jerky movements suggested physical power that was barely—and perhaps unwillingly—restrained: he looked as though he had started at the bottom of his trade and pushed himself through to the top, purely through iron will and wiry muscle.

Jane too was pale as chalk, and remembering what she'd

said about Julia in the gym, and worse, what Greg had said about her relationship with "the Julias in the world," it was no wonder she was shaken by what Mr. Whiting had just told her. I'd only heard the end of the conversation and wondered what might have prefaced that.

Stammering and trembling violently, Jane seemed unable to master herself and that's when I decided she needed some help. I decided to make being an American work for me for a change. I barged right in.

"Hi, uh, Jane? I got those pictures you wanted? Oh, I'm sorry, I didn't mean to interrupt, or anything, but I figured you'd want them right away."

I don't think either of them heard me approach and I startled both of them past recognizing any of the inane words I said. They both stared at me uncomprehendingly. Suddenly aware that they were not alone, that the shell that their emotion had created around them had shattered and the rest of the world was seeping back into that space, each reacted differently.

George Whiting seemed to shut down, get smaller, recede into his own body. The emotion that had made him seem larger than he was interrupted. The emotion I saw in his eyes was gone, or at least shuttered up, no longer visible to the outside observer; all that was left now was the anger of feeling one has been made foolish, having deep emotions suddenly exposed. This wasn't much more attractive than what I'd seen before, but at least it was aimed at me and not Jane. Part of me felt guilty about intruding like this—the man must be in unspeakable pain at the sudden loss of his daughter—but Jane looked as though she was ready to collapse, and she was my main concern.

"Do you mind?" He turned on me and I almost stepped backward, the force of his personality and words was so strong. I decided immediately that I didn't ever want to cross this man. "This is a private conversation."

Shouting on the open street in the middle of town on a

crowded work site doesn't fit my definition of "private," I thought. George Whiting must have had the same thought, for instantly he flushed to the color of a fire engine, an alarming display of passion, and turned to Jane once again.

"Don't you ever imagine this is over," he said in a low voice that hummed with power, his pointing finger within an inch of Jane's nose. "Don't you even *dream* it."

He waited a beat for the message to sink in, and then turned and marched off toward his car with a stiff-necked, stiff-legged gait that might have been comical had anyone else tried to imitate it, but as executed by George Whiting, it spelled out a danger signal as clear as any display of fangs or claws in the animal kingdom. He got into the brand-new bottle-green Jaguar and roared off.

I thought about how rough the construction trade could be, how some of my friends had been asked by the contractors who hired them—out of federal or state regulation, usually—to ignore certain objects discovered when a site was tested prior to building. Had been asked to deemphasize things that would have held up work. It left a bad taste in my mouth, and that was just on my insulated side of things—everyone was always telling stories about the mob, or even just shady practices, trimming the quality of materiel, etc., never mind pulling strings in local government. So there was a lot to look into, perhaps, when it came to George Whiting. And my friend Kam, Brian's boss and one-time roommate, was always pointing out to me that "only criminals and politicians drive Jags." When I asked him about his own XJR—surely he was not a criminal, just a chemist?—he corrected me gently. "I would never dream of driving one in London. I'd as soon wear a pair of green wellies in town. But in America, well, everyone wants to be an outlaw, don't they? That's different."

Obviously, Mr. Whiting didn't share Kam's advanced theories of aesthetics.

I turned back to Jane, who was not watching George

Whiting's departure, as I had been, but was staring at me, white-faced and trembling.

"What have I done? Oh, God, Emma—" And with that, for the second time that day, she burst into tears.

Oh no.

Not at all knowing what the proper British etiquette might be in such a situation, I decided to fall back on what I knew would be appropriate at home. I hugged Jane despite the fact that I'm not a huggy person; I rather suspected that if I'd been through the day Jane had been having, I'd probably not mind someone at least trying to comfort me. And as we stood there for what seemed like a long time, Jane's sobs grew steadily more harsh, not lessening, as they might have. I wondered how long it had been since she'd let herself have a good long cry. I also began to wonder about Whiting's accusations and Jane's reactions to them: What would have happened if I hadn't shown up? It was particularly worrying in the light of Greg's description of Jane feeling hunted, pursued by turks younger than herself. Jane had once upon a time, three days ago, mentioned to Andrew how much she would do to protect her position and reputation. And now, as much as I didn't like to think about it while my friend was wracked with sobs, I had to consider, seriously, the question of just how far Jane might have gone to do just that.

Chapter 10

BY LUNCHTIME, HOWEVER, IT WAS AS IF NOTHING AT all had happened during the tea break. After two minutes of crying, Jane had abruptly pulled away from me, and in a strangled, annoyed voice, explained that she needed to use the loo. I stood there stupidly for about ten minutes, fully expecting she'd come back and explain what had happened with George Whiting, and only then realized that wasn't going to happen when I saw her across the site, quite composed, helping Bonnie with her notes. Then I felt angry, waiting for her like an idiot. I ate the sandwich I'd bought in the cafe that morning, sourly watching Jane eat the one I'd bought for her, since she'd been too distraught to think about preparation earlier.

And when I went over to Jane, determined to ask her if I might have a quiet word with her, she looked at me straight in the eye and said that yes, she'd be delighted, only she was quite busy at the moment, could I possibly—

I said, "Yes, of course," more abruptly than I meant, but far more politely than I wanted, turned on my heel, and didn't quite stomp over to where my work was waiting for me, much neglected that morning and now a perfect diversion for me. I was just trying to sort out how I could possibly be sympathetic to Jane *and* still want to shake her—and in what proportions—when thankfully, the dirt began to speak to me.

It is precisely that kind of quiet moment, when things outside you recede and things in the ground start to make a little more sense than they had just bare minutes before, that is the very reason you put up with the all the dirt and trouble of doing the work. I fell into that easy rhythm of scraping at the soil—it all seemed to come out perfectly level now, I would have bet there was no more than a centimeter's variation across the entire unit—and observing what I had exposed; writing my notes was painlessly simple, the words came readily and precisely. I also knew that I would remember the moment perfectly, years from now. It was the sort of thing I'd come to England for, since directing my own projects, although having a different sort of thrill, didn't often allow me to do my own digging. These moments were precious.

There were very few stones now, so it was the change in the sound of the trowel on the ground that alerted me that something was happening. The soil had become darker and more humic, looser and softer, so I wondered if I hadn't encountered the disintegrated shroud or the rotting wood of a coffin. I would have to watch for coffin hardware and the remains of wood; if Beatrice had been buried in a shroud, I might find straight pins as well. I took a few preliminary photographs, even though there was really nothing to see yet: it was still only evident through touch and sound.

When I looked up again, I glanced at my watch and was faintly surprised to see that it was most of the way through the after-lunch break. Although it wasn't unusual for me to get so wrapped up in my work, most of the crew was already gone, and I noticed that Jane had not bothered to remind me to stop; she was positioned as far from me as she could be without actually leaving the site. Well, good, I thought, slamming my pencil down, I didn't want to eat lunch with her anyway. But then I noticed that she and Greg seemed to be more comfortable with each other again; something had been repaired since that morning while I was otherwise occupied, perhaps only minutes before, because I saw Greg reach over and squeeze Jane's hand briefly from his seat on the ground, as good as a declaration to anyone.

And then, typically, Trevor chose that particular moment to reappear. After an absence from his work of nearly three days, the chunky pain in the backside walked with uncharacteristic haste to his work area and settled in without a word. I wasn't terribly close by—he had been positioned in an area to minimize damage through neglect or incompetence, after all, and I was right at the heart of things. But even from where I was, I could see the other significant, noticeable difference in Trevor that perhaps had been the real reason he'd waited until most of the crew had cleared out during a break. Even from my distance, I could see a very clean, very new, very white bandage across his nose. Where had he been to get that? And what else had happened in the meantime?

Not even bothering to be discreet, I watched the little drama between him and Greg unfold. At first, Jane caught at Greg's hand, not wanting him to speak to Trevor, but he gently disengaged himself and went over to the student. Although I couldn't hear what they were saying, I could imagine very plainly what was going on between them. Their actions were very clear, and I filled in the dialogue for myself.

Greg gestured. *Where the hell have you been?*

Trevor kept his head down to his work and didn't meet Greg's eyes. *Nowhere.*

And what the hell have you been up to? Greg gestured at Trevor's face. *What happened here?*

Trevor shrugged. *Fell down the stairs. Tripped over the cat.*

After only a moment or two of this fruitless interview, Greg's shoulders heaved in a great sigh. Trevor kept his head down, focusing on his notes in an uncharacteristically studious fashion. Finally, Greg gave up and walked away.

The other students returned from the pub, filing back in small groups, and it was Trevor's failure to rise to their collective bait that decided me that something besides the broken nose had profoundly changed the heretofore loudmouthed student—possibly something to do with Julia. I decided that I might try finding out a little more about what had happened to Trevor later on this evening.

Once the other members of the crew were back to work, always a little bit less energetically than at the beginning of the day, somewhat slowed by beer and the idea that there was only the merest splinter of the day left to work, Jane came over to my area. I now saw definite traces of something showing up in the grave shaft and was optimistic that it was an undisturbed burial. I gave her a perfunctory report and we discussed my progress in a businesslike fashion: two professionals who might only just have met, considering the changing soil, the possibility of hardware. Then Jane colored briefly, looked away, and said hurriedly:

"About this morning. Sorry you got drawn into that. Bit of a nuisance, really—"

Bit of a nuisance? "Jane, that was *George Whiting,* wasn't it? He was talking about his daughter Julia, right? What did he say to you before I got there? He was purple!"

I thought she wasn't going to answer for a moment; she was watching as tools were collected for the night. Her face was a study in noncommunication. "It's still a bit too fresh to me. But you're a good friend, Emma. You've been really splendid through all this. I just need some time to sort this all out. A little time, is all. Let me buy you a drink tonight, and then we can talk more—all right?"

I didn't think that the pub was the best place for a private discussion, but I was going to hold Jane to her promise. With relief, I said, "Sure. That'd be fine."

But as work finished, it became immediately clear that Trevor, still quite unlike himself, wasn't going to be a part of

the evening pub session. "Where you going, then?" asked
Bonnie, who was one of the few people still willing to speak
to him on a social basis. The others, emboldened by his
downcast manner and bandage, had done nothing more than
direct a few caustic cracks in his direction.

"Nowhere," he said. "Piss off."

"You needn't get your nose out of joint," she said huffily,
then laughed at her own unintentional joke.

Trevor didn't even spare a scowl for her but set off in the
opposite direction from the Prince of Wales. This was new, I
thought. Then it occurred to me that I was seeing a lot of de-
viations from the norm today: Trevor's rejection of the usual
pub, Jane's cracking and her later cussedness toward me, the
friction between her and Greg, and the presence of the very
angry George Whiting on the site, confronting a woman
whom, by all rights, he should have been very happy to
avoid. I had already tried to ask Jane what was happening to
no avail and Whiting wouldn't be likely to answer my questions, so I decided that it was time to see if I could find out
from Trevor what had had such a profound effect on him.

I realized that I had taken it upon myself to look into
things, ask questions of people who didn't want to answer. It
occurred to me that Sabine had noticed what I hadn't—that
after Jane's interview with the police, I'd easily, uncon-
sciously, slipped again into the role of being the one to sort
things out. Greg's behavior was another spur, as were Andrew's absences and then Trevor's. On top of those pictures
of Julia and the modern skeleton with the tip of a knife
lodged in it—the list was getting very long. I needed to find
out what was going on, and if no one would tell me, then I
would find other avenues to explore. Jane just didn't understand: I could help her with this.

I caught Jane's eye as I picked up my bag. "I've got an errand or two to run. I'll meet you at the pub, okay?"

She looked puzzled and almost said something, but then
changed her mind at the last moment. "All right, then."

I let Trevor get a block or so ahead of me, and since he

didn't expect anyone to follow him, I had a pretty easy time of it. Though I supposed there was no real reason even to stay out of his sight.

After a few blocks, I noticed that this section of Manchester was a little more run-down, a little less nicely kept up than the sections I'd spent my time in up until now. The doorways were strewn with discarded and stained wrappers from fast food joints, and there were beer cans, taller and with more colorful labels than the ones we had at home, mingled in with them. I still wasn't quite used to the idea of being able to walk around with a beer in my hand, if I wanted to. Where I came from, you got a warning from the cops if you even thought about liquor in public. I paused to cross the street—again, carefully reminding myself that the traffic was going to be coming on my right. Graffiti began to appear, mostly raillery against the local police, and the longer I followed Trevor, the more the buildings took on a distinctly seedy appearance. I sped up a little, not so much to keep Trevor from getting out of sight, as to suggest to the loitering youths that I knew where I was going and that I had a purpose in being there. They didn't say anything to me, though they did turn quiet as I passed, and one clucked at me; this was followed by laughter in the group. I wasn't fooling them or myself.

Before too long, Trevor turned into a pub and I followed him, grateful to be getting off the street. The Fig and Thistle was not as well marked as the Prince of Wales—there was none of the landlord's pride in the exterior—but even the gloom inside didn't faze me at first. The Prince of Wales had been dark too, but then I began to realize that darkness was cozy rather than dismal. Even so, I really should have been more aware of what I was getting myself into.

Trevor was at the bar, paying for a large glass of clear liquid, as the bartender put away a bottle of nondescript vodka. The student drank off half his glass. As I went over to Trevor, I tried to catch the bartender's eye, but he looked straight at me and walked past without stopping. Mentally I tried out a new word that I'd heard someone use when talking to Trevor: wanker. Never mind, I had other things on my mind than drinking.

I pulled up next to Trevor, who choked when he recognized me. I sat down and waited for him to stop coughing.

"Sorry," I said. "Didn't mean to startle you."

"What the fuck are you doing here?" He whipped his head around wildly, perhaps trying to see if anyone saw us together.

"Just thought I'd try a change from the Prince of Wales. Though I don't think the bartender—landlord? publican?— would you say—"

"I wouldn't say bollocks," he sputtered.

"—Is as nice as Ian. Still." I tried to get the attention of the barman again, with no further luck. "That's quite a nose job you got there. What happened?"

"None of your bleeding business! Why don't you piss off?"

I decided that the direct approach would be best. "Where have you been the past couple of days? I mean, it doesn't take two days to get a nose patched up, unless of course you went in for cosmetic surgery, in which case you should be more careful about going out into the sun, not that there's been much of that lately. Is there someone you're trying to—"

"There's never a moment's peace from you bloody women, is there?" Trevor slugged back the rest of his drink, slammed the glass on the sticky wood of the bar, kicked back his stool, and left.

That was when I noticed just how quiet the rest of the pub had become. I watched Trevor leave, and looking around me, I saw that I was the only woman in the pub. Every eye in the place was on me, there was no friendliness in any of them, and every one of the other patrons had observed my brief row with Trevor. There was, however, amusement in two faces that I was startled to find I recognized. I swore under my breath and turned quickly around, pretending that I hadn't seen anyone I knew. The bartender, now watching me intently, sauntered slowly over to my end of the bar, a cigarette dangling from one side of his mouth.

"Pint of bitter, please," I said, thinking quickly, hoping that he would serve me this time, hoping I would be allowed to sit at the bar and the others at the table would get up and leave without passing me. I really should have just left.

"Ladies don't drink pints of bitter," he said loudly, mockingly. A few chuckles were heard from the tables. I shifted uncomfortably, wondering what was going on. "In Britain, ladies have halves of cider."

"Well, it's a good thing I'm an American, then, isn't it?" I said, then cringed: I had been trying for banter, but it came out as more of a challenge than I intended. I decided that if I was going to get out of this, I had to stand my ground. "Just the pint, please."

The bartender held my gaze for a moment longer, then pulled out a pint glass and managed the optic in a careless fashion. The result was a glass that was only three quarters filled, about half of that foam.

"Two pounds fifty," he said, and although I suspected the price had been inflated for my benefit, I put the money on the bar without arguing. Call it the unladylike-American tax.

"Emma, come join us," called the voice I had hoped not to hear. I took a sip from my miserable pint, and resigned, turned and walked over to the table. As heads turned to follow my progress, I began to wonder if whether I mightn't be better off with my two companions, as much as I had hoped to avoid either of them: Maybe their company would get me out of the Fig and Thistle without further incident. It was an unattractive sort of hope, but then I found myself in a situation where any hope at all was welcome.

Avery and Palmer sat together, smirking amusement evident in every one of their features. Palmer indicated a chair. "Have a seat," he said.

What the hell were these two doing together? "Maybe just for a moment," I said. "I told Jane I'd meet her." I wasn't keen on mentioning Jane in front of Palmer since he'd spoken against her, but I did want to give the impression I'd be missed.

"Course you will. I can tell. You're a social sort, aren't you?" He didn't wait for an answer, but leaned across the table conspiratorially. "This isn't the sort of place for ladies to be social, though, if you get my drift."

"Well, the bartender certainly didn't seem to appreciate my presence," I said. The foam in my glass had just settled enough so that I could see there was only about a half a pint of beer.

"Oh, anyone can see that," Palmer said, nodding. "But what I have to ask is what brings you here in the first place? The Prince of Wales is much more your speed."

"Just trying to catch up with Trevor." I shrugged, looking around. Attention was still on our table. "Seems he's had a rough couple of days—"

"Someone cracked him a sweet one, didn't they?" Palmer mused thoughtfully. "Wonder what he did to deserve that. He probably put his nose where it didn't belong, and that's how it got flattened."

I swallowed. This sounded exactly like the sort of thing he'd said to me in the car the first day we'd met, but I couldn't understand what his interest in any of this was. I shrugged. "I can't imagine Trevor being at all curious. He probably did just trip over the cat, as he claims."

"Possibly, though I don't see that miserable little sod as an animal lover. What do you reckon, Avery?"

Avery the photographer hadn't said a word. He looked up from his drink, something I could smell from where I sat was coconut-flavored Malibu, and he grinned. It was an expression that spoke of toothy Halloween masks, perhaps even less attractive than his behavior in the darkroom. He shook his head.

"But one does wonder what would have happened, if he was the sort to extend himself, doesn't one?" Palmer took a long drink. "It would be a shame for him to find out the hard way."

Avery hadn't done anything this whole time but turn his glass around and around in place on the table and stare at me. Piqued, I stared back, not blinking, not hostile, not smiling. He slowly removed his hands from the glass and raised them in front of his face. At first I thought that he was going to say something—his hands seemed to shape a prayer—then I realized he was now holding an imaginary camera. His right index finger snapped down briefly, and Avery smiled faintly, his thumb automatically advancing the imaginary film as he lowered his hands into his lap, still gazing at me.

I turned back to Palmer, disconcerted. I swallowed as shallowly as I could, and when I realized that I was clutching the edge of the table, loosened my fingers ever so slightly.

"How is it that you two know each other?" I asked, taking a sip of my beer.

"Oh, well, it's a small world, isn't it?" said Palmer comfortably. "Everyone knows everyone else, knows all their business too. A very tight-knit community, our little neighborhood, always has been. No use for outsiders. We know everyone's troubles, where all the skeletons are—"

I started. Palmer noticed this with interest.

"Oh, yes. All the skeletons. Who's doing well, who's had to scrabble, who might have tiptoed across the narrow line of the law, who's married to a nutter. Whose daughter is dead." He said that last with such a satisfaction that my blood froze in my veins.

"You're not a fan of George Whiting, I take it." I was as careful as I could to keep my shaking from becoming obvious.

Palmer shrugged elaborately. "Now that you mention it, I'm not. I was a lowly employee of his, once upon a time. Man fired me on suspicion of thievery. Some copper wire went missing from one of the sites."

"Didn't help it was found in your garden shed," said Avery in his cartoon character voice. He laughed silently into his glass.

"I have no idea how it got there to this day," Palmer averred solemnly. "And that was the first time I went to Hackmoor as well, bastard."

I suddenly understood that Hackmoor was a prison, recalling Palmer's earlier description of his limited travels.

Palmer continued, increasingly heatedly. "But the point to that is, the man's got above himself. He's no better than any of us, and because he happened to come into a bit, he thinks cake comes out his arsehole. Worse than that, he forgets how things were done, how a bloke, seeing a bit of loose copper about, thinks to make himself a spare quid or two. Some might congratulate him on having an entrepreneurial spirit, seeing as it's really not doing anyone any harm. No harm in the world; it's the punters what pay for it, innit? But others take it personal, where there's no malice intended. But there is now. Malice aplenty. I'll wager he got what he deserved. Didn't he?"

With those last words, he looked at me with a hatred burning in his eyes that shocked me to the core. He blinked and something else was there, interest or calculation.

He began to tap on the table with his index finger. "Now you might remember that I suggested that you shouldn't get mixed up in your friend Jane's business. It's complicated enough as it is. And yet here you are, poking about where you're not wanted, and for the life of me, I can't imagine why you'd want to go and ignore me. Seeing as I've got your best interests at heart."

I stood up. "It's probably because I can't imagine why it's any concern of yours, either Jane's affairs or my best interest. Or in fact, why you care at all. Maybe if you answered me that, then I'd have some reason. Until then, I'm just not impressed."

"I'll tell you why you should be impressed. Your friend Jane will be just fine on her own. She's the sort to use people, then toss them aside. She's done it all her life, by all accounts, and she's moved here to Marchester; she's doing it now with that poor sod of a husband of hers. She probably done it with Julia Whiting too. So she'll survive just fine; her kind always does. And she wouldn't think twice about using you the same way. There's a big hole where her heart ought to be. And that's just for starters."

He stood up now and leaned in close to me; panicky as I felt, I tried not to move away from him. "What my interests might be is no concern of yours. If I find they become such, you'll wish you'd never been born. That's a promise."

I shrugged, showing carelessness I was miles from feeling. "We'll see." I raised my glass and took a sip of the beer. It wasn't very nice beer and I noticed my hand was shaking. As I set it down, however, wondering how I was going to just walk away from the Fig and Thistle, a shout from the bar caught the attention of everyone in the pub. The bartender was shouting at a young, disheveled man who was coming from the back of the pub.

"Here, you! I told you I was sick of your coming in here all the time, using the gents as a bathhouse! I don't want your sort in here!"

"Here, now," said Palmer, with interest. The quiet that had settled on the pub during our conversation was now animated with little gestures and nods toward the bar. Something was brewing, and everyone knew it.

The young man, small and slenderly built, had curly dark hair that was badly in need of cutting. "I ordered a whiskey. What more do you want? I'm not hurting anything."

"I don't care if you ordered a general strike! Get the fuck on your bike and don't come back, you little—"

I didn't wait to hear the rest of the harangue. I set my glass down and walked toward the door. Alas, I made the mistake of looking back. Palmer was still unusually interested in the young man arguing with the bartender, but Avery was watching me. He reached over and brushed his fingers along the rim of the glass from which I'd been drinking.

I groped for the door and got the hell out of there.

As I hurried down the street, no longer caring whether I

attracted any undue attention, I forced myself to consider Palmer's chilling words: "He got what he deserved, didn't he?" The horrible simplicity of his equation, a dead daughter repays a jail term, was so natural to him that I had to wonder what he might have done to bring it about.

"Oi, you!"

The voice behind me was male, one I didn't recognize; I walked faster, trying to decide where I should head if things got dicey again. There weren't many options, as straight back was the only way I knew that might possibly lead me away from trouble.

The voice called out again. "Steady on, there! I want a word with you!"

I hurried along, wishing I'd worn my sneakers instead of my work boots.

"You, Yank! Hold up a moment, damn it!"

I couldn't think of anything I was less likely to do and further increased my speed. I heard footsteps following behind me. I felt in my coat pocket for something I could use to protect myself and seized a ballpoint pen, flicking the cover off with my thumb.

I heard hurrying footsteps behind me. "Shit, I'm not going to—I just want to ask you about Julia!"

That was possibly the only thing in the world that would have slowed me down that evening. I continued to walk, but slower now, and waited until the footsteps were just behind me, then whirled around to face whoever it was. The young man who'd been banned from the pub, surprised, stepped back a bit, which was the way I wanted things. I pressed my advantage, not knowing how long it would last.

"What do you want? Why do you think I can help you?"

He hooked a thumb back toward the pub slowly, so as not to startle me, I guessed. "I heard you talking with those two . . . back there. I heard her name. Did you know her?"

Though the light was dim, I could see he was not badly dressed, but had given his clothes hard use lately. He moved with barely contained patience.

"I never met her," I said warily. "I'm working on the same dig as she was, is all. Who are you?"

He shook his head. "It doesn't matter. I just came back to see her and I was too late. Why were you talking about her?"

I had to be careful here. "A friend of mine has been questioned about Julia's death; I'm sure she's not involved and I'm just trying to find out how to prove it."

"How do you know?" He stepped forward eagerly; I stepped back just as quickly, and brought my hand out of my pocket, still clutching the pen. I probably looked more crazy than dangerous, but I was willing to let that work for me as well. The stranger put his hands up.

"I don't want to hurt you, I just wanted to . . . I don't know, talk to someone who might have known Julia." He sighed and rubbed at the back of his head. "Who might be able to tell me how she died. If you find anything, will you let me know?"

"Why should I?" I took a step back again, not entirely because I was scared, but in part because I was no longer in a state to trust anyone.

"Because I think we're working toward the same end. Look, I'm sort of . . . camping out while I'm here. I don't particularly want to make my presence here known. If you find anything, leave me a note in the cemetery at St. Alban's. You know the place? There's a big oak tree by the river side of the churchyard. Leave me a note under a rock at the base of the tree. If I find anything, I'll let you know too. Same way."

"I'm not making any promises," I said, backing off in the direction of my escape route. This was getting surreal.

"Me neither." He turned away. "The best day's work Julia ever did was to leave here. I'd like to find out what it was that brought her back. And then got her killed."

As the stranger ducked down an alley, I turned and started jogging back toward the center of town, putting as much distance between me and the Fig and Thistle as possible. I didn't slow down until I was just outside the Prince of

Wales and then paused just to catch my breath. The rapidly lengthening shadows cast an unwholesome cloak over landscape that was more happily familiar to me. It was nearly seven, though I was surprised to realize that it was as early as that still. It seemed clear to me that the young stranger was probably the person who was sleeping rough in Sabine's churchyard. Now I was left asking myself, not so much about his curious lodgings or his desire to avoid notice and the police, but as to what his interest in Julia Whiting's death was.

Chapter 11

THE SCENE THAT MET ME UPON ENTERING THE PRINCE of Wales was so far removed from the one I'd just left as to leave me stunned and speechless with relief. I was back where I belonged. The wooden paneling that had struck me as so dark before I now realized glowed from polish and care, adding not light but luster to the room. The glances of the habitués were passing and idly curious rather than suspicious. And best of all, there were faces that I recognized and that welcomed me.

Jane and Greg both cried out "Emma!" simultaneously and waved me over. They were holding hands, practically sitting in each other's laps, a vast change from the barely polite silences and obvious avoidances of the morning. Even as I walked over, I wondered how they had reconciled—and over what, exactly.

I sat down with more of a sigh and a bump than I meant. Looking at my friends, I started to laugh and they joined in.

"Long day?" Jane asked.

"Way too long," I answered.

"What will you have, Emma?" said Greg, as he pushed back his chair.

"No, no, it's my round, I believe," I said hurriedly. I had never bought a round the last time, and suspected that it was my turn. "You're having two bitters?"

"Learns fast," he replied. "Yes, please."

"And two bitters for me too." Jane giggled.

I looked at her. Giggling? "And a bitter for Jane."

It took me a moment to get the attention of the bartender, Ian, but only because it was a busy Friday. "Half a tic." He handed a whiskey and two gins to a young woman dressed in a business suit, who was being teased from a table on the far side of the room to universal laughter. "Now, what can I get for you? Wait, a moment, you're with the professors, right? Then that's two bitters—and what else?"

"Just another one of those, please. And one for yourself." I'd learned from watching Greg that this was the proper way of tipping in a pub.

Ian beamed. "Well, ta very much indeed. You're from the States, right? Do you watch the American football, then? I love it, myself." He began to pull the pints. "Huge place, America, you don't know till you're there. My brother was in Texas, a year or two after he left school, the late seventies, it was. I went to go visit him on the holidays, just a tyke, I was. I didn't know nothing. I got to New York and called him from the airport. Asked him which bus I should take to get to Houston! When he ever told me it would take four days to get there, did my jaw ever drop! I was gobsmacked! You ever been to Houston?" He handed me the drinks, and I paid up.

I shook my head. "Never. Like you said, it's a big country. I live on the East Coast, Massachusetts."

"Oh, yeah? The Patriots, right?" He smiled and raised his eyebrows expectantly.

"Right but . . . I'm afraid I'm not much for football." I looked down at the beer. All these pints were perfectly drawn, the amber body still settling in the glass. I'm sure

Brian could have described how and why the minute bubbles were moving up from the bottom, leaving an exact quarter inch of foam at the top, with an elegant physics equation or perhaps a concise statement about the reaction between the carbon dioxide and the air pressure outside the cask, or something like that. All I knew was that these drinks were about as far away as one could get from the Fig and Thistle without actually heading back again.

"Thanks very much," I said, and moved back to the table. The bartender waved even as he hurried to another patron waiting at the other end of the bar.

Those drinks went down quickly and were followed in rapid succession by another round, but by this time, I'd learned to order half-pints of beer or cokes. It was with some exasperation that I realized that Jane showed no sign of starting the talk that she'd promised. Worse than that, my stomach was empty; I'd had no dinner before I'd gone chasing after Trevor and got entangled at the Fig and Thistle. It didn't seem that Jane and Greg had eaten either, but they didn't seem much bothered by the fact, chatting as they were about everything under the sun but archaeology, Julia, or Marchester. I decided to take matters into my own hands.

"I'm starving," I said. "Let's go out and get something to eat. Someplace quiet."

For a moment Jane looked at me with a calculating clarity that seemed quite out of place in the giddiness she'd shown all evening. She glanced away, and I watched her face change again, to relief. "Look, there's Simon. Oi, Simon! Over here!" A short, fair bloke started with recognition, waved back, and hastily joined us.

Simon was a friend of Greg's from school, I was told, and appeared to be every bit as affable as Greg. After yet another round, courtesy of Simon, I was starting to get fidgety and Jane saw this, I'm sure, because she kept launching into anecdote after anecdote, so that no interruption was possible. I noticed that Simon was equally frustrated, because he was trying to get Greg's attention by raised eyebrows and the like, getting more and more anxious as another half hour went on. Finally, when Jane stopped to draw breath—and another three ounces of beer—Simon jumped in.

"Greg, would it be possible to have a word at the bar? It's about the, er . . . thing."

Greg blinked and then shock registered as he understood what his friend was talking about. Neither Jane nor I knew, that was for sure. "Oh, certainly. Ladies, if you would excuse us for just a moment?"

"Why excuse you? What are you talking about?" Jane said. "Why can't I hear?"

Long pause. "It's a surprise, Jane." He kissed her very tenderly on the head. "We'll only be a moment, and then we'll go out for Chinese, or a curry or something, okay?"

His wife rolled her eyes, unmollified. "Well, go ahead, keep your grotty little secret, but I'm not about to—"

"I need a breath of air anyway," I said immediately. "You guys take the table and Jane and I will take a little stroll. Come on, Jane."

Jane got up reluctantly and then snagged her foot around the stool, falling. After another five minutes of checking her ankle and assuring her that she was fine, I was pleased that Simon and Greg shooed us from the pub, but wondered greatly what the "thing" was that needed to be so urgently and privately discussed.

The quiet outside the pub was as immediate as a blow. Not wanting to lose my momentum or my chance, I began walking briskly eastward, past the site, and down toward the new church. Jane was forced to keep up simply because I refused to slow when she asked me to. I kept going until I reached the field where I'd seen Sabine and young Tedman playing football and found a bench facing the river. I sat down and patted the space next to me. Heaving a great sigh, Jane sat down, as far from me as she could.

The moonlight shone on the water, still as sluggish as ever. I sat for a moment, watching the lights on the other side of the bank winking through the low clouds, and the humidity around me suggested that a low front was just starting to edge into Marchester.

"Jane, I'm really worried about you. You seemed so distraught this morning. Why don't you tell me what happened between you and George Whiting—it was he, wasn't it? Tell me that, tell me what went on at the police station, too. You'll feel better if you can talk it out, I promise you."

Jane made a face. "God, ever since Princess Di. Talk it out, get it out, and you'll feel better."

"Yeah, well it's true."

"Perhaps." She set her jaw and looked away from me. "I rely on myself to get through these things. I take responsibility for myself and I don't need anyone else."

I half-nodded, noncommittally. "You don't even need Greg?"

Jane looked scornful. "Just because we're married doesn't mean I expect him to look after me."

"Greg seems to be the type who likes to look after people," I said. "I mean, look at the way he thinks of his Auntie Mads, at the cafe. He is very thoughtful of her—"

"Oh, well, he would be, wouldn't he?"

"—But when she started to say something that was in the slightest bit negative about you, he shut her down. I mean, it must be very hard for him, to have picked the only person in the world who won't let him help her."

Jane shook her head vehemently. "Oh, I let him help me. I *do*. You saw me tonight, not a word about work, paying all that attention to him? What more does he want?"

I thought that Jane's attention to Greg might have served many purposes and it was a Band-Aid, maybe, but no solution to the sort of problems they had in their relationship. Greg probably was also interested in something a little deeper than flirtations at the pub and I hoped that he never figured out that he was, at least from my point of view, just another entry on Jane's to-do list.

"He doesn't mind your work," I said. "He just wants to be a part of it, to help."

"Every time Greg tries to help, he only makes it worse," she said stonily.

"I find that hard to believe."

She canted her head decidedly. "It's absolutely so. Our house, for example. It's really *his* house, and he thought it would save money if we stayed here, but it really just narrowed down my options, tied me to this part of the world."

I looked around Jane's part of the world, thinking that a house *and* a job was a far-off dream for many of my teaching friends. "And what's so bad here?"

"Well, the university's nice, but not really first rank." Jane was all but pouting. "It's too far from the center of things—"

That's what e-mail is for, I thought. That's why *you* make the department into something special. It's the department, more than the school, after a certain level.

Jane continued. "And the people. Everyone's too much in each other's pockets. And they hate me—"

"You mean like George Whiting."

"Oh." Jane started, then snuck a guilty peek at me. She slumped. "This isn't the first time we've butted heads. He's been annoyed with me since I slowed down his work. Why the bloody man couldn't realize that you just don't go plowing through a medieval smithy, largely intact, mind you, is beyond me. So he retaliated by having some of the Unit's money pulled by the council. Later on, when he proposed another site for a launderette, I was very pleased to stand up at the council meeting and explain why the site was inappropriate, seeing as it was up for nomination for protection. So it's been like this forever; he's mad, his wife's worse."

"I was wondering whether you couldn't, I don't know, smooth things out through her—her name's Ellen, right?"

"Not a bit of it. Bloody cow had the cheek to fly in my face, try to get me to drop Julia. Said it was a disruption to the family. I ask you!"

We were getting off the track, I thought. "But this morning, he was blaming you for Julia's death. Why would he say that? How is that possible?" Even as I asked, I could feel my hands growing colder and clammier. Maybe it was the night air on the river, maybe it was what I was asking Jane.

There was a long silence between us, only partially filled in by the night noises on the river. I could hear something rustling in the weeds, and farther away, a frog croak seemed to echo, intensified by the still air.

Jane stared in front of her, chewing on the inside of her lip, her face drawn with fatigue. She said quietly, "The man is distraught, that's all. Julia and I . . . we both generally behaved badly around each other, for all the reasons people do. I'm so sorry for that now, because I'm sure there was nothing really wrong there. It was just so easy to be tricked into thinking she was more mature than she actually was. It's no more complicated than George wanting to find some reason for the death of his daughter. I'm not surprised he looked to me; he blames me for everything. I'm responsible for Julia going into archaeology, I'm responsible for Julia's death . . ." She waved her hand about, frowning; Whiting was just one more wart on her imperfect life.

"And do the police believe him? Where've they left it with you?"

"I don't know what to believe." She snorted. "The police 'have no further enquiries at this time,' and I mustn't leave town. That's all they'll tell me."

"What did they ask you about, then?" I picked a long blade of grass and began to tie it into knots.

"Just things like timing. Where Julia was at certain times, what her relationships were like with the rest of the crew." Pause. "Where I was the night of the murder."

I paused in my grass torture. "That was your birthday dinner, wasn't it?"

"Yes, yes, the night I stormed out on Greg," she said, and began scuffing a deep rut into the ground underneath the bench. "They were terribly interested in that. I was just walking around that night—"

"Whereabouts?" I thought of the newspaper article describing Julia's last known movements.

"Just all over the place, even as far as the university. I told you all this before. I wasn't going anywhere in particular." She looked up sharply and stopped kicking at the dirt. "Not near the construction site on Leather Street, not near the Grub and Cabbage, if that's what you're asking me, Emma. I just walked and thought. I didn't see anyone. I didn't meet anyone, just like the afternoon I was done at the station. I didn't see anyone, didn't run into anyone I know."

The more she said it, the more I went cold: The lady doth protest too much, methinks. "What were her relations like with the rest of the crew?" Even as I changed the question, Jane was getting more and more impatient with me, I could tell.

"I don't know." Jane dismissed the question, then, after a bit of hesitation, tried to tackle it, unable to resist the challenge. "Julia wasn't well liked. Certainly not by the girls. She was always a bit shy, which puts people off, and once she came out of her shell, she came off as too much the brain, which doesn't often sit well."

She shrugged restlessly. "Some of the blokes had crushes on her, probably. She could be very intense and people seem to be attracted to that. Until they realize it has nothing to do with them, as they inevitably found out."

I wondered whether this wasn't something that had also characterized Jane's life and then thought again of the pictures of Julia in the darkroom.

"Was she involved with anyone?"

"Emma, I really don't see what any of this has to do with you!" She stood up now, very angry. "Why do you persist so?"

I threw the knotted blade of grass away from me. "Come off it, Jane. All I'm trying to do is help, if not Julia, then *you,* at least. Why is that so hard to understand? What are you so scared of? Me? What am I going to do to you?"

Jane got up a little unsteadily; she hadn't been drinking halves. "I understand, I do. Of *course* you want to help. But it's all under control, thank you."

I was angry now; how dared she patronize me like this? "Jane—"

"Emma, you simply don't understand it's not how we do things here." She turned and headed back down the river path toward the site. I sat, really feeling the chill of the damp air now, and pulled my coat closer around me. So much for England in June; I had been hoping for the springtime the poets wrote of—blue skies, warm grass, sweet strawberries, and cool cream—but was beginning to suspect it was mythological. I hadn't had dinner for the second night in a row and was starting to feel the effects of the night's excitement and beer. It was a nasty feeling, being alone in an empty part of town, between two graveyards, arguing with my only friend here.

A splash and another rustling down in the tall grasses by the side of the river startled me, and I jumped up and hurried back up toward the main road. I didn't want to run into Jane on the river path and I didn't want to stay put. Once I got onto the road, well lit despite the creeping fog, I also began to worry about my indiscretion about talking with Jane in so open a place. Yes, it was quiet and lonely, but only this evening I'd learned that there was a lot more traffic, indeed, residence, behind the church than anyone expected. Thinking about the splash again, and now unable to recall having heard the sound of a fish or bird before or after, I hurried down Church Street, back to Jane and Greg's house.

Where there was no one home, of course. Presumably, unless she'd gone for another one of her long, unattended, and unthinking rambles, Jane had met Greg and Simon back at the pub, where they were presently debating the virtues of Indian versus Chinese food. Confident that Jane would make some excuse for my absence, I overcame my habitual reticence about making myself at home in someone else's house and started looking into putting together some dinner for myself. A lump of brie—I don't think Jane would have had anything so common as cheddar—an apple, and a piece of bread, with a nice glass of orange juice, and my spirits rose considerably. I felt much more my old self, much more where I belonged.

My spirits fell back to their pre-dinner low levels. I wasn't back where I belonged, I was back where I fit best so far, which still meant I was as far on the outside as ever. I had no idea what was going on and needed to find out, but was confused by subtleties of culture and the complexities of someone else's relationship problems. I was confused because Jane was my friend, and Greg too, but not the same way that I had friends at home. Even Kam, who had been raised in England, seemed a little more accessible to me, in some ways. Though to be completely fair, he wasn't caught up in a murder investigation. That got me thinking about how much I didn't know about Jane or anything else at all.

I glanced at my watch: eight thirty. Brian would be at work, and I owed him a call. Hell, after tonight, I owed myself a call. It was getting expensive, all these calls home, I thought, as I dialed what seemed like an inordinate number of digits. The phone began to ring. It might be cheaper, in the end, to have Brian fly over—

"Chang," came the abrupt answer.

"Jeez, hon, couldn't you at least say, 'Brian Chang,' or even a simple hello? You wouldn't sound quite so mean. When you say 'Chang' like that, it sounds like someone threw a wrench into a bucket."

"Hey, Emma! Hang on a sec—Roddy, you get going and we'll talk tomorrow. I saw that! Put it down. Get your own flasks buddy."

I heard a door shut in Brian's office. "What's up, babe?"

"Nothing. I just thought I'd give you a call, since you said to."

"Uh huh."

"So how's Quasi?"

Long silence. "You must really be homesick, if you're asking after him."

I wilted. "Oh, I am. I feel so lost. Every time I think I understand what's going on, I don't."

There was a long silence on the other end of the phone and I heard the tapping of computer keys. "Brian, are you listening to me?"

"Yes. You said you feel alien, foreign. I'm sorry about that."

He didn't sound particularly sorry, I thought sullenly. "Hey, I'm looking for a little support here! And well, you just sound like a dink."

He laughed, music to my ears in spite of my irritation. "Emma, you *are* a foreigner. You *are* alien. You say the same thing when we visit my folks in San Diego. Did you think England would be less of a difference than California?"

"I don't know."

"Did you think you were going to blend in? Pick up on every nuance automatically?"

"No, of course not. I just thought I had a better handle on everything than I do."

"You probably have a better handle on things than you think. Definitely better than most people. So what do you do at conferences? Or when you're visiting Ma and Dad?"

"Work it. Make the most of being exotic."

"Right."

I traced a pattern in the straw rug with my toe. "Well, maybe."

"Just don't sweat it, right? And sometimes, it's better to let other people assume you know less than you do. You can get away with more then."

"You're right. I hate it when you're always right." I punched at one of the couch cushions.

"What can I say? It's my cross to bear."

"So how are you?"

"Good. Lonely. And if it's any consolation, the cushion

apparently didn't agree with Quasi all that much. He's been lying low since yesterday, but he managed to hark up a lot of cotton stuffing all over—"

"Please let me just assume that it will be cleaned up by the time I'm back in two weeks, okay? I need that right now."

"Hey, speaking of which—Kam is going to be visiting his mother in a week, so I gave him Jane's number so he could give you a call and you guys could hook up. Keep your ears peeled for that."

"Cool! Is Marty coming too?"

"Do you think she'd let him visit London without her?"

"Ha!" I paused. "How about you? Could you come too?"

I heard a sigh. "I wish I could, but I've got all my vacation saved up for the trip in August. Trust me, it'll be worth it."

"You still won't tell me where we're going?"

"Nope. But you'll love it, I just know it."

"And I should bring a bathing suit."

"Why would I want to go anywhere cold when all I have to do is wait a couple of months?" There was another pause, and I could feel Brian's mood shift. "Emma, you don't know these people all that well, do you?"

"I've known Jane for years—"

"Yeah, from conferences. Once or twice a year you run into her in some neutral academic territory where everyone has to be nice to each other. Maybe you both had a bit too much to drink and got giggly over someone's new article, or something. I'm just saying, be careful, okay?"

"I'll be okay." I hated admitting he was right about this. "I promise. I'll just work from the known to the unknown, just like in the field. I miss you. Something awful."

"Me too. Come home soon."

"Just as fast as I can."

After I hung up, I realized that tomorrow was Saturday, the day of the fox hunt. But as much as I was looking forward to seeing Jeremy and his house again, I had the sinking feeling that I'd also be seeing a lot more of Palmer as well. With that happy thought, I dragged myself up to bed.

Chapter 12

I WOKE UP THE NEXT MORNING IN A SWIRL OF CONFU-
sion. The dreams I'd been having were more intense than
ever, somewhat threatening, somewhat confusing, always
just beyond my ability to understand them. This was further
complicated by the fact that after a moment, I realized that I
smelled coffee brewing. I hurriedly pulled on a pair of jeans
and bolted downstairs, lest the odor prove to be a phantom.

Of course I should have remembered that no matter how
often or how hard I wished it, coffee never brewed itself:
Jane was downstairs waiting for me. I came to that realization just as I hit that squeaky last step, so there was no
chance of fleeing back to my room. Clever trap, Jane, I
thought. It was really unfair, though, to lure me into a poten-
tially heavy conversation before I was fully human.

"Good morning." Jane poured me a cup of coffee from
the coffee press. It was a peace offering; she must have
picked it up yesterday.

"Hey."

There was a long pause hanging between us and I took
the opportunity to stoke up. I honestly couldn't decide

which of us needed to do the apologizing and suspected that I owed her at least a small one. Which was why it was such a surprise to me when just as I drew breath, Jane had already begun.

"I'm very sorry about last night. I had no right. I can only attribute it to being a little overtired and a little hungry. Possibly a mite tiddly."

I shook my head. "I shouldn't have been pushing you—"

"No, no, look, I'm a big girl," she interrupted. "I am, occasionally, able to govern myself sufficiently to account for those factors. You have been a tremendous help to me, to us, and I wouldn't want you to think otherwise. I know you're just trying to help, and it happens to be in exactly the way that tends to scare me off, you know? So please forgive me and I'll try to do better."

"Sure, no problem." I was still a little befuddled; this was all happening pretty fast. "So you and Greg will be coming with me today? To the fox hunt?"

Jane's face darkened. "Um, I rather think not. I've got too much work to catch up on—especially where Bonnie's concerned, alas—and I'm still not ready to show myself at a social gathering. I wouldn't be any fun. But since we haven't rung to say we won't be attending, I'll ask Greg to run you over, so that we don't disrupt his lor—Jeremy's plans—"

With that I heaved a sigh of relief. No private audience with Jane and Palmer in the same room. Something unknotted in my stomach and I realized, chagrined, just how worried I had been about that possibility.

"—And you should give us a call when you get done. All right?"

"Yes, thanks. Er. Any idea what I should wear?"

Jane cocked her head, considering. "I've never been to one of these affairs, but I understand they're not terribly formal. You won't need hunting pinks or anything like that. I should dress, well, as one should dress for running through fields and woods. Trainers, I suppose, trousers, of course. A good warm jumper, at least—I mean, you know, a sweater, cardie, whatever you call them. It will be cool again today, I think. Coldest spring we've had in ages."

She put away the dishes she'd just washed; apparently she and Greg had already eaten. "Anyway, I'm going to get up to work. Just call out when you're ready to go."

After worrying too long about what I should wear, I settled for jeans, sneakers, and a colored T-shirt that I wouldn't mind sweating in too much, with a sweater vest to go under my barn coat. And since I am not a fashion plate by any stretch of the imagination, I simply confined myself to figuring out how to look as presentable as possible before and after a good run. Finally, as a sop to my new resolution not to worry about blending in, I dug through my suitcase and pulled out my new hat, a broad-brimmed canvas hat that would have been better at home fishing on the other side of the Atlantic, but which would be just the thing here if the skies opened up.

Greg was waiting at the bottom of the stairs when I came down. He looked me up and down and shrugged almost imperceptibly. Mentally I stuck out my tongue.

"Very smart. I haven't a clue as to what to tell you to expect, but I'm sure that Lord Hyde-Spofford will look after you. He means it all to be fun, so I am sure it will be. Shall we?"

Greg's car was vintage, dark burgundy, and meticulously maintained, and reminded me of a small rounded station wagon. The way he behaved around it—pausing to inspect a stain that might have been a scratch, picking a leaf off the fender with a frown—suggested that it was not only vintage but much beloved. The logo on the grille showed some wavy lines and a stylized quadruped.

"Morris 1800," he said, as if I should recognize the reason for his pride in that fact.

"Oh. Very nice."

As we drove along, Greg craned his head past the steering wheel, peering up at the sky. "Those clouds don't look good. We'll have rain before the end of the day."

"How do you know that?"

He shrugged. "Lived here all my life."

We drove on a bit farther.

"What are you up to today?" I asked. "Working, like Jane?"

Greg frowned. "No, Jane hadn't said anything about that to me. I'm off to visit Aunty Mads. She's been very poorly lately."

"Oh?" I recalled not having seen her at the cafe the last morning I'd been there, where she was clearly so much a fixture.

"I suppose at that age, you're bound to have a setback now and then, but she's always been right at the top of her form, so we're all a bit concerned about the past couple of weeks, of course. So I'll run over and check up on her."

"I know she'll appreciate that. She seems terribly fond of you."

"She'd do anything, she's always said, for me or Gran either. We thought we'd lose her when my Gran died, but she just seemed to transfer all her attentions to me and she rallied."

I began to recognize the surroundings from the last time I'd been here, detoured by Dora. The hills were rolling, unbelievably green, and dotted with sheep; occasionally we passed a field of brilliant yellow, which Greg explained was rape bloom or *Brassica napus*. We traveled along in companionable silence.

"Any news from Andrew?" I said. "Has he finished his report on the modern skeleton yet? I'm sort of surprised that he hasn't been more forthcoming with his conclusions about it; I mean, it really did look like evidence of a murder to me."

"No, I haven't seen anything yet," Greg said. "Have you asked Jane? He'd probably hand it over to her first, as the project director."

"I asked Jane; she said she wasn't worried about it, it was Andrew's responsibility—" I began. Some of my impatience with this laxity was seeping through, and Greg cut me off.

"Well, there you are. You do understand, Emma, that in Britain, we usually leave the specialists to their work. Not the same degree of hands-on oversight as in America, you see; we find that those in charge can't be taxed with every detail and so we don't try. Everyone has his or her own job. It works out very well."

"I understand the system is different," I said, a little stung by the implied criticism, "but you can't tell me that you're not personally curious about this skeleton, can you?"

"Of course, curious, but it honestly has nothing to do with me, professionally or personally. So there's no point in getting worked up over it, is there?"

I didn't answer.

"You know, Jane's told me what a help you've been to her. To us, really," Greg said abruptly. "I really think we're—Jane and I, I mean—going to pull through all this horrible mess, and that's in part thanks to you. I can't tell you what it means to me. To us."

I had the strangest sensation that I was being dismissed rather than thanked; surely Greg couldn't believe that everything was really all right? "Well, I'm glad if I did anything to help, but we won't really know everything's okay until Jane's been cleared, right?"

Greg shrugged and pretended to listen to the engine carefully, speeding up a little, then slowing down, as if trying to locate the source of an imaginary noise. "The police will find that out soon enough. There's no way that Jane will remain their prime suspect."

"But what about Trevor? Doesn't his absence—and his nose—suggest that something's up at the site?"

"You must be joking." Greg seemed quite genuinely surprised. "I can't tell you the number of times I've wanted to have a go at him. And no, in case you're wondering; it wasn't my doing. Though I'd like to shake the hand of whoever is responsible."

"And what about Andrew? He's been missing for—"

"Andrew? Andrew came home last night, late, and I'm

sure I'm not telling tales out of school, the worse for wear. He does that, sometimes, and every time we take him back. He's just too good with the bones to show him the door." Greg said all this with the blandness one uses to gloss over a suspect fact.

I sat, puzzled and fuming over this, but Greg wasn't about to let me think of another objection: As far as he was concerned, everything was hunky-dory. His complacency about Andrew's lack of report and Julia's murder bothered me. Worse than that, it made me question why I was getting myself involved in any of this.

"And now you'll be able to focus all your energies on Mother Beatrice, won't you?" He looked at me hopefully and downshifted. "I see that that burial nineteen is shaping up very nicely and we have great hopes it is indeed she. You mustn't worry about Morag and the other sillies, either, they're just looking for a bit of attention, you see."

I shrugged. "It's hard to please everyone, or even try to take everyone's ideas into consideration, isn't it? A site is a complicated thing, in the public sphere."

"I don't see why that's so important, though," he replied curtly. "We have the license, our plan has been approved, and that should be that, shouldn't it? Everything else is just catering to special interests and I really think work will grind to a standstill if every crackpot has to be treated as though his ideas are equally valid, don't you? We have to face facts, that there is one right way, and that's that."

"But how do you know that? I honestly don't know," I replied, looking out the window. Hello, sheep. "I think we have to consider the public, the audience, but I think you draw the line differently, every time, on every site. And I'm not sure how you can tell what's right, when you're right."

"Rubbish," he said. "Science is science."

We pulled up in front of Jeremy's house, which was even more imposing than I remembered. "Call if you want a ride home," Greg said. "We should be in."

There were several other cars of every stripe ranging

from another, very tiny, Morris to a Range Rover to a Mercedes sedan. As I stepped up to the open door, I noticed a bottle-green Jaguar pulling up the drive; I hurried inside. I had no desire to find out if George Whiting was driving that particular car.

Palmer was waiting for me there in the entryway. I all but skidded to a halt, but the threatening presence that had so intimidated me in the Fig and Thistle was nowhere to be seen. Palmer approached me with the strict disinterest of a well-trained servant.

"If you'd be so kind, his lordship would like a moment of your time. In the library." Palmer indicated a room at the far end of the hall and I scuttled off away from him. I was curious about Palmer's language and posture. His words were a little forced and I knew from my previous visit, and everyone's opinion, that Jeremy didn't require that sort of formality. For some reason entirely his own, Palmer had decided that this was the way someone employed in a great house ought to behave. And why was he still playing the role of butler? Surely there ought to be more staff. I tucked that question away for later consideration and entered the open door to the library.

"Ah, good morning, Emma!" Jeremy was dressed even more outlandishly than I was. He was actually better suited to the occasion in a raspberry pink track suit and very technical running shoes, bright acid green, no laces, and held on the foot with elasticized panels. "Ah, you see how effectively I'm kitted out for our event today. No one should ever lose me, no matter how thick the fog gets. I do believe we'll have time for at least one good run through, however, before we get the rain."

He spoke of the coming rain with as much assurance as did Greg, I noticed. "I'm looking forward to whatever chance we get."

"There you are, American optimism," Jeremy said, nodding authoritatively. "I love it."

I never thought of myself as an optimist, but perhaps, culturally speaking, I was. Something else to think about.

He gestured to my head. "And I adore your hat—do you fish? If you do, you must come and try my little stretch of river. Even if we don't catch anything, there's no spot prettier on the whole estate—but I'm getting off track again! I have something for you."

He took an envelope from the desk and handed it to me. I looked down at the florid handwriting on the envelope and immediately recognized it as Dora's.

"Please go ahead and read it." Jeremy nodded. He busied himself with some papers on his desk.

The hand inside was equally elaborate, but perfectly clear. That was the thing about Dora, I thought: She might do things extravagantly, but you always understood that it was done to a specific end. The trick was to discover her purpose.

"Dear Emma," I read to myself, *"It suddenly occurs to me that the third picture on the right hand wall of the entrance hall bears further study by you. You've probably already noticed this, but on the other hand, you do tend to get very wrapped up in your little bits of trash and layers of dirt, Emma, and although pretty, in a quaint, antiquarian sort of way, this behavior causes you to lose sight of the big picture, so to speak. However, I won't bore you with the details, they'll be obvious enough to you on your examination of said picture. It's just a portrait with the usual idealized window and background, rather boring, very parochial (don't tell Pooter I said so, he's besotted with anything Marcastrian), but not without a certain charm of light, but I think you'll find it very interesting. Must dash, the plane won't wait an instant longer and the Italians won't thank you for keeping me. Dora."*

"It's something about your pictures," I said, folding the note into one of my pockets. "She claims that there's something important about one of the landscapes that I should see."

"Then you'll have to have a good squint at them when we get back, if you like," Jeremy said instantly. "What is it that you should be looking for?"

"She doesn't say," I replied. "She assumes that I've already noticed, or will do immediately upon viewing it again."

He cocked his head and clucked. "Isn't that like our Dora? But we wouldn't have her any other way, would we?"

"Well . . ." I was ungracious enough to start, but Jeremy interrupted me, quite convinced, and set all argument aside.

"She has her little moments, I grant you, but she wouldn't be Dora if she didn't, now, would she? And we've quite enough uninteresting people in the world without wanting to turn her into another one, don't we?"

"You're right," I said, but secretly I thought there were moments when Dora could stand to be a little more boring.

Palmer stuck his head into the room, avoiding my gaze altogether. "Whenever you're ready, my lord. The other guests are all assembled outside."

"Excellent, Palmer. We'll give you, say, a ten-minute head start?"

"Very good, my lord."

"And do ask Rachel to circulate with the drinks again. Well, Emma, let's get things under way, shall we?"

"I'm afraid I've been monopolizing you."

"Not at all. Once more around with a cheering cup, and away we'll go."

We exited out to a part of the garden that ran alongside the house, a gravel way that led out to formal beds—presumably those in which Jeremy had found his sherd collection—and ran up to a garage that had once upon a time been a stable. About twenty people had congregated there, some rather jolly from the hunt cup, all talking animatedly. The chat fell off gradually as it was realized that the host had arrived on the scene. Jeremy rubbed his hands together in eager anticipation.

"Good morning, good morning! Just a few more moments and we'll begin. We have a newcomer today, and I've no doubt that you'll make Emma Fielding feel welcome in our little group."

There was some polite clapping to accompany the discreetly curious glances in my direction. Jeremy excused himself to greet other guests and I looked around me to see if there was anyone I knew. I only recognized Sabine without her collar, who nodded hello, but was busily chatting with parishioners. Several people introduced themselves and we discussed the probability of rain interrupting our event. A few spoke knowledgeably about archaeology and I was reminded of the accessibility of it to more people in Britain than in the United States. People were dressed in everything from athletic wear to tweeds, but all wore shoes made for uncertain terrain. I suppose I shouldn't have expected to see more people I knew because the population of the dig, my whole world at the moment, was only a tiny percentage of the rest of town.

And then there was the baying of dogs as they were led out of their runs by the whip. All of a sudden, Dora's inquiries after Roxie and her pups made sense to me, although I assumed mother and babies wouldn't be participating today. There wasn't actually a horn sounding, but all at once there seemed to be a buildup of excitement among the animals. Then we were off.

The chaos was controlled, but it was chaos nonetheless. The dogs stayed more or less in one body, but this was loosely described and got looser the deeper we went into the woods. One foxhound caught a scent and with a triumphant yelp that made me cover my ears, he moved with some of his fellows away from the main part of the pack, which continued on. With some good-natured hallooing and cursing, the human party split up, some still following Palmer, some trying to round the strays up. I followed Jeremy's group for a while, and then watched as things disintegrated further, as chatting about neighborly affairs and hunting down straying dogs and the removal of snagged clothing from briars took precedence over following any scent. As I tried to follow the banter that went back and forth in Jeremy's group as we all ran along, in-jokes that had obviously evolved over many such weekends, I realized that no imaginary fox had ever been less threatened.

I had been running alongside and chatting with a young man in his twenties who introduced himself as Rory. He was dressed in camouflage fatigues and a torn black concert T-shirt that read "Scraping Foetus Off the Wheel" in bold red letters. The name of the band alone made it entirely possible to overlook the fact that the T-shirt, either of antique vintage or extraordinarily well worn, was held together with safety pins and a piece of electrical tape. The young man's hair was bright metallic blue. As we ran along, I found myself wishing, in a peculiarly grown-up fashion that unnerved me, that Rory would buy a clean T-shirt and stop putting on so much eyeliner, because he really seemed very nice and had such good skin. We had been discussing the possibilities of his coming holiday in France when he abruptly measured his length on the path with a heartfelt "Fuckwad!"

I trotted back to see what the matter was. Rory's boot lace had broken and when he snagged his foot on a root, he stepped straight out of his Doc Marten boot. My suggestion of retying the lace together was as sensible as it was useless, for the laces on both boots were already too short from being previously and repeatedly broken and reknotted, until there was nothing but knots left. The offending lace was dirty and meant for a banker's brogue, the other was a girl's shoelace, pink shot through with silver, neither of which would ever have been the right length to begin with. After a few moments of fiddling about, Rory gave up.

"Well, pissflaps. I reckon that's it for me. I'm going to head back and suss out what's for lunch."

"Oh, well. It was nice to have met you, Rory. I'm sorry you'll have to miss the rest of the hunt."

Rory shrugged. "There'll be others. Uncle Jeremy always asks me when I'm home."

So Jeremy was his uncle? Did that mean young, colorful Rory also had a title of some kind?

"Very nice to have met you, Emma. I'm pretty sure if you follow this same path the way we've been going, you'll happen on the others soon enough."

And as he limped off back the way we'd come, the boot slapping against the bottom of his right foot, I was absurdly pleased that he had not called me Mrs. Fielding, as he might have and which drove me crazy. That honorific always made me feel absolutely wizened, and I kept looking around behind me for my mother when I heard it. Dr. Fielding had its place of course, but the increasing occasions on which I was called "Mrs." these days just reminded me that I was now further away than ever from the point in my life when I might have worn obnoxious concert T-shirts. Each "Mrs." brought with it a tiny pang of recognition that I was no longer "just starting out" but "well established." I still thought of myself as twenty, but the rest of the world saw me as thirty-two, next stop forty, and I was pretty sure I didn't like that.

I realized I knew better than I admitted where Jane was, and if I was going to be perfectly honest, I also would admit that every time I heard "Mrs.," I pushed myself just that little bit further, trying to distinguish myself from it. I knew exactly what was driving Jane and me both, and I didn't like it. It was like the treadmills at the gym, and we both had to learn to step off.

I had been immersed in these thoughts and had lost track of the voices of the others; soon I realized that I was alone. I wasn't especially worried, as there were paths to follow, and after all, a pack of dogs and a crowd of people do leave some trace behind them. I walked for a few more minutes, listening carefully for the dogs and voices beyond the bird song, when I heard something else that made me stop. There was a hiss followed by the smell of sulfur: someone, quite close by me, had struck a match.

My heart was in my throat: Something told me not to call out. I can't say that it was the spirit of the occasion, because no one had bothered being very quiet up until now: This was more of the chase than the hunt. I suppose it was just that I realized suddenly that apart from that noise, I'd heard nothing else, none of the careless, ambient noises that humans make when they are simply standing. No breath, no shifting of weight, no rub of fabric.

Someone didn't want to be heard. Right up until the moment they'd struck the match.

I turned around abruptly. Palmer was standing behind me, lit cigarette and matchbox in one hand, the extinguished match in the other. I realized that I could also detect another sharp smell, this one definitely animal rather than mineral.

"Not lost, are we?"

I thought: I can yell, if I have to. The others would be close enough by to hear a really good scream, if it came to that, wouldn't they? But I was far enough away not to hear their shouts or the dogs and their racket. Then I realized my mouth was already so dry from running that I might not be able to make a noise if I had to. I tensed up, wondering whether tearing headlong into an unfamiliar forest was a good idea.

I swallowed. "I guess I'm not so lost if I've found you."

Palmer stuck the burnt out end of the used match into his mouth briefly and then carefully replaced it in the box, which he tucked away into a shirt pocket. I realized he was practicing good woodcraft by not littering.

"Well, there are no prizes for finding the fox here, I can tell you that," said Palmer heavily. "I know the dogs don't know it; they can't help themselves, poor buggers. It's all in-

stinct with them. But I want to make very certain that *you* understand that." That last he said with slow, careful emphasis.

Any second now, I thought, bracing myself.

"All this rushing about, looking for things that really
aren't there. Seems a bit of a waste of time to me."

Palmer stepped forward. I, unwillingly, stepped back a
pace, all too ready to spring away, if necessary.

"I suppose that's his lordship's privilege, though I
wouldn't stand for a pack of strangers poking into my business, nosing about the place. I don't stand for it, simple as
that."

He means me, I thought, trying to keep my eye on Palmer.
I tried to remember whether the way behind me was clear.

Palmer stepped forward again. "I've work to finish
here—"

Here it comes . . . ready now. I tensed, nearly on tiptoe,
as if anticipating a starter's gun. The hunt's horn.

"—So you'd best be getting back to the house."

It took a minute for that to sink in. "Wh-what?" It wasn't
at all what I'd been expecting and it knocked me off my
balance.

Palmer looked up into the sky, held out an experimental
hand. "It looks like rain. You do have enough sense to get
yourself out of the rain, don't you?"

"I . . . huh?" I looked behind me, looked up into the sky,
confused.

"Turn yourself around, go back the way you came about
fifty yards. Pass through the clearing, and then follow the
path on your right. That will take you to the edge of the
woods, and you can find your way back well enough from
there. If not, the others will be back this way shortly. The
rain will wipe out the trail and the dogs won't know what to
do with themselves."

He grinned, knowing he'd got me wound up, and then
wiped his nose, showing off the scars on the back of his
hand, just as the sky, as if by command, opened up and the

rain began to pour down. At first, all I could hear was the rain on the leaves, but as the downpour grew heavier, cold drops began to penetrate the canopy and pelt us both.

"Looks like the fox gets away today, at any rate." With that, Palmer picked up the burlap which had been soaked in fox scent and passed very close by me as he headed off into the woods, vanishing within seconds. I turned, stupefied, and not knowing what else to do, followed his directions out of the woods.

I made it to open ground shortly and, to my relief, heard the others—humans and animals alike—not far behind me. As I waited for the rest of the hunt to catch up, I felt the rain weigh down my coat and beat onto the stiff canvas of my hat. That sound reminded me of camping in the rain, and as I scuffed back through the duff and underbrush, I wondered whether the fox that had gotten away today was Palmer or me.

Chapter 13

A S IT TURNED OUT, THE OTHERS MADE IT BACK TO THE house just ahead of me; I had been ahead of them but had come out at the far end of the garden rather than closer to the house where we'd begun. Inside there was a rack for dripping coats and hats and a mat covered with muddy shoes at one end of a long gallery, where the members of the hunt were busily descending upon a buffet groaning under sandwiches, quiche, and, I was grateful to see, a steaming kettle of soup. After a moment's hesitation, I took off my sneakers, joining the rest of the stocking-footed crowd as they mingled under the collective watchful gaze of generations of Pooter's ancestors.

It seemed that, at last, Jeremy had gotten his way; I bit into one of the sandwiches and found that it was cheese and pickle. The "pickle" here was a brown, lumpy, vinegary sauce that took me aback at first, so very different was it from the pickled cucumber slices I was used to. After a couple of bites, I realized that the sweetly sour taste nicely complemented the cheddar and, washed down with a bottle of beer, was quite heavenly.

I saw Rory and he waved; he'd knotted a dishcloth around his boot rather than finding a piece of twine. I thought about having another sandwich, but decided to try the soup instead. It was a curried carrot that drove the last of the cold and damp from me. As I ate, I heard a despondent sigh next to me.

An older man, in a tweed jacket and corduroys so worn there were patches of wale rubbed away, stood next to me in his wooly-stockinged feet, pondering the soup with dismay. His hair was more salt than pepper, wiry; he had overlong eyebrows that curled in mesmerizing directions. Add a round, almost non-existent little chin and a hooked nose and it all made him look quite owlish. He looked at me and shrugged, smiling sadly.

"I suppose it's warm and wet, but soup to me means 'chicken' or maybe 'split pea,' " he said in a mournful tone. "I don't hold much with too many spices. They unsettle me so."

"I was just about to return my bowl; can I take yours for you?"

"Oh, that's very kind of you."

When I returned from the buffet, Jeremy was talking with the older man and quickly introduced me. "Now, Emma, I'm very glad that you've met Gilstrap here, I was meaning to introduce the two of you. He's a very fine historian and I was just telling him how you were working with Jane Compton, eh, Edward?"

"Not really an historian," Mr. Gilstrap said, "but I have spent quite a bit of time studying the town and church records of Marchester and I dare say I know them as well as anyone."

"Not really a historian!" Jeremy said. "Don't let him fool you! He's the recording secretary of the Marchester Historical Society, has been since anyone can remember!"

"Pooter here has been telling me that you were going to look at the pictures in the hall. I was wondering if I could join you? I do like to have a look at them every so often. I'd like to publish a little pamphlet on them sometime, as a souvenir of the city, but it is so costly to print photographs and I am getting a little too old for such a project—"

"By all means, join us," I said.

"If you're ready, Emma," Jeremy said. "We'll spend a few moments with the pictures, and then be back for dessert before anyone knows we've gone."

We wound our way through the house back to the front hallway and I marveled again at the range of beautiful things in the house. I wondered whether, given sufficient funds and thirty generations' time, I could have put together as nice a collection.

"Here we are," Jeremy announced. "Actually, I'd better not tarry. If you think you can find your own way back, I'll just leave you to carry on. I really shouldn't leave the others, not when Jenny Ruggles is going to tell us the story of how she was thrown at Daddy's hunt in 1954."

Mr. Gilstrap chortled. "No, you couldn't miss that. You've only heard it forty times, so far."

"Then you'll be joining me?" Jeremy asked mischievously.

"Good God, no. I was there in 'fifty-four and it wasn't that funny then; it gets worse every year. Please don't trouble yourself on our account, but go, a willing lamb to the slaughter."

Mr. Gilstrap and I strolled along the entryway from the far end, meaning that we were traveling backward through time, each picture a little earlier than the last, moving from the nineteenth- and twentieth-century landscapes to the earlier portraits, until we got to the end nearest the door. The first five pictures were portraits, of men who looked like clergy; they might have been prominent townsmen, but they didn't look like connections of Jeremy's. All the Hyde-Spofford portraits in the long gallery where lunch was being served had a similarity about the nose and the chin that marked the family right to the present day. Now that I considered some of Rory's features beneath the makeup, I recognized the similarity he and his uncle bore to the pictures. But these portraits—the ones that showed views of Marchester in the front hallway—all depicted a landscape behind them, most likely the lands over which the men held sway, and in each of these the old abbey was still standing intact. It was in the third, the one Dora had indicated, dating to more than fifteen years after the lightning strike and devastating fire, that the abbey was first shown as a ruin.

I told Mr. Gilstrap about Dora's letter. I peered at the picture and he put on his glasses and squinted at the plate that had been screwed into the frame, sometime in the nineteenth century by my guess. He read it out loud: " 'Frobisher Cholmondeley, 1449–1521, c. 1520, Artist unknown, English.' Well, that's obvious! Look at that chin! Those watery eyes! Only a fellow countryman could have captured them so accurately."

I studied the portrait, close enough to smell the must of old wood and paint. "He does look a little porcine, doesn't he?"

Mr. Gilstrap snorted. "Like he shoved all his siblings away from the trough. He seems to have done all right for himself, at any rate, making it to threescore and ten years in a time when most people didn't live nearly as long as that. But do you see what your friend was after you to find?"

I shook my head. "Not yet. I wonder if it hasn't something to do with scale or aspect, or something."

"Well, I see what catches my interest. Always has done." He grinned, quite pleased with himself.

I shook my head and smiled. "What's that?"

"The river," he said triumphantly. "That's always been the thing that's determined how the town changed through time. Even in my day, the river was the important thing, all that free power? But there's lots in the history that you can't see in the church records, or the tax documents, or you won't, unless you learn to see between the lines. For example, I mentioned that the factory was important during the war. Can you guess why else the river was so important?"

After I tried "water power" and "communication" and "trade," I gave up.

"You're nearly there," Mr. Gilstrap said. "Smuggling, of course. The black market. Very busy around here. The war was an extraordinary time. Mads Crawford, she could tell you all the stories. She was the one who was here, I was off at infantry training. But she and her friend Caroline Green, later Ashford, were right dashers in those days. Practically running things at home—most of the men in the service, of course, many killed in the raids, a few gone missing and no one knows what happened to them, whether they got caught in a bombing, or ran off or what. So the ladies were running the show at home and it was hard for them to give that up when the war ended. I tell you, although some of the blokes didn't care for what the ladies had learned, in the factory and the home reserves and all, I liked a girl with dash then. Still do. But if you ever want to hear what Marchester was really like back then, buy old Mads a glass of something stronger than tea and you'll get an earful, I promise you. But let's have a look at your picture here."

As far as portraits went, it wasn't very good. Frobisher Cholmondeley's fingers were interlaced and rested on his lap like a pile of fat white sausages, his cheeks both plump and wrinkled, and his mouth small and insipid, possibly even beyond the art of a better painter to flatter. His robes and hat were flat blocks of color, with no fold or even a bit of braid to distinguish them.

But looking over the sitter's shoulder and out the window, it was possible to see where the painter's real interest was: outside the room in which he worked and down on the field before the abbey. The tiny block of landscape in the upper right hand corner, less than one-ninth of the entire picture, was a jewel in miniature. There was only one tree, to the far left of the window frame, but each of its minute leaves was painstakingly rendered in a range of colors that was inconceivable, given the principal figure in the foreground, which was an almost childish cartoon. The patch of green meadow that spread out before the abbey—still standing at this point, shortly before its ruin—was lovingly depicted, the minute dots of bright color immediately suggestive of wildflowers. The stones of the abbey buildings must have struck the painter as part of the landscape, for they were as carefully drawn as the natural features had been, and the river was a bright, lively slash behind the abbey ruin that immediately drew the eye. A few small buildings could be seen across the river, small both as a matter of perspective and in social consequence next to the abbey, like the diminutive portraits of slaves next to the kings and queens in Egyptian wall paintings.

"Looks like the lad wished he was outside with the cows by the river," Mr. Gilstrap murmured. "Anywhere but in that room with himself there."

I was confused, a little annoyed at being waked from my reverie. "What lad?"

"The painter, of course. Although I'm assuming it was a lad, most painters must have been at that time, mustn't they?"

"I don't know," I said. "I suppose you're right. His emphasis is really down in that field, by the abbey, isn't it? That's where all his energy and focus are. I suppose that's what Dora meant, when she said that I would find it out."

I spent another few minutes staring at the landscape, but could find nothing of what my infuriating colleague might have meant. The abbey ruin seemed to be along the same stretch of river, its orientation the same as the one now indicated by the last bit of standing wall, and although the field had been filled over the years with more and more houses and small businesses, it all looked maddeningly correct to me.

Damn Dora! I thought vehemently. Why couldn't she have just told me her idea? Why did she always have to be grandstanding?

"I give up, for the moment," I said to Mr. Gilstrap. "I just don't see what I'm supposed to see."

"I can't make out anything unusual, myself. Nice of your friend to be so specific, wasn't it?" he said dryly.

"Well, that's just her way." I was annoyed to find myself defending Dora against just the same charges I'd been laying at her door an instant ago. "If you want to see what's for dessert, I'll be along in a moment."

"I think I will; a cup of tea would do me just right about now. Very nice to have met you, Mrs. Fielding."

I smiled. "And you, Mr. Gilstrap."

I took my notebook out of my pocket and made a note of the information on the brass plaque before I made a hasty sketch of the painting. I'm not much good at drawing freehand—any virtue in my artifact drawings or plans is strictly a matter of hours of study and too many erasures and measurements—but did a fair enough rendering of the sitter and the view out his window. I made the most effort with the buildings, the river, and the abbey, because they were the things I'd want to draw on later, so to speak.

When the disturbance down the hallway intruded upon me, I had been too much in my own little world, immersed in a four-hundred-fifty-year-old landscape, a detail no more than four by four inches of the whole picture, to move discreetly away, as I should have. Ordinarily I would have claimed eminent domain and since I was there first, waited for the others to apologize and move on, but I wasn't on my own turf and I really did not want to interrupt George Whiting again.

"—If it had been anything but archaeology, if it had been anyone but that bloody Compton woman, it would never have happened," he insisted, quietly for him, but quite loudly enough for me to hear. He was standing so close to her, almost as if he'd been leaning on her while he cried.

"George, you know that's not true. You know that's not the point at all—"

I was surprised at how stern Sabine Jones sounded; she was not in the least intimidated by Whiting, personally or physically. Despite the hole in her sock and the dried leaf caught amidst a tangle of blond hair and combs, she had a force of personality that insisted you take her seriously.

"—So why don't you let me help you? As for Ellen, you know I can help you there, if you'll let me . . ."

Whiting's voice was muffled now, but I could make out a bit. "I can't . . . It's all I can do to—"

As surprised as I was to see George Whiting so deflated, so unlike the strutting, aggressive figure I knew, I didn't wait to hear the rest of it. Having no place to hide, I turned and was about to head back down the hallway toward the gallery where the luncheon was being served, when I saw Palmer at the other end. Our eyes met, and without hesitating, I instinctively turned and hurried back toward the entryway and the front door. Perhaps if I hurried past, Whiting wouldn't recognize me and Sabine mightn't say anything; they needn't know that I had heard any part of their conversation.

As soon as my feet hit the marble floor, I knew I couldn't go out the front door: I was still in my stocking feet and it was pouring with rain outside. I hesitated again, but slid forward on the cool stone floor. It was a horrible moment when the vicar and the contractor broke off to stare at me, and I wished I could sink under the decorative marble tiles.

"I was heading out . . . I forgot my shoes," I said, knowing just exactly how inane I sounded.

"Emma, perhaps I'll save introductions for another time," Sabine said, smoothly and pointedly.

Which was fine with me. I nodded my head and turned to go, ready to face an army of Palmers, when George Whiting looked up. His face hardened as he recognized me.

"Oh, no, I know well enough she's another fucking archaeologist. She's in with Jane Compton, I know that well enough."

Something about the way he kept harping on archaeology struck me, but I had no time to consider it now. "Mr. Whiting. I'm very sorry for your—"

"Don't ever waste your pity on me!"

"George, get hold of yourself!" Sabine hissed.

"—Loss, but the other day, I only wanted to help my friend. Surely you can—"

"I only wanted to help my friend," he lisped back at me, face contorted. "Isn't it a kind and decent thing to want to help its friend! You don't know anything of my loss, and that's well enough with me. You've shown more interest in it than some others who have more right have done. All I can say, missy, is that you have a lot to learn about choosing your friends, and even more about choosing your enemies! For you needn't worry yourself about Jane Compton"—he spat out the words like he'd eaten a bug by accident—"that nasty bitch will devour you before she disturbs one hair on her head! And as for me, if I catch you near me or mine again, I shall very gladly ring your neck."

He turned and slammed the heavy front door open and stormed out into the rain, not bothering to shut the door behind him. I stood, the cold of the marble chilling my feet, blinking.

Sabine shook her head and sighed. "Emma, get your shoes. I'll give you a lift home."

After making my good-byes to Jeremy, I found my shoes and coat and tried calling Jane and Greg. No one was at home, so I met Sabine out at her car, which smelled of her hand-rolled cigarettes. We drove back toward Liverpool Road through the rain, not speaking until something finally forced me to ask: "Sabine, what was George Whiting doing at Jeremy's? Surely he wasn't there for the hunt, not so soon after his daughter's death?"

"No, of course not." There was a long pause from the right hand driver's side, interrupted by the squeak-thump of the windshield wipers. She perched right on top of the steering wheel, not a very confident driver. "No, George had come to drop off a check for a fundraiser, a dinner that Pooter's having in a month. He'd promised to get it to Pooter early, to pay the deposit for the caterers, and he didn't trust the post with a sum so large."

"Oh."

She darted a quick, remonstrative glance at me, then immediately turned back to the road. "That's the kind of man he can be when . . . under other circumstances. Julia's murder . . . and everything, well, you have to forgive him, Emma. He's in horrible pain."

"I see." And I did, but then again, I couldn't afford to be as forgiving as Sabine Jones. She hadn't seen Whiting threaten Jane, call her a murderess.

We pulled up to 98 Liverpool Road. I noticed all the lights were off in the house; Greg had told me that they would be home all day.

"Thanks for the ride," I said finally.

She leaned back in her seat, glad to have the break from driving. "Not at all. I had to get going anyway. I must get ready for tomorrow."

I wrinkled my brow. We weren't working tomorrow, as far as I knew . . .

Sabine laughed. "Tomorrow's Sunday, you heathen. My busy time, well, the morning, at least, so I must polish up the sermon tonight. Cheers, Emma."

"See you."

There was no one at home. I went up to my room, noticing that Andrew's door was open now. I remembered that Greg had said he'd come back last night. Why they put up with him I'd never know. He didn't seem to be all that hot at his job; he hadn't even prepared a report for Jane yet about the skeleton we'd worked on my first day, as far as I could tell. I wanted to see a copy of that and the police report, particularly to see what he'd made of the twentieth-century button. There was something about the stratigraphy, too, that I wanted to double check. I didn't care whether Jane and Greg were unconcerned; I wanted to see it for myself.

I sat down on my bed and stared at the ferny green Laura Ashley wallpaper. I was too wound up to sit and read the novel I hadn't finished on the plane, so I took out the file on Mother Beatrice that Morag had given me and went down to the kitchen to read it. But I couldn't get comfortable in the chairs, and the empty room had that same hollow loneliness that had given me the shivers the day I'd found the pictures of Julia in the darkroom. The parlor, perfect for lounging with a glass of wine, mocked my studiousness on a wet Saturday afternoon, and it was impossible to juggle the contents of the file while struggling to sit upright in the soft cushions of the couch. The whole place echoed of Jane and Greg and I decided that if I didn't feel at home here, I could at least move to neutral territory. I got my coat, umbrella, and file and reasoned that since there was no library that I knew of within walking distance, I might as well go to the pub, someplace where nobody knew my name. A quiet pint and an hour or so of anonymity would be just the thing I needed, as Greg had suggested, to get better acquainted with Mother Beatrice, as Morag saw her. Alas, as with so many of my plans on this trip, it was not to be.

Chapter 14

PLEASED AS I WAS WHEN IAN THE BARTENDER AGAIN recognized me in a friendly fashion, I couldn't help but be a little disappointed when I heard my name called out from across the room. A small group of Jane's graduate students were sitting in the corner waving to me. I recognized the two who'd asked me to sign books for them, Nicola and Will, and the Scottish Gareth, and Lucy, who'd told me about Andrew and the worm ritual.

"Join us, Professor Fielding," Nicola, the small brunette, called.

Since they all scooted aside to make room for me, I didn't think I could refuse without being impolite. Still, I reasoned as I took a sip of my beer to keep it from sloshing, maybe it would be nicer to have the pleasant company of barely acquaintances on such a dispiriting day.

Then, of course, there was the awkward silence as everyone struggled to think of something to start the conversation. "Is this a regular Saturday thing for you all?" I asked.

"No."

"Yes."

"Sometimes."

"We're just meeting tonight before we go off to the cinema," Gareth explained. He hooked his overlong hair out of his eyes with his pinkie, revealing a skull and crossbones earring. "It beats sitting around and drinking and making fun of my burr. Are you meeting Professor Compton and Greg here?"

"No, they're out. I just came to do a little work, get out of the house, you know."

"D'you always work on the weekends, even when you're on holiday?" Will asked.

"Well, this isn't so much a real vacation for me as a chance to visit with Jane and do some documentary research at the same time. My husband and I are going away at the end of the summer, before classes start."

"Where are you going, then?" Nicola said.

I had to laugh. "I couldn't tell you. Brian's keeping it a surprise."

"Oh, isn't that lovely?" Lucy said. "So it's not all work and no play for you, then. It seems that Jane is always slaving away. I like archaeology, but I don't want a job that is going to keep me from having a life too." She blew out a sigh that lifted her bangs from her forehead.

"You seem to do pretty well for yourself, Lucy," Gareth pointed out. The rest laughed. "I haven't noticed you in the library lately."

"Well, it's summer, isn't it?" Lucy replied. "I do my work during term and then a bit of fun and then off to dig in July. I'm not like Julia, but I do all right. No one can say I can't."

"So there was nothing else for Julia?" I asked noncommittally, taking another sip of beer. "No job, no outside interests, no boys?"

"Are you joking?" Will said. "The original girly swot."

"She was pretty dedicated to her schoolwork," Nicola agreed. "Didn't often come out with the rest of us."

"Now, that's not fair," Lucy protested. "You're all making her out to be, I don't know, standoffish. She was really brilliant and she was very shy, but she wasn't horrible or anything. She had other interests, she just didn't go for the usual things that we do. But a week or so back, she and I went to get a reading done. You know, for a laugh, had our tarot cards read."

"You never did!"

"We did so, Gareth. She was looking pretty down about something; I think she'd been on the phone to her dad." Lucy looked sad. "Masses of problems in the family, I reckon. And so I just sort of suggested it, mostly to try and cheer her up."

"So what'd they say?" Will asked.

She settled back and toyed with the coaster under her beer. "It wasn't what I thought, it was all very flashy, high tech. Gave us recordings and all, didn't they? I mean, they didn't do us together, but I just asked about grades and you know, whether a certain someone was coming back from Jordan soon to sweep me off my feet—"

Here there was some laughing at an inside joke. "So what did the psychic say?" I asked.

"Oh you know." Lucy waved her hand. "Usual. Loads of work ahead of me, but I'll succeed in the end."

"And was that with regards to a first or Maurice, d'you reckon?"

There was some playful scuffling between Lucy and Gareth. Nicola said, "I'm sure Julia was asking about exam questions or the like. I mean, I never saw her with a boy. Twenty-two and no men in your life? What's the point?"

"You are being mean. She was perfectly nice; she helped me whenever I was having problems with my theory. I hate theory. And she did so have a boyfr—" But Lucy clammed up very quickly.

"Come on, you can't just leave it there." There was silence in the group after Will's pleading, hoping to force her into an answer.

Lucy hesitated. "I wasn't supposed to know. She . . . well, I'm sure it wouldn't do her any harm now, poor thing, but she was seeing someone . . . someone she wasn't supposed to be seeing, and I wouldn't want to get him in trouble, would I? Besides, I think she thought it was nearly over, so it doesn't matter, does it, so I would never say to anyone. No call to."

Oh, yes, there was plenty of call to, I thought. Good God, it makes all the difference in the world.

"Come on, who was it?" Nicola said. "Whisper it to me, I won't tell anyone . . ." She winked at the rest of us.

"You can be such a bitch, sometimes! You don't care about anyone, do you, Nicola?"

And with that, Lucy shoved her way out from the table and out of the pub.

"Lucy, come on! God, Nicola." Gareth ran after her.

"And I think we'd better be heading off. Sorry, Professor Fielding. I guess feeling about Julia is still running a bit high for Lucy. For all of us, really." Will paused awkwardly. "Enjoy the rest of your evening."

"Thanks."

I found myself alone again, but with a whole new set of worrying thoughts. A boyfriend she wasn't supposed to be seeing? Who might have been ending things, she or him? This put a whole different light on the situation and suddenly, I wanted to meet the young stranger who'd accosted me outside the Fig and Thistle again. The thought of Greg's unwonted and unpleasant volubility of Wednesday evening also sprang into my mind. What had he said, "I tried to give her the space she wanted . . . I don't like to think how I tried"? Whose space had he tried to respect? Had he meant that he didn't like to think how hard he had to work to put Jane from his mind or that he didn't like to think, literally, about what he'd *done* to try and ignore Jane? Had he had an affair with Julia? Or was it something much worse than that? Had he killed her, to take some of the burden from Jane?

Greg loved Jane, that much was obvious. He'd repeatedly

said he'd do anything for her, and frankly, it was a little scary to see the changes he went through the other night. I wasn't sure how to explain it. I knew how much I loved Brian, so much that I felt like I had to shut down that part of my life when I was away from him so I wouldn't be overwhelmed by what I was missing, what I was so used to having near to me. I would try to fill that void with work, to make the time pass faster, and that worked to a certain extent. But it was like having a limb amputated and trying to ignore that it was gone. I could function perfectly well, for a while, until that next phone call came and I remembered what life was usually like. That was the hardest, just after the phone calls. And I knew Brian felt the same way as Greg, he'd do anything for me, though he'd never said it like that.

The difference between Brian and Greg was that Brian was sure I'd come back. Greg wasn't sure about Jane at all.

Greg was desperate.

What if Greg had tried to remove some of Jane's fear of being outstripped for her. What if he'd tried to remove at least one of "the Julias in the world"?

One horrendous thought immediately liberated me to think another. I recalled Greg's rapid changes in mood that evening, and, at the end, how various degrees of anger, sadness, and despair had vanished or seemed to with Brian's phone call. All of it was gone in an instant. Had all that emotion been some kind of show, a distraction, like a bird dragging its wing as if wounded, to lead a predator from the nest? Had Greg been trying to draw attention to himself because I had been getting too close to finding out something about *Jane* and Julia? Surely Jane wasn't that insecure . . . but she had told Andrew not to underestimate what she would do to protect her position . . .

I shuddered and shoved my beer glass away. I couldn't put the thoughts away from me so easily, though I decided I couldn't pursue them any further at the moment. Merely thinking them had been enough; they wouldn't fade and I knew I would eventually have to come back to them, with a more critical eye and a firmer resolve. But for now, I could convince myself that I would still be doing justice to my involvement in this mess by studying Morag's file of information about Mother Beatrice.

The file folder was an old one, pale lilac in color; the fine creases that had been worn in from being carried about were darker, giving the thing the look of flesh, aged and veined. Longer than the files I was accustomed to, to accommodate the longer A-4 paper that was standard in Britain, the folder also felt different, a little less rigid, maybe. I catalogued these details casually and opened the file.

There wasn't much in it, really, and everything there was a photocopy, presumably of Morag's original findings. Nice as it would have been to have the originals—to get as close to the same experience as Morag had had in handling them—I noticed a few things about the copies as well. The first one, for example, was a copy of a newspaper clipping that had been held in a clear plastic sleeve to protect it. The image of the sleeve, and the lint and dust that clung to it, was like a film, a thin veil over the image of the clipping, which looked quite dark and crepey with age. Even if someone hadn't written the date in pen in the corner of the photocopy, June 12, 1908, I would have guessed that the newspaper article was old by the fine web of lines across it and the old fashioned style of the print itself. Even the tone of the article, a little summary of the history of antiquities and curiosities of Marchester, felt creaky to me, personal and didactic, almost conversational in style, as if an old professor was used to lecturing spontaneously and unchallenged on any topic, a far cry from the impersonal reportage of today. "And, if the visitor is pleased to turn to his left and follow the river past the new church of St. Alban's—noting the lovely windows, designed in 1732—he will come upon the ruins of Marchester Abbey—" The photocopy had been carried around for a long time.

The next photocopy was several pages long and from a book of late nineteenth-century vintage on the history of

Marchester and Marchester-le-Grand by Geoffrey Reese. These photocopies were from the section on the churches and several paragraphs that had been underlined in pencil described the abbey and in one line, the presence of Mother Beatrice and her works there. One poetical turn of phrase caught my eye: "And she tended the poor and the sick, the living and the dead, all the days of her life." That reminded me of the newspaper article I'd just seen, wherein a line ran very similarly: "And for the rest of her life, she tended the poor and the sick, as well as the living and the dead." It seemed perfectly clear to me that the author of the newspaper article had read, digested, and used the text in the book by Mr. Reese. I wondered if the phrase hadn't come from a translation of a description in Latin or old French, and this would explain its slight oddness to modern eyes. There was an asterisk and I would have checked for end notes, but whoever had copied the section hadn't also included the notes section or the title of the book for me to note.

A much more recent encyclopedia article about Marchester and other towns in the central south coast had but a single line, stating that among the events of the late fifteenth century was a line from another, uncited church history describing a falling out between the abbess and the church fathers, who had at first cut off then reinstated funding to the abbey after Mother Beatrice's time. This one had someone's—presumably Morag's—flowery handwriting in the corner, where she recorded the date and the name of the volume: 1987.

Even more recent than that was a clipping from a magazine, *The New Pagan's Almanack,* only about five years old, that had a very amateurishly done pen-and-ink drawing of a medieval-style lady—complete with a veil and wimple and embellished with background whorls—who was meant to be Mother Beatrice. The article was two pages long, one page of which was devoted to the title and the picture, by "Rowan Blessingtree," who claimed to channel denizens of the spirit world. The article was poorly written, and the few facts that

I was aware of from my readings on the abbey were badly
mangled; dates were off by fifty years or more, names were
misspelled, and a picture of a brooch was at least two centuries too early. This seemed to be where Morag was getting
most of her information about Mother Beatrice; as far as I
could tell, the information that she'd been persecuted for her
supposed pagan beliefs was based on none of the information that I'd seen; Rowan Blessingtree hadn't even read the
old book by Reese. Like the other photocopies that were in
the file, this article had no bibliography or a notes section.

There was nothing else. I sighed and stacked everything
carefully back into the file, reminding myself that I should
show it to Jane, so that she could check it out, if she hadn't
already. She might even know the source of the quote in the
local history and the newspaper story, I thought. Maybe
she'd want to make a copy of the article about Mother Beatrice, just for a private souvenir—it would be very interesting
to see whether she could explain why some of these notions
had found their way into print. From little mistakes like this,
whole histories had been diverted down wrong paths. Misin-
terpretation—cultural or translational—was probably responsible for more historical inaccuracies than anything
else. I should also show her the picture I'd drawn of Jeremy's painting and Dora's note. Maybe she could make
something of that.

I thought about having another beer, but then checked my
watch and realized that it was very late. I needed to make an
appearance back at Jane and Greg's at some point, and it
might as well be now. With another sigh, I put Morag's
folder under my coat and headed out once again into the
rain, hoping that I wasn't making any of those little mistakes
that would send me chasing after wild geese.

The next morning, Sunday breakfast was a rather more
elaborate affair than usual. It took my mind off my worries
and also made up for another round of early morning night-
mares, just the same as the ones that had greeted me each
dawn for the past couple of days. Jane had gotten up and

made strawberry crepes for us, complete with a rich filling that I suspect was at least half sour cream, half cream cheese, and half crème fraîche. Better than that, Jane brought out the Bodum coffee plunger again and I was as content as I could be. For the moment. No sooner had we finished, lingering another few moments over the empty dishes and a lazy, show-offy argument about a crossword clue in the Sunday paper, than Jane announced that she had to get right to work.

I expected Greg to speak up at this point, but he didn't. So I did. "On Sunday too? I was—"

"Afraid I won't be able to make it out to the site tomorrow," Jane broke in, her voice brittle, avoiding my glance. "It's back to the station for me, I'm afraid, and another bloody round of questions. So I'd like to get things sorted today, try not to lose too much time."

I dropped the fork I'd been toying with with a clatter. How could she do this, prepare a breakfast like the one we'd had, make pleasant and erudite conversation, and then casually announce that she was going in for a second round of questioning about a murder? It was clear to me that Jane was unhappy about the situation, but her capacity for compartmentalization was nothing short of miraculous. I would have sent everyone off to the pancake house and then retired to a hot bath with a bottle of whiskey. No, that wasn't fair to Jane: when I had been in a similar situation, I'd behaved almost as—what? Coolly? Competently?—when I'd packed up the field school and decamped Penitence Point. Except that I remember losing my cool a little more often, letting the ragged veil slip a little more noticeably.

What's more, did I, as a house guest, need to refrain from asking too many questions about one's session with the cops? As a friend, was I obliged to? And I couldn't help but wonder what the police made of an interviewee who was so cool, so self-possessed. "What do they want now?" I asked.

"Trying to confirm a few things, is all they'll tell us," Greg answered. "Though if you ask me, I think they've a lot

of cheek." He turned to his wife. "There's absolutely no reason for this, not even circumstantial evidence to link you to
Julia's death. And I think it's time we called the lawyer who
was recommended to you by Sabine."

Jane nodded agreement and pushed back her chair. "You
can look after yourself, right, Emma? I feel awful about not
being able to spend more time with you, but I'm afraid it's
just bad luck." She made as if to shift the dirty dishes to the
sink, when I stopped her.

"If you want to get to work, go straight ahead. I'll take
care of these. Greg, what are you up to this morning?"

"Actually, after I get done tending to Hildegard's tank, I
thought I'd see if Aunty wanted to go to church. She was
very blue yesterday, I've never seen her so down. I'll take
her in for one of Sabine's shockingly liberal sermons and
see if that doesn't fan her up a bit."

"Is she coming for dinner tonight?" Jane said. "Mads often comes for dinner on Sunday nights," she explained to me.

"I shouldn't plan on it," Greg replied. "I don't even know
if I'll be able to get her to go to church with me."

"Off you go, then," I said. "I've got this under control,
and I'll just go for a bit of a stroll later, so we're all set."

"Thanks so much, Emma. I knew I could rely on you,"
Jane said.

I looked up from clearing the table. My friend's words
had been perfectly level. Not a break or a hitch or a hesitation or any emotion of any sort whatever. Her face was hard
and I thought I saw a peevish look vanishing as I watched, as
though my own self-reliance was some irritation, some
threat to her. She went upstairs, followed by Greg.

I shrugged and put the rest of the dishes in the sink, looking around for the dish detergent. I found a heavy white bottle marked "Fairy Liquid," strangely industrial looking for
its purportedly ethereal contents, and squirted some of the
green liquid into the hot water. If my friends were going to
slide so comfortably into their accustomed roles, Jane the
workaholic, Greg the St. George in search of a lady to de-

fend, then I could at least be graceful enough to get on with the the one I'd assumed, which was—what? Nosy Parker? Optimistic, can-do American? I didn't know. But apparently I did. Even before I knew that I had a plan, even before the dish liquid had risen up in a steamy froth of bubbles, I realized that I was going to use the newspaper article about Julia's death and disappearance and retrace her steps as closely as I could.

I borrowed Jane's map of the town, Marchester A–Z (momentarily confused when she'd pronounced it "aytozed"), and found where Julia's apartment had been. It was on the other side of the river from the site, in a part of town that was busy during the week, with small shops and a local market nearby. It was in a run-down block, but not worrying, more like "cheap and cheerful." After mustering a little courage, I went up to the front door and looked at the names next to the buzzers on the intercom: "Whiting, J." was on the third floor. I went back across the street and looked up at the third—no, fourth floor—Jane always referred to the first floor as the "ground floor." There were curtains over the two windows. One was made out of a large piece of cloth, a dark blue Indian-looking print, and the other was also dark blue but not matching otherwise; they hung askew. It would have been walking distance to the university from here, with the site even closer. It might have been Julia's first place on her own, after a lifetime in her parents' home, school dormitories, and university housing. The hopefulness of place made me unbelievably sad. To someone on her own for the first time, it would have seemed a palace, all the necessities at hand.

Next I checked the map to see where 375 Green Cross Road was. Although it was quite a piece away from the apartment, back over the bridge and to the east of the site, the new church, and Julia's house, I didn't mind the walk. In fact, I found myself walking more and more slowly toward the Whiting residence, my stomach knotting itself until it sent tingles up my spine.

The Whiting house was in a cul-de-sac that appeared to be secluded from the rest of the town, hidden by a cleverly maintained stand of trees. The metaphorical distance between Julia's apartment and this place could not have been greater. In fact, the difference between number 375 and the other places in this upscale neighborhood was striking. Number 375 was older than most of the houses in town, but was still only of 1920s vintage, an elephantine mock-Tudor in superb condition: no flaking paint, no shabby, lived-in gentility, none of the relaxed, benign neglect that characterized the rest of the street. The lawn and shrubs I could see in the front were maintained with a precision that I found off-putting. The grass was as smooth and green as a cut emerald, the half dozen evergreen shrubs that hid the foundation were topiary mounds, their bottom branches trimmed a uniform six inches from the ground, so that the effect was one of a row of hoop-skirted ladies coyly showing their ankles. There wasn't a stray leaf or branch lying underneath the trees, not a flower that leaned out of its rank, and crabgrass would have been ashamed to consider showing itself there. I began to think that there were undergardeners who remained concealed until a pine cone dared fall, and then ran out to scoop the errant vegetation up in a fluid motion, like the ball boys on a tournament tennis court. The notion that a child's ball or a pet dog would have been prohibited from this space sprang to mind. The whole facade announced: we are immaculate, we are respectable, we have arrived, and you will never see the seams where we snuck in. *Noli me tangere.* I thought longingly of the happy mess I'd left at home and experienced a profound pang of homesickness.

The windows were darkened and there was no sign of life anywhere on the grounds. I walked past and tried to peer into the back yard—*garden,* I corrected myself. From the small patch I could see through the wrought-iron fence, the back mirrored the front. No patio for parties, no much-loved garden shed housing the noisy old lawn mower, no deck furniture in this eerie place. I tried to imagine what it would be like to grow up in such an inhospitable house and suddenly could see how, if it had not been born in this place, Julia's quietness had stood her in good stead here. Such an inhuman precision would drive anyone to find quiet corners and unobtrusive amusements. It seemed to me that even the birds didn't bother to nest anywhere near here, or maybe it was just the rain that prevented me from hearing their song.

The next stop was the pub Julia had visited the night of her death. The Grub and Cabbage was nothing like either the Prince of Wales or the Fig and Thistle. On the edge of this tony district, it was of new construction that looked as though it had been poured from a bottle of "Acme Instant Public House." It wasn't open yet, so I headed for the next stop on my grim pilgrimage: the construction site.

A little farther on, away from the center of town and the dig, was Leather Street, a place that was full of new houses and the blank gaps where old buildings had been torn down to make way for new ones. In the middle of it all was a huge area fenced in with chain link that reached ten feet into the air, barbed wire around the top. There was only one gate, a massive sliding thing on wheels that reminded me of Hollywood evocations of medieval castles, fastened with a massive chain and padlock. I walked all the way around, just to make sure I wasn't missing some other entrance, and couldn't even find a hole where kids might have crawled through to play on the dangerous site or rob scraps or whatever kids might have done. There was no way in except for that gate, and there was no way through the gate without a key. As his house had demonstrated to me, there was nothing sloppy about the way that George Whiting conducted himself, but I didn't recall the police stating the construction site had been broken into. How had the murderer gotten in with a body? Or had Julia reached the construction site under her own power?

Having spent some time near construction sites—archae-

ologists are often called in to investigate what they uncover—I could tell that this was extremely well organized.
Trailer for plans and meetings, sheds for storage of tools,
piles of raw materials, cranes hoisted compressors into the
air to keep them hanging safely out of reach. Foundations
poured, rebar jutting up like claws into the sky. Dust making
everything a uniform color, save where bales of brick sat
like a thick, angry scar on the ground. There were two skips
or Dumpsters, new ones, it seemed, off to the side of an older
one, still festooned with the blue and white tape that warned
a police investigation was taking place here. I wondered
whether work had been allowed to continue here and made a
note to ask. If it hadn't, it struck me as a double blow to the
man: kill his daughter, then rob away his livelihood. Which
seemed to me to be an incredibly dangerous thing to try with
George Whiting. But what if that had been the goal in the
first place . . . ? Who would want to hurt him so? Palmer
sprang easily enough to mind, but I made myself think the
next fearful thought: Jane? Both had their reasons for hating
him. He had never shied from hurting either of them when it
suited him.

I walked around the construction site again, as much to
make certain that I hadn't missed another entrance as to give
myself time to think. I also tried not to look as suspicious as
I felt; it was ghoulish, what I was doing, but as far as anyone
else was concerned, I was only out for a walk. But as I
walked, any worries that I might have been watched slowly
dissolved, and between that and my growing confidence, I
began to relax, not move so skittishly. There were very few
people on the street, and most of these seemed to be hurrying, nicely dressed, to church at ten o'clock. The other
noises that I could hear from the street, strangely muffled
roars, I soon identified as the sounds of a televised soccer
match. The fact that these were occasionally overwhelmed
by anguished cries or violent cheering confirmed this for
me. Good. With any luck, for the next hour or so, I might
just be left largely unnoticed.

I was on my way back around to the front gate when I saw her. She stuck out as much as I did on that deserted street; more so, because her behavior was so erratic. At first I thought it was Morag, but it wasn't. I was fooled by the raincoat that reminded me of her dark, flowing clothes. This woman was taller, and had graying hair, and was dressed in street clothes that grew more distinct as I moved closer: skirt, blouse, shoes, stockings, all quite ordinary, upper-middle-class wear, well made but badly fastened and worn. The thing that was extraordinary was the woman's face—suffused with loss and grief so pervasive that it should have been a model for the theatrical tragedy mask, so openly emotional that I was automatically uncomfortable, more so, now, in this place where self-restraint in certain matters was a matter of national pride.

The other thing that was so alarming was her posture. She clutched at the fence, her arms out wide, and whether she was thinking of climbing up or tearing the fence down, I don't know, but her grip on the fence was so intense that I could feel the faint vibrations as they traveled through the cold aluminum links to where I'd stopped. Arms outstretched, she wept in agony, sobs that wracked her body and were communicated down the fence in increasingly loud waves. The fence was sturdily built—it had to be—but the woman succeeded in making that uncaring metal hum with her emotion. The hulking machinery on the other side, the bulldozers and cranes, remained unmoved.

I watched this, hoping that she would wear herself out, calm down, but it only seemed to build as she went on. I was closer now, moving much more slowly, wondering what the hell I should do, when I began to hear the words she was saying.

". . . Quiet now, it is quiet now, and there's no more strife, but I've lost my little girl and she's not here. She's so lost and I am lost and the quiet is horrible—"

What should I do? Ring a doorbell? Another roar went up from one of the houses and I knew the soccer match was still on. Finally, I thought I'd better just ask the woman herself if there was anything I could do. I think also that I was trying to deny that I knew who she must be.

"Are you—?" Don't be an idiot, Emma, of course she isn't. "Is . . . is there someone I can call?" Vaguely, I was aware of a car engine in the distance.

The woman turned to me and stopped speaking. She looked at me without comprehension, though she still clutched the fence like it was a life preserver in stormy seas.

"Can I help you? Can I call someone—?"

There was a revving of an engine as a car pulled up right alongside us. A dark green Jaguar. George Whiting got out of the driver's side and ran over to us.

I froze and acknowledged to myself who it was I was talking to.

"You can't call anyone. We're all lost now," the woman said to me.

Whiting seized the woman's left wrist. "Oh, Jesus, Ellen, what are you trying to do?" He saw me, recognized me, then yanked at her hand with a rough curse. The woman shrieked and banged herself against the fence, clutching at it with all her might. Whiting swallowed, and with forced patience, carefully prised her fingers off the links, one by one, until he had that hand free. "Ellen, Ellen, come on now. You don't want to do this. Come now, love."

I saw the blood then, coming from where the fence had torn at her palm, staining his hands too. Ellen Whiting writhed against her husband, but it was easier for him to remove her right hand, even while he still held her other wrist pinioned. He was a good deal shorter than his wife was but so very strong, and something about his insistence seemed to drain some of the fight from her. But as he started to lead her toward the car, the engine still running, she began to scream.

"Julia! Juu-lia! Juli—"

Whiting, with something that looked like practice, forced

his wife into the car and gently shut the door, cutting off the rest of her cry. He then turned around to me.

By this time, several doors had opened up and people were starting to peer out to find the source of the racket. George glanced at them, no more, then spoke to me.

"You remember what I said before." His words were low. "Bloody archaeologist. Don't you ever say a fucking word about this. Never."

And that was all. He was at the right hand driver's side before I could blink. He slammed that door and then gunned the engine. So overwhelmed was I by what I'd just seen that I just stared. As the Jaguar tore past me, I could see, briefly, that Ellen was no longer screaming, but sat, looking back at the fence, her bloodied hand pressed against the window as if in farewell, smearing the glass.

Chapter 15

IT MIGHT HAVE BEEN MY AWARENESS OF THOSE TWITCH-
ing curtains or the sudden rumbling of my stomach that
spurred me away from there. That is what I told myself; in
reality, I was driven away by the shock, the raw emotion of
what I'd left behind. Pain, madness, fear, anger were danger-
ously exposed like a wire with the insulation chewed off it.
What was most startling, what stayed with me longer than
Ellen's nearly mute misery, was the way that George Whiting had behaved toward her. He approached the scene with a
familiarity that bespoke weariness and a tenderness that
spoke of an abiding love and patience I wouldn't have imagined the man possessed. I recalled Jeremy's words—"rough
around the edges, but no worse"—and realized, in this instance, at least, it must be true.

And then there was Whiting's constant reference to archaeologists. It was so out of place with what he should have
been concerned with—a murdered daughter, a more than
distraught wife—that there must be something more than his
antipathy toward Jane behind it—

No, I realized. Blaming Jane, ranting about archaeologists, it was just noise, I was willing to bet, it was a necessary distraction, like Shylock crying over his lost ducats to mask his distress at Jessica's betrayal. Julia Whiting's profession was a minor thorn in her father's side, given the present circumstances, but focusing on that kept Whiting from thinking about the horrors that had lately enveloped his life . . .

I fled. I decided to have another look at the Grub and Cabbage, but promised myself I wouldn't stick around if it turned out to be like the Fig and Thistle.

Nothing could have been less similar. Despite the fact that it was a clean, well-lighted place, it was stuffed with all the appurtenances of a pub, but none of the life. I got the same feel from it as I did from certain theme restaurants in the United States, where clutter was scientifically accumulated and situated to produce a maximum level of inoffensive nostalgia. People came to this haven of hanging plants, toby jugs, and horse prints because it was conveniently situated on a busy road with a large parking area; they didn't know or care to know the name of the guy behind the bar, a pimply faced lad in an ill-fitting black bow tie and clean white shirt, who looked bored and out of place as he cut limes and washed glasses. From my seat, I watched as patrons entered—mostly couples—pausing at the door briefly. They were nonlocals passing through, it seemed, for a swift half and "real" steak and kidney pie. The waitress who took my order smiled briefly and asked if I thought it would stop raining soon, but didn't appear to hear my answer, her eyes focused somewhere past me. All in all, it seemed to me to be an excellent place to conduct an illicit affair and I wondered whether Julia hadn't arranged to meet her boyfriend here after her visit home and whether he met her before she was killed. The police in the newspaper article mentioned she'd stopped here, and left shortly thereafter.

I finished my half pint and plowman's lunch. It wasn't bad, but it sure wasn't good. The cheese was curled at the edges and the salad was wilted; I wondered whether the cold plate didn't indicate that it had been stacked with countless identical others in the industrial fridge. I had another look around. Maybe it was the way I'd spent my morning, maybe it was how it had finished, but the place seemed to me to be almost as gloomy as my evening at the Fig and Thistle. I certainly didn't feel threatened here, but equally, there was nothing inviting in this place, nothing that made me want to ease back in my seat and relax for a while. It was more as though I felt like I was part of a demographic being serviced. I never would have stopped here, ordinarily. So why hadn't I just walked back to the center of town, to the Prince of Wales? I could have ignored a grumbling tummy for another twenty or thirty minutes. Easily.

The answer was simple. I wasn't here to eat. I was here to ask questions. To investigate.

In that moment, I knew what Sabine had been after, why she'd been so angry when I'd first asked her about people in town. I threw down a bank note and some change and hurried out of there.

I found the vicar in the graveyard behind the church. Reverend Jones was still in her cassock, surplice, and stole, her hair was neatly pulled back and in as tidy shape as I had ever seen it. She was smoking and looking so tranquil under the oak tree that I hesitated. If Sunday morning was her busy part of the week, then how much more precious would the quiet moment after that be? I had just decided to turn around and come back another time, when the gravel I stepped on shifted and rattled. Sabine turned around quickly, a little irritated.

Her face relaxed only a little when she saw me. "Hello. Come to see me?"

"I don't want to bother you. This must be like Friday night for you." I noticed that her stole was embroidered: one side was covered with a multitude of tiny, finely wrought sheep. On the other was a shepherd carrying a single lost sheep. Someone had put a lot of handwork into that.

She waved me over. "There are no Friday nights in this

job. On the other hand, that also means there are no Monday mornings, really. Come on, have a seat." She patted the stone wall she was leaning against.

We sat there quietly for a while, Sabine smoking, me looking at the gravestones. I'd seen that there were a couple of good ones in the churchyard—meaning early ones with ghoulish, instructive carvings of winged hourglasses and skulls—but most of them around where we sat were from the nineteenth century. Yawn—I could get that at home. Rain ran down the stones and pattered on the leaves of the oak tree that sheltered us, and the calm was quietly wonderful. Of course it couldn't last.

"This is a marvelous place," I said. And it truly was, even in the gentle rain. I looked over my shoulder, across the river. The sky was closer, a more intimate sky than I was used to at home, and the green of the trees on the other side of the river in town was accented by the wet. A little sun and a cow and we would have had a Constable.

We sat quietly a moment longer.

"Maybe you can explain something," Sabine said. "When I used to go abroad more often, Americans would find out I was English and tell me how much they felt like they were coming home when they came to England. It always confused me. I don't suppose they were talking about genetic memory? That's a bit much, if you ask me. But they do tend to say it quite a lot. Why is that?"

I thought about it for a moment. "It is memory."

She frowned, not convinced. "You don't *really* think it's something passed down, do you?"

"I don't think it's so much genetic memory—I mean, not all Americans are descended from English colonists, right?—but a kind of cultural memory that gets built in school. You're taught English poetry and plays and literature, some of those images are bound to stick with you, become iconic. You watch enough Merchant–Ivory or Brideshead or even just PBS, and the landscape gets reinforced without you really paying attention to it. So that's why people think they recognize things and places and feelings when they get here. I don't think it's anything more than that."

"Hmm. Possible. Better than anything I came up with, I guess." She knew that wasn't why I was here.

I took a deep breath. "How did you become a priest? You'd been in geology before?"

Reverend Jones raised an eyebrow and stubbed out her cigarette. She reached under her robes, pulled out her papers and tobacco, and rolled another, looking at me curiously. "The two aren't unrelated. Nothing is, I suppose. I was on holiday, in Turkey. There was an earthquake. I was trapped for several hours under the rubble of the building I'd been in, a little cafe. It was gone, utterly destroyed. A pile of wood scraps and clay brick rubble. The owner, who was the only other person in there, was killed. Though not right away."

She was silent for a moment.

"That's where you got the scar?" I prompted, gesturing to the pale line over her brow.

"Oh, no. That? Tch, no, I got that playing rugby."

I had a distant image of a herd of burly men tossing a large white ball and slamming into each other with bone-crunching intensity. It wasn't such a stretch for Sabine, I guess—she enjoyed sport—but far from the peaceful quiet of the graveyard in which we sat. "You played rugby."

"At school." Sabine stuck her cigarette in her mouth and, hands freed, pulled up one leg of her trousers, revealing dark green nubbly socks. Rugby socks, I supposed. "Still miss it."

I realized that she had worn her rugby socks under her robes when she'd given her service that morning. "Got psyched up for your sermon today, did you?"

She grinned. "It is a bit like getting tooled up for a match." Then she resettled herself and looked serious again. "No, I wasn't badly hurt, aside from a lot of bruises and a broken collarbone. I was very lucky."

"And that's how you knew," I said.

"No, not a bit. It wasn't because I had survived and others hadn't. It isn't that simple." She seemed to struggle for her words. "I had always been religious. Very casual about it, but I believed nonetheless. My true conversion, if you will, the thing that solidified my faith, wasn't something I noticed right away. It was days after the quake, really. And my calling came even later after that."

I was determined to have it from her. I didn't care how personal it was, I needed to know. "It was the . . . what can I call it? The power of the earthquake?"

"No, it wasn't that either, though let me tell you, I never want to go through that again, believe you me. Even when I figured out what was happening, why the room, everything was shaking so much—even with my training, it took a moment—all I could think, as I tried to reach the door, was: "Bugger, I'm done for." Not very scientific, not very eloquent last thoughts, as I imagined they might be."

"So *how* did you *know?*"

"It wasn't because I knew something. It was because I stopped needing to know something. It was because I stopped being afraid. Oh, I don't mean I wasn't terrified at the time, I was. You can't know how bad it was. It was weeks after that I noticed, that little background hum of worry was gone. That everyday fear that always seemed to hang over me had vanished. The uncertainty, the anxiety that was always niggling away at me, gone."

"Well, I guess something like that put things into perspective for you—"

She broke in impatiently. "No, Emma, it was more than that. And before you ask, what was it, how do I know, I will tell you, I don't know. All I can say is that it was the most sure I've been of anything, ever. On very good days, in prayer, I am that sure again. It's called faith."

"I see." I didn't really.

Sabine didn't believe me either. "Let me try this. When you are working on some theory or other, it doesn't always match the data as soon as you know it's right, does it? You just really know, it feels right."

I shrugged; I had to grant her that.

"Well, it's just the same. It is that conviction that while I don't have all the answers and never will have, I am absolutely right on this one point." She looked at me. "So what is it that you are so unsure about, that you need to ask someone else how they know what they know?"

Suddenly, all my resolve leached away. "I feel stupid talking about it."

Sabine snorted. "Please don't let that stop you."

"First of all, let me explain: I'm not that religious—"

"Okay."

"I mean, I have ethics that I feel pretty strongly about, just nothing, you know, organized."

"Emma, it's okay."

"It's just that . . . lately . . . I've been feeling like . . . I'm in the middle of a lot of things. I keep finding myself in the center of . . . stuff."

Sabine gave me a sarcastic look. "Now I know you're better able to express yourself than that."

I took a deep breath. "Death. Lately, I'm finding myself surrounded by a lot of death."

"And why does that bother you?"

I looked at her. "Well, jeez. I mean, that's enough, isn't it?"

"Not really." She shrugged. "I find myself near a lot of death—"

She didn't get it, I thought. "No, I mean *violent* death—"

"Yes, that too. So do police officers, fire fighters, ambulance drivers, doctors, lots of people."

I spread my hands. "Yeah, but why me?"

"Ah, the eternal question."

"No, you know what I mean. Those others, they get in the middle of things because of their work, because they choose to. It's part of their jobs."

She nodded. "They asked for it."

"Well, yeah." I picked up a leaf from the ground and began pulling the stem from it.

"Assuming that you don't believe in a Godly plan, I think it's because you can." She carefully stubbed out her cigarette and immediately began rolling another with deft efficiency. "We talked about perspective before—well, rather, I was talking about it. You were ducking it—and I think we've come back to that. Death isn't unusual, we're just better at hiding it, pretending it doesn't happen these days. I think you just find yourself 'in the middle of it,' as you say, because of how you look at things. It seems a natural progression to me. Your job is, at times, to be a professional outsider. Mine too, really, except I haven't the luxury of distance, like you do."

"It's no luxury," I said. "You have to work hard to care about the dead, they're so removed from you."

"Yeah, but you have to work harder to care about the living," Sabine replied, "because they're much more likely to piss you off. But I digress. You've set yourself apart, you have a certain set of skills, and you have your 'strongly felt ethics.' That lets you see things others mightn't and you find yourself inclined to act upon them—even if you don't know why—because of those pesky ethics. The question is, you find yourself in a position to use these skills, where perhaps no one else can or would want to—I'll bet you don't get any prizes for your interest—"

I was reminded of Palmer's words: There is no prize for finding the fox.

"—So I'm left asking: What are you going to do about it?"

I stared at the river. Maybe the answer was out there.

After a minute, Sabine said, "It's not a rhetorical question, Emma. It's something you need to think about."

I threw the shredded leaf away. "I know. I have been thinking a lot about it lately. And I've come to this conclusion: I think part of it is because of something I went through, not too long ago. A very dear friend of mine died. Was murdered. I wanted it solved, for obvious reasons, of course, but also so I could have it settled in my mind, so I would no longer be suspected of it, for the sake of a lot of people. A lot of reasons. Because I felt so much of that, I know what these folks are going through, and I know, somehow, that I can help, especially since I know what it must be like for Jane to be accused . . ."

"And what if Jane is guilty?" Sabine pressed on. "Do you think you'll feel that strongly if you find out she's guilty? What happens then?"

Even though I knew the answer, I couldn't say it right away. "Even if she's guilty, I have to know. I realized that today when I was sitting in the Grub and Cabbage. Do you know the place?"

She wrinkled her nose. "Mmm. Awful."

"Yes, well. I realized when I was sitting there, that I wouldn't have been there at all, if it hadn't been for the way I felt about these things. Something about how horrible and fake it was made me wonder about how you knew something, knew it was real, or good, or you had to act on it. The way I've been acting on what I know and what I'm trying to find out."

Sabine looked amused. "And what do you want from me? Benediction? Absolution?"

I shook my head. "I just wanted to let you know that I wasn't trifling with this. With anyone. That's all."

"Okay." Sabine quashed out her cigarette on the heel of her shoe—just a little flash of dark green nubbly sock there—and picked up the butts carefully. "If I think of anything that might be of help to you, I'll let you know."

"Okay. Thanks." I buttoned up my coat. "See you."

"Bye."

I put my hat on and headed back out into the rain.

"And Emma?"

I paused, turned.

"God bless you."

* * *

It was only after I'd walked a couple of blocks away that I recalled my meeting with the young man outside the Fig and Thistle. I ducked back toward the cemetery and looked around, feeling pretty silly. Sabine was nowhere to be seen. Feeling even goofier still, I returned to the oak tree, thinking that I would check for a note and leave a message myself, asking the stranger whether he was Julia's boyfriend.

I got there and found the rock he mentioned; it looked like a piece of the tumbling wall that surrounded St. Alban's churchyard. I took out a piece of paper and scribbled my note, saying I'd let him know if I came up with anything else. But as I lifted up the stone to place the little folded paper under it, I saw another piece of paper already there. As I unfolded it, taking care not to rip the damp and blurred paper, I realized that it contained the answer to my question, as yet unasked.

It read, "She was seeing a bloke named—"

Oh shit. Oh shit. Oh shit.

I finished reading it, my heart sank to the bottom of my shoes. It was signed, "Stephen," possibly as a gesture of trust. So now the stranger had a name. I crumpled up Stephen's paper, tore up my first note, and wrote another one to leave in its place. "Thanks. I'll look into it. Emma."

It was with a very heavy heart that I headed back to Jane and Greg's house.

It didn't seem as though anyone was home, and I decided that I'd better act on my information before I lost my nerve. Here's where the rubber meets the road, Emma, I thought. Here's where you find out just how committed you are to this inclination of yours. Time to put up or shut up—

I realized I was stalling as I stood outside the bedroom doorway. I tried the doorknob; it turned with a small jerk and a squeak that I imagined echoed through the house. I pushed it open and was greeted by the heavy smell of feral cologne and unwashed clothing. I went in and looked around, trying not to feel like the intruder that I was.

The room was very similar to mine, with pretty wallpaper and lots of clutter that wouldn't have looked out of place in my office at home. A pile of dirty clothes lay over in the corner, spilling untidily out of a laundry sack. And there was a heap of fieldwork bags full of tools at home in one corner. Books were stacked in piles next to the bed. The thing that caught my eye, however, was the smaller bag on the bureau, the one that resembled the others but that looked like it was set aside for other reasons, next to a collection of scent bottles and other toiletries.

Without thinking about what I was doing, I picked up the bag, which was nothing more than an old army surplus satchel with a long shoulder strap. The dry rough canvas was a shock beneath my cold, clammy fingers. It didn't belong with the others there, and something about its size, its feel, told me that it did, at one point, belong with a twenty-two-year-old girl.

I don't think I could have hesitated more than a heartbeat. I undid the buckles on the flap quickly, and without thinking, dumped the contents of the bag onto the bed. I picked through the tangled heap of belongings, deciding that this had been used as more of a backpack than a pocketbook; there was no wallet, no keys, nothing of the immediate necessities that a woman kept near her. Nothing the police would have missed, really; they were more concerned with her missing wallet. They would have been much more interested in where this bag had been found.

A couple of notebooks, all the A-4 size I'd come to recognize, and a file with photocopies of articles and notes on them, all very carefully organized. With a shock, I realized that the articles were a couple that I'd written: Julia had been reading up on me before I arrived. I sat down to peruse the photocopies. Her margin notes were tiny, meticulously printed, as though a computer had inserted the metatext onto the article. I read a few of the comments. Next to the paragraph describing some of the maps of Fort Providence was:

"Typical American-brand post-processualism." Next to the section I'd written speculating on the demise of the colony, she'd written, "Why must they always resort to fiction? Trespassing on Borges."

I grinned humorlessly, and next to Julia's comments, mentally inserted: "Superior disdain common to untried youth." But that didn't mean I didn't agree with her, and I found myself wondering: if I couldn't help but respond this way to written comments I'd never been meant to see, what must Jane have felt having this kid in class?

The other things were far less personal or far more personal, depending on how you looked at them. A small silk purse that contained a couple of tampons. A toothbrush, a clean pair of pink cotton panties, and a pair of blue socks. All very clean and careful, cottony and childish. The things seemed so homely and ordinary that they nearly broke my heart. Where had I been when I was twenty-two? Just finishing undergrad, working with Oscar during the summers, developing my own rather strident opinions—my opinions were still strident, perhaps but at least now they were tempered with a little perspective—but still going home on weekends. A fledgling adult with a safety net; Julia's had been fatally torn.

There was a bit of folded paper, which I had to be very careful when unfolding: the creases in the lined paper—torn from one of the notebooks, I guessed—were furry with age and almost ready to fall apart at the worn seams. There were some lines from a poem, "Church Going," by Philip Larkin, written out in that tiny, meticulous print: "A serious house on serious earth it is,/In whose blent air all our compulsions meet,/Are recognized, and robed as destinies./And that much never can be obsolete,/ Since someone will forever be surprising/A hunger in himself to be more serious,/And gravitating with it to this ground,/Which, he once heard, was proper to grow wise in,/If only that so many dead lie round." I wasn't surprised that Julia had been attracted to this poem. If I remembered correctly, the narrator enters an empty church and considers whether, once the church has fallen to ruins and is lost to memory, the place will still seem hallowed by history, hope, and death. Julia had carried this around for a long time; perhaps, like Morag's file, it was a talisman of belief.

The last thing was a clear plastic cassette holder, with the tape inside. The label was cheaply printed and said, "Tealeaves and Broomsticks, 341 High Street, Marchester, MX6. Psychic Readings, Tarot, Crystals."

I heard a door slam downstairs. Instantly, I jumped up, stuffed the cassette into my pocket, and began shoving the rest of the things back into the bag. The little purse with the tampons went sliding off the duvet and under the bed; with a curse, I reached under and grabbed it, along with a handful of dust kittens. I shoved the little purse, dust kittens and all, into the bag and tried to do the straps as quickly as possible, but my fingers seemed to grow clumsier as I heard the footsteps climb up the stairs. Footsteps heading inevitably, I knew, for me.

Okay, I can't dodge out of here now, I thought in a panic, anyone coming up the stairs will see me leaving. How can I minimize what looks so very bad indeed? Still no answer, as I shoved the last strap through its clasp and slammed the bag back onto the bureau. Shit! I realized that the strap was draped over the edge and the bag had most certainly been turned around the other way when I'd come in! I had just turned it around and rearranged the strap and was removing my hand at the instant I saw him step into the doorway.

Ours was once again mutual shock, and I couldn't suppress a small yelp of surprise. Andrew wasn't nearly so ladylike.

"Jesus Christ! What the hell are you doing in here?"

"I . . . I . . ."

I watched as Andrew's eyes traveled from my face to where my hand was frozen in midair, hovering over Julia's bag. His face, which had been comfortable in his accustomed mask of self-satisfaction and arrogance, suddenly went blank with shock. Surprise seeped in and was quickly followed by a look of such sadness that I, even as I saw my moment, faltered.

Oh, God. I hate this. Aloud, I said, "This is Julia's, isn't it?"

He didn't even bother to deny it. "I didn't even think of it, didn't even notice it there. It's just become . . . a piece of the furniture. A part of my life. She snuck in under the radar before I knew it, and before I realized that I loved her, she was dead."

Orpheus seeing Eurydice vanish from the pine forest might have looked this stricken.

I shivered. "What's it doing here?"

"She left it behind. The week before you arrived, before she went missing. We'd been arguing again. It was close to the end of us being together. I didn't think she should be going to see her parents again, I didn't think it was good for her. She wanted to know precisely what say I had in the matter."

I waited.

He shrugged. "I didn't have any right in the world, I knew that. No right in the world, then. But that didn't stop me from trying to talk her out of it. Anyone could have told her, it wasn't a smart thing to do." Andrew leaned his elbow on the dresser, rested his forehead in his hand. He looked defeated.

"Why not?"

He looked up, away from me, at the opposite wall, then leaned against the dresser. "There was no way to patch up what had been going on there. Maybe later, but it was still too soon . . . there was just too much anger there to be mended. It could only make things worse. But she was just so stubborn . . ." He clenched his fists.

"So why did you try?"

"Poor Julia. I owed her that much, I reckoned. We'd broken up, were breaking up, about to break up, whatever. We both knew it was over. I'd . . . behaved badly throughout the affair. I'd been . . . someone . . . I'd been distracted. She was a lovely girl, there was so much to love. Once you got through to her, once I realized how much she had hidden behind her quiet exterior, you couldn't not. She was so bright—and I'm not just talking about her brains—you just had to look a little more closely and you could see how kind she was, how eager she was to try new things, new ideas . . . she could see right through me and she loved me anyway. I didn't deserve her. It took me too long to figure it out. Now it's too late."

"The first night I was here, when you broke in on me—"

"I gave Julia a key to the house. Sometimes, when they were out, she'd meet me here. I was extremely drunk and for some reason, I thought since the door was shut, she might have come back to find me."

I could hear the rain echoing off the pavement below us outside. A cold wind picked up and blew the light curtains out into the room, refreshingly clean after the musk of the cologne.

I wet my lips and swallowed. "Did you kill Julia, Andrew?"

He closed his eyes. "No. I hurt her badly. I should have been—"

Suddenly, as though he was again aware that I shouldn't be in his room at all, Andrew seemed to snap out of it. He reached for the bag. "I'll just take that, thank you."

"Don't you think the police ought to see it?"

The osteologist glared at me. "Where do you think I'm taking it? Don't you think I want the murderer found?"

"I haven't the faintest idea."

He seemed to consider that for an instant. "I suppose you shouldn't. I'm taking it to the police. You do recall the fact that I actually occasionally work for the police, don't you, Professor Fielding?"

"Yeah, when you don't go missing for days on end—"

"I have other work to do, you know, but those days after I found out . . . well, you can rest assured that I couldn't bear to be near . . . the site. And that at least two of those days were spent answering questions down the cop shop. And don't look at me like that—don't you think I know you'll go running straight to them if I don't take the bag to them?"

I shrugged. It was out of my hands, unless I wanted to try and wrest the bag away from him.

Andrew seemed to summon some reserve and he tried very hard to win me over to his side by turning on the charm. "Look, they do know about me and Julia, but the rest of the world does not and I would truly appreciate your discretion in this. Nothing good can come of publicizing our . . . relationship."

I recalled that his last absence had also coincided with Trevor's. "Does Trevor have anything to do with this?"

"Yes." He didn't look as though he was going to say any more.

I sighed. "Let me rephrase that. Tell me what Trevor has to do with this. What happened to his nose?"

"*I* did." He grinned unkindly. "Little pillock saw us one evening and tried to blackmail me. The night I understand she . . . Julia . . . her body was found." Andrew hesitated, then continued fiercely. "He announced that I would keep him on the site, in Jane's good graces, or he'd tell. He folded as soon as my fist touched his nose. That put an end to it. Should have done it long ago, on general principles."

"How come you didn't tell Jane or Greg where you were going to be?"

"They didn't know about Julia and, excuse me, I don't answer to either of them—"

"They're your friends! You live with them!"

He stared and seemed to debate how to respond to me. "We have a long association, but they don't pry into my business and I do my best not to intrude into theirs. I don't answer to them, and I don't reckon that I answer to you either. Now if you don't mind, I'd like to leave, and I guess I need to keep my door locked. So if you please . . ."

I scooted past him and stopped outside my doorway.

"If you're so concerned, you might as well give Jane and Greg the message that I'm going down to the Hewett Street police station." He paused. "You might cross me off your list of suspects. Detective Chief Inspector Rhodes has crossed me off his." He locked his doors and brushed past me; a moment later, I heard the front door slam

I fingered the tape cassette in my pocket. Detective Rhodes had crossed him off his list? That's exactly what I was afraid of.

Chapter 16

A COUPLE OF HOURS AFTER ANDREW LEFT, JANE, Greg, and I sat down to dinner. While the food was great—I ate with the appetite that comes with having eaten too many nonmeals too recently—the conversation was stilted. Every time we tried one topic, it was curtailed with bad news. I asked after Auntie Mads, only to find that she was very sick and Greg was increasingly anxious that it was her heart. She wasn't even trying to go to the cafe anymore. I asked how Jane's work had gone and learned that she'd spent the whole day frustrated; some of the measurements from the site maps weren't adding up. Greg asked me how I'd occupied myself. I couldn't very well say that I'd been out following in a dead girl's footsteps and watching her parents struggling with their sorrow in public. I'd looked around the house for a cassette player, but by the time I'd found out how their stereo worked, both of them were home and I surely didn't want to play that tape from Julia's bag in front of them. Not until I knew what it contained.

Monday morning came around and I realized that I'd woken up from my fifth morning nightmare in a row. Again, it was nothing more than momentary glimpses of alarming and peculiar images incoherently strung together. I was simultaneously observing and being a dark-haired woman, whose face alternately shifted from Jane's to the grainy black and white image of Julia's face as I knew it, moving about a gray landscape, looking for something, while all the while the faceless masses crowded around her, pressing closer and closer until I felt that I was being crushed under them.

I woke up in a sweat, swung my legs over the side of the bed, and waited until my breathing slowed down. Vivid dreams aren't all that common to me; usually I sleep like a log and have vague, uninteresting memories of climbing up hills or eating ice cream or sweeping. Really mundane stuff that makes me jealous when Brian tells me about all the surround-sound, 360-degree movies his brain stem plays for him. So when I do dream, I try to pay attention to it because I figure my subconscious is working extra hard, tugging at my shirt tail, trying to get my attention.

This time it wasn't too hard to see what was going on. I felt the pressures of being in the middle of Jane's troubles, overwhelmed by the possibilities I saw for suspects, and perhaps a little angry with the hostility that I felt from people who either were my friends, and should have known better, or were strangers, who ranged from the ambivalent to the downright threatening, and who really ought to have been more polite to me, in my humble opinion. No wonder that the REM sleep was coming thick and fast and in Technicolor.

The weather had finally cleared up, and although the rest of the site was very muddy, the tarps largely had protected the excavated areas. The crew seemed quite used to the wet, and so it was with a very little extra effort that work got started.

About ten o'clock and the tea-break, I looked up to see Morag walking toward the gate. I looked around quickly; Jane was still at Hewett Street and Greg was absorbed in his notes. I caught her eye and gestured emphatically that I

would meet her on the other side of the fence. I dug her file
out of my case, and heart sinking, remembering that she
wouldn't be very happy with my opinion of her research,
picked my way through the site. Although she was in the
same style of long skirt and peasant blouse, she was in dark
purple today, with none of the trim that had enhanced her
dress before. Her sleeve rode up and I could see the green
vine tattoo clearly; it was a lovely, complicated thing.

"You're getting close, aren't you?" she said. "I can tell, I
feel Beatrice's presence much more strongly today."

"Well, I'm moving down at a good rate," I replied. "Nothing yet, though."

"But even you must be able to feel her, now. You don't
feel a warmth, a tingling, anything?"

I sighed listlessly; this would go nowhere. "Not the way
you mean."

"No change in your vision?" Morag seemed surprised.
"A sense of movement where there seems there should be
none? No strange dreams—?"

I really was not interested in being probed so. "Look, I've
got your file." I handed it to her. "Thanks for letting me look
at it."

"Now do you see what I mean?" Morag was eager for my
support.

Here we go. "I'm afraid I don't. This is a start, but it
doesn't really support your notion. You need more proof."

"Well, what's this then?" She waved the folder.

"We don't know the sources of all these. You need primary sources. All of these are secondary, so we don't know
what these writers were using for data."

She furrowed her brow. "Primary?"

"Primary data, primary sources are sources that were directly connected to the event you are interested in. A diary,
someone recording what they saw, what they heard. A tax
record or court record or some other kind of legal document.
Even a painting can give you that kind of information,
though as with anything, you have to be careful that the

painter wasn't prettifying things or trying to get some other message across. Folk songs can be useful, photographs are great."

"And so what I've got is . . . ?"

"Secondary data, something that someone who wasn't alive at the time, maybe a historian, has put together. Secondary sources are interpretations of primary data, and in order to evaluate them, you need to know what was used as source material. Secondary sources are good when you are trying to learn some information—it's been organized and interpreted and digested for you—but in order to learn how we know something, why it is true, you need the contemporary data."

Morag threw her hands up in the air, as though she thought I was deliberately trying to frustrate her. "What more do you want? In school they told us you needed five sources to back up your thesis statement—if I get one more, will you believe me then?"

"Look, it's not a matter of quantity here," I explained. "These writers you're using, they need to support the same idea, here, if they listed what evidence they'd used, for example, to come to these conclusions . . ."

"Oh, I know what Rowan Blessingtree used. I called her and asked."

"Oh, good," I said, though I was thinking just the opposite. I didn't want to get mired in this. "What did she use?"

"She has her information through her medium."

I blinked. "I beg your pardon?"

Morag warmed up to her subject excitedly. "Mother Beatrice is one of her contacts on the other side. She came to Rowan and told her of her history, told her of her persecution, told how the abbey was burned down to punish her for worshiping the Goddess—"

"Morag, for one thing, the church was burnt down in 1504, twenty-two years after Mother Beatrice—"

"It could have burned more than once—" she suggested.

"But not without leaving some much more concrete data.

An event like that, a building as important as something like the abbey being destroyed, not only leaves evidence in the documentary record—think about what that would have meant to the people here—"

"There could have been a cover-up."

Frustrated, I tossed my braid over my shoulder. "But not in the archaeological record, where it would take one hell of a lot of effort to expunge such an event, and honestly, all of that work would be visible too. I don't think there was a cover-up for anything." Especially not something as illusory as Morag's theory.

Morag was getting more and more excited. "But it is coming straight from the source! That's exactly what you were telling me about! What more could you want? It is communication directly with the woman herself—"

"Morag, I said it might be evidence if more than one person could share this vision, if we could all have a look at it and evaluate it with the same thing on the table, but visions . . . just don't work as evidence." I looked away, across the site.

She clasped her hands. "It's evidence to me, even if it isn't to you . . . I know, I know in my heart, I've had a vision that tells me it's true, and you'll see I'm right too."

"But . . ." I tried another tack. "Look, I don't think that archaeology is a science in the same way that physics or chemistry is. You can't repeat the experiment of excavation, for example. No one's going to be able to re-dig your site and confirm what you've found, so that's why we publish everything and try to be as clear as possible about how we've established our theories. But I do believe that certain scientific principles do hold, and one of them is that you need lots of different types of evidence to confirm something. From different sources, from different ways of looking at things."

"But this is *my* different way of looking at things," she insisted.

"Yes, exactly. But it's only one way. So if you found

other corroborative evidence to suggest it, for example, in church records or town court documents or in a diary or something, then I'd be more inclined to accept what you're saying." I felt like Wallace Shawn arguing for the slight advantages of Western science over mysticism in *My Dinner With Andre.*

Morag continued on, convinced she had me now. "But I also remember from school that you can't ever prove something, you can only disprove it. By finding the ways it couldn't have happened."

"Well, yes. But—"

"So you can't conclusively prove my theories are wrong, can you?"

I hated this sort of argument: I was constrained by what I knew had been the best model so far for humans learning anything, about the past, the microscopic world and the stellar: the scientific method. I was forced, by my own beliefs, to admit their shortcomings. Morag, unfettered by her beliefs, could use that constraint against me, while never applying it to her own arguments.

"No I can't," I said with a sigh. "But none of the evidence I've seen so far—besides Rowan's article—suggests that I ought to consider that an option in the first place. Look," I said hurriedly, "why don't you look at the documents that Jane's been studying? Most of them are available at the library or in the public archives. See if you can't find out some other reason that might suggest what you say. That's only fair, isn't it? I looked at your data, now you look at mine."

She sniffed. "I don't know why I need to, but if they'll let me, I see no harm. I'll prove I'm right, someday, Emma. Even by your narrow standards."

I could tell she was disappointed in me, but hardly discouraged. "Good luck to you. I've got to get back to work. Let me know what you find."

"Oh, don't worry about that. I'll never be far away."

*   *   *

Maybe it was because I had the distraction of my meeting with Morag, and I wasn't working against myself in my head, but I found the groove that had so carefully hidden itself from me on Friday. The tedium of fieldwork is necessary if you are going to have the joy of discovery, but when you can't get the rhythm going, it's more than misery. On the other hand, on the days when it works, it's beautiful. Friday, I'd been chasing the level down in a spiral, always trying to bring the next corner down to the right level but only by the end of the day somehow managing to get all four at the same depth at the same time. Today, it was as though I had a built-in laser sight, the hand of a jeweler, and the concentration that a surgeon had jolly well better have. It was just before lunch when the stain that I'd been following began to change, ever so slightly, and darker stains began to show up.

Then I hit bone.

I swallowed and took a deep breath. I scraped away, every so gently, trying to follow where the lighter stain led, trying not to increase the damage to the bone that had been assaulted by time, soil chemistry, and the elements for over five hundred years.

At one edge, the bone ran out, the soil returned, but by moving again from where I saw the bone, in the opposite direction, I picked up the trail again and exposed a section of bone that broadened and seemed to be denser than the edge that I'd initially discovered. It curved away again, but this time with a line that was distinct, that suggested if not an intentional, manufactured form, then at least a true structure, created by nature and not some trick of the soil.

A little more cautious work, now bringing out a piece of bamboo, next a brush. I put my tools aside, and stood up and looked at my work from several feet up. What I saw was an arc of bone that surrounded the cavity where this person's left eye would have been. It gave me the impression that whoever it was—and I had my fingers crossed that it was Beatrice—was regarding me with the same unblinking interest with which I inspected her.

I suspect that even if I had been on one of my own sites, I wouldn't have hollered the traditional triumphant call of "Look what I've got!" With bone, in my experience, you're just always that little bit more cautious, both out of respect for the dead and out of a need for security. Nothing like the announcement that you've got human remains to start the storm, where you have people protesting on the basis of everything from respect to the irrational fear that the bones will automatically be contaminated somehow and you have to start worrying about the crazies who think that having a real human skull on their mantelpiece would be a cool thing. So it wasn't strange that I didn't holler, and I'm glad that my instinct saved me there, because when I finally found Jane, back from her trip to the police, I saw that she was talking to a reporter.

She wrapped up then, and he went over to the gate to finish scribbling in his little notebook. I called her over; she cocked her head. I raised my eyebrows. She picked up her pace.

Jane had almost made it over to my units when Morag's words preceded her: "You've found her, haven't you? You've uncovered the remains of Mother Beatrice! Let me see!"

Not only did every head on the site, including the reporter's, swivel around to see what was the matter, but Morag, heedless of her own safety and our previous warnings to her, was running through the gate and across the site. Not a wise thing to do, tearing through an area pocked with deep holes and covered with loose dirt, piles of stones, and tools; nigh on suicidal, given the immediate tattered state of Jane's self-control.

"I want to see—" Morag said, huffing and puffing a few meters short of where we were; I was surprised at how well she could move in her skirts and little boots.

"Morag, get your lardy backside off my site and behind the barrier!" Jane roared as she stomped right past me. "Go, get, you stupid cow, before I—"

The other woman put her hands on her hips. "Before you what? What are you going to do, go to the police? That's a laugh, considering how much time you've been spending down there recently!"

"How do you know about that?" Jane said. She slowed but didn't stop coming toward us. "No one—"

"Oh, I've got my little ways. Now let me see." She bent over, back to Jane, reaching a hand for one of my brushes.

Before I could move, Jane had reached the unit. She didn't stop when she drew up to Morag, but grabbed her around the waist, as though they were fond schoolmates, swung her around, and all but scooped the other woman up, rushing her off the site. It was efficient, well timed, and a fatal mistake. I could barely tear my eyes from the scene, but felt compelled to turn around and see whether the reporter had picked up on any of this. He had, and was staring as shocked and excited as the rest. The entire crew gasped, astonished by Morag's daring and scandalized by Jane's response.

Let it stop here, I prayed. Jane, just calm down, Morag, just go away. Jane, just calm down—

I almost passed out with shock when it happened just like that. Almost.

Jane made it as far as the gate when for some reason she stopped dead, as if all her momentum had immediately been expended. Morag, on the other hand, seemed to swell with her outrage. You could almost see her skirts and peasant blouse expand like a balloon as she sputtered incoherently. I could only pick out the occasional word—assault, rights, police—from the verbal torrent. Jane stood there and took it, a still look of horror on her face.

I started to walk over, but Greg beat me to it. "Morag, it's time to go."

She drew away from him. "Don't you touch me! I'll press charges!"

Greg hadn't touched her, hadn't even raised his voice. "And then we'll press charges for trespass and nuisance and anything else we can think of, so let's call it quits, shall we? We don't let other visitors behind the barrier unaccompanied, so you shouldn't feel slighted, though I will say you've done your best to assure that you'll never be invited back. Just go back to work, cool off, go have some lunch."

"You'll be sorry for this," I saw her mouth. "No matter what else happens, you're your own punishment, you two."

"That's fine, Morag." Greg nodded. "It keeps it simple for Jane and me. Time to go."

With that, Greg walked Jane away. Morag stared a few more moments, then turned and left. Slowly, the crew returned to their work, and although their murmuring was indistinct, I knew that they were all comparing versions of what they'd just seen.

Jane took Greg's hand from her arm, but gently, and she went over to the reporter, who hadn't moved a whit. I watched them talk for some time, Jane's hands clenching behind her back. It seemed to be an argument, perhaps a negotiation, for after a long period of exchange, I saw them shake hands and the reporter left. Jane, looking purely white now, came over to my unit. Her dark hair was plastered to her cheek and her gait was unsure.

"Jane, I didn't mean to—"

"You didn't," Jane said, sweating more from emotion than effort, I believed. "You didn't even say a word, remember? It was all bloody Morag."

I rubbed my forehead, then shifted uncomfortably. "What's the reporter going to do?"

"He'd just come back to check on some details; the article should be out tonight or tomorrow, I guess. I got him to promise he wouldn't write anything about the bones or the fight, unless it came up later, somehow, say if Morag makes a big noise about it. I expect we'll be picketed, perhaps, by flocks of druids or leprechauns or what-have-you. I told him he could say that we are closing in on the burial and he gets first dibs on it, after we've removed the bones. I just don't want that kind of press right now, not when the skeleton's just been uncovered. I've also made a lot of other promises, some involving my firstborn, etc. I really don't want this to get out yet."

She paused and collected herself. "So that's she, is it?" Jane nodded her head toward the small bit of exposed bone that had just caused so much trouble.

"Yes, I think so. Bit of occipital ridge showing, I guess."

"Well, good, then. Excellent. Well done."

Jane's words were hollow and brittle. I looked up at her. She wasn't looking at the bones but over at the gate.

"Jane—?"

"Jesus, Emma, did you see what I just did? When did I become so fucking awful?" She pushed her hair off her face and left a smear of dirt on her cheek.

I wiped some stray crumbs of soil from the edge of my trowel. "Jane, you've had a bad time, Morag was behaving badly—"

"Never mind Morag. I'm talking about *me*. I manhandled her, all but punched her on the nose. I *hauled* her off the site—"

As fine an example of frog-marching as I've ever seen, I thought. "She'd been repeatedly told to stay out of the area, she was endangering herself and the site. I've had the urge myself."

Jane spun around to face me, her face ashy, her eyes filled with fright. "Yes, but the difference is, you never acted on it. You don't give in to your baser instincts; I just did. In a horrible, public display of physical aggression. This is a civilized place, I've always thought of myself as *civilized*. I'm well aware that I'm bossy, a bit competitive perhaps, but I've never just . . . I mean, for God's sake, Emma, I'm *Labour*."

I really shouldn't have. Jane's face had gone from blank

almost to the point of tears, and it was just plain inappropriate of me, but I couldn't help myself. Maybe it was nerves, maybe it was just the way she said it.

I began to giggle.

Jane scowled. "Well, it's true."

The giggles got worse, turned into chuckles. She stomped her foot, very angry now, but mostly because she knew just how stupid she sounded. That just made me laugh all the harder.

Jane tried one last time, a feeble sop to her pride. "Good socialists just don't—"

The tears were running down my cheeks now. I was nearly doubled over and could barely catch my breath. "They don't . . . what? Don't . . . assault the . . . masses?"

By this time, Jane had given up and now shrugged, a little abashed. "Okay, okay. That was a little pompous, perhaps . . ."

I straightened and wiped my eyes. "Jane, that was world-class."

She grinned, still embarrassed. "It was hoped at one time that I would pompous for England, finally take the gold away from the Germans at the Olympics."

"What happened?"

Jane shrugged again, this time tiredly, not bothering with the game anymore. "Oh, I don't know. Lost my focus, I guess, or developed too much focus, perhaps. Emma, I don't know what you've been thinking, how you've been getting through the past week or so, I've been so determined to just face this whole mess out. I've been so wrapped up that I haven't been—"

"Don't worry about it, Jane. It's understandable."

She shook her head. "Emma, let me finish, okay? I've been trying to make it go away by dint of will and that's not going to happen. So I just have to get through it somehow. And I hate it but . . . I can't do it alone."

We stood quietly for a moment, almost as if out of respect for what Jane had just admitted.

"There's always Greg," I said. "If you still want him."

Jane looked even more tired now. "I know, I know. We've got to have a long talk, as soon as possible. Something's not right between us now—"

Wondering what the "something" might be sent a chill through me.

"—And I'm going to fix it." She paused, thought about what she'd said. "We're going to fix it."

And then there came the moment that is never easily traversed, hanging between a momentous event and everyday life. We didn't hug, we didn't share a moment, we didn't punch each other in the shoulder. Being who we were, we both looked away and then got right back to business.

Jane squatted by the grave shaft. "Well, the head's in the right place, pointed toward the west, to see the second coming."

"If it is in fact articulated." I hated playing the devil's advocate, but it came as second nature to me.

"Oh, don't worry, the rest of the postcranial skeleton will be there. And it's your job to find it before lunch."

I checked my watch. "That's about ten minutes."

"Okay, all right then, you slacker, you. You can have until the end of the day. Get to it."

By the end of the day, I hadn't exposed the rest of the skeleton—that was just too big a job—but I had uncovered the rest of the skull and what might yet turn out to be a clavicle and a couple of ribs, and took the measurements and a preliminary photo. The jaw hung, as if dropped in shock or embarrassment or horror, and even though I knew it had to do with the muscles deteriorating and letting go of the mandible after death, I wished it looked a little less dramatic. Dean Avery hovered around just beyond my peripheral vision, waiting till he was summoned to take more detailed photos. I was hard pressed to keep my attention where it needed to be and keep from bending over with him behind me. Finally, as much as I hated realizing how much I was letting him control my movements with his camera, I let him take a few shots of the skeleton at the close of the day.

I could tell that Jane was serious about what she'd said that morning, because instead of stopping at the pub, she suggested that we pick up Indian take-away and eat early. Even though I got the mildest thing that could be found on the menu and even though I loved the layered spices and textures of the food, by the end of the meal I was sweating and my face had gone red. Jane and Greg, each having ordered a vindaloo with three little red peppers next to the name on the menu, ate it with practiced and careless rapidity, with no apparent side effect other than both of them blowing their noses just once.

Greg shoved his plate away saying, "Good, that."

"Do you mind if we leave you to your own devices again this evening?" Jane said after they cleared up. She continued confidentially, "I need to have a good long talk with Greg. There's a lot I need to find out about where his head is at, lately."

"Well, why don't you stay here, then? I'll go down to the pub, or a movie, or the library, or something."

"No, we'll go out. It helps me to think, if I'm outside. Besides," she confided, "I want to keep an eye on the site. I don't want that nutter Morag coming back and messing about."

I shook my head. "She was rude this morning, but I think that was just excitement. I'm sure she wouldn't—"

"I'm not so sure. Someone who can't stay where she's told . . . besides, I'm sure I made matters worse today and I just don't want to take the risk. And it's dried out nicely since yesterday. We'll sit by the river and talk and see what we can't sort out. You'll be all right?"

"Oh, yes. Don't worry about me," I said, following them to the door. "I've plenty to keep me occupied for the evening. Take care."

"Cheers, Emma," Greg said, and shut the door behind them.

I figured I had an hour or two, at the least. I ran up the stairs to my room, grabbed the cassette tape that had been in Julia's bag, a notebook, and pen, and ran back downstairs to the living room stereo. It took me a minute to sort out the controls, and I finally realized I had to flip the switch on the wall outlet before the stereo would power up, but then I shut the cassette into the stereo and settled back to listen to Julia's card reading.

Chapter 17

THE TAPE WAS CHEAP AND THE MACHINE THAT HAD been used to record the session was probably only one generation away from reel-to-reel; the clatter of the plastic as the buttons were pushed and recording started was very clear, but the voices were fainter and it was difficult to catch all of what was being said over the mechanical hiss and vibrations so faithfully recorded along with Julia's voice. Although I was alone in the house, I had turned the volume so low that I could barely hear it; merely listening to this private moment was intrusive enough, a discourtesy that made me feel like the worst kind of voyeur, but the possibility of broadcasting it for others was unthinkable. But I was in this for good or ill, so I got up, turned up the volume, rewound the tape to the beginning so that I could hear it properly, and retreated into the couch cushions. Curiosity and embarrassment, whether for me or Julia, I could not have said, mingled with the hope that I might get some kind of lead; I didn't believe in anything the psychic might have predicted, but I did hope that Julia herself might give me a clue, a voice beyond the grave. The reading began.

"This is a card reading for . . ." There was a pause and a ruffling of paper. "Julia, done by Alicia at Tealeaves and Broomsticks on June__." The psychic's voice was high and firm, convincing, reassuring. Professional. "Julia, although I see you've had two other readings here before with Erin, we've never worked together, so I'll begin by telling you about myself."

A loud, rapid flapping noise filled the parlor at 98 Liverpool Road, and I realized that Alicia was shuffling cards repeatedly, very close to the microphone in the recorder.

"In addition to being gifted with the sight—I'm clairvoyant and empathic, I read from the heart—I also read auras and I do connect with the spirit world. My family has always read in this form to create balance, inside and outside you. If a spirit is walking with you on the other side and makes him- or herself known to me, I will take their messages for you."

I frowned and tucked my foot underneath me; what was Alicia, some sort of answering service?

There was an indistinct childish murmur from someone; it must be Julia. I strained to hear her, and was a little surprised when I realized how much I'd assumed about her, that her voice would be loud or aggressive.

Alicia responded, "No, not ghosts, but spirits. These are all around us, they are always looking out for us, and they are benign. What you see on television and the movies is mostly nonsense made up to scare people and that . . . well, let's not go into how that makes me feel. Anger clouds one's gifts." The shuffling of cards resumed, followed by three slaps of thin cardboard on table.

"I see here that you are a very grounded person, you feel at your best outside, and you need to be near nature to connect with the other side. Do you garden? No? When you are outside in your dreams, that's when the spirits will find it easiest to guide you. Right now, I see you're making transitions in your life, your career, and these are where your heart area lies, this is where you are truly you, and this is definitely where you will stay and be happiest.

"Do you have a particular area you'd like me to focus on today? Money, love, job—"

The small, girlish voice said, "Relationships."

"All right then, relationships. If you ask me about a particular person, I will try and read what their intent is for you." I heard Alicia take several deep breaths. "I am focusing on relationships for Julia now, focusing on Julia now, I am clearing my mind and making myself open, focusing on Julia."

I heard more cards being laid briskly and murmurs from Alicia that were oddly reassuring, almost lulling. "You in the past, you in the present, you in the future, what surrounds you now—there's a lot of energy around you at the moment and things are very unclear to you. A lot of energy. There's so much activity on many fronts; you're at the center of many, many things, some of which are known to you, some of which are not—"

Oh, lordy, I thought. That leaves just about everything in the world open to Alicia. Isn't everyone at the center of a lot of things they don't know about?

"—And I see that you're just recovering from a financial setback, you are struggling at your job—no, you're at university—"

"I'm doing a graduate course," Julia corrected her in a near whisper.

"Yes, I see you struggling there, it's harder than you thought, but you will eventually triumph there and in your chosen career. I see that you are a very creative person, someone who is involved in the arts in some way, the visual arts, painting, photography—?"

My ears pricked up at that last, thinking of Avery.

"No, not really," came the indistinct reply.

"Well, then that is something you will discover in the future."

Well, none of that was very helpful, I thought. Anyone looking at a young woman with bags under her eyes and a bump on her middle finger from writing might tell that she was a student, and doesn't everyone in graduate school struggle and worry about money? Although, from what I understood, things didn't seem all that tough for Julia, academics-wise.

I heard Alicia slap more cards down. "People around you are confusing to you now, they are making demands of you and you're not sure whether they have your best interests at heart."

"Yes." A sigh followed here.

"Well, I see that some do and some do not, but only you can decide that. You need to step outside yourself, clear your mind of the surrounding noise, static, all the confusion, and see how you need to respond here. With regards to your work, you carry a lot of stress with you. You tend to worry quite a lot, but what I can suggest to you is that you let things go, don't focus on the negative or be judgmental, and everything will be made right."

I yawned and looked down at my notepad. I had written nothing down yet.

Alicia continued, "You are on the cusp of many changes, new beginnings are manifested around you, and I find that you need to let go of what is valuable to receive what is valuable. It will be hard to walk away from what you know best, people will say that you are acting out of character, acting foolish in their eyes, but by doing so, you'll become freer, in every way."

"Could you possibly be a little more specific?" I noticed a note of impatience in Julia's voice. "I'm really having a hard time with my boyfriend, my instructors, my family, and I don't know what to make of it. I don't know how to begin to fix any of it."

"Part of the reason that things are so unclear for me is that they are so complicated for you," Alicia chided. "Let me concentrate and I'll tell you what I see."

There was a pause, followed by three more cards being placed, and then three more. "You are at the center of a lot of thoughts and intentions lately, many more than you know, but there are four very strong people in your life who are thinking a lot of you lately. Two men and two women."

I obediently scratched this down on my pad, waiting for Julia to comment on them.

"The women . . . the women are very unclear to me," Alicia continued. "Both of them are very strong willed, older than you—in authority, maybe, bosses, parents, teachers? One is working for you, but in a very clumsy way. You don't always see eye to eye, but she is looking out for you. The second is outwardly very hostile and is trying to keep you back; her feelings are mixed though."

I noted this down: possibly Morag and Jane? What about her mother, perhaps? But which was which?

Julia echoed my desire for details, pressing Alicia. "Do you know what their names are? Are they at work or outside it?"

"Names aren't coming to me but they are both deeply interested in your work, for different reasons. And now the men . . ."

I heard more cards being put down, then it sounded like they were being rearranged. "Does the letter A mean anything to you?"

"My boyfriend's initial," Julia whispered.

"Are you involved now?"

My heart pounded as I waited through Julia's hesitation. "I . . . I'm not sure. I'm not sure he loves me, but I think he might."

Shuffle of cards. "He does, but he doesn't know it yet. He doesn't know why he loves you and not someone else. He feels a great deal toward you, but he is a confused, angry man." Several more cards were put down. "Very angry. He is split, emotionally and psychically, and you should be very careful of him."

"What do you see? For us?"

"To sit here and tell you that there won't be troubles, well, I wish I could. I do see a new transition taking place, but you are both still connected."

"We are in the midst of breaking up, I think."

"That may be what is going on now, but what I see is the future, I can't say how far ahead. Because the thing is, I think that he will finally come to decide that he loves you, and then everything will change for him. You too. Lots of change, and if you can hang on through all that change, stick to your guns, because you know what is right for you, you'll be fine."

"I hope so. I think we could be good for each other. I'm just honest enough for his good, he's just strong enough for mine."

Whoa, I thought. That was some pretty advanced emotional reasoning.

There was another flutter of cards. "Has he broken a date lately?"

"No, not him . . . but someone else has."

"You're also close to this other person?"

"Very. We don't see each other as much as we'd like, but I was supposed to meet him for a drink and he didn't arrive. We've got a fallback plan, and I'll try again and meet him tomorrow night."

I noted this down excitedly; this reading took place the day before Julia's murder.

"Well, this is a younger man and he didn't mean to miss the meeting, it wasn't his fault. He is thinking of you often and he wanted to see you."

I heard Julia sigh. "He's not the second man, then?"

"No, that's all I see of him."

Who was that, then? I wondered. That first sounded like Andrew for sure, though. I wrote down "angry, dangerous, split emotionally." It didn't sound too far off from everyone's opinion of him, so far, and I had his own admission of the affair. How dangerous was he?

"The other older man . . . he's married . . . he sees you as the source of all of his problems, a thorn in his side, if you were not in the picture, he believes his life would be easier."

I caught my breath. Could it be Greg?

"He too needs to decide where his heart is, because he is distracted by too many emotions that are outside his character. Do you know an older man who worries a lot?"

A short laugh from Julia. "Too many."

"Well, keep an eye on them. This one will lead you astray. He wants to help you, but he's going to lead you into trouble, however inadvertently. His work is terribly important to him."

That made me think of Julia's father, George Whiting, or, then again, perhaps it was Palmer—but of course, I was dealing with only the people I knew who knew Julia. Who knew who else I might be inadvertently omitting?

I heard a few more cards being flipped over and there was another worried, muted question from Julia, and I strained to hear her. It was so frustrating having to try to translate what Alicia meant and to try and guess what Julia was asking based on her responses.

"No, no. That card always worries everyone but when Death shows up in the array, it doesn't necessarily mean death as we understand it." Oh! But it had in Julia's case, I thought sadly. "It means the end of something, and can often be a good indication of change that will be good for you, you making positive decisions, you removing yourself from harmful situations, and taking good, healthy, positive steps. In this context, I think that you will be able to resolve a lot of things very favorably in the next six months or so . . . I can only suggest that you try and put all that confusion behind you and do what your heart tells you."

I shook myself, surprised at how lulled I'd become by the hypnotic effect of Alicia's voice. Do what your heart tells you? That doesn't help much, I thought. Apparently Julia didn't think so either.

"I could have gone to the university counselor and got the same advice," she said, nowhere near as relaxed as I'd become; she sounded quite annoyed. "I just wish I knew what to do. I mean, I'm only twenty-two—"

"Would you like to make another appointment, perhaps

go back to working with Erin? Maybe she'd see things a little more clearly for you."

"No, don't bother—"

And with that, the tape ended.

I shifted my weight off my legs uncomfortably. That last bit of Julia's frustration was heartbreaking and it answered for me the question of why she might have gone to a card reader in the first place. She sounded confused, and who wouldn't be, I wondered. She was very young, she was having an affair with one of her instructors, she was on the outs with her family, and at odds with her adviser, who seemed to hold most of her future in the palm of her hand. I had always had Oscar to talk to, then my sister Bucky, then Marty, and Brian, of course, later, but from what I could tell, Julia wasn't close to or even casual friends with her classmates, and all the people who she might have reached out to—parents, lover, advisers—were ambivalent at best toward her.

And I believed that one of them had eventually killed her.

I didn't actually believe anything that Alicia had told Julia, there were simply too many vague statements, things that could have been applied to anyone. Anytime she even came close to the mark, they were things that could have been clues available to any canny observer. But what I could do, I realized, was focus on how Julia had responded to those questions, and identify what she had asked about. Maybe there's where I would find some sort of clue, through Julia, that would tell me what she was thinking about just before she died.

I listened to the tape several more times. Julia had asked about ghosts as opposed to spirits, her relationships, whether the women Alicia mentioned worked with her or not. She'd corrected Alicia in terms of her work and interests (and Alicia had immediately gone back to the last thing that had given her a positive response, I noticed). Julia'd admitted that she was involved with someone who wasn't sure about her, but Julia wanted to know if it would last, whether he would decide he loved her. It sounded to me like she loved

Andrew and hoped the relationship would continue, though she didn't think it would. She was worried that people close to her didn't have her best interests at heart and she wanted to repair the rifts that might be between them. She knew too many older men who were anxious. She'd asked about the card depicting Death when it had appeared in the array.

Julia wanted specifics; she had questions she wanted answered but wasn't getting the responses she sought; she sounded impatient. My take on it, based on how Lucy had described it at the pub, was that Julia had gone to the psychic on a lark the first time, had gone back the second time because she thought she was getting somewhere, and was becoming disenchanted with that source by this last visit. She was a kid struggling for answers and she didn't know how to find them.

She and I both.

I got up and rewound the tape, then recovered it from the player. Sitting back down, I realized that I felt as though I'd been messing around with the cards or a planchette myself; the air in the parlor was full of guilty curiosity.

One thing was for certain, I needed to talk to Andrew again. I frowned. Actually I needed to talk to Andrew about a lot of things, including the first, modern, burial we'd worked on. He had said, however grudgingly, that he would let me see the report he prepared for the police, and it had been a week. Of course, he hadn't been around much, but that in and of itself was something I wanted to ask about as well. I uncurled myself from the couch and rubbed my eyes. I really wasn't looking forward to another interview with Andrew, especially not with the questions I knew I had to ask him. Where had he been, who had distracted him from Julia . . .

I thought a while longer, unproductively, and eventually heard the front door open and slam shut. I looked at my watch: it was eleven o'clock. I flipped the pages of my notepad so that the night's notes were covered up.

"Hello?" I called.

"Bugger!" came Jane's reply.

"I beg your pardon?" I went out to the front hallway, where Jane and Greg were staring at the front page of the newspaper. They looked tired and wrung out from their long talk, but now both were frozen with shock.

"I'm sorry, not you," Jane said. "That poxy little reporter's gone and splashed news of Mother Beatrice all over the front page! He promised he'd wait!"

"He promised he'd try," Greg corrected. "I believe there are things called editors and deadlines that suck away personal volition."

"Well, it's too late to do anything about it now," Jane said. She folded up the paper and threw it on the stand. "Everything was nice and secure when we left the site. But the crowds will be out tomorrow, that's for sure." She turned to her husband. "We'll never get any work done."

"Yes, we will. I'll go out early tomorrow, to check on things as well. Everything will be fine, Jane."

Jane looked very tired, but she smiled at Greg. "You're right. Everything will be fine."

"I'm going up. Coming?"

"Yes, in a minute."

"Night, Emma. Sleep well."

"Night, Greg."

We watched Greg go up the stairs. "So how'd it go?" I said.

"I dunno." It was strange to see Jane look uncertain about anything. "At least we've got to the point where we are saying out loud that there's a problem. And I think, we've got it established that it's on both of our parts—I mean, if Greg won't speak up and tell me he's upset or thinks I'm wrong or what have you, I have no way of knowing, right?"

"Well . . ."

"You know what I mean. And we've established that we do really know that we both want the same thing, which is good. We have a hard slog ahead of us, and the real bugger is that we have to figure out how to get there from here, isn't it?"

You can't get there from here, I thought, but had the good sense to keep it to myself. "So now what?"

"Counseling, I suppose." She traced one of the patterns on the wallpaper. "But we've agreed to wait until we're done in the field. No sense piling things on, Greg says, but I can't help wishing we could just get into it and get it over so we can move ahead, strike it off the list."

I looked at her.

Jane nodded halfheartedly and shrugged. "All right, all right. I suppose that's part of the problem. I'm off to bed. Good night."

"Night, Jane."

I barely got a lick of sleep that night, despite the late hour and the eventful day. When I did sleep, I was wracked by dreams that afforded no rest; when I wasn't dreaming, I was staring at the clock in a decidedly wakeful fashion. Finally, around four o'clock, it was as though someone had hit me with a sledgehammer. I fell dreamlessly asleep and stayed that way until Jane pounded on my door the next morning. I fumbled into my clothing, drank Jane's bad coffee until I could see straight—despite my protestations, she wouldn't let me make my own ("nonsense, Emma. You're on holiday. Let me spoil you a bit." Spoil me a bit of coffee, I guess she meant)—and then followed her out into the gray morning.

Jane, in spite of the gloomy light and threat of a drizzle, in spite of yesterday's events, was practically skipping to the site. When I caught her smiling at her reflection in a shop window, for no particular reason that I could see, unless it was to bestow a beam of radiance on a display of socket wrenches at the ironmonger's, it all became dismally clear to me.

"You know, you might want to tone it down a bit, or

everyone will know you didn't go right to sleep last night," I suggested grumpily.

"God, I hope we didn't bother you. Something—stress, catharsis, something—just lit us up. Shagged ourselves stupid, we did." Jane giggled, and I resisted the urge to slug her. "It was magic."

"And on a school night, yet—"

But the look on Jane's face stopped me. I followed her horrified glance to the site itself, where a police car was parked, blue lights swirling.

"Oh, my God, Greg!" Jane began to sprint toward the gate, the door of which was hanging open. "Greg!"

I took off after her and we arrived at the gate at almost the same time.

Greg was talking to a cop, his face ashen. Jane threw herself at him. "What happened? Are you all right?"

"I'm fine, but . . . Jane. When I got here, the gate was opened—" Greg swallowed. "I'm fine, but someone's dug up the site . . . and they . . ."

"They what?"

"They took Mother Beatrice's bones."

Chapter 18

JANE SEIZED GREG BY THE SHOULDERS. "WHAT DO YOU mean they took her bones? *Who* took the bones?"

"We don't know yet." Greg ran a hand through his hair. "When I got here about seven o'clock, I found the chain had been cut clean through and the gate was open. As soon as I got in, I could see that there was some disturbance by Emma's unit, burial nineteen. And when I got over there . . ."

He shook his head in amazement. "It was just a mess. It was just torn apart, like a bomb had gone off there."

That image actually reminded me of something, but I had no time to concentrate on that. Jane had already decided who was responsible. She paced back and forth, and finally pounded her fist into her hand.

"It was that bloody Morag! She must have—"

"Morag didn't do it," I said.

She whirled on me. "Of course she did, Emma! It was to get back at me, for yesterday. And plus, her sort, she was probably just dying to get her hands on some human bone—"

"Jane, hang on a second, it doesn't make sense," I interrupted. "Greg said it looked like a bomb went off. For one thing, you know Morag's feelings about Mother Beatrice are reverent, more than anything else. Do you think she would have torn things up like this?"

She stopped in her tracks, staring in disbelief. "Emma, she's a *witch*!"

"Come on, Jane, listen to yourself. From the little that I know about neopagans and witches, they don't mess around with necromancy or anything like that. It's just not what they do, it's more of a worship of nature and its order—"

"Bollocks!"

"Pardon me." The youthful-looking PC interrupted us for the first time, his slight form filled out by the strict lines of his uniform. "I'm PC Whelton. Am I correct in assuming that you are talking about Morag Traeger?"

I nodded.

"Yes, we bloody well are!" Jane said.

He scratched the tip of his nose with his pen and I was again struck by the idea that the constable resembled a schoolboy. "Well, I can assure you that she wasn't involved in this in any way. Can you suggest anyone else who—"

"What do you mean, she wasn't involved?" Jane demanded. "How the hell can you tell?"

"For one thing, your friend is right." He nodded toward me. "Wicca is an ancient matriarchal earth-based religion worshiping the Goddess in her three aspects of maiden, mother, and crone. Some also worship her Consort, the Triple God, to maintain an idea of balance in all things. The principle tenet of Wicca is, 'An you harm none, do what you will.' "

I noted that PC Whelton was very well informed, reciting these facts with considerable ease.

"Since Wiccans believe that every action you take, good and bad, affects you and others on many levels, they are very careful and very thoughtful not to do harm. So when you get down to it, I'd say it was a lot more restrictive than some of your more better-known religions."

He pursed his lips like a disapproving teacher. "And as for the sort of thing you're suggesting, well, it's as dirty a notion, as bad an insult as accusing a Christian of eating babies. The worst sort of misguided prejudice, you might say."

Jane wasn't convinced; she looked like she was one breath away in search of Morag herself. "Whatever, I don't really care. Morag has plenty of reason to—"

Oh, Jane, stop, I thought, all of a sudden. Don't go there. "Jane, I think—"

She didn't even hear me. "—Want to get back at me."

PC Whelton clicked the top of his pen, ready to write. "Oh? And what might that be?"

Jane, too late, realized what she'd gotten herself into. "We . . . ah, we had a disagreement yesterday. Got a bit tetchy."

"Did you indeed?" the PC said with polite interest. "How tetchy?"

Jane was silent.

"I see." He tapped the notebook thoughtfully. "Since there were no official complaints, I'll just suggest that you both mind your manners a bit better."

"What?" Jane struggled with this, but finally had enough sense to keep her mouth shut. "Well, yes, of course."

Greg and I both sighed with relief, but Jane didn't keep her mouth shut for long.

"But how can you possibly tell that she wasn't here?"

PC Whelton continued calmly. "Mr. Ashford says that the break-in happened between eleven PM and seven AM. I can assure you that Ms. Traeger was nowhere near here. So why don't you tell me who else might be interested in causing you trouble?" He shot his cuffs, preparing to take down Jane's statement, and I got a look at his watchband, which startled me.

Jane briefly mentioned George Whiting. I thought of Palmer.

"So just how can you claim that Morag wasn't responsible for this?"

Oh, Jane, I thought. For heaven's sake, think about what you've just heard!

"I give you my word, she was not involved."

Jane was frustrated, but realized she wasn't going to get any further. After the rather subdued end of the interview, the PC, typically, assured us that everything that was possible would be done, but then reminded us that it was unlikely he would be able to find anything out, given the lack of clues. "If we do find anything," he said, closing his notebook, "it will be because someone else comes up with some information."

I decided it wouldn't do Jane any good to tell her that I'd seen a pentacle worked into the design of PC Whelton's watchband. What good would it have done?

By this time, the crew had arrived and were informed of what had happened in the night. Jane told them that if they knew of anything, they should come to her immediately, but none came forth. Then she said, if they should hear of anything, she would be happy to take the bones back, no questions asked. The crew shuffled and looked at one another, but there was still no response. They had just enough time to get their equipment and notes from the shed when the dark sky opened up and it began to pour. After thirty minutes, Jane, thoroughly dispirited, dismissed the crew for the day and as they repacked the shed, Greg put the finishing touches on a makeshift tent of tarps and probes. The three of us squatted under the clear plastic, supported by my mammoth screen, Kong, and surveyed the damage to the vandalized grave shaft.

"Well, that was money well spent," Greg said, trying to sound cheery. "I believe we could weather a hurricane with your screen here, Emma. Let's see what's here."

It was every bit as bad as it looked. The rain buffeted the

plastic, finding in every little tear an opportunity to funnel
into the unit and make mud pies of what was left of my careful excavation. We scraped away the loose dirt as well as we
could, and found a few small bones and teeth that had been
overlooked. There were a few unidentifiable fragments of
copper, possibly clothing fasteners that had been destroyed
during the robbery.

"It was dark," I said. "Whoever was here wasn't very organized."

"Right," Jane said. "It wasn't the bones they wanted so
much as to confound me."

"I'm not so sure of that, pet," Greg said. "I had a look
around with PC Whelton. This was the only burial that was
bothered."

"So?"

"Well, if it was meant as sabotage, would they have bothered with removing the bones? Why not just trash them, tip
the loo over, collapse the other shafts? So I don't think it was
personal. I'm betting—and the PC agrees—that it was either
kids who wanted the bones, or some nutter. They didn't stay
long, that's for sure. So I don't think it was personal. For
some reason, they came straight here, to burial nineteen."

Jane rested her head on her knees. "It sure as hell feels
personal," came her muffled reply.

Here was the point where I should have pointed out the
fine old truism: Archaeologists aren't interested in things,
they're interested in stratigraphy. We had the notes and the
photographs, all we were really losing, really, was the information that would have been a part of the demographics—
how many males, females, age at death, general health and
diet, cause of death, that sort of thing. The fact of having
found Mother Beatrice was really much less significant—
technically. Emotionally, well, that was another matter. I
was too depressed myself to trot out platitudes. It had been
exciting to be on the trail of an individual, someone who'd
had a local reputation. A woman of power and impact from a
time when women were meant to go unnoticed.

Then Jane surprised me by trotting them out herself. "It's only one burial, really, when you get right down to it. The rest of the site is in good shape." She paused. "I just feel completely done in, that's all. Absolutely knackered. It's all been too much."

We sat under the plastic, feeling thoroughly worn out and beaten, and listened to the rain pour down and turn the site into a minor imitation of the Somme. Then Jane giggled to herself. Greg and I exchanged a worried look.

"Picts and Romans," she said.

I looked at Greg for an explanation, but now he was grinning too.

"Romans and Saxons," he said back. He caught my eye and tapped at the tarp over our heads, which promptly dumped a pint of water down into one end of the destroyed unit. "Or sometimes, when we were very ambitious and had something we could burn, Britons and Vikings."

"Ah," I said. "Cowboys and Indians. Oscar made me arrowheads, spears, everything." Now I grinned, remembering. "Mother hated it."

"So what's the plan now, Jane?" Greg nudged her.

"Oh, I'm going to sulk in my lab and wash sherds," she said. "You lot can do whatever. I need a chance to regroup."

"Where's Andrew today?" I asked.

Jane frowned. "He had some work to do in his lab on the bones from that modern skeleton. You'd think he'd have finished by now. We expected him on site later today."

So now Jane was interested in the report, I thought. "Where's the lab? I had a notion I'd like to run past him. About the stratigraphy." And the modern skeleton, I added to myself.

"Over at the U.," she said. "That's where I'm headed, if you want to join me."

"Sure."

We drove over to the University in Jane's tiny cramped car and soon saw a modern looking campus of concrete geometry, the only color came from flyers advertising student activities, protests, and flat shares. Even these were tattered and drooping from the rain, hanging limply from the staples that held them to the notice board. Very few people were here during the summer term, and those who were out were hurrying from building to building. Jane parked and led me toward the science building, but instead of heading to the front door, she went around to the back, selected a key, and opened a basement door. It seemed to me that it was the same in England as it was at home: Archaeologists always got the basement spaces.

The rain ran down the steps and into a drain, but that being partially blocked, water ran under the basement door. Jane didn't seem to notice, and I saw that there was another, newer drain just inside the door, which most of the water traveled into. The lowest shelf in the metal shelving in the storage section was fairly high off the ground however, I noticed, to prevent any damage from more disastrous flooding. Apart from that, the lab was actually pretty nice: lots of neatly marked acid-free boxes from previous jobs, and still room left for the current one. There were six tables spread out with artifacts in various stages of being cleaned and labeled, in two rows of three butted up end to end. At the head of these were a desk and bookshelf—Jane's, presumably—like the royal table overseeing the lesser guests at a banquet. Everything was in immaculate order. There were two sinks fitted up with heavy-duty screens to the far side, and a fume hood, which, by the look of the disconnected plugs and conduits, probably wasn't operational. The walls were festooned with posters showing various types of pottery, the regions of the different tribes in Britain before the Romans, and a tattered poster for British Heritage showing a stately home and its grounds—it reminded me a bit of Jeremy's place. This last poster had been further defaced by generations of hopeful young archaeologists, who'd drawn, in various levels of accuracy and believability, sketches of excavations on the grounds of the place. One discovered a pile of gold, another an intact Viking ship; the Eiffel tower poked out of another unit, and in another area, a perfectly executed section of stratigraphy, complete with roots and rocks, and at the very bottom of the pit, what looked like a crumpled sports jersey in maroon and blue. A tiny caption read "West Ham's Hope." I shrugged, not understanding, and turned away.

Jane dumped her rucksack onto her desk, flopped into her chair, and landed her feet on her desk before she rolled away too far. She hit a button on a battered radio and Stravinsky began to pour out at high volume. I wrinkled my nose—I prefer my classical stuff to predate 1850—and she obligingly turned the radio down. She leaned back and rubbed her forehead with her fingertips.

"I really am just going to sit here and think a while, Emma. If you want to see if Andrew's in, his space is on the fourth floor on the left hand side. Take the lift up, you can't miss it. Just knock before you go in—he's a bit dodgy about visitors. And if you would tell him about our plans for the day, I'd appreciate it."

"What time are you going to leave?"

Jane shrugged. "I don't know. When a thought hits me, I guess. If you get bored before then, just catch the 257 bus—it leaves right from the front gate—and it will drop you off on Church Street, by the bridge, not too far from the site. I'll come up and look for you, and if you're not there, I'll assume you've gone."

"Okay. See you."

I found my way through a dimly lit corridor to the lift, which, when I pressed the button, seemed to make more noise than necessary. When the fourth floor light went off and the doors opened, I saw that the rest of the building was cleaner, but still trapped in a funk of 1970s industrial utility, a nonaesthetic. Clearly, Marchester was one of the "redbrick universities." I found the door on the left that said "Human Osteology Lab" and knocked twice. Hearing a grunt that might well have been Andrew's version of a welcome, I pushed the door open and went in.

Unlike the lab in the basement, this room appeared to be used for storage, though I knew it must not be. No posters. No books that I could see, though Andrew must need them and I was really curious to see what he used for references. No paper or drafting tools, either. There was nothing that I could see besides rows of tables, stacks of more acid-free boxes, a bank of lockable storage cabinets, and a desk, with nothing on it besides a computer. No mouse pad, no pencils, no plants. Nothing. And if any room had ever needed music to soften the work done here, it was this place, and there was none. Those I know who regularly work with human remains are convinced that a certain respect, even reverence, is due to those individuals they study, but the bareness of this room seemed even to deny the humanity of those still living.

The only other piece of furniture in the room was a chair at the desk, and the only thing on that was Andrew, who was staring attentively at the screen. Seeing me he promptly turned the monitor off, so that I might not see his work.

"What do you want?" He made no pretense at all to be pleasant and more than ever, Andrew had the look of a funerary monument, cold, pale, hard-featured, and sorrowful. He also looked exhausted, and I had an unaccountable urge to stroke his head, as if some touch might thaw him, but I knew well enough that such a rude trespass would get my fingers snapped at.

"Jane's called work for the day—"

He crossed his arms. "The rain should clear up later on."

"Someone broke into the site last night."

He sat up straighter. "Oh, Christ. Is Jane okay?"

"She's upset, but I think she'll be okay." I looked at him. He hadn't asked about Greg, his best friend, and he hadn't asked about the skeletons, reputedly the object of his professional obsession. Remembering the photos of Julia in the darkroom and their close resemblance to Jane, I was stricken with a sick feeling that there was a very unpleasant, very logical reason that Andrew had been attracted to Julia. "Jane wasn't there when it happened, if that's what you mean."

"No, of course not—"

I couldn't tell whether he was agreeing with me or disputing something else.

Andrew settled back down. "What did they get into, the tool shed?"

I shook my head. "Worse than that. Whoever broke in tore up Mother Beatrice's grave. Or what we assume was Mother Beatrice's grave. Nothing but mud and a few phalanges left."

He leaned forward and took several deep breaths, as though he had received a physical blow. "Oh, God. Any idea who might have done it? Why?"

"None so far. I was going to ask you the same."

"I've not a clue."

Well, so much for that. I guess I was surprised that Andrew was being this helpful.

I decided I needed to plunge into murky waters and find out exactly what was below the surface. "Before, in your room, you'd mentioned a distraction. Who was distracting you from Julia?"

He relaxed back into his chair. "None of your business."

At least I knew it was a who and not a what. "No, it wouldn't be if I wasn't trying to help Jane." I looked him in the eye. "It was Jane, wasn't it?"

His expression told me everything. I recalled how vehemently Jane had denied meeting anyone after her row with Greg, the night of Julia's murder. "Oh, God. You two were together the night of Julia's—"

"No, it's not like that!"

Andrew covered his face with his hands, then sighing, rested them in his lap as he stared at the empty desk before him. "It's not like that at all. That night, I was out walking, waiting until I was to meet Julia back at her place. I was . . . trying to figure out just who it was I was in love with. It was a hellish night for me. When I saw Jane, wandering exactly the same as I was, it seemed to be some sort of sign. It was then, when she told me that she'd had yet another domestic with Greg, that I realized, after all these years, that I didn't love her anymore. It was like chains falling away. I could leave at last. I would never have to worry over whether I would make a fool of myself and my best friend. It was over. Jane assumed I was drunk again by the way I just stood and stared at her, and I was, but it wasn't booze.

"I told her, just go home, sort things out with Greg. I suppose I could have been a little more understanding, but she hadn't known, I don't think, how'd I felt all these years, and I wasn't about to explain that I needed to find Julia immediately and tell her how much I needed her. So Jane gave me a few choice words about my selfishness that were truer than she knew and turned on her heel. I ran back to Julia's apartment to wait for my girl to come home."

Andrew inhaled suddenly, making a horrible noise that was half a gasp and half a sob. He held that breath until he controlled himself again. I realized how that room dwarfed him and how the faint smell of his aftershave seemed like too futile a gesture to establish a living presence in that cold place.

I swallowed. "So you weren't the one Julia was going to meet at the Grub and Cabbage?"

Andrew shook his head. "No, I wasn't going to see her until much later, at her apartment. When she didn't show, I got worried. I mean, any other girl, if she gave me a miss like that, I would have figured she got tired or was pissed off at me or something. Not Julia. Stuck with anything until the bitterest end. When she didn't show I began to get worried. And when she didn't stop by the next day, I knew something was definitely wrong."

"You don't know who she was going to see there?"

"I have no idea, but maybe her parents would do. They were the last to see her before she died, I suppose. I didn't like her going there by herself, though. Her parents are both barking mad, and her father is downright violent. Wicked temper on him. I personally wouldn't want to do anything to get on his bad side. God knows how his wife gets on with him. I would have gone with Julia, but there was the small matter of how her father would react upon making the discovery that his only daughter was sleeping with a member of university staff, someone nearly twenty years her senior, and an archaeologist to boot. Any boyfriend at this juncture would have been a problem, I think, but I was definitely a nonstarter. She said she was meeting someone else after, and who that was, I didn't know. It wasn't like her to keep secrets, really. Keeping us a secret was troublesome to her."

I thought about that, and then remembered the cut chain on the archaeological site.

"Did Julia have access to her father's keys? I mean, to the construction site? I was wondering. The paper didn't say whether the construction site had been broken into. If it hadn't been forced, would the murderer have had his own key to the yard, or did he use hers?" The next question hung unasked between us.

"I knew she had the key." Andrew rested his elbows on the desk now, interlacing his fingers and making a steeple out of his index fingers. "From when she worked for her dad. I don't know who else might have known it, she wasn't close with anyone, really. But everyone did know she'd worked for him, so . . . I think George Whiting is the most likely candidate, if you ask me, but I don't even want to think about it anymore. All I can think about now is that if I hadn't been so slow to sort things out, maybe she wouldn't have felt compelled to see her parents. If I had realized I'd gotten over Jane long ago, if I had realized that I wasn't just larking about with Julia as some sort of . . . gesture, this never would have happened."

"You don't know that—"

"Spare me. You don't know anything at all."

I was about to leave, then realized I'd better ask the other question that had been preying upon me. "What's up with the pathology report on the modern skeleton—can I see what you've done? You promised I could."

"Jesus Christ . . ." Andrew paused, then continued mechanically. "You asked, and I said, I'll see. I've run into a few snags. It's going to be a while. Besides, whatever I do is only ancillary to the forensic pathologist's work."

I walked over to the counter, but it was completely clean of anything—there was nothing to occupy me. "Well, what about the one for Jane, then? I had a thought about the stratigraphy. About the stones on top and the dating. I think the scatter, if I remember it properly, was from the bombing that leveled the remains of one of the abbey walls, right? So if the scatter was on the surface, and we were finding stones mixed into the burial, wouldn't that have to date it pretty close to right after the bombing? Not long enough for any later trash to get mixed in with it, though. That's why I think that modern skeleton we were working on is war vintage."

Andrew gave me a long look. "Interesting thought," he said finally.

"Well? Aren't you going to do anything about it?"

"I'm not in any hurry." He leaned back again, and I couldn't understand why he seemed so relaxed about all this.

"And why is that?"

He watched me, sizing me up, maybe. Maybe trying to figure what would shut me up, get me out of his hair. "Because Greg has enough on his plate at the moment, and I personally don't feel I should add any more grief to his life presently."

My stomach did flipflops and then settled with leaden dread. "Why? Who is it? Why do you say Greg would—"

Andrew smiled, an unpleasant smile that was pure schadenfreude, so pleased to have someone else feel as horrible as he must. "Trust me. It will probably come out eventually, but not if I have anything to say about it, so I'm certainly not going to tell you. No one in Marchester would thank you for pushing your nose into this. I think you should leave now."

I shot Andrew a dirty look and got out of that mausoleum of a room as quickly as I could. The rain was still pouring down, which was fine with me. The bus came along within a few minutes, and I almost missed it, so intent was I on my thoughts. I stared at the gray streets as we rolled along, trying to put some order to my thoughts, the repeated "thank yous" of the conductor a counterpoint to the windshield wipers. An unfamiliar two-toned siren in the distance reminded me how far away from home I was.

Just then we passed Fitzwilliam Street, which I remembered from Morag's business card. I pulled on the cord and had some luck for the first time in what felt like weeks—the bus stopped a few blocks down. I got out, put on my hat, and hurried down the road until I found number fifteen. Fitzwilliam was a busy street with a few shop fronts and restaurants at street level and what looked like professional offices on the floors above, converted from nineteenth-century row houses. The building at number fifteen was in the ubiquitous gray stone and an estate agent's office occupied the ground floor, flanked by a Greek restaurant on one side and an Indian one on the other. A tidy address plate by the bell listed "Marchester Interactive, Web Site Design and Construction, first floor," and, since the door was open, I hurried up a flight, curious as to what I might find.

It wasn't decorated, as such. I suppose the room I walked into off the hallway would have been the apartment's living room, in its former incarnation. Now it looked as though it might have started off as a reception area but gradually became additional workspace for a growing business. There was a single fabric and chrome chair next to a rubber tree plant, which was all that remained of the reception area. Crowded along each of the remaining three walls were three mismatching desks arranged so as to give the illusion of privacy, but that had long since passed away with the growth of the company. Each of the desks had a computer and a printer and a harassed-looking young employee sitting at each one typing like forty, none of whom even noticed that I'd entered the room at first. The place was a haphazard mess, probably only negotiated and understood by its denizens. Cables snaked around the place like Christmas garlands and there was no attempt to disguise or hide them. In fact, there were some tinsel garlands draped along the cables that ran across the wall and I couldn't decide if they were meant to be a cheery disguise for the wires or had merely been forgotten since Christmas. On each of the two side walls, there was a doorway, leading off to other rooms, presumably. One of the desk owners was on the phone, a strawberry blonde with a pointed face whose narrow build was overwhelmed by her fisherman's sweater.

"—In the middle of a death march, no one's slept for a week. I can't believe we're this close to the deadline and they're still adding features. Well, now, you'd think this wouldn't happen *every* single time, wouldn't you? Yeah. Of course it's Tim on their side of things who's the problem; stupid wanker's never shipped anything. He doesn't know his arse from a hole in the wall. Mmm. What can we do, though? They keep giving us work—"

That's when she noticed me. Blushing to the roots of her hair, she said hurriedly, "I've got to go—cheers, love." She hung up quickly and turned to me, annoyed, running a hand over her hair, which did nothing to help make her look less frazzled. "Can I help you?"

"I'm looking for Morag Traeger."

She shuffled some papers, a bit snotty at having been interrupted. "Do you have an appointment?"

"Um, no, but I—"

Morag appeared in the doorway. She, too, must have been feeling the pressure of her project: her hair was unruly beyond artistic wildness, her eyes were reddened, and she looked as though she hadn't had much sleep. She also looked a bit uneasy at seeing me. "What do you want?"

I could have sworn I heard the clatter of typing slow down just a bit; the woman who had been on the phone was lucky enough to be able to see what Morag looked like without having to sneak a peek out of the corner of her eye. "Here to see you, Morag."

"I guessed that. Well?" she asked me.

"I was wondering if I could talk to you for a minute."

She looked at me. I did my best to look harmless. She spoke to the others.

"I've just put the kettle on, the water will be ready in a moment. If you can wait half a minute, I'll run down to the Greek place and get lunch." Back to me. "Come with me. You've got one minute."

I followed her to the adjacent room, which was distinguished by having a door and only one desk, which was so tidy that at first I thought the place must be unused. Then I saw that there was a nice carpet on the wooden floor, and few calming prints on the walls. The place had a residual whiff of incense, possibly from Morag herself; it certainly didn't come from the fresh cut flowers in the vase on the mantelpiece. The desk had a computer, with a stylus and pad: That's right, I thought. Morag was a "creative lead," whatever that might be. Even the books that were pulled from the shelf—a couple of design books and a Pantone color chart—were neatly stacked. One on the top of the pile was *The Visual Display of Quantitative Information* by Edward Tufte, and there was a Post-it note stuck to the cover, so tidily printed that it looked like a computer had printed it. Whew! Morag certainly must have something on the ball, I thought, to help found a growing company and keep up with all those eager young things in front. I had a quick glimpse at the framed photo on her desk; Morag and a short man with dark hair and a beard, both cloaked in full black robes and holding intricately carved staffs. Morag sat down.

"You've heard about Mother Beatrice," I said.

"I was there, remember? I—what is it, Raj?"

A very natty Indian man, in his twenties and dressed in stylish 1970s retro, had poked his head through the door. "We need to talk about my design for—"

"Give me ten minutes, would you?"

"Righto." He looked at me with frank curiosity, then departed.

Morag got up to shut the door, then she returned to her desk. "As I was saying. I'm not about to apologize to you, though I admit, I may have been out of line. I got too carried away—"

I did my best to ignore the fact that Jane had been the one to carry her away. Since Morag didn't see the pun, I wasn't about to advertise it.

"Your friend Jane is the one who—"

"I'm not about to apologize for Jane." I sat without being asked. "Things got out of hand. But I'm not here about that. I mean what happened this morning, or rather, late last night."

Morag shook her head and shrugged. "I don't have any idea what you're going on about." She turned to her monitor screen, losing interest in what I had to say. She tapped a few keys.

I kept my voice matter-of-fact. "The site's been vandalized and the bones of who we think was Mother Beatrice have been stolen. Someone dug her up."

She whirled around, her eyes wide, her mouth working. It took a moment before she could speak. "Oh, Lady, how horrible. Who wa—? Wait, you don't think—?" She stood up, unsure of what to do with herself. "I had nothing to do with this! That is not our way!"

I didn't get the impression that too-earnest Morag could be that good an actor, but I couldn't afford to take anything for granted. I shrugged.

"I swear to you by all I hold holy, it wasn't me or any of my coven!" Morag said. "You must believe me."

"Why must I?"

"No matter what you think, witches don't ever fool with that sort of thing. Raising the dead is just what you see in bad movies. Witches never seek power through the suffering of others and we don't believe that we can gain power only when someone else is denied. What you're talking about, accusing me of, is about as far away as you can get from the tenets of love and trust that I embrace. And think about the Threefold Law."

I shook my head. "I've never heard of it."

"We believe that all our actions, good and bad, are repaid threefold. There's no way I'd so something so ugly, even if I didn't believe in karmic repayment."

I was silent.

She sat down and looked out the window. "We get blamed for things all the time, people make up the most outrageous stories about us, about what we do or what we will do. It's the worst kind of prejudice, persecution. It might be kids, it might be Christians, trying to get us into trouble."

I realized at that instant that while Morag usually puffed up with self-importance at any confrontation, there was none of that here. This was too significantly meaningful to her.

Morag turned from the window as it dawned on her: "Jane Compton thinks I'm responsible."

"After yesterday, I'm hard pressed not to blame her. It looks very bad. You should talk with her, iron this mess out before it escalates."

"It would be hard. She's not an easy person to talk to. I assure you, it wasn't me or mine."

I thought of PC Whelton and the watchband I'd seen, the one with the pentacle on it. I suddenly realized that I had no particular reason to believe him, either. I didn't know what his agenda might be. And there were so many agendas. "Who could it be, then?"

"Jane has made so many people prickly, both professionally and personally—" Morag said.

"Personally? Well, she is a bit driven, but—"

Morag shook her head. "I'm thinking of something else. I mean, symbolically, don't those bones suggest anything else to you?"

"What do you mean?" I looked at her narrowly.

"Whoever dug them up really wanted to disrupt Jane's

work, and that would be a profound hurt to Jane. The fact that it was that burial that was dug up makes it seem quite personal. I'd be thinking about Andrew, if I were you."

I shook my head, trying to figure out how that might work out, given what I'd discovered in the osteology lab. It didn't fit. "What? Why would he dig up those bones?"

Morag shook her head in frustration: I hadn't understood her. "I'm not sure that he's the one who did it, though it's not outside the realm of possibility. I wonder if it isn't so much a professional matter as a personal one. Andrew's been in love with Jane for so long that she was bound to find out, eventually. Maybe she's known all along. Anyone with a pair of eyes to see that would have known, if they wanted to. Maybe, finally, Greg Ashford's found out too."

Chapter 19

MORAG WALKED ME OUT, ON HER WAY DOWN TO THE Greek place. I was glad she did, because I was somewhat in a daze. I walked along the street, trying to reconcile Morag's suspicions with what I'd been considering. Somewhere through the fog in my brain, somewhere out in the fog of the real world, I heard honking behind me. I ignored it—it wasn't for me this time, I wasn't anywhere near a zebra crosswalk—but then heard a familiar and presently unwelcome voice call out behind me. "Emma! Get in, I'll give you a lift!"

I was quickly running out of space on my "would rather not run into" list, but Greg was right at the bottom of that list, at the moment. I didn't know how I could look him in the eye, knowing that his best friend was in love with his wife, and not knowing whether he knew and might have done something about it. At least he was still acting nominally friendly toward me. I waved and got into the car, a little surprised at just how very wet I had become; water streamed off my coat and hat and I soon created puddles on the floor.

Greg saw me looking at the wet footprints. "Don't worry about it; the dear old Landcrab don't mind the wet. A motor for all British seasons, she is." He patted the dashboard, then, turning back to me, frowned. "If you don't mind a quick stop, I'm going to knock up Aunty Mads—"

He just means visit, I reminded myself hastily.

"—As I'm really worried about her. When I called this morning, her neighbor was in and said she's really gone into a decline."

"I'm very sorry to hear it," I said.

"Thank you. I've been calling around social services this morning to see if I can find a visiting nurse to come round. I don't want to drag her to hospital if . . . if it's not going to do her any good."

We drove in silence for a moment.

"So I'm just going to meet the nurse, make sure that Aunty's settled in as comfortably as possible. Are you in a hurry to get back home?"

"Not really. I'm happy to go . . . only, do you think Mads would mind?"

Greg frowned again. "If she's feeling fit for company, then it's no problem. If she's low, and not feeling fit to be seen, you can sit in the parlor. It won't take long, only I want to make sure that I meet the nurse and get things settled."

"Oh, of course, no problem at all. Please, don't worry about me."

We pulled up to a little row of houses, and I recognized that we were just a few blocks from the cafe. Greg got out and reached into the back. "Give me a hand, would you?"

He handed me a couple of plastic grocery bags marked "Sainsbury's," and I followed him up the front stairs. He let us in with his own key; in the hallway, an aroma of long-lived-in house swept over me, scrubbed linoleum and old varnish, sachet, milky tea, and boiled vegetables.

"Hallo?"

A voice called, "In here, Greg." A stout middle-aged woman met us at the door to the kitchen.

"Mrs. Haywood, this is my friend Emma Fielding. Emma, this is Mrs. Haywood, Aunty's neighbor and very good friend."

"Very old friend, at least." We shook hands.

"How is the patient, then?" Greg said, as cheerily as he could.

"Well, not very well, I'm afraid. I won't lie to you, Greg,"—she lowered her voice—"I just helped her to the loo and it's completely wrung her out. She's in bed again. I don't think she's been up since before I got here this morning. She's very bad off, I think."

We all stood around for a minute. "Well," Greg said.

"She's very old and very tired. I think she's had enough," Mrs. Haywood whispered, nodding solemnly. "Is the nurse coming?"

"Yes, I was able to track one down this morning. She'll be here on the hour."

"Well, that's good, at any rate. A nurse'll be able to make her comfortable. She's not doing very well, you know, recognizing people. She kept calling me Moira, which was her sister's name, I think. I've just put the kettle on, but if you don't mind, I need to get to work. Are you all right here, for a bit?"

"Yes, yes, of course." Greg looked distractedly down the hallway. "We're not working today. You've been so kind, Mrs. Haywood."

"No, no. Only, it's a bit sad, to see her so," she turned to me, "with her being so much a part of the town, do you know what I mean?"

I nodded.

"Still. Well, I must be off, but I'll stop in after I've done at work." She picked up her coat and umbrella. "Still raining out, I see."

"Probably a bit longer. It will clear up tonight, be nice and hot tomorrow."

"So it will. Ta-ra, Greg."

"Good-bye, Mrs. Haywood. Thanks again." He closed the door behind her.

"Do you want me to make the tea? You could go check on her," I offered.

"No, you won't know where anything is, and I must put this lot away before it spoils. Let me just look in on her."

He hurried upstairs and was down a moment later, looking concerned. "I think she's almost asleep, but not quite yet. She is a bit out of it. I don't like to leave her alone . . ."

"Well, I can sit with her for a minute, if you don't think it will bother her."

"No, and I'll only be a minute." Greg was relieved to have a plan. "I want to keep an eye out for the nurse as well."

I crept upstairs and peered into the room, which looked as though it hadn't changed much since the 1950s. Large cabbage roses formed stripes on the wallpaper and the furniture was a mixture of cheaply manufactured goods from the end of the nineteenth century and the beginning of the twentieth. Aunty Mads was in the middle of a narrow bed, a faded and much washed cotton nightgown on her thin shoulders showed above the covers. The varnish and sachet smell was very strong in here, the place where she was most herself. There was something else too, though I hesitate to give it a concrete name: it was really more of a state. It was the absolute quiet of a room in which someone had given up.

I had to overcome a tremendous sense that I was intruding before I could step over the jamb, but Mads stirred and opened her eyes and called, "Jane? Is that you?"

I sat down in a chair set next to the bed; the linoleum beneath the rag rug creaked in protest. "No, it's Emma. Her friend. Can I get you something?"

"No, ta very much." She reached for my hand and I gave it to her, because you don't not give someone your hand in a room like that, at a time like that. I could feel the slight bones of her hand beneath the fading envelope of flesh, her skin, dry and warm and papery, slid loosely as she grasped my hand tightly.

"Greg's here, too," I said, hoping that familiar and loved name would stir a little more recognition from her. "He's in the kitchen—"

"No, dearie, I don't want my boy now. Leave him be, for a moment. I want to talk to you, Jane."

I tried once again, reluctantly, as gently as I could.

"I'm Emma . . . Aunty Mads."

"I know you are, dear. But I want to talk to you. It's about my boy and what's going to happen to him."

My stomach contracted.

"I want you to look after him the way I've always looked after him. You can be hard, Jane, but I know you love him. He worships the ground you walk on, which ought to be enough for me, but he's always been so precious to us. So precious. When his parents died, back in 1974 now, it killed his grandfather just a year later. They can call it a heart attack, if you like, but what's the difference between that and a broken heart, I ask you?"

She sighed. "When that happened, I thought that his gran Caroline was sure to follow and I couldn't let that happen, now, could I? After all we been through. So I told her, 'Caroline, you take hold of yourself! You have to, for Greg's sake, poor lad, and I'll help you.' And she let me and we raised our boy."

Time was compressing for Mads, expanding and contracting between the immediate and more distant pasts. But she never let go of my hand. I could hear Greg in the kitchen, closing cabinets and fussing with the tea things now.

"That's how it was between us, you see," she insisted, as if I had gainsaid her. "We was always there for each other. She was there for me, when my young man died in France and Greg's granddad Scotty was off in Africa. I thought it would kill me when I got the news, but she kept me going. And now I was able to do the same for her. Return the favor, you see, but neither of us would ever say that. We didn't talk about it, not like you people today talk about everything. It was just what you did for a friend as good as that and we both knew it. We would have done anything for each other. And oh, Jane, we did."

I tried to imagine for a moment that nothing worse would follow, that this was just the way she had of saying goodbye, but I couldn't maintain the illusion. Little weak tears began to run down her cheeks, getting lost in the wrinkles and making her face damp.

"Shh, shh," I said.

"Jane, give us the little tin there on the nightstand." She gestured to it, my hand still in hers. "The toffee tin."

I picked up and handed it to her. Something heavy and loose rattled in it. She took it in both hands and tried to pry the lid off. She handed it back to me without a word and I opened it for her. She took it and reached inside; then handed what was in the box to me.

I looked down in my hand. It was a large gold ring, a man's ring with a big blue stone, square cut, in the middle. It was real, there was no doubt of that, but it was showy, a thing made to grab the eye and hold it. Its vulgarity was its only purpose.

"You take it now, Jane. I wore it on a chain, hidden like, a long time, until it started to bruise me when I got old—never get old, Jane, it's horrible thing to get old when you don't feel old yet. But you take it now, because I don't need to worry about where it come from anymore."

I started to go cold, afraid I knew exactly where it had come from.

"I never felt guilty about it, not when I done it and not since then. Not until you started to dig last month and I began to worry that you'd find him. Sebastian Hall, I mean. It was only then, years after anyone should care, that I began to feel scared, like. Like we'd done something wrong. Like I was a murderer. And I couldn't think why, except that me and Caroline were always very careful never to mention it, even in passing, like. You'd think I was beyond caring what happened to me, but I worried what Greg would think if he found out. Not that he'd ever think any harm of anyone, dear boy, but I just couldn't bear the thought of him not understanding about me and his gran killing someone."

I could hear the doorbell and prayed Greg wouldn't come in. That the nurse wouldn't come in. Not yet.

"It sounds horrible to say it, 'kill someone,' but we knew we was right to do what we done. I never thought twice about it and I don't think Caroline did neither. She never told her husband, Scotty, I don't think. Men don't always understand about women who are attacked, do they? I mean to say, Scotty was a lovely boy, but if you heard that another bloke—a rich one, a powerful one—tried to force your girl, well, with you being so far away and him being there and rich and all, you might wonder if she'd started something herself, know what I mean?"

I nodded, though she wasn't really paying attention to me.

"They get ideas in their heads about things, so it's best not to say sometimes, no matter what the truth is. I was staying with Caroline then, I couldn't bear to be on my own after the news, and since I didn't want to lose my job, I stayed with her instead of going back to my people after the news about my own poor young man.

"It was during a raid. I heard her scream, bloodcurdling it was. I run downstairs and there he was with her on the front room floor, her skirt all up around her waist."

She paused, and I needed the break almost as much as Mads did. She kept shaking her head, like she couldn't quite believe the memory was as terrible as it was. She took a deep breath and continued.

"I could barely think, the noise outside was that bad. Sebastian Hall'd been a nuisance before, he was always after Caroline to take things from him, sugar, eggs, tins of fruit—filthy stuff, off the black market—but she never did. We were good girls and we never dared guess where he might have stolen the things. He always had enough petrol to drive, and that game foot of his, what kept him from serving, never seemed to slow him down, did it? It did not! But he never came round the house before that night.

"Caroline was a big girl, made me look like a little bird, and she couldn't shift him, no matter what she did: He was too strong. I didn't stop to think. I ran into the kitchen, picked up the big carving knife, and stuck it in his back. He turned around—it didn't stop him—and Caroline bit him, scrabbled away as best she could. I stuck him again, in the front this time, and then he started to go wobbly in the knees, staggering about. The last time, I stuck him hard, and that's when the knife stayed in him. I could feel how hard it hit the bone, how it felt like it does when you stick a chicken the wrong way and get caught up on the backbone."

I smothered a gasp; it was exactly the analogy Andrew had so callously made.

"There was an awful lot of blood and he just went over. We took his wallet off him and hid his papers in a jar of preserves down in the cellar. We decided we couldn't dump him in the river—too many bodies washed up from further upstream, and we didn't want to run the risk—and so we decided to bury him down by the old abbey walls. Everyone gave out it was haunted and we figured it was wasteland now, anywise. What with all the rubble from the bombings, we hoped he might be taken by someone caught in the bombing if he was found.

"The only problem was his ring. Everyone knew it, he was always flashing it around. Only it was stuck on his hand, we couldn't get it off. Imagine the shame of it: getting that fat during rationing! And it was Caroline came up with the answer. 'We cut it off him, joint him like a beef.' That was easier than we thought, in spite of all the blood that was already all over the place, slippery like, but what to do with the ring?"

She breathed laboriously. "It was too valuable to throw away, too well known to sell. So we decided to keep it, in case the need should ever come, we'd have it and take it into London. And I kept it, because I hadn't a man going to come home and ask about it. I never did marry. It just wasn't in me, after my young man died. I'd had enough of worry and loss.

"I suppose that's why Greg's always been that precious to us. He brought me and Caroline together again, poor little lad, after his parents died in that dreadful car accident. I suppose I haven't been too fair to you, on his account, but I don't never say I'm sorry about that. You'll have him the rest of your life, if you're lucky, and I only wanted him for the little time I had left. You look after him now, and you be very good to my boy."

She groped for my hand. "Just don't tell him, don't you. He's a sweet boy, but he might not understand. Men don't always understand . . ."

She was starting to fade a bit now, rambling a little. I swallowed.

"You know," I said, close to her ear, as gently as I could, "if anyone was going to understand, it would be Greg." I could hear the nurse and Greg still talking out in the kitchen.

Mads tried to shake her head; she clutched at my hand, with her last bit of strength. "Never tell him! You understand? Do that for me. Only—Jane? It's a relief now to have it off my mind, these past weeks have been awful hard for me. Ever since he told me where you was going to be digging up. It's a wonderful relief, when I'm so tired."

She patted at my hand again, missing the first time, then catching hold of it again. "You do whatever you like with the ring, Jane. It doesn't matter now. Just look after him. He's my good boy."

She fell asleep then, still clutching my hand. The ring burned heavy and sweaty in my other hand. Greg and the nurse came into the doorway then, pausing.

Very, very gently, I slid my hand from Mads's.

"She's asleep," I said. I got up and met them; the nurse went in and fussed about Mads, smoothing out the blanket, checking her pulse, looking around the room.

"What were you two talking about?" Greg said.

"She told me to look after you," I said. I tried to smile, my eyes brimming.

Greg looked startled.

"She thought I was Jane." I wiped my eyes with my sleeve.

The nurse looked up and nodded. Greg said, "Mrs. Haywood said she's been in and out like that for a day or so now."

"Well, that happens, at the end, doesn't it," the nurse said matter-of-factly. "She'll sleep a bit now, so why don't you show me around and I'll settle in."

"I'll wait in the front room," I said. I hurried down the hall, wondering whether I would make it before the ring, which seemed to be growing larger and larger every minute, slipped out of my hand. I stuck it into my pocket and wiped the sweat from my palm, sitting, staring, and letting my mind go blank until Greg was finished.

He came down the hall with the nurse. "And here's my number at home, should you need it," he said to the nurse. "Any little change, please call me."

"I will. Don't worry, Mr. Ashford, I'll make your aunty as comfortable as possible."

He nodded and we left at long last. I was left wondering who to tell—and what I should tell. Worse, I was now more than ever in a position to ruin my friends' lives in so many ways.

Dinner that evening was a nightmare. Every time I instinctively went to bring up some of what was on my mind, I found myself confounded by the knowledge that I couldn't say anything of what I'd learned to either Jane or Greg. Every bite half-choked me. I was acutely and miserably aware of just how much information I had that I shouldn't have, and how secrets are a burden. Problem was, sometimes secrets need to be revealed to do good, sometimes they have to stay secret, and a burden, in order to do some good.

I wasn't at all certain which sort of time this was. So between me, snared in indecision, Greg, quite down about Aunty, and Jane, just tired of trying, the meal was largely spent in silence, the three of us pushing our food around on our plates in an approximation of dining.

That was the best case estimate, though. It might well have been that I was seated at dinner with a friend who was also a murderer.

We just gave up trying in the end. As Jane put away the leftovers and Greg was absorbed in arranging the heat lamps over Hildegard, I decided to give my one idea voice.

"Jane, can you get ahold of your reporter friend?"

She gritted her teeth and closed the small refrigerator with a slam. "He's no friend of mine."

"But you could reach him, right?"

She nodded.

"Maybe you can use his little overeagerness in publishing the story about the discovery of the skeleton to some good end."

Jane turned, eyebrows raised, lips pursed. "You'll have to tell me what good can come of it."

"Well, I was just wondering. On the off chance that it was someone interested specifically in Mother Beatrice's remains—"

"And not just in foxing me?"

"Right. On that chance, what if we put a bit in the paper that said that the bones that were taken were not Mother Beatrice's? We could say that you'd got the location wrong—"

Jane crossed her arms over her chest, cocked her head, squinted at me in disbelief. This was not going to be an option for her.

"—Or that the bones that were taken were from a later burial and Mother Beatrice was right beneath. Or something like that."

She looked skeptical still. "And what exactly would that do?"

"I don't know, exactly. I just had the thought that maybe if they weren't Mother Beatrice's, maybe whoever stole the bones might dump them, or return them, or something. It's a faint hope, but it might stir up a response. The reporter could ostensibly be reporting on the theft itself, and isn't it good that nothing important was taken, that sort of thing."

Jane didn't look like she was buying it. Greg was a little more optimistic, on the other hand.

"Well, it's better than nothing," he said. "I can't think of anything else worth trying. Can you?"

"No." Jane thought a bit more. "I'll give it a shot. God knows the little scoundrel owes me that much. I'll try to get it in for the afternoon paper tomorrow." She went over to the phone and dialed the number. After some vigorous to-ing and fro-ing, along with the thinly veiled threat that the reporter's premature article might have been responsible for the vandalism and theft, Jane got what she wanted.

"Well, that's sorted. It'll run tomorrow afternoon. Who knows what might come of it, but we'll give it a shot, what?"

The phone rang, and Jane, probably expecting some further argument from the reporter, answered brusquely. "Yes?"

Her face changed almost immediately. "Yes, yes of course. Just a moment, please." She covered the receiver. "It's for you, Emma. Says it's Kam?" She handed me the receiver and mouthed "very posh sounding" with a suggestive roll of her shoulders. It was the first time I'd seen her smile and mean it all evening. She and Greg went upstairs to the parlor.

I grabbed the phone like it was the last life preserver on the *Titanic*. "Hey Kam!"

"How are you, Emma?" His voice was strained.

My shoulders slumped. "Oh, you know."

"Yes, Brian told me. Probably not a good time to talk about that?"

"It's not." It wasn't really private in the kitchen, with peo-

ple in the living room, and I was glad that I wasn't going to
have to give voice to all my grim thoughts. It was also very
nice to talk to someone whose life or reputation I didn't hold
in my hand. A loud background noise came over the phone,
like a treeful of excited birds. "What was that?"

There was silence on the other end of the line, followed
by a sigh. "Mariam. And my mother."

Since Kam almost never called my friend Marty by her
proper name, I could only assume that he was annoyed with
his fiancée. Little alarms went off in my head: Theirs had
been an unhurried engagement, which looked to many like
nerves on Marty's part. I knew better, but while they were
due to be married next spring, this sounded like real trouble.
"First visit not what you'd hoped?"

"Oh, Emma." Kam sounded absolutely defeated and my
heart broke for them both. "They get on like a house afire."

I hesitated. "Um. You'd think that would be a good thing,
wouldn't you?"

"It is, it is. I suppose. But, well, frankly, Emma, and I tell
you this in the confidence of our long friendship, for years I
have been my own man and I liked it that way. My mother, it
is true, was the one person who could make real demands
upon me and I, glad to be able to oblige her, would do so,
most frequently. The fact that there was 3,000 miles of
ocean and a lengthy flight between us made this easy. Everyone was happy."

"Ah."

He continued on confidentially. "Mother encourages me
to be rather more experimental in dress than I would ordinarily care to be. I could, however, in the past, wear the
neckties she chose for me quite happily when I visited, and
she was happy never knowing that they languished in my
closet at home. I could take her to the 'hot' places whenever
I visited, and then quite simply retreat to my quieter haunts
when I returned to Boston. A small price to pay, to please
her, and so filial duty was easily discharged. I could always
go home."

I tried to offer some consolation. "But you had been afraid that they wouldn't get along . . ."

"It's true. I was worried that Mother would find Marty's flamboyance *de trop*; I was worried that Marty would be put off by Mother's quiet, sometimes daunting, rectitude. I was prepared for uncomfortable silences, though doubted it would ever come to anything so unhappy as outright hostility. It's so much worse than that."

He had to say it out loud, I thought. He has to own it. It's the only way.

"Emma, they've ganged up on me."

I would have giggled at the piteousness in his voice, if he hadn't been so truly despondent.

"I should have recognized it. They're exactly alike. In the glow of courtship, I never realized that when Marty chided me for acting like an 'old poop' when I admitted I didn't share her love of Versace, it was exactly the same as when mother would gently remind me that I was a young man and that I ought to dress less like her generation and more like my own. I never realized, when Marty was trying to drag me to all those places where she could see and be seen, that it was precisely analogous to Mother asking to be taken to some scandalous club she'd read about in the papers. While I thought they were so very different, the fact is that they've embraced each other as readily as oppositely charged magnets. It's a catastrophe. Emma, I'm done for."

Just then, I heard my best friend's voice cry out in delight. "No! Not Mills and Boon!" whereupon I thought I could hear the usually unflappable Kam actually grind his teeth. "I'm going to put a stop to this right now."

"Kam, what's Mills and Boon?"

"I'm afraid I need to ring off. When are you coming up to London?"

"Friday."

"And you're staying in Bloomsbury?"

I recited the address of a small hotel I'd never been to before. Kam didn't approve.

"Well, it's a bare step above Russell Square, but an important step, I suppose. You're sure you won't stay with us? There is plenty of room . . ." He trailed off hopefully.

There was no way I was going to introduce myself into that maelstrom until everything had been sorted out and Kam finally gave way to the inevitable. "No thanks, it's closer to the libraries than Mayfair. Maybe next time. I'll call when I get in."

My friend sighed. "Very well. Early dinner Saturday night all right, then? Any place in particular you'd like to go?"

Kamil Shah was polite. He also knew I didn't know London at all, and more than that, he knew I didn't know any of the quietly luxurious places where he felt most at home. He was counting on me. He was an old friend, so I gave him what he sought but couldn't ask for.

"No, Kam. You pick."

Chapter 20

IN SPITE OF THE DIVERSION OF BEING ABLE TO THINK about what might come after the Marchester dig, which had let me fall asleep when I tried to later on, I was wide awake around four in the morning. It was very warm in my room and since I knew, reluctantly, that there was no chance of getting back to the land of Nod, I sat up and looked down at my suitcase. I had kept it so tidy and organized for the first few days, a gesture to being in someone else's neat house; now laundry and papers had begun to spill out of bounds, creeping across the floor with the slow inevitability of a glacier. Perhaps it was because my little borrowed room was the only place where I felt the least bit at home, and distracted by what was going on at the site and my nagging questions about Julia Whiting's murder, I had let it go unchecked. Easy enough to sort it out and do some laundry before I left for London.

I got up, put things in order, and then, seeing I still had another couple of hours until I actually needed to be up and about, took out a notebook and started to try to impose some order on my unruly thoughts. Starting was an excellent notion, but I got no further than taking the cap off my pen and putting it back on again. I was too tired to think straight, so I gave up for the moment.

It was quite hot by the time I dragged myself downstairs for a bath and my breakfast. I was up before everyone else so I dug around until I found Jane's coffee and coffee press, and made some to my own specifications, which, after nearly two weeks of malcaffeination, was nirvana. I thought of those Chinese illustrations of gods, the ones where the celestial beings are traveling around on little clouds, quite regally apart from mortal earth, and thought I knew a little of how that felt. I felt swift, sure, sapient, and sharp. I resisted the urge to rub some of the grounds into my gums. How could I have deprived myself for so long?

Greg came downstairs, dressed but rubbing the sleep from his eyes and jumped when he realized he wasn't alone. "Oh. Hallo. You're up early."

Maybe he noticed the divine light blazing forth from my eyes, or maybe he saw the grounds and kettle steaming behind me. "Found the coffee things all right then? Good."

He busied himself with tea things for himself and Jane and fed the tortoise Hildegard, and I heard footsteps thumping toward the door upstairs pause, then turn around and head downstairs toward the kitchen.

"Is that coffee?" Andrew asked his friend in disbelief. Then he saw me. "Oh."

"Want some?" I was in far too good a mood to deny anyone.

"Yeah, all right, since you're offering." He poured himself a cup, drank deeply, and began to cough. His eyes streaming, he finally regained control of himself. Andrew glanced at his cup and then stared at me.

"Fuck me. That explains a lot." He turned to Greg. "I'm off, then."

We heard the door slam, announcing Andrew's exit. "He comes off a bit rude to people who don't know him well," Greg said, shrugging slightly.

"He comes off a bit rude to those who do know him well," I answered.

Greg's eyes widened.

"I'm sorry. That was uncalled for," I said. "Andrew's got a lot on his mind at the moment."

"Oh? How do you know?"

I realized I couldn't tell Greg about any one of Andrew's problems—the ones I knew about, at least. "Why else would he be so grumpy, unless he were preoccupied?"

He nodded. "I suppose you're right. He's been talking for some time about making a move up north, going to work with a friend up there. Company, not a university program."

"Why hasn't he, then?"

Greg shot me a sharp, questioning look. "I suppose he's just used to life down here in Marchester, is all. No real reason to make a change." He picked up a couple of mugs of tea. "I'll just bring this up to Jane then. We'll be down in a half a tick. Help yourself to the muesli and such, if you like."

"Thanks, Greg."

I ate my breakfast and wondered: Perhaps Greg didn't know about his friend's infatuation with his wife. Then again, maybe he did.

When we finally headed out to the site, I was shocked at how warm it had suddenly become. While the weather had been cool and tending to rain for the past ten days, now it was nearly eighty degrees, just before nine in the morning. The really appalling thing, I observed walking down the street, was that the populace at large was generally ill equipped to deal with this happy turn of events. Many people were in summer clothing that might have been appropriate at home if the mercury had been closer to one hundred: women were wearing short shorts and tank tops, very small children were in their bathing suits, men were clad in Bermuda shorts. The amount of paler than fair white flesh exposed was quite startling, and since I didn't get a whiff of sunblock, I realized that most of the population of Marchester would be proudly sporting first-degree sunburns by the end of the day. I passed one particular couple and shuddered: She was wearing an entirely out of date and ill-advised tube-top that made her look like a sausage escaping its casing and he wore some sort of sleeveless T-shirt that appeared to be made of netting that barely covered a truly world-class beer belly, a thing of pride he'd been crafting for years. It wasn't good sense about being in the sun or even a deeply ingrained Yankee Puritanism that made me flinch: It simply wasn't right.

"Jane, can I have a string vest like that man's?" Greg whispered after we passed. He grinned at me behind his wife's back.

"You even think about it and you're done for," she replied indignantly.

There was little for me to do at the site. I sifted through the destroyed unit and found a couple more teeth and a clothing fastener and a couple of pins, but nothing more. Everything that had been in the grave had been taken. I decided to take the rest of the day off to do my laundry. Jane was fine with that; since I had only another day left, she wasn't too keen on me starting up something that someone else would have to finish after I was gone.

The next day, Thursday, I helped out the students, where I was needed, but space was tight and soon I found I was at loose ends. There was one thing I had to do, though, before I left. I picked up my backpack and waited for my chance as I worked on my notes. As soon as Dean Avery bent over, however, I whipped out my camera and took his picture. With a telephoto lens. He heard the click and spun around. I waved and he glared at me.

Taste of your own medicine, I thought. "You made it look like such fun," I said. "I'll send you a copy. I'll send you a hundred."

I didn't want to waste the sunshine, though, and after a moment's inspiration, was reminded of the view of the

abbey ruin that I'd copied down from Jeremy's painting. I
wondered from where the perspective was taken: had there
been some kind of manor opposite the site on a hill, or was
the picture merely some sort of artistic convention? I decided that I would have a walk around and find out.

It wasn't hard to find the location of the rise; it was just
opposite the site on the same side of the river. There was
nothing but houses there now, newer and more expensive
than the ones down by where Jane and Greg lived. There was
nothing to indicate there had been a house there from which
the ruins of the abbey might once have been seen and the rest
of the view was blocked by the city's growth over the centuries. Thinking once again of Sabine's words about the two
of us being trained outsiders, observing things from different
perspectives, I also saw that the trip hadn't been a total waste
of time. I realized that I would sit up tonight at the site and
see whether the planted newspaper article about Mother
Beatrice's bones managed to stir up any effect.

Jane had wanted to have a good-bye dinner for me that
night, considering that the next day I was going back to London, but no one was really in the mood for it. So it was just
the three of us at table, excellent food in front of us, with the
least imaginable air of celebrating or farewell. Everyone was
so wrung out that there was no point, and Greg kept making
halfhearted comments about how much fun I'd have when I
visited next time. My stomach tightened at the thought of a
"next time." It wasn't long before everyone found his way
up to bed, whereupon I changed into a dark T-shirt, jeans,
and sneakers, made a thermos of coffee, and with my flashlight, quietly closed the door behind me on 98 Liverpool
Road.

The air was still warm, even at ten o'clock in the evening,
and there was not a breeze to be felt. My footsteps echoed
on the empty pavement, and the only people I met seemed to
be hurrying to or from the pubs, islands of light and muffled
noise that marked each quiet block. It didn't take me long to
get to the site, and I realized that even if I had wanted to, I

wouldn't be able to watch from inside the locked enclosure: I didn't have a key. Still, I reasoned that I would be less visible if I situated myself among the small trees and weeds outside the compound, not easily visible from either the road or the path along the river, or even the river itself.

Again, I tried to order my thoughts regarding what I knew about Julia's death. The people closest to her seemed to be the ones most intensely antagonistic to her, and it seemed to me that all of the high feeling she engendered, simply by being who she was—bright, opinionated, young, passionate, and demanding—obscured the truth better than the most carefully contrived false trails. Julia might have been the main source of so much of this emotional turmoil, but there was enough fallout from Jane and Greg's marital problems, Jane's conflicts with Morag and George Whiting, and Andrew's misplaced affections to compound matters significantly. History fed into it all too, what with the connections between Palmer and Whiting, Palmer and Avery . . .

I dozed off briefly, then awoke with a start; the ring that Aunty Mads had pressed into my possession was biting into my leg through my jeans pocket. Eventually, I knew, I'd have to do something about that too, but the possible ramifications against a sick old woman and my own friends were daunting. I drank more of the coffee, wishing it was a little warmer, a little more comforting.

It was getting to around three o'clock in the morning and I was starting to think that I was on a fool's errand. More than that, I had been suspecting I had been out of my mind for some time. If it was someone who was interested in Mother Beatrice, good, but there was little chance of him going back to the site after the publicity; if it was someone interested in hurting Jane, either by impugning her character or disrupting her work, then there was even less chance of his reappearing. But I decided to give it just another half hour before I packed it in; as long a shot as it was to be out here, I had a much better chance of learning something than if I'd stayed in my room. Besides, it was long enough since pub closing time to be assured that anyone out would not be strolling idly, but on his way *somewhere*. Any later, and whoever might visit the site would start running into milkmen and paper carriers and the like; anyway, that was how I was rationalizing it.

Still, there were less attractive places for a stakeout, if I wanted to grace my misguided vigil with fancy names. If I squinted, blurring my vision slightly, I could imagine away the chain-link fence around the site and focus on the low line of ruined abbey wall, the moonlit river beyond that, and the occasional light across the river. Very nice and Romantic, with a capital R.

That thought actually woke me up: it was very romantic, but romance and ruins were more of the eighteenth and nineteenth centuries, not the sixteenth. I recalled the presence of the ruined abbey in Frobisher Cholmondeley's portrait. Why was the ruin depicted there, and not the new church downriver? Or his private lands, perhaps, or his library, as many a proud churchman might have shown? The fact of the ruins being shown in the painting made me wonder whether he hadn't been one of the churchmen in conflict with Mother Beatrice and whether, years after her death, the destruction of the abbey seemed to be some vindication of his side of the squabble. I tried to recall the dates of Mother Beatrice's life and whether there might be some overlap there, but the picture and its subject certainly bore some further consideration. I'd have to remember to tell Jane. I yawned hugely; if I couldn't have answers, I wanted my bed and three hours of sleep.

The coffee I'd drunk was long gone from the thermos, but now making increasingly urgent demands on my bladder, so I considered the porta-potty. There are few things less inviting than a portable toilet in the dead of night: They are not places where one feels comfortable groping about. I thought about turning on my flashlight and then realized that unless I wanted to climb the fence with the flashlight in my mouth, it was the bushes for me. I found as secluded a spot as I could and tried to get down to it.

If using a public convenience as impermanent as a plastic lavatory during the day requires a certain element of cultural training—everyone, including those on the outside waiting for their turn, does her level best to ignore what is going on and is not muffled by permanent walls and doors—then going *outside* those thin plastic walls at night, with the comparative dead silence of an abandoned site around you, is downright eerie. I actually found myself unnerved by the quiet, and the small noise that I made caused me to feel terribly exposed. It was the only time I suffered from anything remotely resembling penis envy: Guys could pull something like this off with relative ease. Hell, it was even socially sanctioned, in some instances, a casual bonding experience. They didn't have the back-to-the-paleolithic, down-and-dirty experience of being so completely exposed to the elements. I never felt so strongly the acute lack of horns, fangs, claws, and defensive armor on humans as I did then, and when something squawked and then splashed down by the river, I jumped a mile. I finished up as quickly as possible, hoping that dear old Mr. Whatsit across the river wasn't an insomniac bird watcher with his binoculars out at that moment, for I had no desire to fog up his lenses. This always seemed so much less complicated when one was camping.

Just as I'd fastened my belt, I heard something. I froze; I was far too tired and susceptible at the moment and didn't want to break an ankle chasing after a river rat or another restless bird. The rustling came again, and persisted, this time, in a regular, strictly bipedal, cadence. Someone was moving through the weed-choked path that ran along the river.

I moved as quietly as I could toward the river to try and get a better look. I had to wait a while after I left the pool of light that came from the street lamp, until my eyes adjusted, but I tried to make the most of that pause as well. The weeds and river were silver in the moonlight. Trying not to panic, as whoever it was moved steadily away from me, I got the impression that it was someone not used to stealth and who was now not especially trying to move silently. A brief break in the steps; the walker stumbled. The path was overgrown but perfectly obvious, even in moonlight. Whoever it was wasn't used to moving on unpaved surfaces.

I followed along, not daring to use my flashlight. There was plenty of light, now that I was away from the street. Not only did some of the lights from across the river break up the gloom, but there was bright moonlight as well. As long as I moved cautiously and tried not to focus too much on the path right in front of me, letting my peripheral vision aid me, I could follow easily enough. A certain amount of familiarity with the path and with moving through woods and fields helped; I was no Hawkeye, but even a little bit of advantage goes a long way if you concentrate on it. Perhaps it was to my advantage that I was not one of Cooper's characters: I was lucky enough not to step on any dry twigs and give myself away.

The figure ahead of me was low and bulky and crouched over. When it paused at the far side of the site, outside the fence, I felt certain that I was on the right trail. I had the impression of someone looking around from the shadows and crouched as carefully as I could, but then the figure moved on. I almost gave up then; it could have been a kid sneaking home from a rave, it could have been a house thief coming home from work: It had nothing to do with the site, it seemed. But then, a brief parting of shadows, a little reflection of moonlight off the water, reassured me and my heart sped up even faster when I saw who it was.

The figure was low because it was George Whiting; it was bulky because he was carrying a bundle of some sort. And now I could tell he was heading down the path to St. Alban's Church.

George made sense, I thought excitedly. He wasn't interested in Mother Beatrice or her story, but he was vastly interested in Jane and her work, albeit in a hostile way. It would have been no trouble for him to break into the site—a good industrial-sized pair of bolt-cutters would have done the job. Perhaps he'd done no more damage because he'd been surprised; perhaps he'd felt only a token display of violence and vandalism was enough, either to vent his displeasure against my friend or to satisfy himself with a response. It had certainly stopped work for a day and put a cat among the pigeons, to say the least. But what was he up to now? Was it possible, as Andrew had hinted, that he might also be responsible for Julia's death? Worse than that, was he trying to frame Jane for it?

I followed along, more slowly now because Whiting was moving more slowly; I could hear the rough rasp of his breath from where I was, nearly twenty-five meters behind. I had to fall farther back when he reached the open field where Sabine had been playing soccer after her math tutorial last week. Once he moved past it, into closer proximity to the church itself, I felt it was safe enough to continue following him, but had to freeze halfway across the field, visible to anyone who cared to look for me, when he stopped just short of St. Alban's churchyard and the low stone wall that encircled the modern cemetery. I waited until he began to fumble his way off the river path, looking for the entrance into the cemetery.

I began to think I knew what was going on. I followed behind as he entered the churchyard and moved hesitatingly across the yard, occasionally tripping over the unevenness of the ground or perhaps a footstone. He stumbled across the yard until he reached the far side, which was sheltered by the huge oak that had been the marker of the makeshift letter-drop that I had used to communicate with Stephen, the young man outside the pub. He dropped his bundle gently, and I could almost swear that I hear the clatter of small, light objects. I wondered if he hadn't been drinking because his breath was heavy and irregular, even for someone who'd been moving as long as he had.

He dropped to his knees by the tree. For almost thirty sec-

onds, I thought he was looking for another note that might
had been left for me. But when I heard the all-too-familiar
ring of metal on stone, I realized the truth.

George Whiting was digging in the graveyard behind St.
Alban's.

From my vantage point behind a large gravestone, I considered what to do. I could feel the cold, rough edge of the
stone beneath my fingers, the cool radiating from the stone
into the warm of the night. I swallowed as I hurriedly ran
down my options. I could leave as quietly as I'd come and
find the police. I could try and startle him, with any luck, en-
suring that he would flee and I could find out what was in the
bundle, though I had a horrid suspicion that I already knew.
I could leave and crawl back into bed, and say nothing to
anyone about any of this.

His progress was slow; there were lots of roots that close
to the tree. I waited a while longer in the hateful paralysis of
indecision. But it was George himself who finally made me
decide what to do. I realized that his heavy breathing and
unsure movements weren't because he was drunk.

It was because he was crying.

Looking back on it, I suppose I had been ready for anything else. Well, anything else providing he didn't have a
gun or accomplices or a plan. This completely disarmed me.
What the hell was I supposed to do with a crying villain?
Then, as though his sadness was communicable, I felt the
weight of what the man was feeling, at what he'd done, at
what he was doing now. It was ghastly, the way his sins
seemed to overtake him now.

I stood up and stepped from behind my headstone, no
longer bothering about trying to be very quiet. He was so intent on his work that it kept him from hearing me. I moved
closer, until I was a few steps away, and then I said, "What
are you doing?"

I stood, feeling incredibly stupid: He was too intent upon
his work and hadn't heard.

Out of habit, I cleared my throat, and this time, Whiting

shot up and whirled around as though I'd fired a shot off next to his head.

"Who's there?" He whipped his head around, straining to see in the dark.

"It's me. I think you should stop what you're doing."

He gripped the trenching tool he'd been using; I could see by the moonlight that his worn face was streaked with dirt and tears. "Who is it?"

I stepped back involuntarily. "Emma Fielding."

"Who?" I could see him peering against the darkness and I turned on my flashlight.

"Jane Compton's friend." I cleared my throat. "The American."

"Oh, good Jesus." His shoulders slumped and he wiped hurriedly at his face, turning it away from me. "Get out of here, why don't you?" His voice was hoarse. "This doesn't concern you. None of this concerns you."

"I'm not leaving without the bones, Mr. Whiting. They do concern me."

"I don't know what I thought I was doing, coming here with them," he said, almost to himself. "I would have been better off just tossing them in the river, bloody things."

"I expect you had other things on your mind," I said, trying to make my voice as steady as possible. I found it hard to speak at all. "Julia's death must be sitting pretty heavily on you."

"Oh, God, you know . . ." He slumped within himself, all the weight of his deeds and conscience heavy on him. "You have no idea what it's been like . . ."

"No. But it's over now. Why don't you just give me the bones, for a start?"

He slung the bag of bones at me, but wouldn't look me in the eye. "Take them." He wiped his nose on his sleeve. "I wish to hell I'd never found them."

The bag was surprisingly light; and I tried to catch it so as not to further damage the rattling contents. I looked at him in disbelief. "Found is a pretty strange word, wouldn't you think?"

"Found is the only word I can bear! Ellen was so pleased, so very pleased." He shook his head slowly. "I hadn't seen her smile for months, you see. I was so hoping she was having one of her good days. But then it all came out. She said, 'Come, George, come and see! Our little girl's come home!' "

My skin crawled. Ellen Whiting had found the results of her husband's vandalism? The poor woman . . .

"Ellen was over the moon, as if everything was back the way it should be. When she ever told me she'd been to the digs, as she called the archaeological site, I thought I'd die. 'I went looking for her at the digs and I found her, George,' she said, 'I've brought Julia back. My girl is safe and quiet, and she won't cause any trouble anymore. I promise.' "

My blood ran cold.

"Then she showed me the bones. She'd dug them up, you see, put them in . . . in Julia's bed. What happened was, I think she understood, at the last, what she'd done to Julia. And so she went looking for our little girl. First she went to the construction site, where Julia "

"Wait—that was when I saw her at the construction site. Last Sunday?"

He nodded, resigned and weak. "That's when she started to apologize for it. She'd had a moment, one when her head wasn't so fogged. She understood, somehow, something of what she'd done."

Oh, my God, no. I felt dizzy, faint, at last understanding what had happened.

"Ellen went back to the construction site to look for Julia. That was the day I began to suspect what had happened. She got out of her room again, early Monday morning and went to the archaeology site. That's when she showed me the bones . . . your bones, there."

I swallowed hard, realizing what George Whiting had

been going through since he'd learned of his daughter's death.

He looked anguished. "She'd done it because she was afraid of how furious I'd been with Julia. She was always trying to keep me from being angry; she of all people should have known that it didn't mean anything, really, with Julia. I *was* angry, I was hurt, when Julia went to study with that . . . Compton woman . . . but Ellen should have understood, it was never as bad as she imagined. Ever since Julia started her program and we fell out, Ellen's turns have been so much worse. I wish I could have controlled myself better, but when you've got a wife who's sick, a company to run, and a kid who's just stabbed you in the heart, so to speak, it's . . . hard not to . . . be on edge."

He'd lost a daughter and a wife, under the most horrifying of circumstances.

Whiting continued. "When Ellen said she'd found Julia, at first I was hopeful, maybe there'd been some kind of mistake by the police, even though I'd identified her . . . her myself . . . Ellen had been so full of remorse over what she'd done—in that moment—she went looking for Julia. And she explained it all very carefully to me: Julia went to the house, two weeks ago this Friday, we had another row, she left. Ellen took her rubber washing up gloves, followed her . . . waited until she came back out from the Grub and Cabbage . . . then she called her, tried to get her to stop making me angry. When Julia said she wasn't coming back, Ellen shoved her against the wall of the alley, cracked her head and . . . smothered her. Stuffed a . . ." He took a moment to choke out the words. "A plastic bag into her mouth. Held her nose. She took Julia to the skip, and brought her wallet back too; for some reason, Ellen didn't want it to get lost. It's in the sack there with the bones and the gloves, I was going to bury that too. Bury all the secrets—"

I was trembling now. "We should go to the police. Tell them what happened. Your wife can get the help she needs—"

That was what snapped him out of his reflections. "No! Julia's dead. That's the worst that could have happened, and it's *over*. What good will going to the police serve? I'm a respectable man, I've made something of myself in this town. I've lost so much, so much, and now you'd take the rest of it from me as well? Do you have any idea what the tabloids would do to us? Surely you'd want to spare Ellen that?"

He slumped back against the tree and slid to the ground, past exhausted now. "I never thought it would come to this. I'd always had my priorities straight—keep the business sound, the family in line, and everything will be well. These past weeks, I've lost so much more than I ever thought possible, you can't imagine . . ." He looked at me. "Can't you just let us alone to solve our own problems? The worst has happened, there'll be nothing more, I swear. I'll find a home, a hospital for Ellen—"

I sat down heavily, too, barely able to believe what I'd heard. I swallowed, tried to gather my wits about me, but George Whiting was just that little bit faster.

He looked up sharply. "You didn't know all this, did you? You thought I'd killed Julia. You'd no idea."

I shook my head. "I thought you'd robbed the site to get at Jane. Maybe. I was out here in case whoever it was was really after Mother Beatrice's bones."

"You're joking! I'm a businessman, for God's sake!" he said, disgusted. "If I want to fuck someone over, I do it with lawyers, hurt them in the wallet. I don't sod about, stealing bits of bone and digging holes." He considered this turn of events ruefully. "So you were just waiting out here and I happened along, is that it?"

I shrugged. "Just waiting" had done the job.

"Christ." Then he seemed to find some hope there. He straightened himself. "See here, if this is all an accident, you needn't say anything, do you? You just go home and let me sort this out. No one ever needs to find out about poor Ellen—"

My anger was enough to put me on my feet again. "Poor Ellen? What about poor Jane? You'd be happy enough to have her convicted, I suppose?"

Whiting made a face, waved that suggestion away. "They'll never arrest Jane Compton. I'm sure they wouldn't. There's no proof besides her hatred of me and her dislike of my girl. And Ellen didn't think about things long; she just did it. Less to cover up that way, I guess. The police have said they're more interested in finding Julia's brother, not that anyone knows where that miserable little sod is—"

I suddenly had a very good idea where Julia's brother might be.

"—So you needn't worry about your precious Jane."

"How can you be so sure?" I stood up. "I think I've relied too much on accident as it is, up till now, to leave anything more to chance."

"Oh, it's very easy for you, isn't it?" he said, recovering himself. "You don't suffer any of the consequences, you don't even need to stop here and see how others fare in your wake! You'll go home eventually, and all this will be a memory of little consequence to you."

I laughed. "Trust me when I say this whole affair has been nothing *but* consequence to me."

He looked as though he was still convinced that there was a way out of this. "It would be very easy to ruin me with this. Ellen's ill, badly ill, but what other harm can she do?"

I was more surprised by his pleading than by his lack of logic. It didn't suit George Whiting.

"I'll find a place for her . . . where she can't hurt anyone, can't hurt herself," he said. "Wouldn't that be better than a lot of fuss that wouldn't serve anyone? I swear to you, that's what I'll do. I won't lose everything I've worked so hard for."

It almost made a bizarre kind of sense, but I shook my head. "It leaves too many people wondering. It leaves a cloud over Jane, Greg, Andr—and everyone. There are too many questions that go begging answers."

He shook his head violently. "No, no, they wouldn't wonder. People . . . people here know how to look after their own, when to keep it buttoned. It would just fade away."

I shrugged. "I'm sorry."

"The hell you are." He spat. "This means nothing to you. I'm telling you, just walk away from this now. I've worked too hard to raise my family up and to protect them now. I won't let you simply destroy it because you think it's right."

He stepped forward, gripping the trenching tool tightly; he raised it, as if calculating whether it would do the job, if he decided it was worth trying. I willed myself to be calm, and, as if by habit, relaxed into a crouch. I had to wonder how far a tough man, who'd spent years fighting for position in town and the security of his family, would go to protect that position and the remains of that family. He'd already, even in the throes of grief over Julia, tried to help conceal her murder by his wife, and it didn't take a lot of imagination to see that the accidental death of a visitor out walking by the river in the dark wouldn't bother him very much in the least.

I sized him up and could tell he was doing the same. He was less than a head smaller than I was, but the muscles that showed under his shirtsleeves were as tough as old roots. I knew how aggressive he could be and had no doubt that if he chose to attack me, I could get badly hurt, possibly even killed. On the other hand, I could see him struggling with himself, balancing grief and fear and anger against the slim possibility of making it better if he should succeed in silencing me, and the much larger reckoning, how very much worse it would be if he tried to kill me and failed. He could see that I was taller, though perhaps not so heavily built as he was. He didn't know about my habit of running and my visits to Nolan, a personal trainer who was teaching me self-defense. He couldn't know these things, but he was carefully considering the fact that I had followed him, had confronted him, and was now apparently calmly waiting for him to decide.

He was wrong there. I wasn't the least bit calm. The only thing that kept me from freaking out entirely was the idea that if I didn't assume a ready posture, things would go that much more the worse for me when they did happen. So it wasn't so much bravery or cool as it was a commonsensical approach to pain avoidance and the knowledge from once having dropped my flashlight on my bare foot, if I chose to lay it upside George Whiting's head, he'd learn I wasn't a pushover.

"This means nothing to you," he repeated. A thought struck him and he lowered the trenching tool a mite with a sly look. "But maybe it does once it's put into the proper framework, eh?"

I did not relax as I tried to read his face. It was with good reason that he'd made himself a success in a very rough business. "What do you mean?"

"What I mean is, your friends seem to know when to keep their mouths shut, don't they? About Mads down at the cafe. I bet you couldn't force Jane's mouth open with a pry bar."

I could feel my heart thudding in my chest and I felt my hands go cold again. I shook my head, tried to keep my voice steady. "I don't think she knows—"

As soon as the words were out of my mouth, I could have died. George Whiting seized on that, more and more sure of himself now.

"But you do know, don't you? I'm not surprised, really. People around here, they know everyone's business, can't help but, in a community as small as this one was once. No one was sorry to see Sebastian Hall go; my dad told me he even gave around he'd had gone up to London after, and everyone assumed he was killed in the Blitz. It wasn't hard to cover up, though they could have done better to drop Hall off at the pig farm and let the porkers finish him off properly. But no one knew and no one cared to know and it wasn't hard to keep quiet after. Poor lasses, what else should they have done? What would any of us have done in their places? Hmmm?"

"I don't know."

He pounced on that. "Exactly."

"But self-defense is different than outright murder . . ." I struggled to derive some sense from the distinction I was making.

George moved impatiently. "My wife is out of her mind, do you understand me? She didn't know what she was doing. I see very little difference between the actions of . . . someone who's lost her mind, and a pair of young girls fighting in self-defense. Who's to say there's a difference?"

I kept quiet. He continued, as if building a proof.

"But let's say your friends don't know. What would it do to Greg Ashford to find out his poor old 'aunty' has been done for murder? Could she stand up to a trial? The publicity might kill her. Could you do that to her? To them?"

I hadn't decided that yet, myself.

"And what if they do know?" Whiting went on. "Might look pretty bad for them, don't you think? What if they were working there as a ruse to help cover up her all too hasty burial of Hall, however long ago? Never mind what it might do to your friends' reputations, there's something called aiding and abetting after the fact, isn't there?"

He watched me for a moment. "It's not as easy as you might think, is it? A little more difficult to come waltzing in and do your damage, when you don't know anyone or care what will happen to them. A little more difficult, now, isn't it? You wouldn't peach on a harmless old lady, but can you really see yourself telling on Ellen now? It's not so easy after all.

"Take your bones, I didn't want them. I just wanted to do right by them, try to undo a little of what my Ellen's done. I see it's got me nowhere. But now you try and see how easy it is to do right, when you've got a little more on the line than you did before. My Ellen won't hurt anyone ever again. I promise. So you take your precious bones and you think long and hard before you decide how to take anything else from me."

And with that, he left me in the cemetery, holding the bag.

Chapter 21

I PICKED MY WAY OVER TO THE WALL NEXT TO THE TREE and sat down heavily on the wall. Now that I had relaxed slightly, I could feel the way the sweat sat on my clammy skin, the way that my heart still raced. I brushed a stray hair out of my face and wasn't too surprised to see how my hand trembled. I set the bag on the wall next to me and it took two fumbling tries with the zipper before I could open it to see if it contained what George Whiting claimed. My eyes confirmed what my ears had already identified: I could just make out two slender arm bones, radius and ulna, jutting out of the jumble of darkened bones that rattled loose in the cloth bag. Since I didn't have anything with me to better pack the fragile bones, I settled for organizing them so that they wouldn't accidentally break each other, moving the skull so that it was at one end of the duffel and sorting the long bones so they didn't act as levers against one another and snap. I didn't touch the gloves or the wallet. Then I rezipped the bag and began to think furiously.

It was clear to me that I had to go to the police immediately: I knew who'd murdered Julia and why, and I also knew why the bones had disappeared from the excavation. But he was right; it wasn't that easy, there was too much at stake for other people. I had to consider that, even if every minute, I risked George Whiting returning with renewed resolve to keep me from going to the police at any price.

He was right about one thing: I was free and clear. I was heading to London in less than a day and could leave this all behind me. But there were others who were not so lucky. At least now I knew that neither Jane nor Greg had been directly responsible for Julia's death, and if they had not been aware of Mads's disposal of the body by the abbey ruins, then there was really nothing that should hurt them now, save for perhaps a little embarrassment. Maybe that would even help Jane, as it never hurts to let those who are intimidated by you see a crack or two in your armor every now and then. If they had been in on it, then it was bound to come out anyway, and if the community as a whole had been in on it, then I couldn't believe anything truly awful would come of this.

Aunty Mads was another situation. If people already knew about it as a publicly kept secret, and the court finding was for self-defense, as it was sure to be, then she had nothing to worry about, either, really. I was much more worried about how she would take the idea of being found out after so many years, however. I didn't see how, after not being able to confess to it openly for sixty years, she would be able to bear it now. But it would be so much worse to have George Whiting dangling the possibility of exposure over her head, I thought. Which would she choose, I wondered: risk having Greg find out what she'd done, or risk having him seen as an accomplice after the fact?

The problem was, I was the one who had to decide. I couldn't leave it, not when I was hanging around a graveyard at four in the morning with a bag of five-hundred-year-old bones by my side and a man's big sapphire ring in my pocket. Whatever would happen to Mads would be lessened by pulling George Whiting's fangs before he had a chance to use them.

That left the man himself and his deranged wife, a woman I'd met briefly, glancingly, once. They would suffer the worst. Perhaps he was right, maybe the worst had already happened and anything more would be adding insult to injury. Maybe there really was no difference between what Mads had done and what Ellen had done, when you got right down to it. There was no premeditation—but who was I to decide that I should pursue things only if the murderer hadn't already suffered enough? If Jane had been guilty, I would have gone to the police, because she was guilty. I had no business splitting philosophical hairs simply because I thought that the Whitings had already been through an awful ordeal. I wasn't a judge of anyone but myself, and the responsibility I had was to do what I thought was right.

I believed I should go to the police, but how did I know that I was right to do so? This wasn't any of my business—

Until I made it my business.

I was no way part of this community—

Until I decided to step up for Jane.

I could throw the ring into the river; I could dump the bones anonymously by the gate to the site, the police would probably find out Ellen had done it anyway—

George said that they didn't seem to know where to look next.

George would say anything . . .

I heard an animal stir by the riverbank and it roused me from my speculations. I couldn't afford to hang around here anymore. I needed to decide.

I didn't need to decide, I realized; I knew what the right thing to do was. I just needed the guts to do it.

Marchester was starting to wake up, ever so slowly. The false dawn lightened the sky and I hopped off the stone wall and began to follow the path back into town, duffel bag in hand. Dew covered the weeds and soaked my sneakers and jeans and I was chilled by something that had nothing to do with the predawn air. I walked past the site, past the turn off for Liverpool Road where I thought wearily of my quiet bed on the third floor, and down toward the Hewett Street police station.

When I was conducting archaeological research, I didn't throw evidence away when it didn't support my hypotheses; when I undertook the responsibility of investigation, I also accepted the fact that things might not turn out the way I thought. It was the same situation now. I didn't like what I'd found, but since I'd taken on the burden of looking into things, I realized I also had the obligation to see it through to the bitter end.

I reached the door and paused. I hoped Jane and Greg would understand; I hoped that Mads would believe I was acting in her best interest, because I had to finish this. It was with a heavy heart, in no way lightened by my decision, that I climbed the stairs and opened the door to the police station, just as the sun showed itself over the horizon.

Chapter 22

A FEW HOURS LATER, AT NEARLY SEVEN O'CLOCK, I
found myself standing in front of the door to 98 Liverpool Road, once again summoning my courage to enter. Finally admitting that the longer I took, the worse it was going
to be, I let myself in and went downstairs to the kitchen. I
sat, too tired even to think about making a cup of coffee,
when Jane and Greg came downstairs together. Both of them
looked haggard, as though they'd been up all night too.
Probably another long night in trying to patch their marriage
back together, now that I knew for sure that they weren't
worrying about worse things. They were startled to see me.

"It's early for you Emma," Greg said. "I hope we didn't
disturb you earlier—"

"I never went to bed," I said shortly. "I just got in and I'm
afraid I've got bad news to tell you."

They exchanged a surprised look but nodded. "It's all
right, you know. I think we already know what you're going
to say," Jane began as they sat down.

I held up a hand to cut her off. "Look, this is going to
suck any way you slice it, but I'm not going to be able to do

this if I don't do it all at once. I'm not sure how you'll feel about me after, but I just have to do this now."

They nodded again, a little confused, and I told them what happened. I couldn't sit; I got up and began to pace. Their eyes widened when I told them about what I saw at the site and about my encounter with George Whiting in the cemetery. Jane took Greg's hand when I told them about why Whiting thought that he might be able to blackmail me—us—into silence. Tears streamed down Greg's face as I told them what Mads had told me, believing that I was Jane. Jane blowing her nose loudly was the only other sound in the room as I finished my story.

"I hope to God you can understand why I had to go to the police, Greg." I finally tore my eyes away from the window and made myself look at him. "I didn't see any other way about it and I didn't think I could take the time to tell you first, because, well, I just didn't want to place any faith in George Whiting's concept of right and wrong, if you know what I mean. I wanted to make sure the police knew every-thing as soon as possible so that there was the best chance that no one would get hurt. I mean, more hurt." I finally sat down again wearily. "I'm so sorry—"

"Emma—"

I ran my hand through my hair, then rubbed my eyes. "I just thought you should know now, because you should be with Mads when the police speak to her. I'm sorry. I don't expect you'll appreciate this, I don't expect you to forgive me. I didn't decide this lightly. I just needed to tell you that I was trying to keep her, everyone, from some greater harm—"

"Emma, listen to me." Greg pulled out a handkerchief, unheedful of the bits of string and paper that fell out. Jane bent over and picked them up absently. "When I said that I hope we hadn't disturbed you earlier, it's because the phone rang so early. About four-thirty or so."

My heart stopped. Had George Whiting made good on this threats to reveal Mads's secret? Had I acted too late?

"It was Aunty's nurse," he said. "Aunty Mads died this morning, very quietly. No one can hurt her now."

"What?"

"Mads died. She's been so poorly, for weeks now." He and Jane exchanged a look. "Now we know it was since we started at the site. She finally gave up."

"I don't understand." I looked from Greg to Jane, and back again.

"It's okay, Emma. It's over."

"Oh."

Jane had been silent up until now. She looked at me and frowned. "It seems you've been going to an awful lot of trouble, looking into things around here. Why? I mean, it's really nothing at all to do with you, is it?"

As familiar as Jane's questions were to me, I couldn't help being vexed by the way she asked me, as if she was more worried that I had transgressed some boundary of etiquette. Still, she had the right to ask, and I'd already come up with the best answer I could.

"We are friends. You were in trouble. I thought I could help so I tried."

"Oh," Jane said, still frowning. It wasn't a suitable answer at all, to judge by her expression. Maybe she was surprised because I had done it and we weren't great friends, only brand new friends, coming from a long acquaintance. Maybe she felt dismayed because she didn't know if she would have done it for me. It didn't really matter; when you got right down to it, it didn't have anything at all to do with Jane.

"Well, thank you, Emma," she said, formally. "Thank you very much." Then, obligation met and discharged, the mood abruptly shifted, and Jane the organizer came back.

"There'll be no work on the site today. I'm helping Greg settle Aunty's affairs and . . . well, they're burying Julia Whiting sometime this weekend. The public's been asked not to send flowers or attend, even, the very small private service, and from what you've told me, that's a blessing too, now. But I thought I'd give the crew the day off so they could have the chance to put this behind them and give us some time to think about Aunty. We've still a couple of weeks left. We're in fine shape for finishing our work."

There was another awkward silence. "Well, I'm going to pack up my things then, and get ready to head into London this afternoon. Unless there's anything I can do to help—?"

"No, no," they both said quickly, just as I expected.

"I left your number with the police, to find me here," I said, apologetically. "And I've given them the number where I'll be in London, if they need to call me back to testify, or clarify, or whatever. Just so you're expecting it if they should call."

"Once I get Aunty's affairs started," Greg said, "I'll stop by Hewett Street, if they don't contact me before then. And we'll need to be in contact with them about Mother Beatrice's bones, in any case."

"Yes, so don't worry about that," Jane said. "It really ties up a lot of loose ends for us, you see. Right. I've got to start calling people. Let's meet up around lunchtime, shall we, Emma?"

"Sure, Jane."

She smiled, tight-lipped and grim, and began to busy herself with her diary and the telephone. I walked to the other side of the room to look at the tortoise. Greg followed, a carrot peeling and cabbage offering in hand.

"You know, I really want to thank you," he said. He handed the food piece by piece into the tank.

I watched as Hildegard began to move as quickly as she ever did to get to the greens. "Why's that?"

"The care you took over people. Worrying about Jane. Worrying how Aunty Mads would be, we would be, if any of this information got out. I mean, it was bound to happen sooner or later, but you took it to heart. And I appreciate that like I can't tell you."

"It's okay," I said. I glanced back at Jane, still busy on the phone.

"Jane doesn't understand why you did it," Greg said,

dropping in the last carrot shred. "It confuses her. Don't worry about it. And don't worry about us. We're going to work things out. It will be hard, we've both a lot to learn. But you remember my friend Simon, from the pub last week? He's going to lend me his parents' holiday place in Cornwall for a week. Jane and I will go down there, away from all the distractions, get started on fixing things. Good thing we're both so stubborn."

We looked down at the tortoise, which was doggedly trying to drag the long piece of carrot across the tank. After weeks of casual glances at Hildegard, I realized how lovely she was, in her way. Her carapace was a domed mosaic the colors of aged ivory and dark lacquer and her bright eyes communicated an intelligence that I hadn't expected. I wondered whether Greg generally had an affinity for hard-shelled creatures or if he just related to Hildegard's capacity for sustained patience.

"I think Andrew is going to look into that job up north," he said. "That will help."

I looked at Greg quickly, but he only shrugged. "It's too easy to hide behind things when there's a third party in the house," he said confidentially. "Always on too-good behavior."

"That doesn't help," I agreed. Greg didn't know about his friend's feelings. Probably.

"Can I feed Hildegard a worm? I'd like to," I said.

"Ermm. Well." Greg looked away, then looked back at me, coloring, with an apologetic, embarrassed grin. "Hildegard is actually more of a vegetarian."

I recalled Andrew making such a grand display of collecting the worms from the students and frowned. "But I thought—"

"Well. It was very kind of Andrew, of course." Greg took off his glasses and polished them carefully. "He was so pleased with himself the first time he brought them home that I simply didn't have the heart to tell him Hildegard doesn't care for worms."

We watched the tortoise wrestle with the cabbage, then I went upstairs to pack.

A half hour later, the phone rang. Greg called out. "Emma, it's for you."

I went downstairs and picked it up. "Hello?"

"Emma, Jeremy Hyde-Spofford here. I was calling to see whether I could entice you to come back to have a look at my bits of things, tomorrow say?"

I could feel my face fall. "Oh, I'd love to, but I can't. I've got to catch a train to London this afternoon."

"Surely you're not leaving us so soon? Why, you've only just arrived!"

"I'm sorry too—"

"Hold on a moment. I was going to run myself up to London tomorrow morning. What say I drive you that evening? We can have a nice long chat about my bits, just the two of us. Would that put your schedule too much awry? I know it's awful of me to ask, but I have so enjoyed chatting with you, however briefly."

Jane and Greg were only going to run me over to the next town and they had plenty on their minds. But it was the fact that Jeremy had said "just the two of us" that made me decide. "I'm afraid I'd be putting you to too much trouble—"

"Oh, no, the imposition is entirely mine upon you. Say you will."

"I'd be happy to."

"Excellent! I'll pick you up at noon and we'll have lunch. See you then."

I replaced the phone and told Jane and Greg of my plans. They didn't seem too upset, really, not with everything they had to cope with. There was still about an hour and a half left and I tried lying down to sleep, but I was far too wound up to do it. So I went for a walk.

I wandered through the streets for a little while; the cafe was closed, a hastily made sign announced, until Monday. I walked downriver one way, then crossed the bridge to the business side of town, walked, and returned the same way, ending by chance or habit at the field next to St. Alban's churchyard. I heard the familiar rasp and ring of soil being shoveled up and dumped aside and it took me a moment to recognize why I should hear that particular noise in this place: Someone was digging Julia Whiting's grave at the far side of the cemetery. I sat down, behind the wall, where I couldn't be noticed, and watched.

As comparatively "new" as St. Alban's churchyard was, it had been filled up over the past four hundred and eighty years. Hence the use of a lone man with a shovel: There would be no room to use mechanical equipment between the existing graves. Soon, however, he was joined by another, who protested that the traffic had held him up. The two fell quiet and worked quickly, methodically, with the ease of considerable practice. They moved down through the ground at a rapid pace, the soil mounding up neatly next to them in a long, low bank. I was thankful that they were silent as they worked.

I thought of all the homely human endeavors that began with the instant of a shovel biting into the earth. Fields tilled for grain, clay dug for pottery, trenches excavated for water, cellars scooped out for storage, and finally, perhaps, a little house fashioned for the last rest. I wondered if the sexton who dug Mother Beatrice's grave beneath the cold stone floor of the abbey worked in reverent silence or whistled tunelessly and scratched himself during the course of what had been just one in a long line of working days. His two modern counterparts seemed to be working faster and faster, and with a start, I realized that they were tucking a length of grass-green material over the berm. They hurried away just as the back door of the church opened and I realized that I was witnessing Julia's Whiting's funeral.

If I stood now, it would be as if a jack-in-the-box sprang open, and I had no desire to draw any attention to myself, no wish to disturb their privacy. I huddled down next to the wall, everything concealed from the eyes down.

There were only a handful of people: Sabine, now appropriately solemn as vicar in her robes, George Whiting; and a few others, none of whom I recognized, unless you counted PC Whelton, who stood with another officer in plain clothes, discreetly at the edge of things. There was no sign of Mrs. Whiting. I realized that this was as close as I had ever been, would ever be, to meeting Julia.

The service was as brief as it was melancholy to watch. I couldn't hear but every fourth or fifth word, and recognized most of those only because of how the funeral rites inevitably become a part of anyone's adult life. I thought then of how robes and words transformed one. Sabine's cassock, surplice, and stole reminded me of Jane's graduation photo and it was right they should: They were both derived from the same medieval tradition. Morag had her robes too—I recalled the photo in her office—and I smiled, thinking that the three women had more in common than any of them might recognize or want to admit.

The breeze rattled the leaves, and my concentration on the scene before me was such that I almost didn't hear the footsteps next to me.

I looked up with a start. The young stranger from outside the Fig and Thistle was there, the one who had left the note in the graveyard signed "Stephen." He looked worse off than before, hollow eyed from little sleep, and his clothing was showing definite signs of wear not so much as clothing but as camping gear. He had made another effort to wash up, though. He nodded to me, as if expecting to see me down there, and then turned all his attention to the ceremony in the cemetery. He leaned forward expectantly, balancing on the balls of his feet, hands clenched into fists, and it was then that I recognized the family resemblance.

The service was over. The few people who'd been there with George Whiting now left and the two of us by the stone wall watched as the Reverend Sabine Jones spoke earnestly to George Whiting. The police pulled back to a respectful distance, and I marveled that it should be the case. Sabine seemed to be the only person he ever let talk to him, advise

him, as I remembered from having seen them at Jeremy's
house that rainy day of the faux hunt. Something about her
insistence touched him this time, because although he responded with no more than a curt nod, body still tense, she
leaned back from him with what looked to be a sigh of relieved satisfaction. Some breakthrough had been made. She
followed George to the door of the church, where the police
joined him.

I got up and looked over at Stephen. "Your father could
probably use some company now, you know."

He shrugged. "Probably. Though he never did seem to
have too much use for me, you know."

"I have no idea; you're probably right. But now's . . . different, isn't it?"

"Yes, I expect so. But it's going to take me a while, isn't
it? I left because I was tired of trying. Tired of arguing with
him when I finally realized I couldn't set things right with
my mother. But maybe if I'd tried a little more, Julia
wouldn't be dead."

I shook my head. "I know from experience, it doesn't
work like that. You can't save people. Julia had other people
in her life who tried too. Who loved her. In the end she made
her own decisions, and in the end it was out of everyone's
hands. It was just a terrible accident."

"He could have done something," Stephen insisted. I
could see how much he took after his father. "He should
have done something. He could have put *her* away, he
should have, long before this, only he didn't, out of pride.
Stupid pride that doesn't mean a damn thing. No one cared
about his name, whether he'd come from money or from the
gutter, no one did, really. It didn't matter."

"It mattered to him. It shouldn't have mattered, but it
did."

Stephen turned away, bitterness over him like a caul.
"Right. And look where it's gotten us."

I sighed. "It would be wrong to think of this as purely
your father's fault, you know. Some of it was beyond his

control. Your mother . . . Ellen . . . he loved her, loves her.
How hard must it have been to watch her disintegrate like
that, then realize that you were the reason she did what she
did?"

I didn't expect an answer and didn't get one. I suppose it
took a lot of gall for me to make excuses for George Whiting, but Stephen didn't tell me to shut up. He wanted to talk.
"What will you do now?" I asked.

"I don't know. Stick around a few days, then head back
up to university; I'm working there through the summer
term. I would like to finish up, but after, who knows." He
shrugged, worn out. "I'll probably call him. Probably. But it
will be bloody awful."

"Probably. You know, if you do talk to him, why don't
you think about having Sabine Jones there? George listens
to her, and she'd be a good person to have on hand."

Stephen shrugged, and then the regularly spaced *thump,
whump* of soil being shoveled onto his sister's coffin began
to fill the silence of the graveyard.

It's that sound, I thought, my own throat constricting, that
idea of finality that will reach him now. I watched Stephen
closely, but he seemed no more affected by the burial than
he had been by the spoken ritual.

We stood a few more minutes; I just couldn't leave him
like that.

"Can you show me the site?" he asked.

I nodded. "I can show you, but the gate will be locked today. I can tell you about it, though, if you want."

He nodded and we walked back down the path toward the
site. We stopped on the river side of the fence and peered
through the links.

"It doesn't look like much, just tarps and beaten down
soil," I said. "But under those tarps are the areas where the
crew has been working, the medieval graves—"

"I know, Julia told me all about it." He gritted his teeth.
"All about it; her work meant the world to her. You could tell

from all the details in her calls and e-mails. Where was she working? She said she was working in the northeast corner."

I pointed out the area opposite us.

He nodded. "She said she had to keep an eye on her friend Lucy, who was a nice girl, but not very good at digging." He smiled a little. "She felt responsible for Lucy's work."

I shrugged. "Lucy is okay; Julia was just that much better. They were finding—"

But Stephen was crying now. He clutched the fence and wept for his sister. It wasn't the sound of dirt on coffin, but the place she had loved and described so well, now bereft of her presence, that did it. He hardly made any noise at all, but his slight shaking rattled the fence. I put one hand on the fence to quiet those vibrations, rested the other on Stephen's shoulder, and closed my eyes.

He stopped after a few minutes and pulled back carefully. He looked away and started to speak, then stopped. He looked at me.

"I was about to say something stupid and cheap, but I won't. I won't do it. Julia was worth more than that."

I nodded, feeling my eyes well up. "I'm very sorry for this all. I—" I reached into my pocket until I found one of my university business cards, crumpled from being in my jeans. "Take this. If you ever want to . . . I've been through something like this, too."

He looked at the card, then grinned briefly. "That's right, your name's Emma."

I smiled a little back at him. "I guess we never introduced ourselves properly, did we?"

"No. But it's all right. Thanks, Emma." Stephen gave me a quick hug, and before I knew what was happening, he'd continued down the path, away from the site. I gave him a moment to get away, then followed the fence all the way around the site to the main road. I didn't realize how rapt I was in my thoughts until I literally bumped into Morag,

similarly preoccupied. There was an awkward moment between us.

"Hello," I said.

She nodded. "I'm just out for a walk. It's my lunch."

"How's the project going?"

"Good, but it will be over soon, thank heaven." There was
a pause; Morag was unusually subdued. She took a deep
breath. "There's no one at the site today."

"No. Work was canceled because of Mads Crawford's
death." I didn't feel I needed to tell her what I'd just wit-
nessed.

"We'll remember her when we have coven next, and Julia
Whiting, too. Pray for them both." She looked down the
path, back where she'd come from. "Pray for healing, the
Lady's mercy."

I thought of Portia. " 'It is twice bless'd; it blesseth him
that gives and him that takes. / 'tis mightiest in the mightiest;
it becomes the throned monarch better than his crown.' "

Morag was impressed. "That's very good. Is it from the
Bible?"

"No." I looked away. "I've got to be going. My ride
leaves soon."

Morag nodded, unsmiling. "The Lady's blessing on you,
then."

"Thanks. Uh, you too." As I walked toward the site and
the main street, I could hear the little ripple of bells on
Morag's scarf receding in the distance.

Jane, Greg, and I were standing in the front hallway saying
our good-byes, when Jeremy arrived. He and Greg took my
bags out, and then Jeremy said he'd meet me in the car when
I was ready. The silence in the hallway was overwhelming.
Each of us was preoccupied with other things and we all
looked dreadful, dark rings under our eyes. I was glad that
there was so little time for good-byes.

"Got everything, then?" Greg asked. "Book to read?

Candy? Motion sickness tablets? Smelling salts?" He smiled weakly.

"I'm all set, thanks."

Greg kissed me on the cheek. "Good traveling, Emma. Take care. Good luck in London and . . . we'll see you in Chicago, next year, I think is when the next meeting is?"

I kissed him back. "That's right. See you then, Greg."

He shifted from foot to foot. "Well, I'll leave you girls to say good-bye, then." He all but scampered away from us upstairs.

Jane and I were left alone together. "Well. Do come again when . . . When . . ."

"When . . ." I chimed in as cheerfully as I could, and fell similarly short.

"When we'll make more time to take you around and see things," Jane finished finally.

I nodded. "That sounds good."

"You know," she said, "I think Greg's got something cooking. A surprise along the lines of the one your Brian has for you. Won't say a peep about it." She looked at me expectantly.

"Yeah, I know."

"You know? What is it?"

"*Jane!* I'm not going to ruin the surprise."

"I hate surprises. I hate secrets." But she looked childishly pleased in spite of it.

"Let me know how things turn out, okay?"

"Of course." Jane quickly kissed me. "Thanks for coming, Emma," she said to the air over my right shoulder. "I learned a lot."

"Me too," I said, shouldering my things. "Take care, Jane."

"You too."

I grabbed my backpack and jogged down to the waiting car.

*   *   *

Lunch was casual, and although Jeremy offered me chicken salad, he confessed that since Palmer was away, he was going to indulge in cheese and pickle. I decided to join him in that and enjoyed watching him eat the sandwich with such relish.

"I'm sorry you didn't get a chance to meet Mother," Jeremy said, after his second sandwich. He wiped a bit of pickle from the cuff of his shirt, but I was of the opinion that he should have left it there. The shirt was a truly horrible red and white striped dress shirt that made him look like a stick of peppermint. "She left directly after her birthday party for Switzerland. She would have enjoyed meeting you."

"I'm sorry to have missed her. Speaking of which, where is Palmer?" I asked. I was only eager to know where he was so I could avoid him, if possible.

"His holidays. I practically have to shove him out the door every year. He never goes away, of course. Doesn't like foreigners, doesn't like anything new or different. I suspect that accounts for his attachment to this place. It makes sense to him, somehow. That's part of the reason I let him help in the house when the other staff are on holiday during the summer; everyone needs to feel they belong somewhere."

"I suppose they do." Perhaps it also explained why he felt such antipathy to me, a foreigner, and Jane, an outsider to Marchester. "Let's have a look at those sherds," I suggested.

"Wonderful. They're just in here."

The pantry was huge, large enough to store service for a very large household and their guests. I could see stacks of plates behind glass doors built into the heavy wood cabinets, and more specialized items, like porcelain wine coolers and silver epergnes that would have been used to create stacked centerpieces of fruit or sweets. Jeremy pulled out a couple of shoeboxes and began to set out his broken treasures for me to examine on a long oak table in the middle of the room.

The sherds were caked with crumbs of dried soil, but that proved no problem; I was able to recognize them almost immediately. There was a wide variety, ranging from nineteenth-century wares with transfer-printed designs in blue all the way back to buff-bodied wares with a bright green glaze, that I suspected were either local English or possibly earlier French wares.

"I hate to be so vague," I said, "but I'm betting this is late medieval and that's just beyond my range of expertise. Where did you find them all?"

"In the rose garden."

I smiled. "Jeremy, you have a very large rose garden. Do you know whereabouts? Which end of the rose garden?"

"Yes, I do!" He checked the shoeboxes. "This lot of the transfer-printed ones, I found them just outside here. The others were further away—"

"Near an older part of the house? An older kitchen area, maybe?" I suggested.

"Now that you mention it, yes! How did you know?"

"People would have chucked broken or unwanted crockery out the door, out the window. They didn't start to get fussy about trash in plain sight until very recently, the past century and a half or so."

"Really!"

I nodded. "It worked out well, really, the pottery would help create a solid surface in the mud, and any bones or food refuse would have fed any animals that were in the yard, or garden. I'll bet you have some that match this later stuff still in your cupboards. Jane or Greg would be able to identify some of this earlier material for you a little more closely."

"I invited Greg to come around some evening when we were loading your bags. He said they'd be happy to come once things settle down. Terribly sad about Mads Crawford, wasn't it?"

"Yes, it was," I said. Sadder than anyone really knew.

"What do you think, Emma?" Jeremy asked, genuinely interested in my answer. "Will they get the remains of Mother Beatrice back?"

"Oh, yes. I know they will."

Jeremy seemed to sense that I wasn't going to say anything more about that—I was going to leave what details emerged to the police. "Speaking of mothers superior, I've had a telegram from Dora. She didn't know how else to contact you and she wanted to make double sure that you'd seen the portrait of Frobisher Cholmondeley."

"Oh?"

He grinned, reached into his pocket, and pulled out a creased piece of yellow paper. "Yes. Apparently she couldn't stand the suspense of wondering whether you'd seen what she wanted you to see. She decided that she shouldn't leave anything to chance and spelled it all out here. Longest telegram in history, I should think. It's all here, have a look."

I took the paper, and despite the fact that the words were printed and not handwritten, the language and the medium absolutely screamed "Dora" to me. It turned out, very simply, that she wanted me to notice the way the ruin's stones were scattered, so that I might be able to tie them into things on the dig; not at all the minutiae I'd been hunting for.

"Is it anything helpful to you?" Jeremy asked.

"Not really. We've got the remains of that wall, of course, and any of those loose stones would have been the first ones robbed out, so it's not much use to us. Still, Dora was thinking like an archaeologist, which is quite something. I've never seen a telegram before, though."

"Rather a flair for the dramatic, hasn't she?" Pooter agreed. "So it won't change your views on Mother Beatrice, will it?"

"No—oh! Jeremy, I did think of something . . . er . . . a while back, and I completely forgot to tell Jane about it!" I told him my speculations about Frobisher Cholmondeley and the abbey ruins, the ones I'd formulated sitting outside the site in the middle of the night. "It seems like a long shot, but it's worth investigating the documents, just in case. Do you mind if—?"

"Not a bit! Use the phone over there, by all means."

I left a message for Jane, and, relieved that I had passed

that lead along, turned back to Jeremy. "Thanks. It may be nothing, but . . ." I shrugged.

"Not at all, you must track down every lead, of course. People in town seem to have so many ideas about the old girl—Mother Beatrice, I mean. Have you been able to suss anything out about her, in particular, I mean? You were the one doing the excavating, after all."

"There wasn't much I could tell from that—it was a pretty brief encounter we had," I admitted.

"I only ask because, well, I seem to recall Mother B and I are connected, way back, you see. I think it's a relation by marriage, third cousins, sixteen times removed, or something of that ilk—I don't really go in for genealogy much, but the family records are all here. I shall be looking into it soon, as it seems there's going to be a lot of interest in Beatrice, once Jane gets her work done. It would be nice if I could do my part to tell her story, and it's a wonderful thing for the community, where everyone can take something from a local figure like that. That's why I ask."

"Oh, of course." I played with one of the sherds, thinking of all the different ideas that I'd run into: was she a mystic, a pagan, a canny politician, a social worker, or a woman who wanted to avoid another marriage? Was Beatrice pious or ambitious or charitable or rebellious? Was there any way to tell for sure, in the absence of her own words, and was it necessary that she should be only one thing and not another? It seemed that everyone—Morag, Jane, Sabine—had their own ideas on the subject. Andrew would eventually reveal what her diet was like, what she died of, and whether she suffered from arthritis or had ever had children. Even Jeremy would have his family's take on her. I grinned and decided to offer up my own idea for consideration.

"Maybe she was just someone who saw an opportunity to do something useful and she took it."

Jeremy thought about it and nodded. "There are much worse epitaphs to have. Now, Emma, shall we head for the Old Smoke?"

Chapter 23

"SO, WE'RE ON FOR TONIGHT?" MY BEST FRIEND Marty's voice came clear, fluty, and demanding across the line to my garishly wallpapered room in the B and B, Saturday morning.

"You bet."

"And so we're going shopping this morning?"

"Huh?"

"If we're going out tonight, we need to get you some things today," she explained. You could almost hear the QED she didn't add.

"I thought one just washed one's hands and brushed one's hair before dinner. Apparently you've added shopping to this little tradition?"

"Emma, what have you got in your suitcase?" My former college roommate was being as patient as she could. "Besides the work clothes and books, I mean?"

She knew me very well, but I wasn't going to give her the satisfaction of admitting it. "I brought a nice skirt for going out in."

"Yep. Made of cotton, too, isn't it?" Before I could speak

up in defense of my perfectly respectable walking skirt, she changed tack. "You haven't let me go shopping for you in ages," she wheedled.

I sighed. "No. My heart isn't often strong enough these days. Look, if you really want to, I will—"

"Yippeee!"

"—But you have to remember that neither my taste nor my credit cards are as extravagantly endowed as your own."

I could practically hear her pout. "Emma, have I ever made you look silly? And am I not the best shopper you know?"

I had to admit she had never made me look foolish, though everything she picked out for me was just a tad more adventurous than what I would have considered. And Marty has a nose for bargains like a pig has for truffles.

"It will be strictly high street department stores, no boutiques, I promise. And you'll get to see Kam's mother again. You know, she's an absolute jewel!"

"Okay, then." Given Kam's description of what had been transpiring between his mother and his fiancée, I was eager to see them together.

A few hours later, we met in front of the Oxford Circus tube station. Kam's mother was a striking woman, was very like him: tall, slender, with a regal bearing, with eyes that were the most penetrating I've ever seen and a mane of silver hair bound up in an elegant knot. We shook hands, and I remembered where Kam got both his lithe frame and his manners.

Then we got down to the real business of the day, starting with a rapid bargaining session between Mrs. Shah and Marty. Mrs. Shah's pronunciation was unmistakably upperclass, but her accent was just musically eastern enough to remind me that she had immigrated to England some time ago. My old college roommate—Marty would have preferred "former college roommate"—was a petite brunette with precise features and flawless ivory skin. She had an air of urbane knowingness in her eyes that reassured and disturbed at the same time. She always looked as though she'd stepped out of the pages of *Vogue*. I was always annoyed that so many of my friends were such clotheshorses; they always made my casual attitude seem just plain sloppy.

"H&M," Marty offered.

"Hmm, no, we're looking for elegant, but not so trendy."

"Selfridges, then."

"Er . . . too . . . youthful," Mrs. Shah said, tactfully—in regards to what, I couldn't have said.

"Right, right, we want a bit of dressing up," Marty said, and I noticed that my former roommate, once and presently a citizen of New York City, was rapidly acquiring a posh London veneer to her speech. It suited her.

They circled around me like sharks critically eyeing the contents of a life raft. I understood completely that I was merely along for the ride, with nominal veto power.

"Harvey Nichols," Mrs. Shah offered. "There's a mid-summer sale."

Marty seemed to waver.

"You get first refusal on the dress," Mrs. Shah upped the ante. "But I pick the shoes."

"Done!" The two women didn't actually shake on it but quickly flagged a cab, telling the driver, "Knightsbridge." We got out and they led me down the busy street, crowded with tourists from every nation in the world. Warm, not as hot as it had been, glorious weather for city walking. And, safely between my two companions, I never crossed the street looking the wrong way.

Except we weren't on a walking tour but a military expedition. My companions clearly knew their way through the store and found the department they were looking for with precise economy of effort. We passed racks of lovely things, each saying "No" with the merest glance, even before I had even registered what was on them. Then Marty paused before a display of sleeveless linen dresses, in gorgeous rich summer colors. Mrs. Shah said "Yes." They rapidly flicked through until they found a peacock green one and hustled me into the changing room. Mrs. Shah looked at my feet and said to Marty, "Six ought to do?"

"Yes, that's right. Maybe six and a half."

"I'm a size eight and a half," I piped up, muffled, as I pulled off my shirt over my face. "Sometimes a nine."

"Yes, dear, but we're accounting for British sizes," Marty explained as she pulled up the zipper in the back. "Thank God it's been cool enough that you've been covered up. Otherwise we'd have to do something about your farmer's tan line. God, that doesn't half work, does it?"

I turned to the mirror, and Marty stepped back. I had to agree with her, it was fabulous. The linen was elegant, the silk lining felt cool and luxurious against my skin. Mrs. Shah reintroduced herself into the changing room and nodded. "That's the one. Here, try these."

I eyed the strappy little nothings she held out for me. "I couldn't walk very far in those."

"You're not meant to go hiking in them, Emma," Marty lectured. "Think: valet parking, doorman, maître d'. As if any man wouldn't give up his seat for you looking like that."

"All right," I said. They'd see how silly I looked when I got them on.

Only I didn't look silly. Although the heels were about three inches, they made me appear almost six inches taller and gave a sexy cant to my hips that startled me. Marty dodged out again and returned with a fluttery scarf, which she draped in front of my throat and down my back. "If you don't fuss with it, you'll be perfect," she said, when I went to fiddle with the scarf. "We'll get you a little handbag too."

Before they arrived back with a ridiculously small evening bag, I had a chance to scope out the price tags. The total was higher than I would ordinarily pay, but quite reasonable, considering how nicely everything was made. Downright cheap, when I thought how it made me look and feel. I practiced walking back and forth in the heels, getting the feel for them, more daring than my usual pumps. It was almost painful to put on my walking-around clothes again, though a bit of a relief to have nice flat shoes on.

After I paid for everything, I found myself escorted over to the cosmetics department, and I put my foot down. "I don't wear a lot of makeup," I explained to Mrs. Shah.

"She doesn't wear any," Marty corrected.

"Oh, my dear, but we don't want you to wear a lot of makeup," Kam's mother replied emphatically. "We only want a hint, the tiniest bit, to show off your excellent features."

"It's only an emphasis, not a mask," Marty said, all her attention focused on poking through the lipsticks. "You really should have just a little. You'll never know it's there, and you'll look fabulous."

"It would be the finishing touch," Mrs. Shah added. "Just a little? For me?"

I suddenly realized why Kam had sounded so beleaguered—there was no escape from these two, once their minds were settled on something. I gave in and bought a lipstick and some mascara and that sort of thing, secretly amazed at how it altered my face: mine and yet not mine. I had to admit, they were right in every choice, and though I hardly felt I would be transforming my everyday life, it was nice to play dress up and feel really sleek for a change.

We found our way to a cab, where Mrs. Shah insisted on treating us to lunch at "this really lovely little place" she favored. "You've been such a good sport, letting us have our way with you, as it were," she said, reaching across and placing a delicate manicured hand on mine. She was the kind of graceful person who could make you feel like you were doing her a favor, when it might actually be the other way around.

Over a mouthful of cold crab salad, I remembered I had a question for them. "When Kam called the other evening, I thought I heard someone say, "Mills and Boon," whereupon there were shrieks of laughter and he promptly changed the subject. What was that all about?"

Marty and Mrs. Shah exchanged mischievous smiles. "We wouldn't tell anyone else in the world," Mrs. Shah said, "but you're one of Kamil's oldest friends. It's just I'm afraid my boy is a tiny bit puffed up at times, and it makes him self-conscious, you see."

Kam? Self-conscious? "Tell me!"

"Mills and Boon are just these light little romance novels," Marty said, "like Harlequins, and they're known for being heavy on the sentiment and—"

"The mildly titillating love scenes," Mrs. Shah finished. "I had a batch of them for the beach, you know, when you want something amusing that you can pick up and put down easily. Mariam asked about them—they're in the guest room—and Kamil, I'm afraid, overreacted. You see, if he hadn't—"

"No one would have known that he used to sneak them in his youth. Well, no one outside the family. I don't know why he can't admit he was just a boy looking for ideas of love and sex."

"I see," I said. This was too good to be true.

"You mustn't tease him about it, though, Emma," Mrs. Shah said. "Not even if he becomes very overbearing about something. Men are such fragile creatures."

"I'm saving it up," said Marty, as though she were planning for Christmas or an artillery strike.

Dinner that night lived up to my new dress. I felt elegant and looked after and had the unutterably blissful sensation of feeling absolutely and completely appropriate to the occasion. I blended in and was astonished at how much of a relief that was. True, the restaurant was never one I'd frequent on my own—it was just a little too nouveau, a little too luxe, a little too everything—but I had all the right protective coloring and the luxury of being guided by Kam's expertise. It actually made me a little sad, to remember how out of place I'd felt for so long. Kam, looking as cool as ever, knew enough not to inquire when I grew quiet, but Marty excused us both and dragged me to the ladies room.

"Okay, Fielding, let's have it." Marty crossed her arms.

At least she'd had the decency to wait until I was out of the stall. "Marty, I really don't want to talk about it. I've just had a rocky couple of weeks, is all."

"Just give me the executive summary." She turned to the mirror to smooth her hair. I don't know whether it was intentional, but her outfit even matched the muted earthy grays and sands of the bathroom's stone tile. "I want to get this sorted out before the cheese."

So I told her briefly of my investigations and the decisions I'd faced at the end of it all. "I may have to go back, and I don't mind," I concluded. "I just don't know whether I made the right decisions, that's all."

"Of course you did."

"Marty, you can't say that. By the time I'd figured out everything, or rather, stumbled over most of the truth, I had it in my power to do a lot of damage to a lot of people, whether I wanted to or not. I think I lucked out—this time. But how do I know if I did the right thing?"

"You made the right choices. I know you did." She eyed me in the mirror as she fixed her lipstick, smudged her lips together, blotted them carefully.

I risked straightening my scarf slightly so as to give myself something to do. My fiddling didn't seem to do any damage. I sighed. "But how do you know?"

"Easy." She closed her evening bag with an adamant snap. "I know you. Now please, let yourself off the hook. I want to get back and have a look at the port list."

"Fine, just as long as you pick. Marty, I can't tell you what a treat it was this morning, to have you and Mrs. Shah do all the shopping, all the deciding. Taking charge, taking care of me. I'm sick of trying to decide what is right. So you choose; tonight, for me, it's any port in a storm. Just so long as I don't have to think about choices, ponder any heavy decisions. No repercussions, no responsibilities, no consequences, nothing like that."

Marty nodded, then her eyes widened, a flush rising through her cheeks. Her hand flew to her mouth. "Oh, shit! Emma! Double and treble shit!"

"What, what's wrong?" I looked around, trying to see what might be causing her so much distress.

"Kam's surprise! It's just awful—oh, he was so pleased with himself too!"

"What is it?"

"He meant it as a treat, just for you. Oh, Emma! They were *so* hard to come by—!"

I was almost frantic now, at her alarm. "Marty! Will you please tell me?"

"Oh, Emma! The Barbican. Kam got us tickets for *Hamlet!*"

Actually, the play was great.

I didn't have much time to think over the next week or so. I hit all of the repositories I wanted, found a few nuggets at some, came up empty a few places, made notes for more detailed research to libraries and houses outside of London on my next trip. Ordinary, satisfying, busy. It reminded me of what I was good at, what I loved about my work.

I talked to Brian a couple of times and he told me that he'd received a call from Dora: She wanted to make sure that I had gotten her telegram and had seen what she'd intended me to notice in the little portrait of Jeremy's. I told Brian about the painting and my thoughts on what it might represent, and it occurred to me then that as annoyed as I'd been with Dora, if it hadn't been for her, I wouldn't have seen any of the pictures. Wouldn't have met Pooter, wouldn't have run into Palmer and the scene between Sabine and George

Whiting, wouldn't have had the chance to see these people outside of the dig. If she hadn't been the kind of person who is selfish and commanding and demanding and sweeps one away in borrowed Bentleys and sends telegrams when everyone else in the world is content with cabs and coach class and phones and faxes and e-mails, I wouldn't have gotten this perspective. So I had to admit, I owed her something for that.

There was occasionally a mention in the news about the events following the discovery of the Marchester murders, but I always switched the channel or turned the page to avoid them. I did have to go back to Marchester one day, but was back in London by that night. It was all so procedural and I focused so much on my answers that it was like a trip to the dentist; you don't really look forward to it, but it was less of a trauma than you had imagined. It was all very clinical, very procedural, and it had an out-of-body quality that helped me not to think too much about it all. I was grateful that I didn't run into anyone I knew.

I managed to keep myself busy and distracted right up until I got on the plane for home, and then there was no more hurrying to meet appointments and make schedules. I had plenty of time to think on the flight, but I did the best I could with a couple of novels and a glass of wine and a nap. Until we started to circle around Boston, waiting for our turn to get into formation and land. Then I started thinking about Mother Beatrice. Who was she? Was she a political creature? An altruist? A feminist? A saint? And how would we, five hundred and thirty years later, ever know for certain? Would Jane, with her aggressive pursuit of facts and radical use of theory, find out for sure? Facts can be subject to interpretation, and theories are pretty bubbles made of thought and personality. Would Morag find the evidence to back up her medium's evidence, signs, and portents, or would Sabine find the truth about Mother Beatrice in reflection or church records? They too needed something more to finally convince. Art, science, faith—even sheer force of personality, like Dora's arrogance or Kam's self-possession—these inform us, but nothing seems to give the whole picture, solve all the problems. Whatever you choose—or whatever chooses you—it's just about enough to get you along through this life.

At long last, though it had only been a twenty-minute delay, the pilot announced that we would begin to descend. I happily went through the ritual of putting the tray in its upright and locked position, readjusting my seat, and miraculously, for the first time in hours, watched the dandruffy head of the person in front of me pull away. I found myself getting more and more excited, and that drove some of my worries away. I would never know, really, if things would have been better if I'd not gone to the police. Maybe some things aren't meant to be known. Maybe the important thing was, I tried as hard as I could and was finally willing to take responsibility for what I'd decided. Maybe the important thing was trying and doing, finding yourself in a situation and trying to make some good come out of it at the end.

The plane seemed to take forever to land. My impatience grew exponentially, geometrically, until I was ready to go ask the pilot why he couldn't move things along just a little faster. Surely a few more degrees of decline, a few hundred more horsepower, wouldn't hurt any? I was already twenty minutes later than I thought I would be, and somehow, after more than three weeks, it seemed unbearable.

Finally, we bumped onto the runway and the effect of the plane braking—the rushing in our ears, being pushed back into our seats—was enough to reassure me that it would be soon, I would see Brian soon, in less than minutes. I could hold my breath if I wanted to, but I didn't want to, because the way I was humming with anticipation, barely kept in check by my seat belt, was practically aerobic. Suddenly, the light went off, the little chime binged, and we were there, and the whole reason for traveling so lightly, the wedging of belongings into tiny bags, was again revealed to me: I grabbed my carry-on bags and threw myself into the aisle. No wasting time at the luggage carousel: I was going to see Brian.

But of course, the line of passengers took forever to move out of the cabin, and then there was the blast of salty Boston air—so refreshing after hours in the plane and the smoggy smell of London—before I was back in the terminal, heading for customs and trying to remember where I'd hidden my passport and forms, but all the time my heart grew lighter, my pulse sped faster and faster, and I knew it was just instants away.

I walked out of customs and then I saw Brian. I knew it was he even before I visually recognized him, it was the way he stood, the way he shifted when he craned to search for me. Then I really *saw* Brian, an instant before he saw me, and I loved how he was anxiously searching for me too. He was wearing the T-shirt that he knows I like best, and I could tell he'd run around the house cleaning things up so we would have time to play when I got home, fussing with things until he could legitimately go to the airport. The crumpled paper coffee cup in his hand spoke of more time killed at the airport, and my eyes began to well at the sight of that sign of anticipation too. Then he saw me and waved hugely, like a kid, not caring who saw, and his smile was like a lightning bolt that cracked my heart.

I pushed forward, as impatiently polite as I could manage, until I cleared the barrier and I could throw down my bags and wrap my arms around him, and he could fold me up in his. I could feel people forced to move around us and didn't care. I could feel my shoulders relax for what seemed like the first time in a month. Next to Brian's smell of newly laundered shirt, and soap, and shampoo, painfully familiar and so long missed, I could tell I once again was plane-grimy and smelled of prepared meals and plastic head-phones and almond scented liquid soap and I didn't care. I began to cry. I couldn't hear what Brian was saying, it was just disconnected words like "love" and "miss" and "back," and it didn't matter that I was probably saying exactly the same thing back to him, over his words. It didn't matter in the least.

Okay, fine. There are some questions that I can't answer, some things I'll never know for sure, and that's okay. I can live with that. Because there are some things that I just know by heart.

JOIN AMELIA PEABODY, EGYPTOLOGIST AND SLEUTH EXTRAORDINAIRE

"Between Amelia Peabody and Indiana Jones, it's Amelia—in wit and daring—by a landslide."
—*The New York Times Book Review*

AMELIA PEABODY MYSTERIES BY *NEW YORK TIMES* BESTSELLING AUTHOR

ELIZABETH PETERS

LORD OF THE SILENT   0-380-81714-4/$7.50 US/$9.99 Can

THE FALCON AT THE PORTAL   0-380-79857-3/$7.50 US/$9.99 Can

THE APE WHO GUARDS THE BALANCE

0-380 79856-5/$7.50 US/$9.99 Can

LION IN THE VALLEY   0-380-73119-3/$7.50 US/$9.99 Can

THE DEEDS OF THE DISTURBER   0-380-73195-9/$6.99 US/$9.99 Can

HE SHALL THUNDER IN THE SKY

0-380-79858-1/$7.50 US/$9.99 Can

And in Hardcover

THE GOLDEN ONE
0-380-97885-7/$25.95 US/$39.95 Can

Available wherever books are sold or please call 1-800-331-3761 to order.   EPP 0302

LISTEN TO
NEW YORK TIMES BESTSELLING AUTHOR

ELIZABETH PETERS

LORD *of the* SILENT

Performed by Barbara Rosenblat
ISBN: 0-694-52510-3
$25.95/$38.95 Can. • 6 hours/4 cassettes

THE GOLDEN ONE

Performed by Barbara Rosenblat
ISBN: 0-694-52509-X
$25.95/$38.95 Can. • 6 hours/4 cassettes

Also available in LargePrint editions
Lord of the Silent • ISBN: 0-06-620961-7
The Golden One • ISBN: 0-06-009386-2

All Harper LargePrint editions are available
in easy-to read 16-point type.

Available wherever books are sold or
call 1-800-331-3761 to order.

www.harperaudio.com

 HarperAudio   ALSO AVAILABLE   HarperLargePrint

EPA 0902